THE WILD HUNT

THE WILD HUNT
AN ANGLO SAXON SAGA
Garry Kilworth

NEWCON
PRESS

NewCon Press
England

First published in December 2022 by NewCon Press,
41 Wheatsheaf Road, Alconbury Weston, Cambs, PE28 4LF

NCP293 (limited edition hardback)
NCP294 (softback)

10 9 8 7 6 5 4 3 2 1

ISBN:
978-1-914953-38-5 (hardback)
978-1-914953-39-2 (softback)

Cover Image by Chris G.

Editorial meddling by Ian Whates
Typesetting by Ian Whates
Cover layout by Ian Whates

PART ONE
ELFLAND

ONE

Winter had gripped the land in a fist of ice. King Eorl's people huddled together in their inneryards, silently worshipping the fires. Wood for fuel was hard found. Men and women had to forage daily, digging in the snow for fallen branches, or cutting deadwood from the living trees. Children shivered in their woollen garments and deer hide smocks, stamping their feet and clapping their hands to keep warm. Many of the warriors wore thick wolfskin coats and hats. The women walked around with several woven layers of cloth insulating them from the cold. They were better able to withstand the freezing temperatures, seemingly more hardy than the men when it came to fending off inclement weather. Indeed it was a mystery to the Angles why their women survived the cold better than strong, burly warriors.

Osric, son of Lord Eorl, had wandered down to the river early, to fish for the evening meal. Osric had cut a hole in the ice, but he had not had a great deal of luck with the inhabitants beneath. He was eighteen years of age, a slightly-built youth who appeared more suited to poetry than hunting or warfare. His features were handsome enough, but there was no strong chin or heavy nose of the warrior to excite a young maiden wanting a husband who could protect her and keep her safe. Indeed, his chest was not oxbreast-shaped nor his limbs oak-bough thick.

There was a wiriness about him, however, and his feet were as light as those of the deer. He could run faster and leap higher than many of the heavier men, and he was clever. His father thought him too clever, as fathers will who are outwitted and outmanoeuvred by a younger man. Osric could run circles around the lord and master of his inneryard when it came to understanding riddles or following the spoor of an extra-cunning boar or realising what was wrong with a sick horse. This of course infuriated King Eorl who, being descended from the gods as all Anglo-Saxon kings were, believed himself to be superior to other men in all things. This included his son, who would enrage his father even further by saying, 'If you claim the Lord Woden as your ancestor, then as your son so do I. It may be that something has jumped from grandfather to grandson, missing out the man in the middle?'

'You, boy,' his father would counter, 'are not even a man. You're a grasshopper, jumping around, leaping here there and everywhere.'

But Eorl loved his son more than he loved the gods, be they Woden, Thunor or Seaxneat, and every hair on the boy's head was precious to him. The youth's mother had died in great pain two years previously, possibly elf-shot by one of the unseen ones, and there were no more children. It grieved the older man that his offspring's form was not shaped for leading a shield-wall into battle, but more for carrying messages down the warrior-line. However, secretly he marvelled at the ingeniousness of the young man's thinking and wondered whether this attribute might be more valuable to a king than brute force? But would the people accept a king who was not a great warrior? That was indeed a worry and gave Eorl many sleepless nights.

Thus it was on this harsh winter morning, with the hoar frost clinging to his hair, that Osric was kneeling on the river ice with a fishing line in his fingers, rather than running with those on the boar hunt in the forest. Indeed, as he looked down into the dark waters through the hole he had cut, Osric's thoughts were not even on the task in hand, but on the comely features of a sixteen-year-old maiden, who had widened her eyes to him as he had passed her by. Girls who showed you the whites of their hazel-iris eyes were tossing out a meaning not difficult to catch. Osric had reached the age of marriage and had been quietly surveying the field, wondering if he liked any of the available girls enough, or indeed wondering if any liked him. Well here, it seemed, was one who was not repulsed by his looks. He was immensely eligible of course, being the king's son. It was likely he would be the next king, since any election from those eligible for kingship – his uncles or cousins – would naturally favour the direct line from father to son. Not a foregone conclusion, but certainly a good probability. Even better were he a sturdy sword-wielder, but though his stature disappointed his father, Osric was still no slouch with a weapon.

There was a creaking sound on the ice behind Osric. The youth turned to see three of his father's thegns, hearth-companions, crossing the edge-ice towards him. The leader paused in his step when Osric looked into his eyes, then came determinedly on. This huge fellow was Wulfgar, a mighty warrior, one of the strongest and fiercest amongst Eorl's people. Wulfgar had a sword in his hand, unsheathed, ready to use. The two warriors with him were likewise armed. He tried to divine from their eyes what their intentions were towards him.

Osric could see blood-splatters on the wolfskins of these thegns. Then he noticed another man, standing in the shadows of the wood on the slope above. Who was that? It looked like Eadgard, one his noble cousins. Yes, indeed it was. Osric was shocked to recognise the man. Eadgard had recently been banished for the foul murder of a whole family in their own inneryard. Eadgard was known to be ambitious: always a braggart, regaling his own virtues as a warrior and a man above those of his fellow warriors – especially those of his puny cousin Osric, who was in Eadgard's opinion far more suited to be a follower rather than a leader. Eadgard must have returned and secretly recruited these brute thegns to his own cause.

'Oh, my poor father,' Osric whispered to himself, with the horror of an image filling his head, 'are you indeed now lying with mortal wound in your heart?'

'Osric,' called Wulfgar as he came unsteadily forward on the slippery surface, 'my lord the armring-giver, your father, is very ill. It is believed he is dying. He requests your presence at his side before he goes to meet Lord Woden.'

Blood was still dripping from Wulfgar's blade, falling on the ice and making spreading stains. Wulfgar followed Osric's gaze and no doubt realised now that the youth was suspicious. He sheathed his weapon, still coming warily on towards Osric, the ice creaking under the heavier weight of the warrior-thegn.

Certain then, that these men were killers, murderers, regicides.

'Does he?' replied Osric, straightening, his feet ready for flight. 'My father looked healthy enough when I left him this morning.' Osric felt a terrible pang of emotional pain. Surely then his father was already dead. There was the blood on their clothes and these men wore the grave look of a business to be done in their eyes and in their expressions. Osric called, 'So why the weapons in your hands? Did he tell you to force me to come, even to the point of striking me with your blades?'

The warriors pretended to look about them, as they expected to see legions of enemies along the banks of the river.

'We must be cautious in such terrible weather, Osric – this is the time when attacks might be expected from the East Saxons, Mercians or even the Bernicians of Umbria. Come, join us quickly and let us talk on the bank. I'll explain better there what needs to be said. Your father will be getting impatient with us. You know how angry he gets when you fail to heed his commands.'

Osric began to back away, towards the far bank. He had not even thought to bring a knife with him, let alone a heavier weapon. All he had were his feet.

'The Umbrians?' he called. 'Come down from the frozen north? They must be in an even tighter grip of winter than us. And the East Saxons love their beds too much to bother fighting in the snow and hail.'

Wulfgar gave him a greasy smile. 'Stand, boy. We're not going to harm you.'

Osric turned and began to slide-glide towards the far bank, the ice becoming thinner and more dangerous as he reached the middle of the river. He heard Wulfgar's angry voice ordering the two thegns to go after him. When he glanced back Osric saw that Wulfgar had become entangled with his fishing line and was sitting on the ice cursing and swearing, trying to free his feet from the cord. The two other warriors were advancing fast. Osric increased his sliding progress towards the bank, beyond which were deep dense woods in which he could lose himself.

When the men were halfway across, Osric heard the ice crack behind him. Suddenly he realised his own weight was half that of the thegns. The ice at the edges of the river was thicker than in the centre. He turned to warn them to go back, but it was too late. Crazed lines appeared on the frozen surface of the river. Then Finnan crashed through and was gone. He never reappeared. Holt had been following him at a fast pace and now attempted to stop. Osric could see the fear on the warrior's features as he slid inexorably towards the hole left by his companion. When he reached the edge, the ice again gave way, widening his exit from the world. His arms went up as he appeared to clutch at the clouds to save himself. The golden armring, given to Holt by Eorl, Osric's father, flashed in the pale light of the winter's day. Holt's face was shocked into a grey mask by the coldness of the water as he bobbed down to his shoulders. He grabbed at the edges of the hole and attempted to heave himself out, only for the ice to crumble. Two or three times he tried to climb out, but it was a hopeless exercise. The ice continued to give way and finally with a hopeless look at Wulfgar, Holt too slipped down to his death.

Osric reached the bank and turned to see Wulfgar. The hearth-companion and possibly the murderer of his father was staring at him from the safety of the edge-ice.

'You can't escape, boy,' called Wulfgar, softly. 'There's nowhere to run to.'

A sinking feeling told Osric the warrior was right.

'I shall do my best,' he replied, 'and if I do manage to get away, you can be sure I'll return.'

Wulfgar snorted a laugh. 'I can't wait.'

And it was true that Osric stood little chance of escape, especially in the dead of winter, with the world locked in ice and snow. His tracks would be plainly visible. He would necessarily move very slowly through the drifts. At night he would freeze. There would be nothing to eat and with not even a knife to hunt with, the possibility of killing game was small. He looked towards the edge of the forest, knowing the trees would not hide him for long, and, with despair in his heart, he struck out through the thick snow. Halfway to the tree line, he stopped to look back at the settlement high up on the ridge overlooking the river. His people were there, friends and relations, who would yet have no idea what momentous incident had occurred. Their king was dead, assassinated. And the king's son might as well be a dog for all the chance he stood of living through the day. There were the wattle huts with the lord's Great Hall rising over them in the centre of the village. That had been his father's house, where Osric himself had been born and raised.

Smoke curled lazily from the distant rooftops to the skies forming a pall over the whole area. The girl whose eyes had entranced him would be busy boiling water on one of those fires, or weaving, or stitching garments, or performing one of many similar chores. Osric's tribe had come in ships two generations ago from a vast but crowded land on the far side of the sea. Now, having crossed the swan-road this was their home. There were people here before them, but they had been defeated in battle and either taken into the tribe of Angles or chased away. Most of those first dwellers had been Celts, but there had been Saxons, Varni, Gauls, Frisians, Franks, Geats – a whole mix of peoples – whose fathers had been in the army of Rome and whose families were embedded after the Romans left. The girl with the eyes claimed Frisian ancestry, but now she was a ghost in his head. He stood no more chance of seeing her again than becoming king of the East Angles.

Once in the forest of oaks and birches, Osric began to stride out, the snow less deep under the canopy. It was darker in there and that gave him some comfort, though he knew any hope was probably false. The path, such as it was, wove through the woodlands taking him south, towards the homes of the East Saxons. Even if he reached them Osric had no idea whether he would receive a warm reception. They were Saxons. They might cut him down where he stood. Beyond them, on the other side of the great river, were the Jutes, a little more amicable. There were other fiefdoms of Angles of course, but a long way from here. Umbria to the north and Mercia to the north west. Too far away to even contemplate. And there was no reason why they would be any more friendly towards him, even though they were of the same stock. All the Angle, Saxon and Jute realms had been at war with one another at some time. There was no guarantee of safety anywhere. Mercia was the most successful warrior-nation, with King Paega at their head. He collected tribute from almost every tribe on the island, south of the land owned by the Picts.

At one point, Osric paused briefly to make a small rustic altar from fallen branch wood. A god post. Standing before it, he said prayers to his favourite god of the Wen, Ing, ruler of the elves. 'If you find it in your heart, Lord Ing, to assist me in my plight, I will make a sacrifice to you when I am able. At the moment, I have no animal and no weapon with which to despatch one, otherwise I would not be pleading for your help empty handed…' It was then that Osric heard the baying of the hounds. His pursuers were close behind him now and it seemed there was little Lord Ing could do, even if he had a wish to save the life of a pathetic youth. 'So,' murmured Osric to himself, 'in the month of Solmonath, the life of a foolish boy will stain the white snow red and his spirit will drain from its treasure-chamber. My ur-law is set for when we are born and when we will die. I must submit to the Wyrd with all the thews instilled in me by my father. My enemies shall not hear me beg for my life, nor find me on my knees, weeping. I shall stand and face them like a man and die cursing their names for their disloyalty, treason and lawlessness.'

Lord Ing, god of prosperity, passion and wealth. Ruler of the Elves:

So what do we have here? A boy, not much more than seventeen summers by the look of him. He asks my help. Do I give aid to youths such as him? Not in the normal way, but there is an intensity in his speech, which always attracts me, for am I not the god of passion? I am feeling generous today: let the sun shine through the canopy. This youth has my attention.

A few moments later, Osric looked down at his feet and saw that the deeper snow was gone: just a light covering over the bracken. Indeed, through the treetops a mottled sunlight was lacing the forest path. It was still cold – bitterly so – but the snow was but a dusting of the undergrowth. And the sound of the chase had given way to an eerie silence. It was as if the world had been reborn into a new day. What magic was this? What strange... His thoughts were suddenly stunned by a sight that stood before him in a glade.

A figure like a man faced him, yet it was not a man. This creature was taller than three mortals standing on each other's shoulders. Its face was as wild and ever-changing as a storm-tossed sea. As if the wind were blowing over a field of long grass sending waves across his features. On its head several yards of long, thick dark hair lashed the air and trees around and above the glade. Its fluid form rippled in the light streaming through the canopy. The being's feet were buried in the oak mast that lay on the forest floor. Osric knew instinctively that this was one of the gods and if asked to guess would have replied 'Ing'. Fear gripped his heart and squeezed it hard, as two willowy arms flailed the air above his head.

'You called me,' cried this nightmarish spectre in hollow tones. 'What is it you want? Speak up. Speak with clarity. You were less than clear in your request.'

'To – to – escape those who would kill me,' said Osric, hoarsely.

'Ah, another who wishes to thwart the Wyrd,' boomed the god, sounding disappointed, for now Osric realised he was in the presence of Lord Ing. 'Unsatisfied with his fate and unwilling to go to his prescribed death.'

'No!' cried Osric, suddenly finding a defiant tone. 'This is not my Wyrd, not my ur-law. I cannot believe that even Woden, god of Wisdom and Lord of the Wild Hunt, would approve of the way this day has gone. My end has been thrust upon me by a man whose lust for power has distorted his honour. These are murderers and criminals who chase me and want my life. I would willingly give up my life in glorious battle, in an honourable war, but I will not submit to the loathsome ambition of a grasping usurper, a man with bad blood in his veins. This is foul work by the lowest of creatures, but without a sword in my hand and a shield on my arm, I cannot even take one of them with me when I leave Middeangeard for the world beyond it.'

'Do not raise your voice to me. Anger does not become you. You know who I am,' replied the figure, quietly. 'Now, you must go. Follow that path on the far side of the glade.'

The baying of the hounds resumed and sounded closer and Osric started to run towards the track indicated by the god.

'Walk, boy! Don't run,' came the order from the god. 'Do you not trust me?'

Osric realised the god was still watching and indeed he slowed his pace.

TWO

Once on the narrow path the sounds of his pursuers dimmed and eventually they were heard no more. Osric followed the narrow track which wound amongst hornbeams and beeches for several hours, until he came to yet another clearing in the forest. In this opening were a group of beings whose beauty astounded him. He stood and stared at them for a long while, during which they stared back.

They were tall slim creatures, caught in the light of a huge deeply-golden afternoon sun. Their hair was long and silvery, hanging down their backs to their narrow waists. Their complexions were pale and their skins almost translucent. Even at a distance he could see their eyes were like chips of ice, sharp and glittering, as they studied him with blank expressions on their faces. They were eyes that filled him with dread, for he knew from old stories that they belonged to the elfen. Every one of them, there were seven altogether, carried a bow and a sheaf of arrows. No words were spoken until he moved and even then it was just a single, 'Come!' accompanied by a long thin beckoning finger tipped by a dagger-like nail.

Osric stepped towards the elves and using the traditional greeting of his people, said, 'Be whole!' Then he added, 'Where am I?'

'Where you should not be,' came the reply.

There followed the tinkling of small bells, which Osric realised was laughter from those he was encountering.

'This is the land of the Aelfen,' said the tallest of the elves, who stood at least a head above the height of Osric. 'No place for a mortal.'

Osric drew himself up to his full height, wondering if he was about to be shot to death by elfen arrows.

'I was told by Lord Ing to follow the path,' he explained. 'I had no idea it led to the land of the elves.'

The group of elves raised their eyebrows and looked at one another, shaking their heads. Then the tallest one said, 'Welcome, Osric. We have been expecting you for hours and we're impatient creatures, being light of foot and forever darting here and there – though some of us only move quickly when we have to...' He glanced at one of their number, an elf who looked down as if ashamed to be picked out. Then this being's feet began tripping away. He did a little dance on the turf as if to prove the accusation false. Finally he gave a sigh and ceased his dancing. When he looked up at Osric there was a radiant smile on his face. 'Welcome indeed,' he said. 'Take no notice of Thorn, he's jealous of my ability to relax and enjoy peace and quiet.'

There was no retaliation from the tall one, Thorn, to this remark and the elves gestured to Osric that he should follow them. They skipped along the forest path with light feet, until they came to a high, frost-covered meadow. Here were more of them, dozens, if not hundreds. They seemed to be doing very little, except talking amongst themselves. When Osric walked out amongst them they stared at him, looking him up and down, but there seemed no animosity in their study. In a corner of the meadow were their horses, milling around, clearly anxious to be doing something. Once the elves had finished peering at their guest, they moved swiftly and purposefully towards the steeds. Each then found his mount and leapt up on its back. There were no saddles or reins, only manes to grip. One, riding a palomino, with its golden mane and tail, raised his bow on high and cried, 'The hunt!' Whereupon the whole field emptied within seconds as the riders charged off over the landscape. Osric was left alone on the hillside, staring down at his old settlement far below.

The hunters returned before dark and the horses were hobbled and left to graze as the sun went down. Nightfall brought out the stars and a gibbous moon, but the cold did not grow any worse. In fact Osric realised that since he had entered Aelfgeard, the world of the elves, he had felt nothing more than chilly, despite the frost and snow. The elves had lit bonfires now, all over the hillside, around which they gathered. Osric joined them at one fire, ignored by most of the gathering. One or two stared at him, as if they resented his presence among them, but for the most part they spoke to their neighbours, or across the flames at others on the far side. They had brought no game with them back from the hunt and Osric was desperately hungry.

'Are we going to eat?' he asked his nearest companion. 'Where is the kill from the hunt?'

'We don't eat the quarry,' replied the elf, seemingly amused. 'How disgusting that would be.' Icy eyes bore into his. 'What do you take us for? Mortals? The deer and boar rise again and are ready to become prey again on the morrow. The excitement is in the hunt itself, not in killing.'

Osric suddenly realised he was probably speaking with a female of this fay species. At least, he took her for a female. She was a much more delicate creature than those who had met him in the forest, with a softer, more musical tone. She was as tall as he was and startlingly beautiful, with a slight figure – but no sign of breasts under her green tunic. When he looked around at others warming themselves at the fire, he saw that all the other females – they could be nothing else, he decided – were flat chested. He wondered if this meant they did not feed their babies with breast milk. Did they even have babies, or were the young hatched fully grown from eggs like birds? How ignorant he felt. He really knew nothing about these magical folk, normally invisible to human beings, except that they played tricks on mortals and sometimes gave them an illness by throwing darts at them. 'Beware the elfen,' his grandmother had warned him as a child, 'for they are devious creatures.'

Staring into the eyes of this being, Osric wondered why he had previously thought the loveliness of a village girl so entrancing. This creature was beyond beauty. She dazzled and enchanted him with her mere appearance. He knew from his mother's teaching that he should not look only at the outward form of a woman, but should also seek intellect and spiritual worth also, but indeed he could not help but feel intensely excited and even aroused under her gaze. She was exquisitely formed and perfectly perfect in his opinion. He would have faced a whole legion of hostile thegns just for a single welcoming smile from this divine being at his side.

'I love your beauty,' he found himself saying. 'The silver hair, the diamond eyes, the clear pale skin...'

'It's seasonal,' she replied, casually.

'What?'

She turned and faced him. 'We change with the seasons. When autumn comes, my hair will turn red, gold or brown, like fallen leaves. My eyes will turn grey as the birds who leave our land and fly off into the darkening skies. Will you find me so lovely when that happens?'

'Of course,' Osric protested. 'You will still be you. And in the spring, shall you blossom like the flowers of the meadow?'

She smiled. 'Oh yes – and when summer comes, my hair will turn to the gold of ripening corn and my eyes to the deepest blue of a July sky.'

'Woden bless us,' Osric said, catching his breath, 'may I be around to witness these miracles of another race.'

16

The elf-girl's name, he was told, was Linnet. 'That's not my real name,' came the follow-up, 'but as a mortal you would not be able to pronounce my aelf-name, so Linnet will do.'

'So,' he asked, 'what about food? I'm extremely hungry and as my hosts, I would have thought you would attend to my needs.'

'You are here under sufferance, mortal,' she replied, sharply. 'We took you in because we were requested to do so. In any event, you wouldn't like what we call food. Pollen and petals from the flowers. Mustard and cress from the ponds. Milk, stolen from the storage jars of mortals. Honey. Sweet juice of flowering nettles. Mushrooms and toadstools. Fruit. Nuts. Clear water from a brook. You need more substantial food than that, I'm sure.'

He certainly did and he was feeling ravenous. Venison or wild boar meat would be good, with bread and cheese, perhaps then followed by honey. He had no objection to honey as such. It just didn't make a meal in itself. He rose to his feet, then said, 'Linnet – my I borrow your bow?'

She looked a little shocked by this request and glanced across the circle of elves at another female, who raised her eyebrows, shrugged, and then finally nodded – reluctantly it seemed.

Linnet unslung the bow from her shoulder and also handed Osric a slim quiver of arrows.

'Look after it,' she warned. 'It's precious and its mine. If you damage or lose it, I can get no other. We are given our bows at our making – you would say birth – and they are ours for life, like an arm or leg. If the bow is ever permanently damaged or lost, then there's no replacement. Do you understand?'

He stared into those icicle eyes. 'No – but I'll look after it as if it were my own head. Is that good enough?'

'It's worth more than your silly head,' she retorted. 'If anything does happen to it, you will indeed lose that part of your anatomy.'

He laughed at this and took the weapon, which was indeed a thing of beauty. Its rainbow curve was a piece of artistry and there were many symbols and figures carved into the willow: animals, birds, wildflowers. A single barn owl's feather dangled from the top end and the grip was bound with silver cord. On inspecting the arrows Osric found that, like those of mortals, the shafts were of good straight ash wood. However, there was no metal at all on either the bow or the arrows, which were pointed with flint and fletched with a jay's blue feathers. The weapon felt light in his hand, having a fine balance, and he set forth into the meadow beyond the forest looking for hares. It was late in the evening and there would be one or two such creatures out for feeding or play near their forms.

He stood in the shadows of the trees on the edge of the wood, using the dappled light for camouflage. Then with two fingers he let out a shrill whistle and quickly fitted an arrow to the cord of the bow. Indeed, three sets of black-tipped ears went up following the shrill sound. The nearest was twenty paces away. Osric had always been good with a bow. He was not a great expert with the sword, but he had the ability to fire an arrow into a target with reasonable expectation of hitting it. However, striking a hare hidden in grasses was not the easiest of tasks. He aimed at a hand-span below the base of the ears and let fly a shaft. The ears disappeared. He ran swiftly to the spot and found, miraculously, a female hare with the arrow in its heart.

'That,' he said, lifting he warm dead creature by the back legs, 'is either very good luck, or I have a magic hunting weapon in my fist.'

He took his kill back to the glade where the elves were gathered. They seemed to have no shelters as such, no huts or houses of any kind. Their horses grazed at the edge of the clearing and the elves themselves simply lounged or sprawled on the grass, or sat on tree stumps, talking in soft voices. They did have a camp fire, though, probably more for the light than warmth, for they didn't appear to be wearing thick clothing and yet they showed no signs of feeling the cold. Osric took his hare to the fire and using one of the sharp flint arrowheads, began to skin the kill, beginning with slitting it lengthwise along its belly, then down the inner side of each limb.

Once he had peeled the skin away from the dead quarry, he cut open its belly and removed the offal, carefully placing the liver, heart and kidneys on a smooth stone at his side. He then looked up, hoping to discover a green branch nearby which he could use as a spit. Glancing around him at the elfen, however, he saw he was being observed with utter horror. One or two of the fabled creatures had slim fingers to their mouths, as if they were about to be sick.

'I have to eat!' Osric said, suddenly feeling guilty – though why he did not really understand. 'I have to have food.'

A collective shudder went through the long-haired beings who surrounded him, and they turned their backs to him.

'Stupid,' muttered the youth, aggrieved, and not wishing to get up and break a sapling from a tree for fear that any other 'living thing' might upset his hosts, he used one of Linnet's arrows to spit his hare.

Indeed, once the meat was roasted it was absolutely delicious, and the guilt he had felt fled from him. Man was made to eat the flesh of animals, he told himself, and he wasn't going to eat salad for the rest of his time among the elves simply because they had delicate feelings. He threw the bones into the fire, where they crackled and sizzled, further upsetting his hosts a little, then he took the bow and went to look for the female elf who owned it. He found her with some difficulty, the elfen all looking very much like one another, and handed the weapon to her with his heartfelt thanks.

'I have eaten now and would like some wine. Do you have any mead?'

Linnet had been carefully inspecting the bow for damage and seemed irritated that one of her arrows had lost its fletching and bore burn marks on its shaft.

'Yes, I heard you had slaughtered a fellow creature, stripped it of its fur coat, then charred its fine muscled form over flames...'

'Charcoal,' he corrected.

'...so that no more will it run like the Hrethmonath-wind over the leas, nor box with its friends in the greening corn, nor mate with its lover...'

'Oh, please,' snorted Osric, '*lover*? I can take all this stuff about dancing through the springtime meadows, but jack hares mate with the nearest and most available jill who manages to turn her rear end towards him. Look, while I am amongst you, I shall be performing the most disgusting of acts, so you'd better get used to seeing me slip behind a hedge to do my ablutions, eating the legs and lights of wildlife and snoring in my sleep. That's what mortals do, I'm afraid, and while we're criticising each other, I find you elves all a bit prissy. You have these wonderful bows, but they're only toys for shooting creatures that jump up immediately after they've been shot full of arrows, and dance off into the sunset.'

Her ice-drop eyes narrowed. 'We also have invisible dart-spears, to throw at mortals and make them sick,' she threatened.

'Yes,' he retorted in kind, his anger overflowing, 'and how cowardly is that? We can't see you, or retaliate, so...' All of a sudden an irrepressible urge flooded his heart and brain and he found to his horror that he had leaned forward and kissed those bow-shaped rose-petal lips that she was using to scorn him. '...so, so,' he fought desperately for something to say to cover his indiscretion, 'so there,' he finished lamely, wondering at his own stupidity. 'That's that, then.'

She touched her lips with the fingertips of her right hand.

'You kissed me,' she murmured.

'Er, I did? Yes, I did. I apologise. It was you. You provoked me. I didn't mean to, but it just happened. I'm sorry. Is that a terrible crime here?'

Osric looked up at the glistering stars set in a black, velvet sky and at the perfectly round, golden moon, as if it were their fault he had transgressed and taken advantage of Linnet and had trespassed on his hosts' generosity in giving him shelter and protection from his enemies.

Osric looked around him, expecting to see raging elves coming at him, to exact revenge for his crime.

'No, no,' she whispered. 'Not a crime. You are a handsome youth. I am a beautiful elf. And now we are in love.'

Osric straightened his back. 'Eh?'

'You kissed me on my lips. What did it taste like?'

Osric licked around his mouth.

'Very nice. Soft and sort of honeyish.'

'There,' her eyes sparkled. 'Sweet. It was a sweet kiss, was it not? You are mine then, and I am yours. We are to be wed and will love each other eternally.'

'Now, just wait a minute...'

A tall male stood over him, his shadow from firelight falling over Osric.

'It is the law and the lore. You are hers forever. If you did not want her, you should not have bonded with her, mortal.'

Osric knew that mortals sometimes married with elves and though he knew nothing of what became of such rare relationships he realised that it wasn't difficult to be trapped on cold hillsides and caught in the thrall of such charming creatures.

Lord Ing:

So, the youth is to marry one of my elves? It sounds as if I was right to save him from being torn to pieces by the hunting dogs. He must treat her well though, or he will answer to me. Every elf is precious to me and no mortal can have dalliances without repercussion following.

Though it was bitterly cold, and Osric felt it right through to the marrow of his bones, he and Linnet spent the night on a mossy bank below a live oak making love. This was conducted sometimes ferociously, sometimes gently, until the grey fingers of a new dawn clawed their way up the sky. Osric was exhausted but deliriously happy, having never been in a woman's bed before this night. Even as a prince and therefore entitled to many exclusive privileges because of his position in society, he had been taught to revere and respect women. To bed one without going through the accepted formalities would dishonour his family name.

Yet, he was a lusty youth and had yearned for a maiden in that way ever since he had come of age. Night upon night his dreams had been artistically wrought, full of naked bodies tangling, tying knots of flesh under the blankets, reaching explosive states of ecstasy time and time again. Sometimes he had woken with his wet seed staining the blankets, for once glad that his mother was no longer alive to witness her son's transgressions. Now those dreams had become reality and the act had not disappointed him. What a night! What a wonderful night! He breathed the fresh cold morning air into his lungs and were he in his own village he would have given any onlooker a display of athletics that would have them wondering if he had suddenly been overcome by lunacy under the full moon.

The night had otherwise been a very cold one for the young prince, and when his energies were finally spent he lay shivering under his wolfskin cloak, though Linnet did not seem to be at all uncomfortable. Indeed it seemed that none of the faerie beings suffered the pain of winter in the same way as mortals. Osric had not seen a single shiver or a rubbing of hands since coming amongst the elfen. Here in their circular glade the snow was but a sprinkling and the frost a dusting of crystalline powder on the forest floor. Beyond the clearing, though, the snow was piled high around the bases of the hornbeams and beeches making it another world out there. After gnawing on the remains of last evening's roasted hare, Osric wandered out of the glade and fought his way through the drifts to the woodland's pale.

From that vantage he looked out at the white world, with the river flowing beneath him, to the hill on the far side. Over there, under the snow were the strip fields of his people, ready for the planting of the vegetables and corn when spring arrived. On the far right were the burial grounds. Had they buried his dear father yet? A wave of grief flowed through him, brief but piercing. Surely not, for they would have to plan a great funeral, a ship burial fit for a king? His father had been the proud lord of his people, the armring-giver, the gold-giver, generous with wealthdeal and they would not simply bury him like a commoner, Osric was sure. Eorl, like all Angle kings, was descended from the gods, and they would surely give him his proper rites.

Indignation flowed through the youth's veins, filling his head with burning thoughts of revenge, as he remembered that his father had been assassinated by a usurper and disloyal nobles. Eadgard and Wulfgar had to die by Osric's hand. His whole being craved to be in battle against these murderers. Yet, he realised the time was not yet right. He was still only a youth and not a full-grown warrior. Osric would have to bide his time and wait for his opportunity to right the wrong.

Over there, in the village, the inhabitants were leaving houses with walls made of overlapping triangular planks of wood. Most of these dwellings had straw-thatched roofs, but there was one darker than the rest made of heather-thatch. This was the dwelling of the girl with the large, soft eyes. Her father was eccentric and liked his home to be different from others, though heather-thatch was not exactly unique. His daughter would be going out to tend the cattle or fetch water from the river, or perhaps firewood from the forest edge. Tears came to Osric's eyes. He would never see that girl again; or if he did, he would be an old man of twenty-five or more.

Even as he watched he recognised some of his friends and neighbours. Then someone came to the doorway of the mead hall, the Great Hall, the place where his father held court and met with his thegns. The place where the villagers would gather for ceremonies and meetings. The place where all the business and entertainment was carried out. There were many villages which had been under the rulership of Eorl. They all belonged to the king, yet his ownership was not exclusive, since the people were invited within to attend many functions, especially wassails and feasting. The man in the doorway stretched and yawned, his eyes scrutinising the surrounding landscape with an owner's eyes. His whole stance said, 'This is my land, these are my people, this my village. Who would dare take it all from me? I am the lord of all I survey.'

Eadgard!

Osric's nostrils flared as he recognised his father's killer.

Eadgard the usurper.

'Suck in the air, you treacherous bastard', thought Osric. 'It's a thing more precious than gold and I intend to rob you of it, just as soon as I am able.'

THREE

It took Osric a few days to realise what he had done. He had promised to marry an elf. The ceremony, he'd been told, would take place in the spring, when there were flowers for garlands and the birds were returned from far off lands. Indeed, what had he done? Inside, he was fearful. He didn't want to spend the rest of his life among the elfen. They seemed to do nothing but go out on hunts (to which he was never invited anyway, since what a mortal killed stayed dead) and lounge around combing their long hair and flashing their beautiful even teeth. Sometimes they went to the village across the river to cause mischief, but again they would not let Osric join them. They told him that while they themselves were invisible to mortal eyes, he would be seen and probably struck down by his enemies. They, the elves, would not be able to protect him. It was best he stayed away from danger.

So had he trapped himself in a world of dissolute creatures, who seemed to do nothing during the day but ride horses and lay about, and at night make love to each other with free abandon, not even bothering to cover themselves from sight? Yes, he enjoyed doing those things too, especially since his lover was herself willing and apparently insatiable, but he did not want that to be all he ever did. There was the glory of battle to consider. No prince worth his salt was going to rule a people without first proving himself on the field of conflict. Then there were other pastimes: fishing, wrestling, war games, feasting, songs, drinking mead, poetry, the admiration of craftsmanship and jewellery, the conversation with friends. Was he expected to forgo all these normal mortal pursuits for the love of an elf? And, he asked himself, did he actually love her, or was he merely enchanted by her? Perhaps both?

One week after joining the elves, Thorn came to see him.

Thorn was one of the tallest of the elfen: a fine figure of a fabulous being, supple and straight as a young poplar, with eyes that could cut through iron.

'Today you will join us. We go to fight,' said Thorn. 'We have picked you out a steed, one that we think you can handle, and you must choose a weapon of some kind.'

Osric had been sitting, hunched under his cloak, staring at the marbled sky and wondering if he ought to go out and kill something to eat. He jumped up, eagerly, realising that here was a real change in the dull routine of elfen life.

'Fight? Fight who?' he asked. 'I can't be expected to kill any of my friends, but certainly I'll destroy those who are my enemies.'

'Thursae,' replied Thorn. 'They have eaten one of us. We must teach them a lesson. Let them destroy each other, or mortals, or even dwarfs – we don't care much for dwarfs – but they must learn to leave elves alone. Now find a mount and get yourself a weapon. I wouldn't advise a club – you won't get near enough to use it. A slingshot, perhaps? Or a spear? Not a bow. We have enough of those. Yes, a slingshot would be good. The Thursae have learned to dodge arrows, but pebbles are harder to see in flight. You could aim for his eyes and blind him, then we will shoot him to death, turn him into a hedgehog with a multitude of arrows, eh?'

Thorn smiled. It was not a pretty sight. His lips curled back revealing two very pointed ones where a human's molars were normally found.

Osric had heard of the Thurse, as he would have called them. There were many stories about these foul giants who were bent on destruction. It was their one delight in life, to demolish the work of others. Whole villages had been smashed to pieces in the night by these creatures. And it was not just men or elves the Thurse targeted. They would stamp on a skylark's nest with just as much pleasure as they would crush a badger's holt. Osric had never seen a Thurse. Very few humans had seen a Thurse just as very few humans had seen an elf. Rarity of sighting did not mean they were not out there, though. There was plenty of circumstantial evidence to show that giants walked the earth and the Thurse were not the only ones. There were also the Ettin. They were not as destructive as the Thurse but definitely giants and definitely to be avoided if a man were to remain with four limbs.

'Are you with us?' asked Thorn. 'Or do you just take hospitality and not give any return?'

Osric was affronted by the jibe. 'Of course I am with you. If I refused to join my hosts in a matter like this I would lose my honour. Honour to an Angle is everything, especially to a prince like myself. Without honour a man is nothing. Are we going to fight the whole tribe of Thurse, or what?'

'No, you'll be relieved to hear that we have isolated the giant responsible for roasting and eating Larch, but still it will not be easy. They are mighty creatures, the Thursae and you will be risking your life.'

'You are not talking to a mere Jute or a Saxon, Thorn. I am an Angle,' replied Osric with dignity, straightening his back, 'a prince, the son of King Eorl. I have been taught to fight with many weapons and not to fear the foe. However, I shall take a spear since the slingshot is not one of them. I know how to handle a spear.'

At midday the elfen were gathered, all on horseback. They bristled with bows and quivers, and indeed, some carried staves on this occasion: strong thick rods of oak. They rode without saddles or bridles, simply holding on to their mounts by the horse's mane and gripping the flanks with their long lean legs. The steeds themselves were quite beautiful animals with sleek coats, fine limbs and high heads. Their manes and tails flowed like silk threads. Any Anglo-Saxon would give ten of his own horses to have just one of these creatures of the wind. Mounting the warhorse he had been given, Osric felt the strength and power that flowed from the beast and into his thighs Osric cried excitedly, 'Oh, this must be the most wonderful of horses!'

'Better hope none of the gods heard you say that,' snorted Thorn. 'There is of course the eight-legged steed Sleipnir, the mount of Grim to consider when making rash statements.'

Yes, of course, the Lord of the Wild Hunt, Woden – sometimes known as Grim – had a horse that thundered across the heavens and was the epitome of all equines.

However, before Osric could mentally chastise himself, there came a shout from one of the leading elves and suddenly the whole troop was racing through the forest. Much of the deep snow had melted a few days previously, but there were still patches on grassy clumps and puddles that had iced over. It might have been a precarious ride if they had not been on horses that knew every crevice and wrinkle of the earth. Osric didn't need to manoeuvre his beast. It knew where and when to gallop and where to slow to a canter. Sometimes, like the others around it, the horse even dropped to a trot or a walk, when the going was marshy and the ground treacherous under hoof. They rode below wide blue skies with just a few streaks of white cirrus like the lazy brushstrokes of a god. On the horizon there seemed a swirl of winds that played tricks with the eyes. Osric noticed that they were following the river, which wound its silvery serpentine shape through the undulating countryside. Had they trapped the giant with his back to the water? Perhaps they intended to drive the Thurse onto the thin river ice and so destroy him that way?

However, the ride finally took them away from the river and up towards the north and at last to the sea. There were cliffs in this region that often crumbled into the waters of the ocean. They found the Thurse they were looking for, clearly lost and hoping to follow the shoreline to meet with some familiarity of scenery. He was standing on the top of a chalk cliff when he heard the sound of the hooves pounding on the frozen ground and turned to face three score elves, all armed with bows and sticks, and one single mortal youth with a spear in his fist.

'Ho!' the giant roared. 'You would brook a Thurse?'

Osric stared up at the face of this monster, who was as tall as a mature hornbeam. He was a thickly-made creature, sturdy in every part, with a great head whose skull was undoubtedly dull, heavy and as solid as a drystone wall. His arms hung huge and long, the hands down past his thighs and level with his great oak-knot knees. The feet splayed outwards, flat and wide, having to cover a vast area of ground to keep this massive lump of muscle, bone and fat upright. A nose the size of a wild boar flared to reveal cavernous nostrils. The genitals that hung between its legs were monstrous and ugly, swinging back and forth with the giant's cumbersome movements.

'We are here to kill you for your murder of one of us,' called Thorn. 'Prepare to leave this world for another – if you have one.'

The giant's thick-lipped mouth sprayed spittle through jagged horribly-broken teeth. The Thurse try to eat anything and often made mistakes. The creature roared out his anger on being confronted.

'I killed no one.'

'You roasted an elf on a charcoal fire then devoured him,' shouted Thorn. 'Do you not recall that terrible act?'

Suddenly the puzzled brow smoothed over and a large crescent smile of satisfaction came over the face of the Thurse.

'Ah yes. Enjoyed it too.'

At this the elves charged forward in fury, loosing arrows at the lumbering creature. They rode swiftly past him at a distance where he would not be able to knock them from their horses. However the arrows did little to harm the giant. As Osric had guessed, the huge Thurse was so well armoured with a thick muscled skin and even thicker bones the arrows hardly penetrated. They stuck in him, sure, but they hung from flint heads which hardly pierced the beast. Also, the giant was very adept at warding off the arrows that were aimed at his eyes, the most vulnerable part of his anatomy. There were a few arrows stuck in his eyelids, but he seemed to have the knack of closing his eyes just before an arrow hit one of them.

Soon he began to tire of this game and continued his walk along the cliff top, irritated but not impeded by the shafts from the elfen bows. They were like gnat bites to a human: annoying but hardly life-threatening. The elves were desperate to bring him down, but they lacked the power needed to fell this creature. After a while they began to run out of arrows and it looked as if the expedition would have to return to the elfen glade without completing its mission. Then Osric had an idea.

'Thorn,' he yelled. 'Get those elves with staves to follow me in.'

He thumped his heels on the flanks of his mount, which shot forward towards the monstrous giant without any hesitation. Osric cantered up right behind the Thurse and was within a few yards of his target when one of the elves cried excitedly, 'Throw the spear now! Throw it!' making the giant turn and look. But throwing his spear like a javelin was not Osric's intention, for that would be no more effective than the arrows had been. He held the weapon like a lance and intended to drive the point full force, with the weight of his steed's charge behind it, into the ankle bone of this great hulk of flesh and bone. The giant saw him and stooped to swipe him from the back of the horse, but Osric ducked down behind the left flank and the huge calloused hand swept by him just catching his long hair. It almost unseated the youth, but he clung on, one hand on the mane, the other directing the lance. Flint head met flesh and bone, jarring Osric and taking him off the back of his mount. He tumbled to the frosted ground and rolled away from a foot that tried to trample him.

The giant now howled in pain and reached down to pluck the spear from where it protruded from his left outside ankle bone.

'Now!' yelled Osric. 'The staves!'

The elves with these stout weapons rode forward and while the giant was bent and plucking the lance from his foot, they hammered on his temple with the ends of their oak staves, pole-axing the creature in the way that mortals did with their cattle. Stunned at first, the giant simply toppled forward. But the fierce pole-axing was relentless and the elves did not give up for a second, thumping with all their strength on the same spot of the giant's forehead. Finally he wailed and groaned, calling out pitifully, 'Leave me alone! Leave me alone!' But elves have no mercy, no compassion when it comes to revenge. They are absolutely cold and ruthless. In a short while the giant lay unmoving, clearly dead, and the whole episode was over. Osric was shocked and a little sickened by the remorseless way they had despatched the Thurse, but at the same time knowing that if such a creature had eaten one of his family, he would probably have been just as unfeeling in his actions as they had been.

The elves physically rolled the giant over the cliff and watched him fall to the rocks and wild waves below. His body whacked the granite then made a mighty splash on entering the surf. It was done. There was no more to be said. Not Thorn nor any of the other elves came to Osric and thanked him or praised his initiative and courage. It was as if they had done it all themselves. On the return journey to the glade they hardly took notice of the youth who had saved them from failure. Even Linnet only mentioned the deed in passing, saying, 'I heard you helped to kill the Thurse today.'

'Yes, I was the hero of the hour,' remarked Osric, grimly, 'though no one seemed to appreciate that fact.'

'We're not proud creatures,' replied Linnet, though without any sense of criticism. 'We do what we have to do and do not expect praise. You wouldn't want me to puff you up, would you? Surely not?'

'Surely I would,' he replied, sourly. 'That's the reward for risking one's life.'

'Boasting. We don't like boasting. Now go and wash before you touch me again – you've got greasy hands from eating that dead animal.'

'Dead *cooked* animal. You make me sound like a wild beast.'

She smiled one of those enchanting smiles. 'You *are* a wild beast – that's what I love about you.'

FOUR

Spring came early. It was still only the month of Hreth when the bulbs threw up their green shoots. Birds began returning from far off places, individually and in bright swarms over the landscapes and lakes. The elfen began to change colour. Osric woke one morning to find his beloved had royal-blue eyes and hair that mimicked the colour of the blooms on a gorse bush. Her skin had darkened to echo the hue of the bark of a larch. It was like waking to find a stranger in his bed.

'Does it happen so quickly?' he asked.

'What?'

'This change – this seasonal alteration in your form?'

She shrugged. 'It happens when it happens.'

'It's very strange.'

'Only to mortals.'

Now that the month of the winds had come, when standing hares were fighting in the fields, Osric had a decision to make. That decision was not whether to stay or go: he was definitely leaving the elfen. What he needed to decide was whether to sneak away without saying anything to anyone, or confront Linnet and explain why he could not stay. The easiest course was naturally to run away without a word, but Osric felt his honour would be impinged if he played the coward. So very reluctantly he went to Linnet and told her that he was going and would not be coming back. Her face fell and tears entered the new blueness of her large eyes.

'You do not love me any more?'

'That's not true. I do love you a great deal. Unfortunately, my darling Linnet, I do not love you enough to give up my life as a mortal. What you're asking me to do is to cast away my birthright, not just as a royal prince, but as a mortal too. I'm not prepared to bury myself in Elfland, here to die of boredom even though I have my loved one at my side. Can you see what you're asking me to do? If our worlds were indeed one place, I would love you until death took me. But they are separate regions which exist side-by-side, but not as one. I must go, my sweet Linnet, or I will indeed waste away. I need to do things that mortals do. I must avenge my father's death. I must wrest the kingship from a usurper and rule a people who need me…'

'Yes, and die in battle.'

'Indeed, if I must, for the right cause.'

She pouted. 'Go then, leave me. I care nothing for you any more.'

'I cannot believe that's true.'

'Can't you? Just as I fell in love with you over one single kiss, so I can fall out of love with you now that you reject me. Go and play your silly war games, but know that if you leave, you can never return. Even were you to find your way back again, I would not want you.'

'It's not as if we're actually married,' he said, 'there was no ceremony.'

'Elves don't need ceremonies. You know that. It was enough that I gave myself to you – and you to me.'

His heart felt as if it were made of iron.

'I'm so sorry, Linnet – I shall never forget you.'

She gave him a wicked-looking smile.

'Oh, I'm aware of that. Every night I shall be with you, in your dreams – and every morning you'll wake and wish you were back with me. You will dream of no other, nor of any other thing – only of me. You will yearn until your heart aches as much as mine does now. You will languish, you will pine, but there will be no respite, because I shall be as a dead mortal to you, never to be seen again.'

Thorn rode with him to where the fiefdom of the elves touched the world of mortals and there bid him farewell.

'Goodbye, mortal – good luck with your quest, whatever it may be.'

It was the first time any of the elves apart from Linnet had engaged Osric with anything like friendliness.

'Goodbye, Thorn. I hope Linnet will be all right.'

'She'll fret for a while, perhaps a long while, but her heart is strong.'

'I hope so. She said she would plague me with dreams until I die.'

'You did well with the giant. We don't praise our own because it's not necessary for an elf to feel proud, but I know you mortals need bolstering on occasion, so I tell you, it was a feat well done. You thought quickly and carried out your plan swiftly and without consideration for you own safety. That's to be admired. For this reason I will speak with her and ask her to let you go. She is feeling vengeful at this moment, but after I have talked with her, I am sure she will allow you your own life. Now go – and try to remember your time with us with affection.'

Thorn then gifted Osric an elfen bow and a quiver of arrows.

'You'll need a weapon, mortal, to protect yourself against your own kind, if not to defend yourself against rogue creatures of our side-by-side worlds.'

'Thank you, Thorn.'

Osric had no more words to give and turned the mount he had been given – the same horse he had ridden against the giant Thurse – and cantered away. Now that he was out of the thrall of the faerie, he decided to name his steed.

'I shall call you Magic,' he whispered in the beast's ear, 'for you are from a magical land, the fiefdom of the elfen.'

Lord Ing:

So, the youth has done the one thing I expected and dreaded. He has broken the heart of one of my children. Do I crush him now like a beetle? Yet, yet, I hear the Linnet calling me, asking me, begging me not to harm the boy. She loves him still, in the way that elves love mortals. So I must be lenient, I suppose, and still watch over him. She has asked me to and I am inclined to favour this unfortunate boy.

The young prince paused on the ridge above the river, turning in his saddle to look around him. Which way to take? Directly south were the East Saxons. Not particularly friendly neighbours. Then the Jutes below the big river, who seemed to go quietly about the business of living. To the west of the Jutes were the South Saxons and beyond them the West Saxons. Osric knew little about them. Then there were the Umbrians: a long way from Osric's home. To the west were the Mercians. Neighbouring the Mercians was the border with the wild Celts, whose princes had been displaced by Osric's people. The Saxons, Frisians, Jutes, Franks and Angles had arrived in shiploads and slowly but surely had taken over the land for farming. They had driven out, enslaved or absorbed any Celts who opposed them. It was a big boiling pot of new peoples who were trying to get a foothold in this land. The last tribes who had invaded the islands a long while back – the Cornish and the Walha who had been pushed out into the south-western corners of the island – were doing their best to send these continental latecomers back where they came from.

Also among the local populations there were descendants of Roman soldiers and their families who had stayed when the legions returned to Rome. They were not all from Rome, of course, since the majority of the soldiers in that army had been auxiliaries recruited from Gaul and the same areas where the Angles and Saxons set sail from once Roman rule in Britannia was at and end. These people too had been absorbed into the tribes of the invaders and had added to the general mix.

Whichever way Osric went, providing he didn't go too far north or west, he would meet with folk who spoke the same language and whose customs and rites were much the same as those of his own people. It would probably be wise not to reveal his royal ancestry, but to travel as a young man seeking adventure. Thus he set forth towards Mercia, a powerful fiefdom with land that had wide borders. The Mercians were Angles like himself, so he could probably slip in without too much notice and find a way to make a living until he was ready to return home. When that would be, he had no idea at this time, but his heart burned for revenge. So far as he was concerned, Wulfgar and Eadgard were Death-in-waiting. His blood almost seared his veins when he thought of those two treacherous warriors. Such a heinous crime could not go unpunished and the punisher had to be Osric.

Osric rode for many days. Magic proved to be not only a swift horse, but one with stamina over long distances. At one point, just as twilight was giving way to darkness, the wandering pair came across a brace of gallows at a crossroads, with two dead men hanging from them. As Osric rode beneath the vile bodies, which had been ravaged by birds and climbing mammals, he heard the two dead men arguing about who was responsible for the murder they had committed together.

'You held the knife! It was you who plunged the blade into the pedlar's heart, not me. Why am I dangling here alongside a man with a black heart? I have done no crime. I am innocent.'

'Innocent?' snorted his swinging companion in hollow tones. 'Who was it stole the pedlar's pots and tried to sell them in the market? Who was it who encouraged me to use the blade? It was you, you filthy wretch, who brought me to this. I am on Woden's tree of death because of you. You were the one who said let's do it, let's earn ourselves a little wealth without having to work for it...'

Osric looked up at the faces now pitted and eyeless. One of them had lost his nose to the pecking of ravens. The other, whose hair had once been long and golden, had lost most of his beautiful locks to springtime birds making their nests. Their ragged garments hung from their emaciated forms, soiled, rotten and stinking of corrupted body fluids. The youthful prince winced and wrinkled his nose.

'Why don't you just accept what the Wyrd have designed for you,' he murmured as the darkness set in. 'You only have each other now. Your failure to accept responsibility for what you did in this life is preventing you from going to the next world.'

'Ha!' cried one of the men whose feet had been pared to the bone, 'what next, world? We can see the monster Hellmouth and he waits impatiently to swallow us into his gut. I think I prefer hanging here, thank you very much.'

'And who are you,' moaned the other dead man, 'to criticise us – you having murdered your father.'

Osric tugged Magic's mane to halt him. 'Who told you that?'

'It's common knowledge,' chorused the hanged men, clearly delighted to have another person to quarrel with, 'every thegn and churl knows that.'

Osric decided to spend the night near the gallows, in case the dead men had more to tell. He hobbled Magic near some lush grass and with his back to one of the gallow's support posts pondered on what he had already been told.

So, Eadgard and Wulfgar had put the blame on Osric for the death of his father and probably for the deaths of the other two thegns as well. He would need to avoid villages close to home, knowing that word had now gone out that he was a patricide. Eadgard and his fellow conspirators would bear testament, all horrified indignation and fury, to swear they had witnessed the murder of the father by the son. It was what such men would do. They would point out that Osric's 'fierce ambition' had overcome the love and loyalty he should have for his father the beloved ring-giver and gold-giver of his faithful and true-hearted hearth-companions, his thegns.

He could hear Eadgard booming in the Great Hall, 'He wanted to be king before his time. We all know that...' Wulfgar and the other plotters would be murmuring "Yes, yes," and encouraging thegns ignorant of the truth to follow them in their condemnation '...and it is ever thus that a son too eagerly seeks power and looks on his father as a barrier to his nefarious aims. Osric must be hunted down and he must face the law which applies to prince and churl alike. Send word to all our neighbours that they should be vigilant in capturing this killer of a king. He has violated his oath and must pay for it with his life.'

All twelve-year-old Angles and Saxons took an oath to obey the law and never to commit a crime. Breaking that oath was perhaps as bad as committing the murder itself. A boy's or a man's word was a sacred thing and to abuse it was to cause great anguish amongst his people, for who could you trust if not your own?

If at all possible they would make sure Osric was dead rather than put him before the court to argue his case. If he were captured alive by another village, Eadgard would send Wulfgar to bring him back home and Wulfgar would of course kill him for 'attempting to escape' and there would be no revision of such a deed.

Oh yes, they thought that because Osric was young he was stupid. He was now an outlaw and anyone could kill an outlaw without repercussion. Well, they were wrong. The gods – or at least one of them – knew that Osric was innocent of such a crime and was protecting him. Why else would there be dead-men soothsayers on the road? Some being was watching over him and if asked to guess Osric would have replied, 'Lord Ing,' the same god who had come to his aid when he was fleeing from Wulfgar and his hounds. This revelation did not mean, however, that Osric was beloved of *all* the gods. He had to be wary and not trust in an invincibility. The gods of the Angles and Saxons were as fickle as ordinary men. Osric remembered his mother telling him the story of Starkathr, a warrior who had crossed the swan-road from the continent and who had settled with Woden's blessing on the island the Romans called Britannia.

Starkathr had been loved by Woden himself, but hated by the Saxon god Thunor, the Lord of Thunder and Lightning.

Woden gifted Starkathr with three normal lifetimes, but Thunor cursed the warrior with committing a terrible crime for each lifetime.

Woden blessed him with riches, but Thunor made sure he never owned a grain of land. Woden awarded Starkathr victory in every battle, but Thunor made sure he was severely wounded in every one of them.

Woden gave him the gift of oral poetry, but Thunor managed to curse him with a bad memory.

Finally, Woden caused Starkathr to be loved by the nobles, while Thunor ensured he was hated by the ordinary people.

It was not enough to be the favourite of one god, a man had to be careful to appease all the gods and not arouse enmity for a stupid word or deed.

Thus it was, while Osric was musing, that a small dragon, not much larger than a bull, landed nearby with a leathery flapping of its bat-like wings. Osric's village had once been terrorised by a dragon much larger than this one, which his father had dispatched in a fierce fight. Dragons often had protective patrons – lone, rogue kings who lived in the fastnesses of dark ironstone mountains and were interested in nothing but gold and jewels – and Osric was mildly interested in the history of this particular beast. He stood up and unhitched his bow in case the dragon wanted to do battle, for although it was small it was not young. There were many species of dragon, just as there were many species of birds. The scales on this one's back and flanks were encrusted with brown, dead, brittle lichen. One of its fangs was missing, the left one, and the ear on the same side was notched and torn. Its tail was long and whip-like, with a curved dagger-sharp tip. Baleful red eyes were fixed on Osric's face and the youth realised he was not going to get away without a fight.

'Do you belong to anyone in particular?'

'I am my own self,' replied the beast, 'and have no master.'

Satisfied, Osric asked that the fiery-mouthed monster to go away, which request was curtly refused. There was a brief but frenzied battle. The dragon tried to get close enough to use its wicked tail, lashing out with a wildness that such creatures employ in place of considered strategy. Osric used the posts of the gallows to duck behind and block the dragon's blows. This particular breed did not have fiery breath and relied on its claws, teeth and tail to kill its prey. It was also very stupid. Any creature with a modicum of intelligence could tell it that in such a conflict – an archer against a close-combat beast – there could only be one winner. So it was: the dragon was slain by one of Osric's arrows. It died cursing the youth, but a dragon's curses are weak and ineffectual. All their strength is in their physical make-up and they have little power to cause spiritual harm, since they pray to no god, nor follow any ideology. They simply exist to cause mayhem and chaos where they can and to instil fear and havoc amongst mortals.

It has to be said that there is some good in the presence of dragons on the Earth. Indeed, they often bind people together in order to fight against a common enemy. Yes, men invaded, fought for land and gold, but, even once they had these selfish needs met, they still found weak excuses to attack and kill one another. Dragons and their kind helped to focus on dangers outside petty wars about nothing but glory and power.

Osric knew that dragons were necessary to the world and though they had to be slain on occasion, he also knew it would be a bad day for mankind when they disappeared altogether.

It grew a little chilly as the grey twilight came in and Osric gathered some dry grass, twigs and with the sparking flints he carried he made a fire. There was a duck tied round the neck of Magic, which had been plucked and gutted, ready for roasting. Herbs were taken out of a small double-sack that was also slung around the horse's neck. Along with the herbs were greens and roots. With these ingredients the hungry prince began to prepare the last meal of the day.

ꜰɪᴠᴇ

While Osric was again leaning his back against a gallow's post, the corpses of the dead men now silent and spinning slowly round and round, back and forth in the evening breezes, another youth was coming towards the same spot. He was thinner than Osric, built even more wiry than the prince, with a pinched face and fierce black eyes. The dark hair on his head was roughly cut and stood up like stiff grass, being heavily engrained with dust that clung to the head's natural grease and follicle oils. His face, it had to be said, carried a good deal of dirt and grime, not having been united with water for at least three days. The youth needed to satisfy his thirst like any other mortal and such water that had come his way had gone down his throat. For all his crafty, cunning appearance he was a lusty stripling and indeed there was, deep down, a basic honesty which belied his aggressive bearing and expression.

His name was Kenric, and he was born a Saxon. Kenric was the dispossessed son of a farrier and, like Osric, an orphan. His father and mother had been killed in a raid by the Mercian Angles and Kenric had hated Angles ever since. He also hated his Saxon kin because they had turned him away when as a young child he was in need of their help, and between them they had laid claim to his father's forge and precious tools, leaving Kenric nothing. He hated the gods for similar reasons, his prayers coming to nought. There were many harrows on the highways and byways, but Kenric ignored them all, refusing to worship. In fact there were not many people or beings that Kenric did not hate, given that he had found no friend or benefactor among them. Always, ever since he was eight years of age, he had been forced to rely on his own initiative and resources, which had sometimes got him into trouble, his enterprise not stopping short of stealing the odd loaf of bread.

Kenric carried with him a sword, a seax made by his father. This was the weapon from which the Saxons took their name. There were several different types of seaxes and Kenric's was the 'long' seax, with multiple fullers and grooves. The edge curved slightly upwards towards the point, the back curved away gently. There were snakes in the patterned blade. The youth could use the weapon efficiently when it became necessary. He was dressed in a churl's smock, tied at the waist with a piece of old string. The smock was of thick wool, which kept him warm on dry nights, but when it rained it became sodden and heavy, and at those times – providing it was not winter weather – he simply removed it and carried it under his arm, preferring nakedness to lumpy wet clothing. This night was clement though, and he was happy to have the wool next to his skin. The sword, in its sheath, was slung on a loop of leather, a baldric, and hung down his back. He could unsheathe it in a split second, should he need to defend himself. When he had the crossroads in his sight, he saw to his surprise a dead dragon, a beautiful horse munching grass and a youth dressed in expensive fabrics and carrying a bow and quiver of arrows. The young man, far too smooth and genteel-looking for Kenric's taste, stood up as he approached.

'Be whole,' said Kenric, using the traditional greeting.

'You also,' came the wary reply.

The two youths stood for a moment eyeing each other.

Kenric nodded upwards towards the two dead men.

'I see you've got comp'ny already.'

'Yes, but they've stopped talking to me.'

Kenric frowned. Was this youth simple in the head?

'Well, be that as it may, do you have any objection to me sharing your fire?'

'You're welcome to join me in my meal,' replied the youth. 'Do you have any wine about you?'

Kenric thought this a stupid question, since he was clearly without anything but the sword on his back.

'No wine, no water, nothin' at all.'

The other looked disappointed. 'That's a shame. I haven't so much as tasted a drop of mead for nearly six months. Just weak elfen wine made from blackberry and elderberry juice.'

'Ah, you're an elf then,' replied Kenric, thinking the boy was more of a lunatic than he had first imagined. 'One of the invisible beings.'

The other youth straightened and screwed up his face.

'Are you daft? Do I look like an elf?'

Kenric took a step back. 'Don't throw insults at your guests, unless you can back it up with muscle.' He put his right hand over his shoulder and gripped the hilt of his sword. 'Who are you, anyway?'

The other straightened his stance.

'My name is Osric, son of Eorl, King of the East Angles. Be careful boy, I have just slain a dragon, as you can plainly see, and am more than a match for a skinny churl.'

Kenric glanced towards the body of the beast and then took his hand off the blade down his back..

'A very small dragon,' He then nodded towards the bow now in Osric's hands, 'slaughtered at a very safe distance. Not much bigger'n a sparrow really. But you did kill it, I can see that. So, you're a prince of sorts, you say? Of the East Angles. We Saxons don't think much of Angles. In fact, as a Saxon churl, I'm probably equal to an Angle prince.' Kenric then stared at the meat that was roasting over the fire with hungry eyes. 'And you'd be skinny too, if you hadn't eaten for two days.'

He could see the other youth smouldering, having received words no prince, whether of Angles or Saxons, should be subject to. 'Look,' finished Kenric, 'let's sit down and talk, and you can tell me why you're wanderin' all over the land when you have a fiefdom waiting for you with the east Angles, eh? Out here,' he swept the landscape with his arm, 'one needs to travel in numbers. The world's crawlin' with thieves and bandits, and all sorts of riffraff. You with your elf's bow and me with my sword make a good pair, don't you think? Heck, I'm starving.'

Osric was still glaring at him, but then suddenly he broke into a smile. It was clear the royal youth normally had a pleasant disposition. Kenric smiled back and then the pair of them grasped each other's weapon hand for a moment, each secretly trying the strength of the other, before Osric let go and pointed at the food.

'You can join me, Saxon, and welcome. No more insults, though. I've had enough of those from the elves to last me a lifetime. What's your name?'

'Kenric.'

'Well, Kenric, I could use a companion, not to say a friend, right at this time. Yes, that's it, sink your teeth into the drumstick. Let the grease run down your chin, but lick it off before it drips into the fire. Ah, too late, it sizzles. Never mind, take a hunk of bread and wipe the rest off before you lose it. No mead I'm afraid. Only water. Good, refreshing stream water in that skin. You see, I've been cast out of my inneryard, into the outeryard by treacherous nobles. They murdered my father and would have killed me if I hadn't managed to kill two of them first...'

'You killed two warrior thegns?' said Kenric, looking up from his repast. 'Small ones, like the dragon?'

'Let's not start that again. Well, I didn't kill them with my bare hands. I led them across dangerous ice and they went through and drowned. The third man, Wulfgar, escaped with his life. Now they hunt me down like a rogue wolf. They know I'll be back to settle with them if they don't get to me first.'

Kenric nodded, stripping the last of the flesh from the bone with his teeth.

'And the elves? They're after you too?'

'No, listen, this is the best part. While I was running from the hounds the great god Ing came to me and guided me to a glade. There in the clearing was a group of elves on beautiful horses – like that one. I call him Magic...'

'Good name.' Kenric had to admit the horse was a beautiful creature.

'Anyway, the elves took me in and I almost married one of them, well, she said we *were* married – a beautiful maiden elf called Linnet.' Osric's eyes went a little misty at this point and there was a catch in his voice, which made Kenric think he might have been mistaken. He had been thinking that Osric was making up a lot of this nonsense, but clearly the other youth believed what he was saying or he wouldn't get emotional. Was he then mad? Who on this Earth had seen elves? Only witches and shamans. Ordinary youths, be they princes or paupers, did not see the creatures from the other side. 'Well,' continued Osric, sniffing, 'I had to leave her if I was not going to spend the rest of my life with Thorn and the other faerie. You know they do nothing but hunt and they don't even kill the quarry. At least, they do kill it, but it comes back to life.'

Definitely cuckoo-brained.

'So, how long did you spend with 'em? The elven?'

'Six months. They gave me Magic and Linnet said if I left her she would cease to love me, but I really couldn't stay, could I? What a waste of a life. Living amongst creatures who think it's hilarious to sour the milk after some poor churl's daughter has spent hours getting it out of the cows? Now I'm an outlaw, without a friend in the world. All the good people of my fiefdom, even those in my inneryard, think I've killed my own father. That's what the dead men told me.' He indicated the two corpses swinging gently in the firelight. 'They told me Eadgard, the man who's usurped my father's leadership, and Wulfgar his henchman, that these two had spread the word that I had done the murder.'

40

'The dead men, these two,' Kenric looked up at the rotting pair, 'told you all this?'

Osric sighed. 'You don't believe me, do you?'

'Let's just say I'm sceptical – that's a good word for a churl, ain't it? Sceptical? I learned that from a monk.'

'What's a monk?'

'Oh, a sort of shaman, a holy man. They have different gods to us. Well, only one actually. They call him, well, *God*. You would, wouldn't you, if there was only one, because he wouldn't need a name, being...'

'Being the only one. Yes. So, you think I'm a liar, Kenric?'

'No, just a bit touched in the head with all that's happened to you – your dad being chopped down an' all that. I'm willin' to let it pass though, without further comment. Is there any more of that bread-cake?'

'No, it's all gone, and I haven't even eaten yet. What are you doing?'

Kenric had got up and had unsheathed his sword. It was not a wonderful blade and probably didn't even deserve a name, but it looked sharp enough. Osric stood up, wondering what the Saxon churl was going to do. Indeed, all the boy did was to walk back to the two gallows and cut the ropes that held the cadavers aloft. The two bodies fell with a sort of squashy sound on the packed-earth crossroads. Maggots sprayed into the air in the moonlight. Bits flew off the corpses, a hand going this way, a foot going another. Kenric got a stout branch that had fallen from an oak and then proceeded to heave the bits of putrid flesh and bone into a ditch, where the carrion could be stripped by wolves and foxes. Then he came back to the fire and sat down with his new companion. The stink from the rotten corpses was very strong, but they were youths who had lived with smells like that all their lives.

'They won't be talking to anyone else,' Kenric said. 'Only out of the mouths of them that eat 'em. Now, want to hear my story? It's not as fancy as yours – no kings, thegns or elves to speak of. My old man was a farrier, which is you'll agree, quite a respectable profession, as jobs go.' Kenric's eyes went blacker than usual. 'He was cut down by an Angle warrior. My mum too. It was a raid and the rest of the village got away, but my dad was hammering iron on the anvil and didn't hear the horn warning us of an attack. The Angles then raped my mother and afterwards stuck a sword in her belly, even though she was carrying my next brother or sister. That's my story, Prince of Angles, and I've hated your people ever since.'

'I don't blame you for that, Kenric,' replied the other youth, earnestly, 'but you know, your warriors do the same. They attack our villages and kill our people. It's all over the land at the moment – raids, war. The Mercians killing the West Saxons and the East Angles doing battle with the East Saxons, and the Jutes raiding the Frisians. Tiw, the God of War, seems to be enjoying himself lately. It's the way things are. Look, we're both orphans now. Let's put aside our birthrights and pledge a grith – a pact of peace between the two of us and be damned to war.'

'Tiw is a great god, though,' said Kenric, looking nervously out into the night. 'I'm sure he's got his reasons for all these battles.' Although the boy did not pray to the gods, he certainly believed in their presence.

'Oh yes,' Osric replied, catching Kenric's tone. 'Tiw is a great god and not to be questioned. 'You know that Tiw lost his hand when he put it into the mouth of the great wolf, Fenrir, in order that the terrible beast could be trussed. The wolf bit it off, clean, severed it at the bone joint. That was very brave, to sacrifice his hand in order to capture Fenrir. Now the God of War is a cripple, with only one…'

'Yes, yes,' interrupted Kenric, thinking his new companion was going a bit too far. 'We've all been told the story by our elders. I'm just saying we mustn't blame Tiw for wanting war. It's his purpose.'

'Yes – it's what he does. You can't blame him for that.'

Kenric decided this was enough to ensure that Tiw did not come down in the middle of the night and cut their two throats while they slept.

'So,' he said, 'elves, eh?'

'Don't keep going on about that,' growled Osric. 'By the way, I did help kill a giant too – not a small one, either.'

'An Ettin?'

'A Thurse!'

Kenric was impressed. 'I would like to have been there.'

'But you don't believe in elves and presumably giants too.'

'I didn't say I didn't believe in them. Everyone does, of course. Otherwise people wouldn't get elfshot with poisonous darts, would they? What I said was you can't see them. But if you *could* see them, and you went out to kill a giant with them, the best sort of giant to do battle with would be a Thurse. They're devils, ain't they? Just for the hell of it. They'll rip down a hut in the night, or break a fence, or throw a boulder onto a bridge and smash it to pieces. All just for the hell of it.'

The two youths chatted on, deep into the evening, until Kenric realised he was getting no answers to his questions and knew that Osric had fallen asleep. To his detriment, Kenric did think about stealing the prince's horse – how did he know he was a prince, anyway, just because the other had said so? – but something about the youth who had given him hospitality caused him to reconsider. So, to his eternal credit, he didn't go through with this crime and, curling his thin body round the remains of the fire, fell asleep also. In the night Tiw came down to have a look at them. Indeed he had been ruffled by Osric's grumbles and the insult of being called a cripple. However, he saw that they were indeed very young men, not yet even a score of years, and was wise enough to realise youths of that age make rash statements without really thinking them through first. The great god warmed his hands on the embers of the fire, then shook his head before leaving. A tawny owl saw him ascend and let out a loud hoot in fright, before flying into the safety of a wood.

SIX

Osric woke first and poked the fire, but the ashes had gone cold. Both youths had slept too deeply to wake and tend it. He then stood up and stretched, staring out over the rolling countryside. Magic was there, not far off, his noble head held high in the morning light. There was mist weaving amongst the woodland trees, which spilled out and drifted across hillocks and down into valley pockets, where it nestled like a warm furry beast seeking a comfortable bed. The birds were already awake, of course, calling to each other. Two rooks sat on the spar of one of the gallows, having fed early on the mouldering remains of the hanged men that lay in the ditch. One of the birds wiped its horny white beak noisily on the lumber. This woke Kenric, who sat up, shivered, and then stretched his limbs, two at a time. He blinked hard, then rolled over and climbed to his feet, peering out over the landscape.

'Someone's coming,' he said.

Osric looked in the same direction and there indeed was a dark shape moving through the mist, coming from the direction of the distant sea. It was a man, tallish, who seemed to be carrying no weapon. Still, the two youths did not want to take any chances and armed themselves with their own war-trappings. When the figure came closer he stopped, to stare at the young men. Clearly he had not been paying attention to his surroundings before that moment and this was the first time he had noticed them. He stood for several minutes, before waving a hand.

'Be whole, boys.'

'Be whole, yourself,' replied Osric. 'Who are you calling *boys?*'

'No offence, no offence. You're young men, I see.'

The stranger had a peculiar accent and he spoke Anglo-Saxon as if he were unused to using some of the words.

'You're no Angle or Saxon. Where are you from?' asked Osric.

The man bristled. 'What's it to you?'

'This is my fiefdom,' snapped Osric. 'You are a stranger.'

The newcomer was not a young man himself. Osric guessed he was somewhere around four decades in years. He had long blond hair, matted and filthy, and wore a blue cloak held up by a clasp on the right shoulder. His grimy face was lined and furrowed and the stubble on his cheeks had wolf-grey hairs among it. Although no weapon was visible, it would be a very foolish person who wandered around in a land not their own without a weapon of some kind. A dagger probably lay hidden in the folds of that cloak, ready to come out with one quick movement. There was a craftiness about the stranger which neither of the two youths liked. A cunning look in the blue eyes, that flicked back and forth, as if seeking an opportunity to benefit from a lapse of concentration on the part of the young men before him.

Kenric said, 'You can stop casting about. You'll get nothing here. Best keep walking or you might end up on one of those death-trees.' He pointed to the gallows and the two rooks immediately took flight, mistaking the gesture for a threat.

'No harm, no harm,' said the stranger. 'To answer your question, I'm a Geat, from over the swan-road, north of the land of the Danes.'

The youths looked at each other, each wondering whether this man was going to be a problem to them.

'A Geat,' said Osric. 'Like King Beowulf?'

The stranger's eyes lit up. 'Yes, yes, you've heard of our king?'

Kenric said, contemptuously, 'Everyone's heard of the warrior who defeated Grendel.'

'Well, did you hear that he also killed a worm, a great dragon? Much bigger than that worm over there.' He pointed at Osric's kill, which made Kenric smile and nod. 'Bigger than three longships end-to-end. That was when King Beowulf was an old man. I was there, when Beowulf and the dragon slew each other. I was one of the king's men, who stayed with him until the death. Most of the warriors ran away when the dragon came out of his lair, but not me. I stayed. Yes, I stayed. I helped the king by distracting the worm when it came forward with its breath of fire. I saw the king plunge the blade into the worm's throat. Sadly the old man was engulfed in flames at the last,' a tear came trickling down the cheek of the stranger. 'A great sadness. A very great sadness. We gave him a wonderful funeral.'

'So,' Osric said, unimpressed, especially by the size of the dragon, 'if you're this magnificent hero, what are you doing running around my father's fiefdom in nothing a but a rag of a cloak?'

'Ah,' the eyes turned really crafty now, 'I have been very unfortunate – very unfortunate. I believed my assistance to the king was of great value, but those who ran away accused me afterwards of not saving the king's life. You can see how such things can be turned around, after the event. Cowards need to salvage their pride and their reputation. They need someone to blame. I am a victim of my own bravery, my own courage. In staying with the king, I became the obvious target for those who slunk away, fearing for their lives.' He let out a huge sigh and turned his face to the sky, as if asking Woden to acknowledge the unjustness of his plight. 'So I had to run and take a boat to some distant place – the boat I chose came here.'

'Where's your weapon?' asked Kenric.

The stranger looked puzzled. 'My what?'

'How are you going to defend yourself on the road?'

'Why, I have none. It was wrested from me by the cowards. I've had no time to get another. I've heard there's a great maker of swords here in Britannia – a smithy called Wayland. I was hoping to meet with this man and have him forge me a blade worthy of my deeds.'

Both the youths laughed at once.

The stranger looked annoyed. 'Have I said something funny?'

'Yes, of course you have,' answered Osric. 'The Wayland that you speak of was a prisoner of an evil king, who forced him to make swords and jewellery for the king and his wife. In the end Wayland escaped, killed the king sons, bedded his daughter, and then, having had his revenge and leaving the king to grieve the loss of his heirs, Wayland vanished into the mists of a moor, never to be seen again.

'How could he do that? Disappear? Surely the king could have hunted him down.'

Kenric replied simply, 'Wayland was an elf.'

The stranger nodded. 'Ah, that explains it. An elf. Yes, elves and dwarfs are good at such things as sword-making. Well then,' he continued, giving the young men a gruesome lopsided smile, 'I'll just have to trust in your expertise with your own weapons, as we travel the road together. What is that like, by the way?'

'It's a very well-laid track used for carts, wagons and walking. The soldiers from Rome made many roads while they were here and for some reason didn't bother taking them with them when they left.'

Both youths laughed again at this joke, which seemed to infuriate the stranger.

'Stop laughing at me or I'll have to do something about it,' he cried. 'I'm a man full grown and you're just boys. You should be treating me with respect. I'm an elder, not a figure to be mocked. Do you want me to teach you both a lesson in manners?'

Osric was the first to reply. 'Hold your tongue, Geat. You're a guest in our land.' Already Osric's plan not to speak of his nobility had gone to pot when bragging to Kenric. 'You're speaking to a man with royal blood in his veins and another with a sword that he can use with great dexterity. No one said you can travel with us. You go your own way, Geat, and leave us to go ours. I wouldn't be surprised if you ended up on one of those gallows before too long.'

The stranger's face then turned into a tragic mask.

'Please let me come with you. Please? I have no friend in the world.'

'Tell us the truth, then,' said Kenric, looking him up and down, 'for you are no great warrior as you pretend to be. You say you were with King Beowulf until his death. That's surely a lie.'

'No, no, I was with him. I was the one who led him to the dragon's cave.'

'Aha!' yelled Osric. 'I know who you are then! You're the one with no name. The thief who went to King Beowulf, hoping to receive a pardon for your crimes if you promised to show the king the treasure cave of the great dragon! Yes, that's who you are, a miserable thief.'

The man looked enraged. 'That's not fair. I held to my side of the bargain. I led him and his warriors to the cave of the worm. I should have been made a thegn for my services.'

'But you ran away,' said Osric, 'as soon as the worm appeared.'

The thief's tone grew shrill. 'You have no idea what it was like. It was huge. Monstrous! And the flames that came from its throat blistered rocks and whole trees were blackened by a single breath. It filled the valley and with one slam of its tail it could have flattened a dozen warriors. Yes, I ran away, but so did all the thegns. All but one, who stayed with the king. I would like to have been that thegn, but I'm not a warrior, I'm a thief – who does his work well, by the way, and could be of use to you as you travel the land.' The cunning look was back on his face.

Kenric now looked at Osric and said, 'We haven't yet agreed to stay together, but perhaps we should, and take this worthless creature with us. He could indeed be useful, eh?'

'There's one problem,' said Osric. 'I have a horse, you don't.'

'Aw, I'm used to walking. 'So's he. I can't think he's ever been on a horse in his life. You don't need to gallop everywhere, do you? You can give your Magic a run and a jump when you feel he needs it, then come and walk him alongside us? What d'you say?'

'But,' asked Osric, 'where will we go? I was heading towards Mercia. They're Angles – you hate Angles.'

'I can put up with them for a bit. Till we become wealthy.'

Both youths grinned. 'Yes,' Osric said. 'That's what we need to do. Become wealthy.'

'And I can accompany you?' interrupted the Geat, hopefully.

'Why not?' Osric replied. 'But you must promise never to steal from *us* – only from strangers – otherwise I shall have to cut off your arms. And I don't suppose you've got a name, so we'll call you the Thief.'

The Thief, who was of course an habitual liar, answered, 'I promise.'

'Now,' said Osric, before they set out, 'I don't suppose either of you has anything valuable, which we might trade for good food and drink? I'm a little tired of game and water.'

Kenric shook his head, but the thief touched a small earthenware vial which hung on a leather cord from his neck, before he too said, 'No.'

Osric frowned. 'What's in the little pot with the cork?'

'Mine,' replied the Thief, backing away. 'It's private.'

'I asked you what it was, not whose it was.'

'An essence.'

'Precious? Frankincense? Myrrh?'

'Neither.'

Kenric suddenly reached out and snatched the vial from the Thief's neck, breaking the leather thong in the process. The Thief let out a yell of indignation and tried to retrieve his property, or to be more accurate the property of the merchant from whom he stole it. He was not successful. Kenric parried the Thief's flailing hands and handed the vial to Osric. The Angle prince removed the wooden stopper from the neck of the container and sniffed the contents. Immediately he inhaled, the prince suddenly reeled and staggered back, then fell in a dead faint to the ground. The oil in the vial spilled out onto the grasses. Osric then simply lay there, looking pale and close to death, while the other two stared at him aghast.

'What is it?' cried Kenric. 'A poison?'

The Thief shook his head, equally as puzzled as the pauper youth.

'Bergamot,' he said. 'That's all. An oil I took from a travelling merchant in my own land across the swan-road. Only bergamot. It's a harmless substance from a fruit called the spiny orange, grown in the far south of the land over the water.'

Lord Ing:

Three of them, now. Do I take them all under my protective cloak?
No, for if I look after the princely youth, the others will also be
secure. Now, I have the boy on his way to the Land of Dead Spirits, to see his father and
mother. Bergamot. In future he will know the key and will need no assistance from me.
Ah, the scent of bergamot!

Osric suddenly found himself high above the landscape, looking down from the kingdoms in the clouds. He began to stride out, wondering where his feet were taking him. He was aware that there were beings up here in the ether. Not just the gods, for indeed he could see Woden's eight-legged stallion, Sleipnir, grazing in the celestial fields out of the sight of men. There were other creatures, too, strange animals and birds, things he had no names for. Some looked dangerous, but Osric was able to keep clear of them since he was on an island cloud with no bridges between it and the rest of the atmospheric elements. The place was the Spirit Realm, where his mother now dwelt. A sudden thought came to him. His father! His father would be here too! He hurried his feet.

Indeed, when he entered the foul forest wrapped in green mists where the spirits of the dead wandered around looking lost and bemused, he sought his parents among them. He found his mother first. As usual she was melancholy, and upset because she could not hug her son physically. Still, she said she was glad to see him, glad that he was still thinking of her enough to visit her prison. Osric did not tell it her it was not by choice, for he hated the realm where insubstantial disembodied souls wandered to and fro, their minds distracted, their memories shattered. They seemed only interested in gathering the shards of their former lives, trying to knit them together, find a solution that would enable them to rest in peace.

'Mother,' he asked her, 'where is my father?'
'Oh,' she cried, looking around her, 'is he here? I have not seen him.'
'Yes, he came not long ago. He said he wanted to be with you.'
'And I with him. But there are so many. So many. It's difficult.'
Osric said, 'We will find him together.'

As they went, he walking, she drifting, she asked him, 'Son, you are a man full grown. Have you found yourself a wife yet? Remember not only to look on her face, but into her heart and mind too, for she is the keeper of your inneryard keys, the keeper of your worldly wealth and your honour. A good wife will remind you when your passions run amuck, that the *thews* of a man – wisdom, bravery, loyalty, truth, honour, moderation, steadfastness, neighbourliness and industriousness – are the real treasures that reside in the chest he carries with him in his frame. A good wife will not shirk her responsibility and shrink back from her duty of telling her lord that he must look to these qualities before giving in to such fiery feelings as revenge and desire. Have you found such a maid, my son, to help you govern your life?'

'I nearly married an elf.'

'An elf?' shrieked this elegant woman's soul. 'May the gods forbid it!'

'But they don't.'

'Then the laws of men should do. Never marry an elf, or any of the mystical creatures of wood, field and fen. Such unions will never thrive. It is difficult enough for two people to live together without giving them the problems thrown up by having to cope with cultures that are not familiar to them. Both will suffer, elf and mortal, and misery will be the only outcome of such a terrible tie – unless – unless the love that binds them is immeasurably strong and is impossibly profound.'

'Well, I didn't succumb to her charms that deeply,' he was pleased to tell her, casually, not wanting to displease his mother. 'I like her well enough, but that is all.'

He lied, of course, for Osric was one of those young men who fell deeply in love with almost every pretty wench that crossed his path. Luckily they found his father soon after that, before his mother could question him further. The older man was sitting alone, staring down on what was once his fiefdom. Far below, the green fields stretched out flat and unreachable, the river winding through them like a silver whip-thong, the woodlands like dark beds of spikes. Eorl was sighing and weeping a little, the tears hot with anger as well as wet with regret. When he saw his wife and son he let out a bittersweet, poignant cry that echoed through the sky.

'My love!' he exclaimed. 'And my living son.'

Osric gave out a cry of dismay. His father's disembodied form looked ravaged and shredded. Whereas his mother's shape, though insubstantial, resembled the contours she carried in life, his father looked torn and ragged. Clearly something had happened to the king after his death because when Osric had left him that morning to go fishing his father had been whole and hearty, and in fine fettle.

'Father, what happened to you?'

'Ah,' came the king's voice out of the flimsy rags of mist that vaguely recalled the form of that man in life, 'they cut me to pieces. They hung my arms and legs from the beech trees down by the river, and my head was weighted with stones packed and sewn into my mouth then thrown to the fishes. My torso was butchered and the meat given to the hogs to eat. Now my disparate parts are scattered over the earth and my unearthly form has become unstitched and hangs in threads as you see.'

Osric was distraught to hear this desecration of his father's corpse.

'But Father, Wulfgar told the people that I had killed you. Did he then tell them that I had dismembered you and treated your body thus? Surely no one would believe it of me?'

'No, they had another body, that of a malefactor, and wrapped it in cloth so that it was unrecognisable. This they told the people was my cadaver. Then they gave the criminal a lavish funeral in my place, a boat burial on the hill. Eadgard wept during the ceremony and cried out that he was distraught, that he would never get over the death of his lord and that he would never rest until his lord's killer was himself in his grave.'

Osric almost collapsed under the onslaught of spiritual pain on learning of this horrible treatment of a once respected and revered king of his people. He fell to his knees alongside his mother, who was also overcome with suffering. The pair of them wept together, while the king himself let out a deep moan of sadness.

When Osric got to his feet, his sorrow had turned to rage.

'I pledge this, Father, that they shall suffer as no men have suffered before. I shall avenge these wrongs with all the strength in me, both spiritual and physical, and will not rest until both Wulfgar and Eadgard are quartered and themselves hanging from the boughs of beeches. This I swear with all my heart and soul.'

His mother said, 'My son, I know you mean well, but...'

Osric did not hear the end of the sentence, for at that moment he opened his eyes and found himself looking up at two anxious faces.

'Are you all right?' asked Kenric, as the prince sat up and shook his head. 'Why did you swoon and topple like a felled tree? Is it a sickness?'

'No – no. I – I think it was the scent of that bergamot. When I smelled it, I was transported. I don't know why.'

'Transported?' questioned Kenric. 'Where to? You haven't moved from that spot since you keeled over.'

'Ah, well, I dreamed it then. Those are my dreams. But they seem real enough. Perhaps my spirit goes wandering, while my body remains here. Anyway,' he got to his feet, 'I feel fine now. We should be on our way. Let's do so now.'

The vial seemed now to have been forgotten and as the other two walked from the spot, the Thief retrieved it from where it lay in the grasses. He rethreaded the leather thong through the hole in the top. Then he searched and found the cork, which was thrust into the neck. Finally, he slung the loop of leather round his neck, knowing that in future he had a means of bringing that arrogant prince to his knees. Yes, here was a weapon, this essence of an orange, which could render a man harmless and at the mercy of anyone who cared to take his life. That was a useful tool to have and not weighty like a sword or awkward to carry like a bow. Useful indeed.

SEVEN

The three companions set forth across the countryside. Osric had never been so far from the sea before and he was uneasy with moving inland. It seemed the landscape grew harsher, stranger and less friendly. There were dangerous mountains to climb – admittedly not high ones – and hazardous moors to cross. On the top of one mountain was an elevated moor. The going was hard, the soft wet peat sucking their feet ankle deep. And it was not just the physical problems of the ground: Osric became aware that they were in a region of the weird and eldritch. There were foul-smelling giant toadstools, fungi which reached the shoulders of a man which were dark and ugly. They formed a canopy over the pathways. These great parasols had twisted warty caps and disgusting vents where grey, crab-like parasites crawled in and out. All three men felt tense and apprehensive as they passed under these fungi trees.

When they came out of this uncanny forest they were on open ground, but above their heads there were hundreds of birds which seemed to be attacking one another. For the most part they were corvi – crows, rooks, ravens, jackdaws, jays – that blackened the sky overhead and occasionally it seemed they deliberately flew into each other at speed. These mid-air collisions caused casualties to drop from the heavens and litter the peat hags with feathered bodies. A stocky-limbed lynx was gathering some of the dead birds in a pile, presumably storing them to take them back to its young at a later time. The boys watched this wild cat warily, but the lynx was uninterested in anything but its heavenly larder.

Kenric asked, 'What's the matter with them? Why're they smackin' into each other like they're at war or somethin'?'

The Thief picked up a rook, then a raven, turning them over in his dexterous pickpocket's long-fingered hands.

'Blind,' he said at last. 'They're all blind. They're not colliding on purpose. They can't see each other.'

Osric shuddered. 'What horrible magic is this? Who wishes such things?'

'Maybe not who, but *what?*' replied the Thief. 'Perhaps,' he said, looking around him at the dismal, dreary quagmire, 'the magic comes from the marsh itself? Such a place as this has been the bolt-hole and haunt of evil sorcerers since mortals first walked the Earth. They would have dropped foul spells where they trod, which sank into the bog and festered there, perhaps to be eaten by the worms and grubs that eventually end in a bird's gullet. Other creatures that live and cross this loathsome moor may fall victim to those rotting gobbets of dark magic that lay decaying in the peat, releasing disfiguring odours that overcome passersby.'

'If that's so,' Osric said, 'the sooner we pass over this wicked place the better, before we too become victims of its stenches.'

Indeed, it was not long before they came across a witch whose nest-hole had been dug under a piece of rough granite as tall as three men standing on each other's shoulders. The entrance was not much bigger than a badger's sett and when she heard voices she came wriggling through this vent beneath the monolith to greet them.

Osric and Kenric had just realised they could not reach the downward path that night. Despite their fear of rogue magic they decided to make camp in a peat hag. Now they were confronted by a hideously-thin old woman with hair down to her ankles. They declined her offer to spend the night in her 'comfortable dry little home' preferring the open air. This sack of bones and hair left the three men and squirmed back down her entrance shaft into the depths of the earth. All the while she was muttering and grumbling about the ingratitude of the young.

Kenric shuddered as he watched her filthy feet disappear in the blackness of her underground nest. 'This is the month of Eostre, the goddess of the radiant dawn – and we have to meet such creatures in Middangeard as spawned by Eortha, the goddess of the earth and the underworld.'

A shrieking laugh came from below his feet and a claw-like hand was instantly thrust upwards through the damp peat to grab his ankle. It tried to drag him forcibly down through the oily, mushy ground. Osric kicked the wrist of the witch whose nails had buried themselves like talons in the flesh of Kenric's ankle. In an instant Kenric's sword was unsheathed and he tried to sever the hand from its arm, but the foul appendage was withdrawn to the sub-earth lair instantly. Moments later the same fingers were snatching at the front nearside hoof of Magic, who simply trod them into the ground. A howl of pain followed. However, the youths were amazed at the distances between the two attempts and realised the witch had a wide network of tunnels running under the bog in every direction.

'We can't stay here,' complained the Thief. 'Once we fall asleep she'll come snaking through that hole, or some other, and slit our throats. We need to move on out of her reach.'

'He's right for once,' Kenric said. 'Can't stay here.'

So they stumbled through the darkness, crossing the peat bog, sometimes sinking to their knees in the soft earth, sometimes falling into great pits in the landscape full of loathsome fluids. There was indeed nowhere to stop in safety. They had to get down from the heights into one of the meadowland valleys below. This proved more difficult in the darkness that it would have done in the light, especially leading a horse. There were times when they were on such narrow ledges they might easily have fallen to their deaths. However, by the middle of the time between midnight and dawn, they came to the bottom of the escarpment, down from the moorland plateau, and were back on grassland once again. The three of them fell to the ground and were instantly asleep, their exhaustion levels having passed that point where any one of them could keep their eyes open and mount a sentry.

Osric woke the next morning with a nagging pain in his side and he soon realised he was being poked by the butt-end of a spear. He sat up to see they were surrounded by a group of thick-set dweorgs, or dwarfs. Some, *many*, of these creatures were hard-toiling, skilful at metalwork, and no problem to mortals. They worked in gold and used gems to produce beautiful jewellery. Others, and these seemed to be such a group, were rogues and bullies, especially in great numbers.

These outlaw dweorgs had skins as rough as sandstone and indeed their features might have been roughly-hewn from stone. Their stubby fingers held clubs or axes or short spears. They were an ugly gang of beings and Osric guessed they had been thrown out of their various clans for crimes or misdemeanours: ejected from underground caves or the mountain-habitations of their kind.

The dwarf with the poking spear, a lumpy, square-shouldered fellow about waist high to Osric, glared at the youth and then shouted in some dark guttural language the prince did not understand. The thick dark hair that sprouted from the dwarf's nose blew back and forth as the creature yelled his unintelligible nonsense at the youth.

'Don't do that,' growled Osric, as he was poked again, 'or I'll have to do something like it back.'

'You, up. All, up,' snarled the dwarf. "You pay gold.'

Kenric was awake now. 'We ain't got any gold,' he snorted. 'You think we'd be sleepin' in this godforsaken place if we had anythin' valuable?'

The dwarf, whose grey hair seemed to have been cut with a blunt sickle, sneered and cried, 'You give horse. We take horse. Yes, we take.' The other dwarfs roared their approval of this magnificent plan from their leader.

'Of course,' said Osric, standing now. 'You take the horse.'

'What are you saying?' shouted the Thief, now also awake and on his feet. 'That's a valuable animal!'

'But,' continued Osric, still addressing the chief of the dwarfs, 'I must warn you that my horse won't like it.'

'I teach him to like,' growled the dwarf chief. 'He learn quick from me.'

The fellow stumped over to Magic who was quietly contemplating the day emerging from the east. The dwarf reached up and grabbed the beast's tail, and attempted to drag his hindquarters round to get Magic's head to face in the direction the dwarfs wanted to go. Magic took great exception to this. He was already incensed at being handled by a creature whose breath stank of rotten food and whose armpits smelled like the dried faeces of cats. Magic's back legs lashed out horizontally, striking the dwarf chief in the chest.

The dwarf flew backwards and landed with a thump on the meadowland. His mouth was agape and his eyes wide, but clearly he was dead. His chest had been caved and the ribs smashed into his heart and lungs. Blood trickled from his mouth as the other dwarfs rushed to his aid. They stood around his inert body, wailing and thumping their own chests with their fists. Osric notched an arrow into the string of his elfen bow. Kenric drew his sword. The Thief looked around him for a safe avenue of escape for a coward fleet of foot and uninterested in standing his ground.

The dwarfs first looked in horror on their dead chief, then they began to scream in fury. They beat their chests and heads with their fists, while screeching oaths and curses at the horse. Instead of attacking the trio of humans, they started running towards Magic. Some of the dwarfs had wicked-looking curved knives, like sickles, which they brandished. Others had what looked like ironwood clubs or maces made with a flint head and oak shaft. Clearly they were going to beat the horse to death and would have done so, long before Osric and Kenric could stop them, when a girl suddenly appeared as if out of nowhere and stood serenely calm in the way of the spitting, snarling, ferocious horde of short but muscled creatures.

'Look out!' cried Osric, fearing for the girl's safety. 'Run away!'

Both he and Kenric started forward, weapons drawn and ready, now having two vulnerable beings to save instead of one.

But the girl, barefoot, with a pale unblemished complexion and wearing only a head garland of white flowers and a white dress that seemed to cling her form as if it were wet, simply smiled. She looked as fragile as a flower herself standing between the charging dwarfs and the horse. Both young men thought this maiden, who was no older than they were themselves, would be trampled to death before they could reach her. Osric stopped and drew his bow, ready to fell the first dwarf that tried to touch either her or his beloved steed. However, before he could loose the shaft, the dwarfs came to an abrupt and strangely silent halt. They stood only an arm's length from the girl, shuffling their feet and looking bashful.

'Go away,' said the girl, in a quiet tone. 'Leave us.'

The dwarfs now wailed, but they turned and walked back, to pick up the body of their chieftain. Four of them hefted him onto their shoulders, he being so muscle-bound that even in death his carcass was stiff. Only his arms dangled down from his square body. The dwarfs then marched solemnly back across the lea towards a distant set of caves in a rocky hillside. The Thief, who had previously bolted in that direction, took fright and circumnavigated this now ruly crowd of hairy beings, running in a big wide circle to avoid coming into contact with any of them. When he returned to Osric and Kenric, he said, 'I was going for help.'

The pair ignored him and turned their attention to the girl.

'Who are you?' asked Osric. 'Don't you know they would have cut you down and beaten your body to a pulp if we hadn't been here?'

'Oh,' she said, with infuriating calm, 'it was *you* who saved me, was it?'

Osric replied, 'Of course. They saw me with my bow, ready to kill any dwarf who dared to lay a hand on you, and they came to their senses.'

'Ah, that's what they came to? Their senses. Yet, you know, bandit dwarfs have very little sense. They're governed by emotions and their silly greed, which is why they've been thrown out of their own community. No, I think they stopped in their tracks rather because I was in their way.'

'But,' spluttered Kenric, 'they would have run right over you.'

'Not if they value their nasty, rough, calloused, lumpy skins,' replied the girl.

The youths looked at each other, then at the Thief, who simply shrugged.

Frowning, Osric asked again, 'Who are you?'

'My name is Sethrith of Mercia, but it's not who am I, but *what* am I that's important.'

'Why,' cried Kenric, laughing, 'you're a young girl, that's what you are – and you shouldn't be wanderin' round the countryside without protection. What in the name of the gods are you thinkin' of? There are terrible beings out here in the lonely areas of the world. The moors and mountains is no place for a woman. Are you a churl, or from some better class?' He stared at her dress. 'Is that silk? I've only seen silk once before. It looks like silk. Pr'aps you're a princess, escaped from an evil abductor? Or maybe you sleepwalk and have wandered from your bed? Have you been – what's that word you once used, Thief? – ostra… yep, ostra*cised* from your tribe for some reason? Maybe you're not even from this land, but was shipwrecked or somethin'?'

She stared at him and wrinkled her nose. Then she said to Osric, 'He's very inventive, isn't he? A very active imagination. But not even close. I'm here because I want to be here. I was indeed asleep when I felt the alarm, but woke instantly and flew here within the moment.'

The boys looked at her helplessly.

It was the Thief who spoke. 'Alarm? What alarm?'

'The horse. It's an elfen horse. I felt its terror in my heart when the dwarfs began to charge at it. I knew it needed me, so I came.' She walked over to Magic, who nuzzled her hand when she reached up to stroke its neck. 'It's a beautiful beast, isn't it? Did you steal it? The elves will destroy you if you did.'

'He was given to me,' said Osric. 'By my elfen friends.'

'Oh, you have *friends*. Elfen friends. And they rushed to your aid when you were in trouble? I think not.'

'They live a long way away from here, otherwise my betrothed...'
Osric stopped and bit his tongue.

The girl raised her shapely eyebrows, her loveliness suddenly turning
the stomachs of both youths to melting butter.

'Your *betrothed*. The story becomes even more interesting and more
unbelievable. You are betrothed to an elf?'

'Not any more. She... I had to leave.'

'Ah, she wasn't beautiful enough.'

Osric replied hotly, 'She was amazingly beautiful, I have to tell you.'

'As beautiful as me?'

The face before him was indeed wonderful and the prettiest face he
had seen on any mortal female in his life. But there was no comparison
between that countenance and the visage of a female elf. It wasn't that
one was lovelier than the other. It was simply that it was impossible to
compare them, any more than you could compare and apple with a
plum. They were a different species. A swallow and a goldcrest. A daisy
and a bluebell. A sprig of heather and a branchlet of broom.

'That's not a fair question,' he grumbled after a long while of staring
at her amazing blue eyes and long yellow hair. 'Not a fair question at all.
Now, you must stop playing games with us and tell us who – sorry *what*
you are.

'Simple – I'm a witch.'

All three males stared at this delicate young waif, frail and defenceless
as a wispy wood anemone, and shook their heads.

Kenric said, 'You're no witch. We've seen a witch, up on the moor on
that plateau, and she was as ugly as a toad and had the strength of a boar.
You share only the same sex as that foul creature.'

'Oh *that* old hag? She thinks she's powerful, but she's a dozen places
below me in the hierarchy of spellers and charmers. I could destroy her
just like this,' and the girl lifted her hand and snapped her fingers. A
lightning bolt flew from her fingers and cracked as thunder in the sky
above, making the youths and the Thief jump back in startled fear. The
Thief even turned and started to run, before his intellect clicked in and
he realised he didn't know what he was running from or where safety lay.
Sethrith continued, 'Why on Earth did the dwarfs cower before me, if I
were not a witch, or indeed some sort of sorcerer? You should never
judge by appearances, boys. And you,' she said to the Thief, 'are a man
full grown and almost as old as the Beowulf and his thegns you left to be
slaughtered by the great dragon. You ought to be ashamed.'

'Shame is something I put in my back pocket many years ago,' replied the Thief. 'It was never any assistance to me when I got into trouble. Yes, you are a witch. I've seen the likes of you before. Are you really that lovely all the time, or is there a grotesque person who emerges in the winter? You witches have many forms. Show us the one you feel the most comfortable with.'

In an instant there was a beautiful peregrine falcon perched on the Thief's wrist, staring into his eyes with yellow intensity.

The Thief let out a yell and tried to unsettle the raptor, but it clung to his wrist with strong talons for quite a while, its claws drawing blood. Then it was gone and the girl Sethrith was back, smiling sweetly. The youths were indeed shocked by the event that had happened before their eyes, Kenric wondering whether they had been hypnotised rather than the thing actually taking place. He had known sages, men who could play with the minds of others, making them believe things that had not actually occurred. Osric though, was still a youth who believed what he saw, and he stared at the beautiful creature before him with great wonder and admiration.

'I would have expected you to turn into a cat,' he said. 'Something soft and furry and warm to look at.'

'No,' she replied, looking deep into his innocent eyes, 'I like the wild excitement of cutting like a crescent blade through the blue air of the sky, swooping, stooping, dropping like a stone on an unsuspecting prey, streaking, hurtling into it with the speed of a barbed arrow and tearing it, ripping it apart, scattering feathers to the wind. If the truth must be out, I like the taste of blood, Osric of the Angles.'

'She is a witch!' he said breathlessly, to himself and anyone who might still be in doubt of the fact. 'This comely young girl is a terrible witch.'

He stared at her, his heart flying from his chest once more.

Lord Ing:

Ah, so now the youth has fallen in love yet again! Passion? He has too much of it, if you ask me. He seems to fall so very easily, though indeed the witch is lovely to view. What do I do here? Do I intervene or let things take their course? Young witches of course don't fall in and out of love at the same speed as mortals and my guess is that she's not over-enamoured with him. Perhaps she may one day reach that state, but for the present...

EIGHT

In Esageard, the home of the gods, there was feasting around the table in the Great Hall of one-eyed Woden, Lord of the Gallows, Lord of the Wild Hunt, God of Poetry and Mantic Ecstasy, Consort of Frige: a god with many titles. The table around which the rest of the gods sat would have covered a fifth of East Anglia and was fashioned from a thousand oaks from the forests below. Roasting on spits over huge fires were oxen from the world below, taken in the night. Eostre was there, drinking mead, as was Seaxneat, Freo and her brother Ing (ruler of the elves, both dark and light), Hreda, Tiw and Thunor – Loki, the trickster god, of course – Helid, Eorda, Wuldor and Frige consort of Woden. Woden himself sat at the head of the table, looking every hand-span the Chief of the Gods, the leader of his clan. Really, the whole Ese was there, as well as those lesser gods from the minor clan, the Wen. The only one who wasn't there was Hama, whose job it was to guard the Rainbow Bridge that leads to Esageard, and as usual he was very upset at missing the Ierfealu, but Woden could hardly leave the gateway to his fiefdom unguarded. One of the several races of giants would snatch at the chance to attack and climb up into Esageard to wreak havoc and cause as much destruction and death as they could manage.

The Ierfealu, the ritual toasts of mead dedicated to the deceased, was halfway through, there being only a few deaths of those who mattered to the gods. The kings of the tribes of mortals – Saxons, Jutes, Angles, Frisians – were all descended from the gods and therefore worthy of consideration at Ierfealu. Woden was particularly displeased about the death of the king of the East Angles.

'What,' asked Woden, 'of Eorl – how did he die? Did any of you witness this passing of a king of one of the Seven fiefdoms?'

Ing spoked up. 'I was there, my lord. The king was murdered by some of his own thegns, and one of them took his place as ruler of the fiefdom.'

'Murdered, you say,' said the Goddess of Love, Frige, mixing the mead with buttermilk to keep her figure full and busty. 'Must this go unpunished?

'Wife and lover,' answered Woden, 'you know it is not for us to interfere with the machinations of mortals. These affairs must be untangled by those who tangle them. We each have our work – Eorde who knows she must watch over the earth and Thunor over his storms – but to interfere directly is not good policy. That leads to jealousies and favourites amongst ourselves and when the gods start getting angry with one another, intrigue and suspicion follow, and before you know it we're at each other's throats. When the gods begin to quarrel, the world shakes and rattles, and men die in their hundred thousands. We do not need a war amongst ourselves. We have enough trouble with the giants and their kind, without creating more problems.'

'Then what's to be done?' asked Seaxneat. 'Do we just let it rest?'

Woden raised his goblet. 'To Eorl, King of the east Angles, may his spirit move through the forests of the dead with all its memories intact.'

There was a clashing of dwarf-gold goblets around the table and then the quaffing of the mead down the throats of thirsty deities.

'My Lord Woden,' called Ing from the far end of the great table, licking the residue of the honey-wine from his beard, 'I did take the liberty of assisting King Eorl's son to escape the wrath of the murderers, Wulfgar and Eadgard. I hope that was not too presumptuous of me. The boy, Prince Osric was in danger of being torn to pieces by hounds. I allowed him to find a way to and reside with a group of my elves before he moved on of his own accord.'

Woden considered this confession carefully, while Ing awaited judgement on his actions, when his one eye opened a little wider. The Lord Woden had once exchanged one of these orbs for the gift of wisdom and those who asked judgements of him knew that he would give them good counsel. He was not a god given to rash wild statements or was too hasty to turn over the facts in his mind.

'Ah, was this the youth that a short while ago sneaked into the forest where all the dead souls of mortals wander?'

'Yes my lord, the very same. He went to see his murdered father.'

Woden stroked his chin as he mused, then he answered.

'Indeed. I shall allow your actions in relation to this young prince, Lord Ing, since it was not direct interference in the affairs of the pursuers. Had you prevented the hounds and their masters from proceeding with their quest, I should have to admonish you Lord Ing. However, rather than positively staying the hands of the predators, you merely opened up a path of escape for the prey. Had they been swifter, more agile, or cleverer, they might have caught their quarry despite your intervention. They have only themselves to blame, these strong-armed felons, for not being cunning enough to catch this Osric.'

'I don't really see the difference,' muttered Tiw quietly to Thunor, 'but Ing has always been a favourite of our lord Woden – which is why he was given Aelfgeard and the elves as a gift for his first tooth. Now you and I…'

'Speak up, Lord Tiw,' growled Woden from the head of the table. 'We can't hear you? Is it a joke? A song? A story? What?'

Tiw jumped. 'A – a song, my lord. A song.'

'Well sing up, let's hear it. Start us with the first line.'

'*O hear the swan-road calling, the sea that shapes the shore,*
O give me winds and wild-waves, to shake its shell-strewn floor…'

The lusty base and baritone voices of the other gods joined with that of Tiw's, followed by the high, sweet tones of the soprano goddesses, as they all strove together to reach the chorus, which resounded through the heavens above the mortals. Men and women in the world below Esageard looked up, surprised to see no black, blustery clouds. They could hear the storm, but could not for the life of them see where it was. Still and all, the sound continued to reverberate through the blue air above the world and finally mortals shrugged and put the strange event behind them and got on with their normal tasks of farming, hunting and killing each other.

The gods on the other hand, grew tired of singing and followed the Lord of the Wild Hunt, when he suddenly leapt from his chair and mounted his eight-legged horse, Sleipnir. The whole bunch of them then went charging around the sky, looking for that elusive celestial boar, Saehrimnir. The skies were full of their loud cries and the thunder of hooves and once again mortals stared up at the clouds, but this time they knew what was occurring. The wild hunt was in progress. There is a spectral element to the wild hunt: ghosts are led by the lord on his eight-legged horse. Woden and his ghosts were chasing a quarry of stray souls through the heavens.

Some said the wild hunt predicted a death in the family, but others argued that if that was so, there would be a death in *every* family, which would not make sense for how long would it be before every inneryard was empty of occupants, they all having died after a wild hunt. The gods needed people, just as much as the people needed gods. If there were no one to believe in the divinities, then the immortals would just fade away.

EIGHT (A)

Eadgard and Wulfgar, back in the royal village in the East Angles, had been busy rounding up Osric's friends and interrogating them. The young men were continually asked whether they had been involved in the plot to kill King Eorl and install their friend as king in his place. What Eadgard and Wulfgar were doing was not of course trying to unravel any conspiracy, for there had been none, but to gauge where the sympathies of the youths lay. They were trying to ascertain whether their coup had been successful in so far as getting the people to believe their side of the story. No word had come back from Osric and there was the hope between the two men that the boy was gone: frozen or starved to death by the terrible winter.

'It has been a long winter,' said Wulfgar, 'and he had nowhere to go. How far would he get on foot in such cold weather? My guess is his body is lying somewhere in the forest, half-eaten by worms and wild beasts. I doubt anyone will even recognise the brat if they found him, even some of these whelps who used to be his friends.'

'I hope you're right,' replied Eadgard, 'but even if you're not, what could he do? Run to some other realm and plead his case? What would a king do if he heard such a story? Nothing. Why risk war with one or more of the fiefdoms on the say-so of a boy found wandering in the outeryards? I think we're safe from Osric, but – but I'm not so confident of my place in the hearts of his friends.'

Wulfgar growled and nodded, taking a bite of the duck drumstick in his hand. 'There's only one that I think we need to watch closely. The bastard son of Eorl that your sister bore…'

Eadgard's eyes narrowed as he remembered that after the death of Eorl's queen, the king had pursued Eadgard's youngest sister, Renne, and though she never agreed to marry him it was widely known they had shared the same bed on occasion. Renne was later very quickly given in marriage to a noble of the East Saxons and was subsequently killed accidently by the flying hooves of a wild horse. The Saxons sent a son of hers back saying he was not one of theirs and indeed the youth did resemble Eorl in many ways: not so much in looks, but in mannerisms and gestures, in his stance and in his shallow-throated laugh. Even the churls could see that this boy, Aelheah, was the son of their king and the half-brother of Osric. Indeed, even the boy's name, Aelheah, meant 'child of the elves'. It was the sort of name given to babies born out of wedlock to high-born women who wished to maintain that they had not been unfaithful to any future husband, but had been an unwilling participant of a sexual union between mortal and elf in the land of dreams.

'Indeed,' agreed Eadgard. He poked the ashes of a fire that had died but not quite lost it's heat. 'I have an idea. Let's say that Osric is still alive somewhere and planning to come back with an army? I think we need to send a warning to him that if he does return, he will face a terrible death. You remember that Geat sailor we found on the beaches, washed up by the sea? Half-dead he was, but we warmed him, fed and watered him, gave him back his life. He told us many stories of his homeland before he left, but one of them has always stuck in my mind because it is such an image as to make most men shudder with horror.'

A smile crossed the scarred and pitted face of Wulfgar.

'I think I recall the custom you refer to.'

'The blood-eagle.'

'Yes.'

Eadgard paced the floor of the great hall. 'It has to be done publicly – otherwise the news will not reach Osric. The whole point is to inform the mongrel that if he ever comes back, this is what he should expect. Bring the youth to the gathering of the fires tonight, and we'll do it then. We'll need two willing thegns to hold him and support the idea of the execution. How loyal are the thegns to our cause now?'

'They believe you are their rightful ruler and that Osric murdered his own father – a patricide with a consuming and bloody ambition.'

That evening, there was the ceremony of the fires, a local custom amongst the East Angles alone. At the height of the proceedings, Aelheah, who was laughing and joking with some of the herdsgirls, not knowing that the evening was going to end in his vile execution, was secured by several thegns. On looking into their faces he knew at once that he was going to die. He was not a well-built youth, not even having Osric's wiry strength, being fashioned more for poetry than war.

'No, no,' he screamed, 'I have done nothing. I have done nothing.'

He thrashed and squirmed like a stoat caught in a snare, his lean body writhing and twisting, trying to get out of the grip they had on him. All the while he was sobbing and calling for help amongst the people. They, however, shocked as they were by the suddenness of the arrest, could do little to help him. Some asked what he had done and were told he was a traitor to the kings, both the old king and the new king, and that he had been condemned to death. 'You will be told of the details of his betrayal and treachery once the execution has taken place,' called Wulfgar, the most senior of all the thegns. 'It is with a heavy heart that we carry out the law, but a warning must go out to all those who think they can plot against the rightful rulers of our realm. These are terrible crimes and require an equally terrible punishment.'

Still Aelheah cried out his innocence. Wulfgar did not gag him as he would have liked to do, because he wanted the horror of the act to reach the ears of Osric, if that youth were still alive. So they dragged the poor young man down to the river bank below, where a strong post had been set in the low tide mud. There in the torchlights, under the stunned gaze of the crowd, they tied him back-to-front to the post. Many thought Aelheah was going to be left to drown by the incoming tide, but were astonished and aghast when Wulfgar sliced open the youth's back to reveal his rib cage. The thegn then cut and snapped away several of the screaming youth's white ribs, during which the victim whose hands were fastened high on the post, finally sagged into unconsciousness: a relief to the watching and listening Angles. Wulfgar then ripped the young man's lungs out of his back and draped them across his shoulders. There they continued to pulsate like the wings of a great mountain-country raptor about to take to the air. This was the 'blood-eagle' execution used by those across the water, in the lands from whence the Anglo-Saxons came.

The light of the torches seemed to enhance the horror of the scene, as it caused the shadows to flicker over the torn red-and-white flesh of the victim's back as he hung slumped from the post, his body like a gutted fish that was still vainly struggling to stay alive. Nearby, in the centre of the mud, the water of the river lapped in the runnels grooved by the retreating tide, the only sound in the silence that had fallen on the watchers. A child started snivelling, then crying in earnest, which caused others of a similar age to begin weeping noisily. One or two of the adults groaned, relieving their feelings a little, letting them out onto the night air. A woman began gasping for breath and had to be supported by friends or family: possibly a maid who was one of those who was fond of the youth who dangled from the post. Still the lungs throbbed and quivered in the torchlight, flapping on the young man's back, fighting to pump oxygen to the heart in his chest. Eventually they would give up, flatten to empty sacs, become mockeries of what they had once been.

Leaving the youth to die, the people finally traipsed back up the hill towards their homes, the image of the execution they had witnessed raw and vivid in their minds. Later he came to consciousness again, that poor frail youth. All through that night they heard the wails and pleadings, the screams and crying, of the young man dying on the post, until the early morning tide brought a welcome end to his suffering. After this event, naturally, there were nightmares amongst the young and even amongst the old, and men and women went about their daily tasks for a long while afterwards with fear gripping their hearts should they be accused of a crime that might merit such a death. Indeed, they hardly spoke of what they had seen except in whispers, and Eadgard's plan of sending a message into the outeryards to reach the ears of the runaway prince was entirely thwarted. No villager ever passed on the events of that night to a stranger and so the plan fluttered and died: was indeed as dead as Aelheah himself, when they cut his pale eelfish-slim body down from the post and hung his severed limbs, torso and head from the oak known as Old-Man-Who-Lives-Forever, the one with the girth of a churl's wattle dwelling.

Shortly after this happening, Eadgard was himself out on the edge of the woodlands that climbed up from the river to the village boundary. As he was musing on this and that, turning over in his mind the next transaction he might make with the merchants who brought goods – jewels and silks from faraway distant lands, too distant indeed for Eadgard's limited imagination to grasp the exoticness of their colour and majesty – a giant wolf emerged from the undergrowth and stood not fifty paces from him, staring at him with large grey eyes. Unusually, the wolf's cowl was as black as charcoal in contrast to its long-haired ashen coat. A chill went through Eadgard and instinctively he looked back to see if there were any thegns within hailing distance. Finding none, he nervously unsheathed his sword and stood waiting for the wolf to advance.

The wolf however simply continued to stand where it was, staring at the ruler with baleful, perhaps accusing, eyes.

Eadgard did not know whether to remain or flee. In the end he realised he could not outrun a wolf, certainly not one of this size. Surely it was an otherworld creature, perhaps lost from the realms of the upperworld? So he stood there, sword gripped fiercely by the hilt, ready for any onrush. But the wolf seemed in no hurry to attack, if that were its itent, and continued to meet the human's stare. There they stood for a long time, until finally something happened which turned Eadgard's blood to freezing water in his veins. The wild beast actually spoke to him in a low harsh voice full of malice.

'You're wearing my sister.'

Eadgard, fearful though he was, glanced down at the wolfskin cloak he was wearing, then looking up again replied, 'It – it was given me by another...' any further words jammed in the back of his throat, unable to find their way out over his tongue and through his mouth.

After this, the wolf said nothing more and eventually turned and loped back into the forest to be lost amongst the shadows of the trees. At the very last minute he saw the shape-change. There was a blurring of the shadows, then the wolf stood up on its hind legs for a brief moment, before the form warped, shimmered, and took on the contours of a female being clothed in foliage, green as fresh spring grass.

Eadgard continued to stand where he was, rooted to the spot even with the dread of the wolf returning. When evening came and settled amongst the hills and fields, he finally turned and walked stiffly back to his realm, nodding in affirmation at a belief that had come to him once his mind had unfrozen itself. He whispered only one word to himself, over and over again. 'Witch. Witch. Witch...'

NINE

The four companions set out once again, heading for the land of the Mercians, where the great Paega ruled. Paega was a ruthless and powerful warrior-king, intent on expansion of his fiefdom. He had already defeated Ogga and the Walha, the Umbrians, several times and his sights were now set on the other five fiefdoms of the Angles, Saxons and Jutes. Osric was hoping that Paega would support him in an attempt to kill or drive Eadgard from the east Angles. The Mercians were Angles too, so Osric was hopeful of a good reception.

As the four rounded the top of a hill they viewed an amazing sight coming up the other side towards them. A mighty army of thousands, some on horseback, some on foot, with a baggage train trooping behind. Now the four could hear the bullroarers being whirled above heads and the drums beating out the rhythm of the march. The warriors, bristling with weapons, were not in columns or blocks of men such as the Romans used to march, but more in the barbarian style of massed men travelling in a loose crescent which stretched for at least a mile wide. In front of this horde rode a thick-set man on a tall horse. He was wearing a wolfskin cloak trimmed with ruddy fox-fur and the legs that gripped the flanks of the horse had twice the girth of any other man on the field. On his head was a silver helmet decorated with animal motifs and skulls and faces of men or gods. A huge sword hung from his belt and a warhammer was slung on a strap over his right shoulder. However, the most obvious feature which caught the attention of all four travellers, was the man's face. It was horribly scarred, as if raked by the claws of a bear, and the lids of one eye – the right one – had been sewn shut and was concave there being no orb beneath them.

'Paega!' exclaimed Osric in a startled tone. 'With his Mercian warbands. See there are the chiefs of warbands and there the young warriors…'

'You know him?' said the Thief, slipping behind Osric and Kenric.

'No – but who else would it be? Sethrith, what do you think?'

Osric looked round, but the girl was nowhere to be seen. When the prince glanced upwards, he saw a half-moon bladed shape, a raptor of some kind, sweeping across the sky and disappearing behind a distant woodland. Sethrith was gone. At that moment he wished they all had her magic and could make the same retreat, but there was nothing for it but to face the oncoming army. Osric walked forward, the other two trailing behind, clearly hoping that the youth would have some influence over the king whose horse plodded towards them. Otherwise they might be slain on the spot or at worst have to join the horde of warriors and follow to wherever it was going to fight whatever enemy it had in mind.

The king reined his horse on being confronted by Osric and his whole army rippled through its ranks until it too came to a shuddering halt. The king used his knees to lift himself out of the saddle to look beyond the three figures in front of him, as if seeking to discover whether they were the vanguard of some opposing force. Finding no hostiles beyond them, he settled back down onto his mount and studied the youth and his two companions with his one surly eye.

'Are you some of my outriders?' he snarled. 'Who do you answer to? Leax? Gastar? What in the name of the gods are you blocking my way for? I'll have you flayed and your skin used for fans. If you are outriders, where are your mounts? Do you have news for me of the enemy? Speak up before I split a skull or two.'

'My lord,' said Osric, his voice a little tremulous, 'I am the son of Eorl of the East Angles...'

'What?' the king once more rose up off the back of his mount, this time he stood, with the horse bowing a little from the centred weight. 'You're an emissary? Your father marches against me? Where is the gutless bastard?'

Osric's fear vanished immediately and his temper flared.

'My father was not gutless – he was a courageous warrior!'

The king dropped back down into the riding position and his left eye gleamed. One of the thegns urged his own steed forward and raised an iron warhammer over Osric's head, about to crush his skull with it. But Paega lifted an arm and stayed the noble's hand. Then he glared down at the youth who stood defiantly in his path.

'*Was* courageous?'

'My father was murdered by several of his thegns,' growled Osric, 'and I intend to exact revenge for that crime.'

'Careless of him,' replied the king. 'A Mercian ruler would never have been so sloppy or soft as to allow such intrigue in his mead hall. Who has taken his place?'

'Eadgard, whose henchman is Wulfgar.'

'Don't know 'em,' said the king. 'The East Angles, eh? I'll remember how weak they are and when I have the time I'll venture in that direction. In the meantime, boy, I'm on my way to teach the West Saxons who is Woden's favourite son. Out of the way, or I'll ride over you and your two kitchen boys.' He spat on the ground and flicked the ear of his warhorse, which had almost fallen asleep and now began to stumble forward, carrying the weighty king.

'Kitchen boys?' muttered Kenric, under his breath, but he was not as hot-headed as the young prince, and kept his counsel. The Thief had been called much worse in his time, so was totally unaffected. Osric however, could not let things go.

'My lord,' he said, grabbing the mane of Paega's horse, 'will you not divert and attack the East Angles and restore me to my royal post?'

Paega smiled. 'Of course,' he cried, 'I have naught else to do this morning. It'll only take a few minutes, won't it?'

The warrior-king then let out a huge guffaw and turned this way and that, inviting his thegns to appreciate his humour. Naturally, they did. They slapped their sides and rocked with laughter. Nothing more was said. Paega spurred his mount and with his fist knocked the youth aside. Osric fell to the ground and was mocked by the warriors tramping past him, following their great war-maker towards a battle from which many of them would not return. Osric finally got to his feet and was buffeted as the troops passed him, still laughing as the joke travelled back down the lines, until finally the rear guard, indeed consisting of kitchen boys, came sniggering past, trying to nudge the standing prince. While Osric had put up with thegns and even churls mocking him, he wasn't having it from greasy lads whose day job was to turn the spitted hog roast. He gave the nearest one a ringing slap around the ear and drew his sword, causing the following river of youths to part and flow either side of him, the laughter having been stemmed.

'Do you think he will?' asked Kenric.

'Will what?' asked the despondent Osric, staring at the baggage train as it disappeared over the crown of the hill.

'Attack the East Angles?'

The Thief snorted. 'He was jesting, Kenric – can you not tell when someone is being ironic.'

'I don't know the word,' replied the other youth. 'Where I come from, people mean what they say, otherwise they get called liars.'

71

'Oh, right,' said the Thief, 'so then why don't you trot after King Paega of the Mercians and tell him he's a liar? And that, my young friend, is another example of irony, or rather sarcasm. Where did the witch go, by the way?'

'She flew into yonder woodland,' said Osric, still in a wearisome tone. 'I'm not sure she'll be back. She's a beautiful maid, is she not?'

The Thief stared at Osric for a moment, then said, 'Ye gods, the boy is in love.'

Kenric also stared at his youthful companion, who stood looking moon-faced in the direction which Sethrith had gone.

'What, *again?*' cried Kenric. 'Yesterday he was in love with an elf!'

'He's one of those,' replied the Thief. 'A youth who falls in love with every young wench that crosses his path.'

Osric turned to them. 'No, no, you don't understand. This wonderful girl is the one. She will be my queen once we have killed Eadgard and Wulfgar. She will be beside me, helping me manage my inneryard, my people. Yes, Sethrith is she who will help me lead the East Angles.'

'A witch,' growled the Thief. 'A witch is going to be queen of the East Angles and the whole realm will welcome her to their bosoms.'

'If she be my wife, yes.'

'Young man, you have a lot to learn about people,' sighed the Thief. 'And also, a great deal more to learn about young women. Now, shall we go down into that valley which is full of the inneryards of the Mercians? What do you propose we do to put bread in our mouths? Beg?'

Osric said, 'I've been thinking about that. Kenric, you said your father was a farrier, yes?'

'That's right.'

'Then why don't we set ourselves up as such? Kenric has the skill he must have learned from his father. He can teach me to assist. You, nameless one, have another very useful talent. We will need equipment to begin our trade. You must go out and find it where it may be. We'll need hammers, an anvil, some iron for the shoes and nails, tongs, various other items including leather aprons. I'm sure that kind of thing is just lying around, waiting for someone to pick it up. What do you say, Kenric. Can it be done? Do you have the knowledge?'

The shorter youth nodded, his intense black eyes on Osric's face.

'I have the knowledge. I can show you the trade.'

'Good. That's settled then. We'll earn our keep and in the meantime I'll be working on a plan to invade my homeland.'

'Settled?' exploded the Thief. 'What? That I should thieve all the necessary tools and put myself in danger of being hung as a criminal?'

'Which you would be,' pointed out Kenric, 'if you stole things.'

'I think I will not do it,' said the Thief, straightening his back. 'No, I will not.'

'It's your trade,' said Osric. 'That's what you do. You've done it all your life. What, if not that, would you contribute to the general welfare of us three? Can you shoe horses? I think not. Can you *learn* to do so? Not at your age. You are past learning. Thus, the only thing left open for you is to follow your chosen profession – stealing things that don't belong to you. It's the only thing you're good at.'

They were now approaching the inneryards of the Mercians, each one having a living-house and outhouses, some wealthier families even having a lesser hall all to itself. There were mostly only women, old men, cripples and children to study them as they entered the settlement, any grown man below a certain age being in the army of King Paega and on his way to death or glory. And studied they were, being travellers and strangers to the region. They were finally accosted by an elderly man who was probably a shaman of some kind. He held them up with the palm of his right hand and glared at them with a malicious gleam in his eyes.

'Where do you think you're going?' he asked the three. 'We want no foreign tinkers here, corrupting our children and fornicating with our women.'

'We are here,' cried Osric, so that all who were witness could hear, 'at the request of King Paega, who told us to come.'

The old man now looked a little disconcerted.

'Who are you? From whence have you come?'

'I am the son of King Eorl of the East Angles. I am here as an emissary to the Mercian people and as a friend of King Paega.'

'Then…' the man's tongue faltered, but after a minute or two gathered itself together, '… welcome.'

He melted into the crowd, many of whom continued to stand around and stare at the trio of strangers who had entered their settlement. Such events did not happen every day. It was an unusual enough occurrence for everyone to stop work and be entertained. However, once they saw that the three newcomers had no tricks to perform nor carried with them any exotic wonderful creatures – no monkey-people from a dark distant land or mina birds that spoke like humans – they dispersed and went back to their chores or relaxations, thinking that something might come of these intruders at a later date, when their cruel, stern, ruthless ruler returned from the wars. If anything were going to happen, it would be then. Perhaps a quartering or at least a hewing of a live body lengthwise with a heavy two-handed sword? If their king lost his war – an unlikely result – he would be sullen and furious, and therefore in the mind to chop someone up. If he *won* his battles, he would be fired up and bumptious to such a degree that he might still chop them up just to see the bits fly. Either way, the humdrum life of the settlement would be enlivened for a day or two.

The trio spent that night in a disused hut with a damaged roof and a collapsed wall, but fortunately it did not rain. There followed an argument as to whether they should sell the elfen bow and arrows, or the sword, in order to get at least a little funding for their forge. Osric won in the end by promising Kenric they would purchase him an even better weapon once they got their business off the ground. The Thief went to the market place to sell the sword and returned with various items, including several chickens. They found the owner of the hut, a shepherd, and bought it from him with a woollen hat. The rest of the week was spent repairing the place until it was indeed habitable.

Next they set up a forge in the field behind the shepherd's hut, making a furnace out of an iron cauldron and clay bricks. The cauldron was large enough to hold a substantial amount of charcoal which could be brought to a fierce enough heat to work iron. Kenric made some bellows out of a leather jerkin and odd chunks of wood: an inventive piece of work that impressed his fellow farriers. Finally, the Thief was sent out to the outlying villages to steal an anvil, hammers, tongs, etc., which he duly did, being one of the most skilful burglars the Saxon world had ever seen. Nothing was taken from the central village where they and the king lived and the stolen goods could be identified, which would naturally have resulted in the gallows.

Osric went out every night at twilight and mournfully sang Sethrith's name to the wind, hoping that she would reappear and end his longing. To the relief of the other two, she did not. Evenings were spent eating and drinking whatever the Thief could manage to filch at the market. (The goose lasted but two days with three hungry mouths to satisfy).

Then one morning they were ready to ply their trade and Osric went out with the Thief to drum up business. They found out what the local farrier was charging to shoe horses and deliberately undercut him. At first no one was inclined to trust these upstarts from another tribe. Who knew whether they would injure their precious mounts? But then a trickle of work came their way and the goods earned began to stack up at the back of the sleeping hut.

'I told you it would work, my plan,' said Osric, excitedly. 'It was a simple scheme but we've made it happen.'

Kenric turned out to be an excellent farrier, following in his father's footsteps, which he had once vowed never ever to stoop to. In fact every time he took up the hammer to beat the red-hot iron, he grumbled and grouched about having to do mean and dirty work, while inside he was born to be a warrior. In his head and heart he was a six-foot stone-jawed wide-shouldered fighter with immense skill at weaponry, whose proper place was at the king's right hand on the battlefield. A noble whose lord relied on him to protect and serve him until death prevented it. In truth he was a slim youth with only an average ability at wielding a sword or spear.

'Smithing is for fools,' he would mutter, 'not for brave young heroes with hearts yearning for songs to be sung about them.'

On the other hand, Osric was fascinated by the creation of iron ore into something shaped to be functional and useful. He watched Kenric's hammer crashing down on the anvil and revelled in the clouds of bright flying sparks that danced in the air like tiny stars. He was fascinated by the heart of the fire that when the bellows were pumped became white with intense heat that drove him back. It seared his face and arms with its waves of hotness. He loved the feel of the heavy hammer and the force of its head when it struck iron. Even the tongs were magical to him, being able to hold a piece of red-hot metal at arms length without danger. Everything about the forge charmed him and he was amazed that when he had his horse shod in his old village he had simply left it with the farrier and collected it later without witnessing the wonderful work that went into fashioning an iron shoe. Even the curved shape of which seemed to him to be a work of art worth studying at length.

However, there was not a great deal of work for them in the village while the young men with horses were all away at the war. One old man came with his workhorse to have it shoed and grumbled all the time about the price he was having to pay, which was at least half of that he would pay to the established farrier. The following morning, though, came a reckoning. There was a yell from outside the shepherd's hut before the three companions rose from their beds. They all stumbled out into the light, blinking furiously, to find a huge man with a hammer in his hand standing with his legs apart and looking very hostile and aggressive.

'I've come to close you down,' growled the muscled man. 'Either you shut up your forge or I cave your heads in. The choice is yours.'

'Ah,' muttered the Thief. 'And here is our local farrier. I've been expecting him.'

TEN

Osric studied the big smithy and decided that without a sword, or a weapon of the long-bladed kind, he might need some assistance to deal with him. He was about to whisper a hastily-thought-out plan in Kenric's ear when the Thief unexpectedly stepped forward and took charge of the dire situation.

'My friend,' he said, addressing the local farrier, 'you need to stay your hand for a short while.'

'And why's that?' growled the dark-faced giant, scarred and pitted with burn holes on his face, shoulders and arms. 'Why do I need to wait?'

'Because, in all good sense, the Mercian army will be returning from the war with the West Saxons. There will be a great many horses to re-shoe. Also, bloody, battles tend to be shambolic affairs, fought over rough ground. Rocks, dropped weapons, discarded helmets and shields, fallen boughs of trees, flints and other stones will all have been instrumental in de-shoeing the warhorses. They will come limping home, ready to be serviced by the farrier. You, sir, who will not have enough time or energy to satisfy all those warriors. You will need assistance. We can provide that. There's nothing so testy as a hero returning from fierce fight, weary and spiritually drained. They will all want their steeds shoed *now*. Not next week, not even tomorrow, but now. They will be angry with those who get shod first – and even more important – angry with you, the farrier, for choosing to do the mounts of others over their own precious horses. Citizens, warriors especially, like to believe they are the most important people in the world, next to the king of course, and you will be swamped by these self-important moody killers of men.'

The farrier stared at the Thief, his mind obviously working backwards and forwards, trying to work out whether the Thief was trying to fool him. It took a while for the Thief's words to sink in, but once they did, the local smithy nodded thoughtfully.

'Once the army has been shod, then I will come back and kill all three of you.'

He shambled away, dragging his sandaled feet across the dusty ground, the big hammer dangling on the end of his mighty arm.

Kenric heaved a sigh of relief, but turned to the Thief and said, 'But he's coming back – we haven't got away.'

'By that time,' said the Thief, 'you will have built up a rapport with your customers. You must make yourselves into the best farriers in the district, so that when he returns to smash our skulls, others will step in his path and say, "Back fellow, these are experts at their trade, unlike you, and if you touch a hair on their heads, you will be struck down by my sword." Besides that, the Frithguildsmen – the keepers of the peace – will be back. The Frithguild will protect us, especially if we're the best in the business.'

'Best in the business,' replied Kenric. 'Yes, we can be that.'

'Or,' added Osric, 'we make a run for it in the dead of night.'

Two days after this, King Paega returned in triumph with his army, dragging behind them a huge rabble of slaves and hostages. The Mercian thegns and churls were cock-a-hoop with their victory over the West Saxons, having killed their king and taken several of the high-born women captive. Not that the Wessexians hadn't put up a good fight and taken a few of the Mercians with them to Neorxnawang or to Hellmouth (that terrible giant beast who swallowed cowards and other miscreants). The Wyrd dealt blows to each army, though not in equal measure, of course, for there had to be a conqueror and a conquered. There were quite a few empty horses and pairs of sandals on the return journey to Mercia. Paega had taken the long way back in order to raid the Jutes and the East Saxons, putting both of them in their places below his. All in all, the king seemed satisfied with the outcome. He had pillaged the Jutes and had found coffers of copper and silver coins, not used as currency in either realm but a good source of wealth none the less, probably taken during continental raids. Some were used as a necklace for his wife, others melted down to make brooches and clasps, and for ornamental figures on the hilts of swords.

Lord Ing:

Fascinating. From prince to farrier. My admiration for this youth increases by the day. There are deposed princes who would sit on mossy mounds and bewail their misfortune until someone put them out of their misery – but not this one. He's not afraid to get his hands dirty, eh? My cousin Thunor would be quite taken with a youth going to the hammer and the anvil, and of course the furnace and its fierce bright heat.

Naturally there were a couple of days when those wives who had lost their men wailed in grief, filling the air with their mournful cries, until King Paega had had enough of the noise and threatened to put to death the next woman who shrieked in sorrow. Things began to settle down. The plunder brought back was exchanged between warriors, some wanting fancy clothes and jewellery, others needing to replace their weapons or mounts. Cloaks of fine wool and even one or two of silk, were worn about the place by proud nobles, warband chiefs. Those in the hands of any lucky churls were hidden somewhere in case they were taken away by superior officers. Weapons were exchanged for agricultural tools and workers went out into the fields to clear them for sowing. It was Weoth, the month of the weeds, when the toil involved backbreaking days of bending over and hacking at the roots of thistles and brambles and other intruders into the fields.

As ever the heightened, the raw emotions of bloodlustfull war, death and near-death, created a schism in the wall between otherworld and the real world. This stirred the unreal creatures from the shape-shifting region which exists alongside the realm of mortals. Unhallowed creatures ventured through the crack and caused havoc amongst stragglers and camp followers. If you were with warriors who offered libations and sacrifices to the gods (Woden rarely being forgotten) you were safe enough from the preternatural world of elves, nicors and giants. If you failed to follow the custom of thanking the gods for victory, or forgot to do so, the consequences were often dire. Men in the outeryard who did not bother with ur-law, the primal law laid down by the Wyrd, were not only harassed by giants and dwarfs on their return journey, but when they arrived at their inneryard even the household cofgodas wights gave them trouble for their sins.

Fortunately this state of affairs worked in the favour of the three companions at the forge. The local farrier's nephew had fallen foul of a nicor, one of those strange-old-man water-horse creatures with green beards and bright eyes who lived on the edges of a waterlands or rivers. Being an adventurous and fool-hardy youth, the reckless nephew had tried to ride the water-horse, and had been duly taken out and drowned in a lake. Nicors do not like to be mounted and the youth should have listened to the warnings of his friends instead of showing off. The farrier was grief stricken and relied on his nephew for assistance in shoeing customers' horses. Thus though he continued to work at his trade, his heart was no longer in the business and Osric, Kenric and the Thief were forgotten rivals of the poor man.

In this feverish post-war atmosphere, Osric was hoping to hear news of a certain witch. He was disappointed. No man he questioned had come across an enchantress as beautiful as the description which unravelled from Osric's tongue (his two companions raised their eyes to heaven and shook their heads at one another). Still he didn't give up asking, even though he was given short shrift by many of the thegns he bothered with the subject.

So it was that many thegns, their new armrings – given them by their king for their services in battle – shining gloriously in the sunlight, came to the forge to have their horses shod. Even the king sent his favourite steed for fresh iron footwear. He later sent for Osric and Kenric and they duly trudged off to the great hall wondering if they had performed the work badly. Instead they found Paega quite amiable. He invited them to take part in the symbel, the drinking rounds, toasts, oaths, boasts, songs, jokes and stories which took place ritually on many nights amongst the nobles who guarded Paega and his family, especially those thegns who were hearth-side companions of the king. The lord of the hall thanked the two farriers brusquely for the job they had done on his favourite steed then promptly ignored them, leaving them to sit amongst a crowd of hostile warriors who thought them upstarts. Indeed, they were told they were present on sufferance.

One particular grey-bearded thegn named Sigeberht, the king's right hand man, resented their presence in the hall. He whispered in the ear of Kenric, 'Brat, you two runts had better get back to your sty before the sow who gave you birth runs out of milk.'

Kenric was startled and replied, 'I may be low-born, but my friend is the son of a king.'

Sigeberht was a man with a great mop of pepper-and-salt hair and forearms as thick as Kenric's thighs. His breath smelled rank, no doubt because the gaps between his teeth had trapped rotten meat from old meals, and his skin was like worn vein-crazed leather. There were two savage-looking dogs, huge sandy-coloured hounds as tall as a man's groin, one on either side of Sigeberht. This man stared hard at Osric who stared back just as hard. The dogs snarled and bared their teeth, sensing hostility between their master and this stranger-youth with flashing eyes.

'Look at me like that boy and I'll take your head from your shoulders,' growled the thegn. 'King's son, eh? What are you then, a hostage?'

'No, a man robbed of his father by treacherous thegns.'

Sigeberht raised his eyebrows and his companions laughed.

'Oh, a *man* is it? Listen, stripling, half-strongs like you have a long way to go before you reach any kind of manhood. Have you killed an enemy in battle? No, I doubt it. Have you even marched with an army? Very unlikely. Have you thrust your weapon into the gaping wound between a woman's thighs? Ha! You are a mere worm, and not the dragon kind, but those that infest the dirt. Now trot out of here like a good little piggie and return to the muck of your sty...'

Osric's face was hot with anger. He leapt to his feet.

'You dare to talk to the son of Eorl, King of the East Angles, as if he were a *hog*? You have a mouth as foul as a bog with your rotten teeth and stinking breath. I have killed giants and dragons, and have ridden the hunt with elves. I have an elfen wife who mourns my departure from her side. I have spoken with dead men and walked with witches. Do not tell me I'm not a man. I ride an elfen horse and shoot an elfen bow. You, on the other hand, ride with brainless oafs and clumsy wielders of warhammers. There is no refinement or intellect in you. You can't even get the lines of "The Wanderer" right. In the third line of the third stanza of the poem, it is *cwithan*, not *modsefan*. You have exchanged the two words for reasons only the gods will be able to fathom, since they make no sense the wrong way around.'

Sigeberht's eyes were bugging from his head at this point. He jumped to his feet and used the drinking horn in his fist to stab at Osric's face. However, the older man was drunk on mead and Osric avoided the blow easily. Sigeberht tried again, only to find his target had moved swiftly away from him. Osric snatched a knife from the feasting table and threw it at his opponent. Fortunately for both Sigeberht and Osric, another thegn stopped the knife from killing its target by thrusting a wooden trencher in its flight path. The point of the weapon stuck in the greasy wood. Thegns, mostly as inebriated as Sigeberht, cheered this feat lustily and stamped their feet, and thumped the table with their fists, enjoying the spectacle of two warriors at each other's throats, albeit one was but a green youth.

Sigeberht threw away the drinking horn, splashing the king with its contents, and snatched up a sword.

'Now, by the hair of Lord Woden, I'll spill your guts onto the floor,' roared the huge thegn.

The king stood up and brushed the drops of mead from his tunic.

'Enough,' he snarled. 'Sigeberht. You've wet me.'

The thegn turned and saw what he had done.

'Ah, forgive me, my lord. But this runt...'

'We've all been witness to what's occurred, my friend, but you can see he's just a boy with a fiery temper. It'll destroy him in the end – or make him king of his people. One or the other. In the meantime, I'd rather you didn't slice open his belly, because I want to hear more about this elfen bow he professes to own.' The king turned to Osric. 'You are the farriers? You and that skinny churl beside you? Is this true? You have an elfen bow? If you lie to me youth, king's son or dirt grubber, I'll let Sigeberht here take your head from your shoulders and feed it to the fish.'

Osric realised how his temper had taken him close to death now. He cooled down. 'Lord Paega, I apologise for causing a ruckus in your Great Hall and for insulting the elderly noble before me. I would not have done so, had his own insults not driven deep into my spirit and raised a fire there. I am sure the queen, who sits over there as calm and sensible as my own mother once did, viewing all this mayhem with a critical eye... '

'Yes, yes. Have you got such a bow?'

'Indeed I have, my lord.'

'And does it hit the target every time?'

'I killed the dragon with it.'

Kenric muttered, 'A very small dragon...' but then shut up when everyone stared at him.

'It never misses,' continued Osric. 'Those who gave it to me told me to use it sparingly, for the elves you know do not like to kill a beast outright. They hunt only to kill for a moment, then the prey gets back to its feet and runs off none the worse for the wound.'

'What's the point of that?' murmured another thegn, but the king waved him silent

'You, boy,' the armring-giver said to Osric, 'will come on a hunt with me tomorrow. There's a giant boar out there that refuses to be killed. It's avoided my spear a dozen times. There has to be a reckoning. We'll leave at dawn. Come on your elfen horse with your elfen bow, and we'll bring that big black bastard to his knees. Sigeberht, Acca, Osulf, you'll join us. No, no,' there was a clamour amongst the other nobles, 'not too many of us, or the boar will never be flushed. If you lot come hollering and yelling, stamping all over the countryside, you'll scare him into a hidey hole. Just the five of us. My hearth-companions only – and the farrier.'

'Then can I kill this upstart youth?' asked Sigeberht, snatching a horn from a neighbouring thegn and taking a long swig. 'After the hunt?'

'We'll see,' replied the king. 'He did a good job with shoeing my steed. I'll have to think about it. My dear wife Beornwynne, my advisor, will give me excellent counsel as always, and since her heart is good, she will probably propose letting the boy live – but then, I'm a man of ill-moods sometimes and find it difficult to control my rage. Woden is the same. I probably got my bad temper from the great one-eyed God of the Gallows and the Wild Hunt, being descended from the Lord of Mantic Ecstasy, so I'm not really to blame if I don't follow the wisdom and advice of my queen.'

However, when it came to it, Paega did listen to his queen. Beornwynne's bloom, her youthful loveliness, had long since faded from her complexion. But she was still a beautiful woman and her wisdom commanded a large following amongst the thegns. King Paega even slept with her on occasion, when he needed strong arms about him to bolster his confidence. Beornwynne, like many queens who have survived many birth-givings, was perspicacious in the ways of the world and family honour to her was paramount for a king and queen. Without honour the walls of public respect crumble and a monarch's position becomes tenuous. Her counsel was of great importance to a husband whose main train of thought ran along the lines of killing anyone who threatened his kingship. Paega was a warrior first and the scholar and sageness in him came a long way behind. He was not unintelligent, but his intellect often took a back seat to his enthusiasm for blood, power and glory.

Beornwynne was a lusty lady and at fifty-three years still very much enjoyed sex. Her husband, like so many older unchallenged men, often strayed into fields of fresh virgins. Like many other potentates he found it difficult to possess absolute power and at the same time be strong enough to ignore fruits forbidden to those who had not the same status. The pair had an unspoken agreement never to question the other regarding extramarital congress. However, that unspoken agreement was accompanied by another unuttered pact: no favour or special advantages were to be awarded or even promised to any illicit bed-fellow. Any adulterous sex was to be unemotional and casual, without any lasting passion. If their agreement was to work, there was to be no falling in love and promoting another woman or man in importance above the wife or husband. The pair were locked together in a life-long marriage that only death would force asunder. Any warrior who thought he was going to advance his position in the court by bedding the queen was sorely mistaken and ended up bereft. Any maiden who thought she might replace the first lady was equally misguided. The king and queen were much stronger together than they were apart – and anyway, they loved one another.

'Sigeberht is simply jealous of the youth's beauty and indeed his years. The boy might be useful to us, being the son of Eorl, and anyway he has come to us requesting sanctuary. In all honour we must offer him the same protection we give to our common churls. If one of my own sons were to request the sanctuary of another of the kings of the Seven Realms, I would expect it to be given.'

King Paega looked into the fathomless depths of his wife's large, wide hazel eyes and nodded. They were alone together in her bedchamber. He watched as she offered libations to the goddess Freo, sister of the god Ing. Freo was the Goddess of Magic and War. Half the slain on a battlefield went to her, the other half to Woden. A great many of the women of Mercia offered evening prayers to Freo, the goddess who wore the amber-lit torc called Brisingamen, preferring to have one of their own gender watching over them during the night hours.

'You're right.'

'Of course I'm right,' replied Beornwynne. 'We must respect thew.'

She was referring to the virtues or honour that every Angle or Saxon of right mind needed to follow to keep their self respect. These were: wisdom, bravery, industriousness, troth or loyalty, truth, friendship, moderation, neighbourliness and steadfastness. The king was not sure under which heading protecting the son of a rival king came but he very rarely questioned his queen's judgement. He found if he got into any kind of argument with her, it eventually strayed into various other subjects and areas and never did come to a conclusion. The queen possessed many mental mazes and led him into them with consummate ease until he was completely lost and wondering how in the name of demons he was going to find his way out again. Certainly there was no going back to the original subject under discussion.

'Yes, my dear, thew must be respected at all times.'

'You must keep Sigeberht on a leash.'

'I will, most certainly I will. The boy will have to do his stint on the wall, of course, like any of our own people.'

'Naturally.''

Paega was referring to Uffa's Dyke, the ditch and earthen wall his uncle had erected thirty years previously to keep out the warriors of Powys. Since then Paega had conquered much of the land beyond the dyke, but he kept the wall manned with his men in case those wildmen in the mountains beyond got uppity and tried a sneak attack on the Kingdom of Mercia. It was a cold thankless task, patrolling the wall, but every warrior had to do his duty, even the king's closest thegns. Only women were exempt from the task, though there were women nearby to feed and give comfort to those males who spent their time staring into the mists of Powys hoping the hairy creatures who lived there would come out and fight to relieve the boredom.

'So, husband, enjoy your hunt tomorrow. If you see any bears, leave them be – they're difficult eating and they can inflict terrible wounds on a man.'

One of her sons, a boy of eight years who had been led by his father to believe that he was a grown warrior, had been killed by a brown bear who took off his eager face with one swipe. The boy, who had been under a servant's supervision, ran at the brown bear with his small seax, as he believed his father would want him to. The bear simply reared and clawed, leaving the child with a mortal wound. The servant, on informing his master what had occurred, was instantly struck on the temple with an iron spike which Paega had been using to lever a flint from his horse's hoof. Two people dead within minutes, a child and a hapless churl, which was not uncommon in the kingdom of Paega the warrior-lord.

'I would have thought,' he said, 'you would want me to kill all the bears in the kingdom after…'

'No, no,' she stopped him from speaking the unspeakable, 'it is never the fault of the animal, for they are simply reacting to what they believe to be danger.' She paused before adding, 'Tomorrow you will have Ramm, my only living son, with you.' She had lost two others in infancy to illness. 'So please be careful to look to his safety.'

He was in half a mind to tell her the Ramm was already a weakling and needed toughening up, but wisely refrained from saying so.

'Yes, yes I'll do that too. In fact, it would be better he didn't join the hunt. I think he prefers fishing to hunting.'

He stared at Beornwynne as he lay on his wife's personal bed while she undressed ready to use it for the night, his eyes on a level with her wide hips and more important to him, what lay between them.

'I think I'll stay here for a while,' he said, his voice a little cracked, 'if that's all right?'

She smiled at him as she slipped, almost drifted, into a silk nightdress.

'Of course, my darling. Stay all night.'

'Yes, I might do so, my love. That would be - that would be fine.'

ELEVEN

Five horsemen rode out of a red dawn, into woodlands and fields where rocky outcrops were flailed by wild braided streams. The man on the lead horse, a high-headed bay with a sheen to its coat which invited stroking, was King Paega. The king had a bull's horn from which he drank mead in large heavy gulps. Three other riders also had drinking horns and were quaffing honey-wine in place of a breakfast. Only the youngest of the group, Osric the East Angle, had both hands on the reins. Osric's head was down, watching the hooves of the horse ahead disappearing and reappearing into and out of the shallow mists which drifted over the ground. None of the men spoke to him or to each other, though one – Osulf – made a startled cry when a churring goatsucker was flushed from the moorland grass. It shot up from beneath the legs of his steed. The king gave his thegn a fierce glare and the man murmured, 'Forgive me, lord.'

Finally, they came to a spinney which was tangled with crooked saplings and had the darkness of the night still trapped in its heart. The king halted his mount on the pale of this thicket. He held up his hand and spoke.

'This is where the monster sleeps,' he said. 'This is where I saw him last, but had only a broken spear for my trouble.'

They entered the outer part of the wood, but after riding a few paces could get no further because of tight thick bambles.

'You stay here,' said the king to his three armringed thegns, 'while I and the boy ride around the far side.'

'I'm not a boy,' growled Osric, but was ignored.

Sigeberht said, 'Lord, you will have no protection.'

'I can protect myself,' snarled the king. 'I need you to beat the brush, so the beast is flushed in our direction.'

'Surely, lord, the dogs can do that?'

'I'm asking you to do it. The dogs have no sense of direction.'

Sigeberht lowered his head in acceptance.

The king then, followed by Osric on Magic, rode out of the thicket and skirted the spindly trees until they were on the other side.

'NOW!' roared the king.

There was a hallooing and bellowing from the thegns as they beat the undergrowth with their spears. A high penetrating squeal came from the bracken within the dark heart of the wood. Then a thrashing sound, which seemed to go back and forth amongst the bracken. Suddenly a huge black shape with wide white eyes broke from the spinney and hurtled between the legs of the king's mount. The coarse-haired ridged hump of the great boar lifted the horse up in the air and Osric heard the cracking of the poor quadruped's ribs. With a whinny full of pain and terror it tumbled over and threw its rider onto the ground. The heavily-armoured lord of the Mercians hit the earth and rolled down a tufted hillock, to lay winded in a hollow. To give him his due, the king was on his feet within a moment, but his sword had been bent beneath him and jammed in its scabbard. He struggled vainly with the weapon as the great black boar, a monster with huge curved white tusks, spun on the turf and came hurtling back again towards the flustered king.

Osric spurred Magic forward and reached the king before the murderous beast was able to gore him. He reached down and grabbed the royal collar, hauling the huge man out of the path of the charging hog. The boar crashed past them, nicking only the king's flapping cloak, leaving in its wake the rank smell of its foul hide. Osric saw up close the farinaceous, thickly-matted hair of the boar with its own dried crap hanging from the feathering of its hind legs. It was an enormous brute, its backbone like the ridge of Striding Edge, almost as high as that of a tall horse. The fury in the wild creature's eyes and demeanour would have terrified any other steed but Magic, whose elfen origins ensured the horse remained calm and untroubled.

Osric flung himself off the back of his steed and landed on his feet next to the fallen king. Wrenching the royal man to his feet, again by his collar, he stood with Paega as the boar wheeled for a second charge. The hunched beast then came thundering straight at the pair, just as the three thegns came round the corner of the wood, their eyes on stalks as they saw the danger to their king. Osric unslung his bow and fed it with an arrow. There was a startled yell from the thegns as they tried to distract the great boar and get it to charge their way. The beast was not to be diverted. It knew its target and hurtled towards it at high speed. Osric drew the bow and let fly a shaft. The arrow sped forth and buried itself in the right eye of the boar. The haft of the arrow travelled a quarter of its length into the skull of the charging animal. The brute let out a horrendous screech as its forelegs buckled beneath its chest. Momentum ensured that it somersaulted through the air, landing with a thump two paces in front of the king and the youth with the elfen bow. There it lay panting out the last few gasps of its life.

Paega finally managed to unsheathe his damaged sword and he plunged it into the boar's body, piercing the creature's failing heart. The king then went to look at his own horse and it seemed the charger's neck had been broken when the boar knocked it flying. Paega sighed, lifting his steed's head to look in its eyes, then he let it drop and walked back to Osric and the boar. He said quietly to Osric, 'We'll send someone to bury my mount. He was a good stallion. He served me well these last three years.'

Osric said, 'Yes,' knowing that a man's horse was revered and loved almost as much as that same man's wife or daughter.

'Well done, my lord,' cried Sigeberht on reaching them and dismounting. 'The beast has been slain by your blade.'

'Don't flatter me,' said King Paega. 'We all know I should have been killed had it not been for the boy's arrow.'

'I'm not a boy,' snapped Osric.

He was ignored, and Acca rode up and took the reins of Magic, who was standing quietly by.

'Here, my lord,' said this thegn. 'You ride the boy's mount. He can come up behind me.'

Osric cried, 'No one rides Magic but me.'

Now they looked at him and he was no longer ignored.

However, the king's attention was drawn back to the boar at his feet.

'We must skin him and take his head back for stuffing,' Paega said. There were murmurings from the thegns and the king then added, 'No, not the boy, the bloody boar you idiots,' as Acca looked down at Osric with a quizzical expression on his face. 'One of you peel the beast and sever its head. I'll ride with Osulf, but in front, not behind. A king can't be seen limping into his inneryard, assisted by his thegn. I need to retain some dignity. And the boy is right. I've seen the look in the eyes of that steed of his. It's a one-man creature. It'll throw me before I've got a leg over its back. Come on, let's get on with it. I need my breakfast.'

And so they skinned the giant hog and flung the hide over the hind quarters of Sigeberht's horse. Acca was given the head to carry on his mount. The king went up in front of Osulf, who held on to his monarch's shoulders with large but strangely gentle hands, seemingly embarrassed to be touching the body of his king.

Lord Ing:

The youth indeed has promise. To save a king from certain death is an act not to be sniffed at. However, kings are notorious for forgetting such debts over passing time. This king is a ruthless, merciless beast of a man who would sell his own daughter – wait, he has already done so with the elder of the three! – into a loveless match to further his own ambitions. If the youth stood in the way of new conquests, wealth or land, then the act would be worth nothing and the boy would be slaughtered.

Osric followed on behind the four Mercians, quite happy with the morning's work, knowing he had acquitted himself with honour. He knew the king was pleased with him, though he also realised that Paega had been humiliated in front of his warriors and a callow youth, and that fact might wipe out any real advantage Osric had gained from his actions.

Before they got back, it started to rain. A massive downpour, which spoiled the triumphal entry of the huntsmen returning victorious from the hunt, since most people remained inside their dwellings and didn't see the king and his men enter with their prize. Osric, soaked through and dripping, went back to the shepherd's hut to join his two companions and to tell them of the morning's events. They listened with keen ears to the tale he unfolded and wondered if their friend would be called forth to receive a bronze or even a gold armring from the king. It seemed to them that he deserved a reward.

In the event, there was no reward forthcoming. Indeed, Osric fell ill of a fever, probably caused by being wet and cold for too long after the hunt, which was the only prize he got from the adventure. That or the local elves were punishing him for using one of their bows to kill creatures of the forest. Osric was never sure what part the elfen played in sicknesses. He recovered by late summer, but no one ever came and thanked him for his part in the hunt. When eventually he was summoned, along with the Thief, it was by one of the nobles to tell the companions that their turn on Uffa's Dyke had come round. Kenric was to stay behind to keep their business as farriers going. This last concession was no doubt because the king had been pleased with the shoeing of his horse and recognised the worth of the forge to his men.

The thegn told the Thief and Osric, 'You will form part of the contingent who guard our border by patrolling the wall built by the great and wise King Uffa of the Mercians, may the gods remember his name.' The man, a short stocky fellow with arms as thick as a badger's girth and a face like a boar, was not unsympathetic to their low mood. He said, 'The time will soon go. At least you are men without dependant families. No wives? No children? Well, none that you are willing to recognise, anyway. Once you're on the wall and the keen wind is cutting through you, you won't be able to think about much more than keeping warm and dry in any case.'

'How long for?' asked the Thief.

'Six months is the usual term, unless you upset the commander and he adds further time. Keep your noses clean and do you work well and you'll be back here by Solmonath.'

So the pair said goodbye to Kenric.

'Look after Magic for me,' said Osric. 'Don't try to ride him though – he'll throw you for sure.'

The two then set out with a group of others for one of the guard posts along Uffa's Dyke. Those on the other side of the wall, the people Romans had called the 'Celts' or 'milk-faces' who originally came from a collection of disparate tribes from the continent, were a dark and savage lot who had good reason to hate the Angles and Saxons, the latter having driven many of them westwards. The Walha princes and nobles had lost their lands to an even more savage people. Now they were not only defending their last more mountainous territory with fierce resistance, but also attacking and raiding those who had usurped them, causing all sorts of problems along the border with Mercia. They strove to recapture their lost lands, but King Paega was just as determined not to let them have even a handful of dirt.

A hundred men made the trek to the dyke and arrived hungry and irritable. Seven of them, Osric included, were immediately selected by the post's commander to go out and find food to feed the whole group.

'You can demand food from the villages, bread and vegetables – no meat, you'll have to hunt for that yourselves – but leave the villagers enough grain and cabbages to keep them alive. It does no good to take all the churls have so that they starve. We're not barbarians. We're here to keep the barbarians out...' laughter from the men '... and as I've already said, you'll need to kill wild game for your meat. It's forbidden to remove cows or sheep, or any domestic livestock. Who does the gathering and who the hunting I leave you to work out for yourselves.'

Once the officer had gone, a big fellow stepped forward and started giving orders.

'You, you and you, go to the villages and get the bread and greens. I be leadin' the other three in the hunt.'

Osric had been chosen as a member of the first group and he resented it.

'I'm a hunter, not a gatherer,' he told the big man, who he now recognised as a butcher's assistant. 'Choose someone else to go round the villages. There's one or two here who've never had a weapon in their hands. This man, for example. He's a farmer. He knows better than me what state the bread should be in.'

'You'll do as you're telt, boy,' said the big man, 'so keep youm gob shut.'

Osric was half the size of this loudmouth, but he stepped forward smartly and kicked away the man's leg at the ankle. The man fell to the ground with a great thump, which knocked all the wind out of him. Osric put his foot on the man's throat before he could gather his breath.

'Do you want a crushed windpipe?' he asked.

The man flicked his eyes as the pressure bore down on his neck.

'Listen to me,' said Osric. 'I'm the son of a king. I don't take orders from churls. I give them. That's not to say they are lesser men than me. One of my best friends is a churl. But I have had the training and I have the skill, and, most important of all, I have a bow here that never misses. I will hunt the deer with two others, I don't care who they are, and the rest will make the trek around the villages. Whose hounds are these milling around our legs? Not yours, or they would have attacked me by now. I'll borrow them for the length of the hunt, if their owner pleases."

He allowed the big man, who someone whispered was called Thark, to his feet. Thark rubbed his sore throat and glaring at Osric said hoarsely, 'I could break youm in two.'

'If I let you, you could,' replied Osric, 'but I'm never going to do that, am I? I will kill you before you get a hand on me, you can be sure of that. My knife is in my waistband at the moment. It will be out within a second and buried in your heart a half-second later. Would you like to try me?'

Thark stood there for a moment, still glaring, then said, 'I got a knife in my belt too and I be good with it.'

'At slicing bacon, yes, not at fighting. You're a very strong fellow, Thark, but if it comes to knives I am lithe and quick, much too quick for a great hunk like you. You could probably break the back of an ox, but I'm not an ox, I'm a warrior born with all the training in the ways of war that you've never had. Don't be a fool. Just do what you want with these others, but don't cross *me* or you'll regret it. Actually, you won't, because you won't be alive to have any such feelings.'

Mouths hung open and the eyes of the other five men and youths were going back and forth, from the face of Thark to the face of Osric. They were enjoying the argument. None of them really cared who won it. Nor were they concerned as to their ultimate task, collecting bread and vegetables, or hunting. In fact the former was the easier of the two, since hunting was a dangerous business, even going out for game as meek and mild as deer. There were boar out there and wolves, lynxes and bears and who knew what else that could rip open a man's belly and feed on his innards?

Thark, his mind as heavy and dense as lead at that moment, realised he was not going to get to be the leader after all, and relinquished the post with only a final dark look at Osric.

Osric said, 'Thark and I will do the hunting then, with you,' he chose a slim youth who looked good at running, 'you'll do as a game dog. That's a compliment, not an insult. You look swift on your feet and are as bright looking and intelligent as any hound bred to fetch shot game. We'll need a few birds for the pot as well as a larger beast. There're a lot of hungry mouths out on the wall. If we do well, we'll make a lot of new friends, and everyone needs friends in a war situation. Someone to pick you up and carry you back if you get wounded on the battlefield. If you make enemies amongst your comrades, then you'll be left to rot in the hands of foes. We need to make sure those who come in tired, cold and hungry have something substantial for their efforts in guarding the realm of Mercia. Do you all agree?'

If they did, they didn't say so, looking at him with the slow mournful faces of men and youths used to plodding out into the fields every day and doing the backbreaking job of sowing and weeding. They were rock gatherers who picked flintstones out of their family plots, who ploughed and dug loam, who collected wood for the fire along with the girls. There was a shepherd amongst them, so Osric understood, who would be used to driving off wild beasts from his flock, and he was the youth he had chosen to come on the hunt. The rest were only familiar with killing the odd hare or game bird that came out of the shaven corn fields at harvest time. If they had encountered a larger wild beast it was by accident, not design, and no doubt they had failed or run away.

Later that day, Thark, Osric and the youth with the long legs and knowledge of creatures of the wild returned with seventeen wildfowls, two beavers, three hares and not one deer but two. There would have been three, but Osric refused to shoot a doe with a fawn, much to the disgust of Thark. However, the big man was warming to the young prince and had now realised that Osric was smarter than he was. It said something for Thark's intellect that he recognised this and accepted it. Princes, he told Osric, are not necessarily cleverer than churls just because they are born the sons of royalty. Some royals and nobles were as dense as a boulder. Whereas Thark had known slaves who were quicker and deeper thinkers than shamans.

The meat went down well. With so many mouths to cook for and feed, the game all went into stew pots. It was easier to get ready and easier to serve than slices or chunks of roasted meat. Beaver wasn't all that savoury when roasted or eaten on its own, but in a stew it went unnoticed. Also stew was simpler and fairer to dish out. One could fill a ladle for every man, whereas slices and chunks might vary in size and amount, and fighting would break out when one was believed to be favoured over another. When every man has a knife in his hand it's difficult for the frithguildsmen to keep order and keep every body whole. Knives that sliced meat and cheese were ideal for cutting chunks from a neighbour.

The gatherers had done their work too and had brought in bread and butter, vegetables, cheese, cream and honey, even visiting villages well over the ten miles around the post.

There were also three prisoners in the company. Osric stared curiously at the captured warriors. They were shorter men than most Angles, but a great deal broader and with longer hair, hair that went right down their backs. They had a darkness about them, not in their skin, but in their eyes and expressions. When they met the looks of their captors they held them with fierce contempt. Wild, wild men, who had fought to a standstill before being taken. There had been twenty of them in the beginning, a raiding party which had killed an Angle herdsman and had tried to drive the cattle over the border. Seventeen Walha warriors had fallen under the swords and warhammers of the Angles, taking nine of the Mercians with them. The Angles were all now in the Hall of Heroes and the Celts had gone to their own strange gods. Osric had been told of an icy kingdom somewhere in the clouds, where the Celts had to continue to battle with monsters, which was why they had to die with a sword or spear in their hands.

The Celts were headhunters, their belief having at its core a reverence for the power of human head. It was not disdain or disrespect that had them displaying the heads of the conquered, but a deep veneration of the preternatural force those shrivelled skin-covered skulls contained. Severed heads of enemies hung by the hair from the manes of their horses and decorated their dwellings. When Osric went close to them, to listen to their speech, he could understand nothing. Their tongue had a rolling lilt to it which sounded almost musical but the words were warped and strange. They watched the Angles closely as warriors were given food and Osric realised these enemies of Mercia were thirsty and hungry.

'Is anyone going to feed those men?' he asked a thegn.

'Men? They're animals, not men,' came the answer.

Osric said, 'I see them clearly as men. Different from us, perhaps, but men just the same. They need to eat.'

'If you want to see them eat, then you'll have to give them your food,' the thegn snapped. 'They're not going to get any from my cook.'

Osric went to the Thief and said, 'I need half your portion.'

The Thief shrugged. 'I'm sure you've got a good reason.'

'Yes I have,' came the reply.

Osric then went to the three Walhamen sitting with their backs to the wall, hobbled at the ankles and bound at the wrists. He laid his wooden trencher in front of them, placed his jug of water next to it, and walked away. When he looked back a short while later he saw them sharing the food between them. They sniffed suspiciously at the cheese and buttered bread, but ate them none-the-less. They quaffed the water greedily and Osric realised they must have been extremely thirsty, not having drunk since the battle. Fighting always saps a man's body of moisture and warriors always come off a battlefield with a raging thirst. It would have been cruel to deny them liquid, even if they were as the thegn said, animals. Later, after the Thief had shared his own trencher with Osric, the prince went to collect his slab of wood and his jug. The Walha in the centre of the three, spoke to him in Englisc.

'Why?'

Osric picked up his trencher and pot.

'Why not?'

'We hate your guts and would have those guts trailing in the dust.'

'As would we yours, if you were not captives.'

'I ask you again, Angle. Why?'

Osric sighed. 'I would not see any man starve or thirst, even if he is the enemy of my people – and actually, these are not my people. I'm a guest here.'

'They make their guests fight for them?' said the Walhaman, with a catch in his voice. 'Nice hosts.'

'I'm an unwelcome guest. My home is in the east. I fled from the swords of other men and cannot go home until I can retrieve my place.'

'Ah. You murdered someone.'

'No, someone murdered my father and wants to do the same to me.'

The thickly-bearded captive Walha screwed up his mouth and nodded in understanding. Then he said, 'My name is Tomos, from Powys.'

'And mine, Osric from the East Angles.'

'Well, Osric, you have shown me and my companions an unexpected kindness and now we owe you a favour. If we leave here alive, then you can expect to collect it sometime. We are a proud people, even if we do steal cattle.'

'Name me a nation that is not proud.'

Tomos nodded hard at this, laughed and repeated the last few sentences to his companions, who also broke into raucous laughter. This drew the attention of the thegn, who frowned and came and told Osric to 'leave the prisoners alone' which Osric did. Later that day the three captives were exchanged for four Mercians who had been abducted by the Walha for just this kind of bargain. The last Osric saw of Tomos, a short but very stocky man with black hair standing stiffly on his head and chin, was when the three were led to the wall and ditch where they would be left to find their way into their own lands beyond.

Thark had also been studying the Walha barbarians when they were still in camp and he said to Osric, 'I had heard they'd be executed. Did you see the way they eat?' The butcher turned to face Osric. 'I'm glad we didn't kill them prisoners of war. If we be doin' it, they be doin' it, and if I be caught by Walhalies I don't mind goin' on to be a Walhalie slave. I be not much better now than if I was a slave. But if we kill them we catch in war, so'll them what catches us.'

The Thief, sitting on a bench the other side of Osric, replied, 'They were not prisoners of war.'

Thark frowned. 'Yes they be.'

'No, they be, as you quaintly put it, prisoners of law, not of war. They came over the border to steal cattle, not to do battle. They're lucky to have escaped justice. What would happen to *you* if you stole a cow?'

'I'd get knocked on the head with a hammer.'

'Precisely.'

Thark looked around Osric at the older man.

'Who be you? You don't speak like us.'

'No, that's because I'm a foreigner.'

'What be you doing here if you'm from the outeryard?'

The Thief sighed. 'Escaping justice, my friend. You see, I should have been executed long ago for theft, for robbery on the road, for stealing this that and the other. But somehow I've managed to avoid having my neck stretched – or as you so eloquently put it, getting knocked on the head with a hammer. That's why I know what I'm talking about. War is when you go to battle and kill as many men as you can before they kill you. You can kill a king on the battlefield and still be regarded as a hero by your enemy. Raiding is when you go out to steal sheep and cows and even ducks if you want to get away quickly. If they capture you doing the first, you are a brave warrior and entitled to live. If at the second, you are a grubby thief, like myself, and the noose or the executioner's hammer is felt to be quite justified.'

'You talk funny,' accused Thark.

'I might say the same of you, friend, but this is your country and your tribe, while mine is miles and miles away.' The Thief sighed again.

TWELVE

The next day Osric went out on the wall with a spear in his hand. He and the Thief were about a hundred yards apart, as were all the sentries guarding the Mercian border. There was a cold wind blowing and while Osric's wolfskin coat was thick and windproof, his face, hands and sandaled feet were uncovered. It was a miserable way to spend eight hours, with only a biscuit to comfort him. He stared out into the countryside beyond, a rugged landscape confronted him. It was grey scene, a depressing outlook, and when it began to drizzle and the mist came in it was even more dismal. The only entertainment, if it could be called that, came from the Walha on the other side of the dyke. Men, women and children, passing by on their way to wherever, paused to turn their backs on the guards and lift their shifts to reveal bare bottoms. Some of them farted very loudly and laughed like crazy.

'Come up here and do that,' cried one or two of the guards. 'I'll kick that arse into the sea!'

Rasping tongues and hoots and obscene gestures were the answers.

Towards the end of the day, when the gloom began to settle over the land, Osric had a visitor. Sethrith, dressed in flowing voluminous veils, suddenly appeared at his side and stared with him at the outeryard which housed the Walha.

'What are we looking at?' she said, making Osric jump since he hadn't noticed her arrival. 'You seem very transfixed.'

'Eh? I'm on guard. Where did you come from?'

'Oh, on the wings and back of an owl. I'm a witch, remember.'

Osric stared longingly at this beautiful woman, who taunted his manhood with her lovely form and face, with her long yellow hair and blue eyes. He stared into those deep eyes and found himself drowning in fathomless pools. Quickly, he shook his head and saved himself from being lost forever.

'What are you doing here? Why have you come to upset me?'

'Do I upset you?' she asked, sweetly. 'I don't mean to.'

'Well, you do. I – I'm very fond of you. It upsets me to have you near and not be able to – well, to touch and...'

'Oh, but you're a married man. You have an elfen wife.'

'Well, it wasn't a real marriage, was it? I mean, all she did was say we were married. There was no ceremony and no witnesses. Linnet just said that a kiss had sealed the bond. I'm convinced that elves and mortals are not meant to be together. It doesn't usually work.'

'And,' she said, ignoring this, 'you've been looking at King Paega's third daughter, the one with the raven hair and dark complexion. Don't try to deny it, for I know you have, because I can see her image still caught, still locked in your eyes. You want her, don't you, as much as you want me? Is there no depth to your butterfly nature? Do you want *every* pretty girl? Shame on you, Osric. You are a libertine. You play with the feelings of young women. Perhaps you need a good talking to by someone who should have taught you better ways?'

'And who would that be?' he growled, angry now.

'Why, your mother of course.' And Sethrith smiled and was gone.

Lord Ing:
Perhaps the witch is enamoured of the youth? Why would she visit him yet again, if not? However, there is something that she does not know. The boy left something behind in elfland, something with his elfen wife. It could make a difference to a young maiden-witch, if she was of a jealous nature – and I never knew a witch who was not.

Osric, now bitterly cold, decided it was time to take a break from his guard duties on the wall. He took out his small vial of bergamot and inhaled. Thus it was not the magic of the witch that sent him on his journey skywards, but the scent-trigger. He found himself once more on the way to the Realm of the Dead, where his parents resided. On his way through the clouds he once again came across Sleipnir, that wonderful eight-legged stallion of Lord Woden, but the steed was being anxiously tended by a good-looking groom who seemed upset. When the celestial stable boy saw a youth passing by he hailed him and called him to his side.

'Do you know anything about horses?' asked the handsome groom, who was no older than Osric himself. 'Something's the matter with my lord's steed. I've been given the job of looking after him. I used to be a hand-servant to Lord Woden's wife, Lady Frige, who likes to have me around. I really don't know anything about horses though and I can't think why I've been given the job of looking after Sleipnir.'

Osric studied Sleipnir, who was standing with cloud up to his ankles, apparently very poorly indeed. The mount was thin, almost wasting away, and looked very lethargic.

'He's constipated,' said the groom, stroking the great beast's neck, 'and there's blood in his urine – and I think he's got a pain in his gut…'

In his mind, Osric went through all that Kenric had told him about horses, for the young churl was not only a good farrier but was versed in the ailments of quadrupeds. It was good for business to know a young horse from an old, a sick horse from a healthy one. Kenric knew the breeds, the problems horses encountered when it came to their physical well-being, and the advice he could hand out to his customers who came in purely to shoe their mounts put him in good stead with them.

Osric inspected Sleipnir's mouth and felt the sweat on his coat.

'What have you been feeding him on?' he asked the groom, a boy who had been killed by bandits while out collecting wood for the fire. 'Do you take him down below, to the world of mortals?'

'Not all the way down. Just so that he can reach the treetops. He likes to graze on fresh elderberries and such. I don't let him touch mistletoe or anything that might harm him.'

'Oak trees?'

'Sometimes.'

Osric asked the youth a few more questions and finally felt he was on the right track and could give the young man's soul a definite answer.

'He looks to me as if he's suffering from acorn poisoning,' said Osric, stroking the beast's nose and wondering if he would be able to tell anyone he had touched the wondrous mount of Lord Woden. 'You need to grind down some charcoal to near powder and make him eat it. The charcoal will help soak up the poisons in his belly. Then just keep him away from oak trees.'

The distressed youth said, 'I didn't realise. Other animals eat acorns.'

'Dogs and horses can eat a little, but easily too much. Don't worry. Do what I say and he'll soon be all right.'

'Thank you,' said the relieved groom. 'My spirit thanks you, deeply.'

Osric said it was a pleasure, then asked wistfully, 'What is she like, Lady Frige? Is she beautiful?'

'As the stars and the moon,' said the youth's soul, going all dreamy. 'Beautiful as a clear night sky full of all the glories and wonders of the heavens.'

'And you – you are one of her favourites?'

'Alas, yes,' came the reply, 'for I used to serve her night and day. Then I was suddenly given this job, of looking after Lord Woden's wonderful steed, by the great god himself. Since then I have hardly had any time to serve my lady.'

'Ah,' said Osric nodding, 'I see.'

And indeed, he did see, as it was plainly evident to anyone but the young handsome youth who used to be the body-servant of the great god's wife.

'Well, goodbye then. I'm off to see my parents in the Realm of Spirits. My name is Osric, of the East Angles, should anyone ask who cured Sleipnir of his acorn poisoning.'

'I used to live in the Realm of Spirits, but not any longer,' called the youth's soul, as Osric strode away. 'Give my regards to any West Saxons you meet.'

Once he had found the misty remnants of his parents, they stood talking to him, giving him the advice that parents always give their children.

His mother said, 'You must be careful in your dealings with young women, my son. There is much unhappiness to be gathered and spread by following every whim which is directed by the fire in your loins.'

'Mother!' cried Osric, turning away his head in embarrassment. 'A mother should not talk to her son in such terms.'

'Loins? My dear child, I wish your father still had use of his.'

His father said, 'Who are these females, my son, who lead you along the path of dalliance?'

'Elves and witches, Father – makers of magic.'

His father looked very disapproving of this, but simply shook his head sadly.

'Do not let other matters turn you from the course you must follow – to revenge me and regain the fiefdom of the East Angles!'

'I'll try not to, Father, but life is life.'

'And another thing,' said the dead king, 'you seem to be puffing yourself up amongst your fellows. Forever telling them you are a prince and therefore better than they are. Sadly, my son, you are no longer a prince. With my death and your flight from our realm, you are nothing but a wanderer. If anyone asks who you are from this day forth, you must tell them *"Ic Eardstapa!"* I am the Wanderer. There is no shame in being one who walks the world, sees sights that few other men witness, experience adventures that few other men have the fortune to enjoy. You will know fierce slaughters, my son, and fearful times, and you must guard your mind's treasure-chamber of thoughts, but you are only an ordinary man now that you are walking the world. Here in the Realm of Spirits I have learned there is no such thing as royal blood. Blood is blood, whether of a churl or a king, just as the sap of one oak is no different to the sap of another. There are great oaks and there are puny oaks, but though they may differ in size and strength, they have the same juices keeping them alive. For me, here, *wyn eal gedreas* – all joy has died. My life, your mother's life, these are in you now, and will be in our grandchildren, be they the children of witches or elves or just plain ordinary wives and mothers who love them.

'Go, my son, and may the runes spell a good life for you. One day you must carve a god-post for your father and mother. I am told that the men who murdered me allow the young warriors to use my skull at the hoodening in place of a horse's skull, simply to demean the memory of their old king. Recover all my scattered bones and fit them together and bury them with all the rituals worthy of a ruler. Pray for us at the harrow altar. Keep to the virtues and honour of the thew. Follow closely the frith. Let not the Attains, the nicors and the Thurses take hold of you and lead you astray. Remember we are here in Neorxnawang, watching over you.'

With a terrible feeling of loss, Osric left Neorxnawang and made his way back down through the clouds to Uffa's Dyke.

When he opened his eyes, there was fighting going on around him. There was a clashing of swords and spears rattling against shields. He leapt to his feet, confused and disorientated, but fell in with the fight. The invaders were driven back, but there were deaths of both sides. Men lay draped on the earthen wall, in the wet grasses and weeds, their mouths open in death, eyes wide and skins taut with the terror of leaving the world. Osric helped to gather up the dead, placing them in carts. They left the Walha men and women to their own people, who came back without weapons, quietly and without any fuss, to take away the warriors of their kin and kind who had fallen in the fray. There was no time for the victors to strip the vanquished of their armrings or any other personal valuables, and, if truth be known, these skirmishes seldom had a victor or vanquished. They were simply clashes in which each side tested the metal of the other and went away with no gain.

Once the mess was sorted out and the afternoon guards were replaced by those who would stand watch for the evening, there was an inquest. Some of the other guards maintained that the Thief had not given the alarm quickly enough. They said the Celts were upon them before they knew it and the struggle was therefore that much more desperate.

'They came at him, at his point on the wall,' maintained an officer of the watch, pointing to the Thief. 'He was not there to give the alarm, but had walked away to do something of his own making…'

Osric realised what had happened. When he had collapsed, as he did when his mind flew from his body and went up into the clouds, the Thief had probably run to see what was wrong with him, thus leaving his post unattended. The Thief was not defending himself but Osric knew he could not allow the Geat to take the blame for what was essentially his fault. Yet, the punishment for failure of duty on the wall was death. It was with some fear in his heart that Osric spoke up.

'Captain,' he said, 'it was I who called this man from his post – I fell to the ground with a pain in my chest and called for him to assist me.'

'Is this true?' the Thief was asked. 'Did you run to his assistance?'

'I saw him fall,' replied the Thief. 'I was afraid he had been hit by an arrow or slingshot stone.'

The officer stared at Osric. 'And where is the pain now?'

'Gone, Captain. An elfen dart, perhaps? I apologise for my grave error.'

'Men have died,' said the Captain of the Watch. 'Saying sorry is not good enough and you know it. You must be punished…' Osric's heart was in his throat as he waited for the sentence. '…you will be beaten with a blade. My judgement is that you will receive thirty strokes on the back and ten on the chest. Clear a space on the floor of the hall. All men remain to witness the punishment. Swayn, you will deliver the strokes with the flat of your sword. You,' he pointed to Osric, 'strip to the waist and lay across the table. Be quick now, we wish to eat on that table and Swayn, try not to let too much blood stain the top. It puts me off my food. Go.'

Osric was immensely relieved he was not going to have his neck broken, but he knew he was not yet out of harm's way. He knew that some punishers did not follow orders to exactitude. Many of them got carried away with the violence of the act, carried away by the lust for administering pain and suffering which sent them into a red-mist trance, forgetting that they should keep the blade of the sword perfectly flat when striking the accused man's back or chest. Should the resulting wound prove fatal, the punisher was rarely admonished since all knew that blood-lust was a necessary emotion in the heat of battle and was ingrained in warriors who wanted to live a long life.

Osric lay across the table with two men holding him down, one by his wrists and the other by his ankles. The man on his wrists was Thark, who had a smile playing in the corners of his mouth. Osric was staring up into Thark's eyes and he knew the big man was going to enjoy witnessing the beating. Swayn was no weakling and since Osric was a stranger to him and of another nation, there was no reason for the punisher to hold back in any way.

The first stroke took all the breath out of Osric's body and his eyes widened with the pain. Tempered metal on flesh causes great weals to appear and those who were watching let out a collective gasp. Even Thark looked shocked and certainly the man with the sword in his hand delivered the second stroke with less force, even though Osric had made no sound himself.

The blows came swiftly after that, *wham, wham, wham, wham, wham, wham, wham,* until Osric heard himself crying out with the pain, tears streaming down his cheeks in hot rivulets to wet the table top below his face. He felt humiliated by his weakness at giving in to the agony of the strokes as they smacked down hard onto his ribcage and shoulder blades. It was the latter which hurt the most as the sword bounced off the corners of one or the other scapulas. He had begun by counting, but lost the figures in a red mist of pain. Then he realised the Thief was yelling out the number despite being ordered to shut his mouth by the captain.

'Thirty-two, thirty-three, thirty -'

'*Stop!*'

The captain's voice rang out and his thick fingered hand shot out to grab the wrist of Swayn, who was delivering a downstroke. No more blows came and Osric, covered in sweat and blood, seemed to collapse internally and lay as a miserable heap of bones, hair and flesh with no one grasping his limbs. When he glanced up he could see through hot liquid eyes the dazed expression of his punisher. Swayn still had the weapon dangling on the end of his arm. The blade was streaked with bits of skin and blood. Swayn appeared to be coming out of a trance, his musty breath rapid and hot, and foul smelling. He almost keeled over, but one of the other border guards held him up, preventing him from toppling over. Then he handed the sword to someone and slunk away, into a far corner of the hall in which it had all taken place.

For some reason there was no mention of the ten strokes on the chest after that. Possibly even the officer had seen enough suffering to satisfy his duty to administer punishment. Indeed, Osric had got off lightly, considering the fact that men had died on the wall and others had been wounded.

Two men then carried Osric to his sleeping quarters, where the Thief tended his raw wounds. The Thief had collected some balm and herbs on the way, while the two guards had been placing Osric on his bed, and turning the youth over – Osric was almost unconscious now – he carefully washed away the blood and gore from the youth's back and applied the cool soothing balm. Osric moaned whenever he was touched, but did not try to restrain his companion physically. Finally, the medication was on, there was nothing more the Thief could do, so he left Osric to try to sleep. Later he returned with some potage, but Osric could not get it down, so once again the Thief went off, this time to go back to duty on the wall.

Three days later Osric was judged by the captain to be fit enough to return to his post. He was still a little unsteady on his feet, but his eyes were good and his voice as strong as ever, so he could yell an alarm as well as anyone. He stood his watch for four hours and then returned to sit on the edge of his cot, calling the Thief to come and talk to him.

'What happened in the end?' asked Osric, in a low voice so that others in the room could not hear. 'The captain stopped the beating.'

'Swayn was bringing down the blade edge-first – he would have cut you in half.'

Osric snorted. 'I doubt even Swayn's that strong, but I suppose he would have caused me great injury. Thank you, by the way, for calling out the strokes. There's no misery like not knowing how long to bear the pain of each blow. You did it in spite of being told not to. Did the captain punish you for disobeying him?'

'No. And as to thanking me, you could have let me take the punishment, instead of owning up. It would have killed me, of course.

I'm not a strong and hale youth. I'm an elderly man. I couldn't have stood those blows.'

Osric shook his head. 'You're not that old, but you are – older. Yes, I suppose when someone reaches your years the body is not so strong.'

Swayn then got up from his own cot and came sheepishly over to stand by Osric's, looking down on the youth he had beaten with a blade.

'I come to say there was no malice in my strokes,' said Swayn. 'I did as I was ordered to do. Yes, it is as this fellow says, in the end I unwittingly turned the blade to the cutting edge – but not on purpose. By that time I did not know up from down. You may think it was simply a matter of laying into your back with the ease of a swordsman, but by the time I reached twenty-eight strokes my arm felt as if it was coming off. The pain in my muscles was excruciating. I could hardly see through the hotness of my eyes. It was all I could do to lift my arm for the next stroke, let alone keep the blade flat and level. Anyway, I wanted you to know...'

'No blame,' replied Osric. 'Perhaps I'll do the same for you one day?'

Swayn stared at him as if trying to gauge whether this was said in spite or humour. Osric grinned to help him decide and Swayn nodded and stretched out his sword hand to be shaken. The two men gripped each other's hands and then let fall. Swayn said, 'We are brothers now. In battle I shall watch your back...' then realising he had not chosen his words well, continued, '...that is to say...'

Osric and the Thief laughed and after a moment Swayn joined in with them. Thark then came over to them and offered his hand also, which was duly shaken, though Osric did not ever think he could regard the big butcher's assistant as a brother. Then all four of them went off to the mess when the bronze bell sounded for the next meal.

That evening Osric was not on duty and wandered away to the edge of the woodland on the Mercian side of the wall. There he stood looking up at a huge full moon that balanced like a disc on the tops of the trees. It was a cold evening, but with no snow and the frost would not arrive until morning. The landscape was heavy with long lean moon-shadows that stretched along the ground: the skyline spiked with the tips of the same trees that were responsible for those dark lanes. Osric stared at the moon, wondering if the queen of that kingdom in the sky was looking back down at him and wishing she were mortal. The youth thought a lot of himself at that moment, believing himself to be a man and hero. A little streak of self-importance and a big slice of overconfidence had entered him, now that he knew he could take pain and shrug it off within a few days. Give me a battle, he thought, and I'll triumph! I'll slaughter my enemies with a stroke of my sword. I'll destroy those who destroyed my father and my right to live amongst my own people. I'll...

A large lean and hungry-looking wolf came out of the edge of the forest and stood there, staring at Osric with narrowed eyes.

Far from being afraid, Osric thought he knew who the wolf was and what it was doing there and even though he was unarmed he was unafraid.

'Ah, you've come to visit me again? Really, Sethrith, we must stop meeting in this way – people will talk.'

The wolf took two steps forward, still staring up into Osric's face.

'Look, witch-girl, I know you by your eyes,' laughed Osric. 'Come on, show yourself in your true form. You can't fool a youth as smart as me.'

The wolf, indeed a starved-looking creature with a visible ribcage and a hanging belly, took three more padded steps forward and bared its yellow teeth, its eyes sharp with intent. A snarl escaped its throat. The hair on the nape of its neck rose and bristled.

'Oh come on...' began Osric, but at that moment a young hare sprang up out of the grass and in the moonlight made a wild dash for the woodland's edge.

The wolf shot instantly sideways and was on the hare in a flash, breaking the creature's back with one snap of its jaws. It then took the limp form in its mouth and without even a single backward glance at Osric, trotted into the darkness of the forest.

Osric remained staring at the spot where the wolf had entered the treeline for quite a while, before saying to himself, 'Not Sethrith. Not a witch at all. A real wolf. A starving wolf,' before turning and walking back to his sleeping quarters feeling suitably stupid, glad that no one had witnessed his foolishness.

Lord Ing:
There's a wolf out there, a giant beast with a grey cowl, underneath whose eyelids is written the secret of eternal life. Gods have no need of such alchemy of course, but mortals have been looking for it for thousands of years. An elixir? A root, a herb, a spice? You would like to know, wouldn't you? Then find the wolf, trap him and hold him fast so that you may lift his eyelids, and read what is written thereon.

By the by, it's no good killing the beast, for the runes fade instantly when the heart stops beating and the blood grows cold in its veins.

The months did indeed pass by, with long boring hours on the wall tempered by brief explosive minutes of high intensity action. Swayn never got the chance to watch Osric's back in battle: the youth was killed by a Walha spear close to the end of his watch one evening. Indeed, close to the end of his time on the wall. Just before the termination of their stint on Uffa's Dyke the Thief and Osric were called away from their posts to take part in a major offensive against the Bernicians. Bernicia and Deira were co-joined Umbrian Angle realms which had been subjugated by Mercia, their kings constantly beaten in battle and killed *ad nauseum* by Paega (and before Paega, his ancestors). But the Bernicians and Deiran kings were forever springing up again and rebelling against the oppression of Mercia. They did not enjoy paying tribute to the Mercian kings and moreover had embraced a new god despised by those who saw Woden and his house as the creator of the race.

A new Bernician prince had thrown Paega's gold-fetcher – the man who collected the tribute due to Mercia – into a pit of wolves and told him to take his gold from the teeth of the starving beasts in that pit. Naturally the gold-fetcher was torn to pieces and devoured within the hour. His bones, those that had not been cracked open for the marrow, were gathered in a sack and back sent to Paega, who immediately executed the messenger who brought them. A courier's life, whether on one side or another, was not worth a pinch of dust in times like these. Those who were chosen for the job made their peace with their gods and bid their families a last farewell before setting out on a mission which could have only one outcome.

Thus, Paega gathered together an army and appointed Acca as its commander, the king too busy fighting elsewhere to go on campaign himself against such an enemy. Acca was a young thegn with high ambition. He took with him almost all the men and boys in his extended family as his cavalry. Osric and the Thief were armed foot warriors, not amongst the churls since Acca recognised Osric as a noble, but still Osric felt aggrieved that he could not be amongst the riders. Three thousand of them set out at the end of the summer intent on teaching Eric of Bernicia a lesson. The new prince had given himself the name Eric-the-

Destroyer, but no one had yet discovered what Eric had so far destroyed. It seemed to Osric that the only thing Eric had demolished was the treaty between his people and Mercia. Osric sympathised with the Bernicians – their pride and honour had been constantly trodden on by the Mercians – but he was annoyed at having to fight in a conflict which was not going to advance his own cause one iota.

The two armies met in a valley on the far side of the border between Bernicia and Deira. The latter had decided to stay out of the battle and quietly went about their business elsewhere, leaving the Bernicians to sort it out. If the Bernicians won of course the Deirans could stop paying tribute to the Mercians and could do so without fear or reprisals, and without having to lose good men in a war. However, the Bernician army was over three times the strength of the Mercians, having three thousand men under the command of Eric-the-Destroyer. Acca had taken with him just the cream of the Mercian army, a thousand of the best warriors.

It soon became apparent too that Eric was an intelligent and resourceful leader who knew how to best deploy his troops. Strategy and tactics had never been the strong point of Mercians who threw themselves headlong into the fight with great heroism and gusto, but relied on their fierceness and bravado to carry the day. They went charging and screaming in with warhammers and battle-axes, swords and spears, unconcerned by their opponents seeming calm and orderliness, only to find themselves trying to scramble over or through cut thorn bushes that Eric was using as a barrier. When the Mercians became entangled and emerged scratched and bleeding on one side or the other, the Bernicians jeered and hooted.

These taunts went straight to Accra's heart and instead of sitting down with the other thegns and working out a good plan for a small army to best a large army, he once again charged hot and raging headlong at the Bernicians with his foot warriors. The Mercians tried to leap over the thorn barrier and were cut to pieces by the triumphant Bernicians, leaving Acca amongst the dead. Osric, the Thief and around seven hundred of the original thousand attackers managed to retreat. However in their headlong flight they found themselves trapped at the end of the long valley with a wide torrential river blocking their final retreat. They were locked in by the Bernicians. Night had fallen and the Bernicians made camp in a semi-circle, ready to finish off Accra's army in a morning massacre. Osric could see their campfires all around, blocking any night escape by the Mercians.

Osric sat down on the cold ground with the Thief.

'Well,' he said, not able to keep a note of despair out of his voice, 'tomorrow will be glorious, but can only end in one way.'

'Yes,' replied the Thief, 'unless we don't leave it until the morrow.'

Osric stared at his older Geat companion, trying to gauge what was behind that remark.

'You think we should attack *them?*'

The Thief nodded. 'Why leave it? Look, you know I'm a coward, Osric. I've run away from more fights than any man on Earth. I admit it. I do not want to die and I'm not ashamed to own up to it. Yes, you are like most men, a warrior and a man of honour, but without men like me you would never survive to old age. I rely not on courage in battle, but on cunning and craft. I am a sly, conniving man and have more survival tricks than a fox. I collect such schemes wherever and whenever I can. This situation, I know I can't flee from. They have us trapped and unless I want to try to swim across the freezing waters behind us, I have to stay and take my medicine...'

There had been Mercians who had attempted to swim the torrent, only for the others to watch them hopelessly swept away and drowned.

'So, I have a proposal to make to you, which you must put before the counsel of thegns gathered under that oak tree.'

'Why me? You should take the credit if you have a good plan.'

The Thief shook his head. 'They won't listen to me. I'm a foreigner, a Geat from across the swan-road, of low birth, not to be trusted. They might think I'm leading them into a trap. It has to be you, a prince and an Angle, a youth with a quick sword blade and a strong heart. Still, you may have trouble getting them to agree, so be prepared to fail, my young friend. Anyway, this is what I learned from a sailor and scholar who came to us from the Mediterranean Sea. This man had read many old books, some of them in Latin, others in Greek, Egyptian or Armenian, and his tricks were more manifold than those of the conjurer-god, Loki, may his name be emblazoned on the curtained lights across the northern skies in winter...'

'Yes, yes, get on with it.'

So, the Thief indeed got on with it and told Osric what the Mercians should do if they were to stand even a chance of escaping slaughter. Osric then went to the thegns and passed on the plan as if it were his own. It was not as difficult as the Thief had envisaged. The bright ones among them got it straight away, but unfortunately one or two were not so intelligent as their companions.

A huge, thickly-muscled thegn called Aedelhun, kept saying, 'Why the clay? I don't get it. Why the clay?'

Osric drew a deep breath and one or two of the other thegns rolled their eyes. The prince explained it all again, until finally another of the thegns, a younger brother of the dead Acca, leapt to his feet and cried, 'Enough. Aedelhun, either come with us or sit on your backside and watch. We're going to kill some Bernicians.' He then stripped off and ran down to the river bank to disguise himself. Others joined him, ordering their churls to do the same. Eventually Aedelhun followed them, still grumbling, 'I just don't get it. Why not just go in and kill 'em? Why all this fuss and bother, first? I just don't get it…'

That night, during the darkest of the hours, when the moon was well hidden behind a thick cloud, several hundred naked white figures hurled themselves into the camp of the Bernician army, emitting blood-chilling screams and eerie moans. They appeared to be figures that had risen from the grave. Only their eyes had any visible colour, looking out red and hot from pits in their faces. Their mouths were like caverns in rock, from which terrible oaths and threats came, followed by the swishing of a sword and the crying of men whose limbs had been severed or whose hearts had been pieced by cold iron. Thousands of Bernicians came out of their tents and began running hysterically this way and that, terrified by the white demons that were flying amongst them, cutting men in half, severing heads, skewering vital organs. It was dreadful chaos and the fear of the otherworld drove hordes of terrified warriors down towards the river and into its deadly swirling currents.

'They're coming in from the sky,' shrieked one demented soul, sound out of his head with fear. 'They're flying down, out of the darkness.'

This cry was repeated over and over again, until the several camps of the foe were scattering over the countryside, running from the foul beings that had descended upon them. The screams and wails added to the chaos and panic amongst the Bernicians, one or two of whom stood their ground but, being abandoned by their comrades, soon gave up the fight and joined in the mass exodus. Dark figures swarmed over the hills on either side of the valley, streaming away into the blackness of the landscape beyond, running, running, *running*. All order, every chain of command, had broken down. There were nobles clutching a bundle of fine clothes, there were churls still in their smocks, there were men wild and naked.

It was not the number of attackers which caused the foe to desert their camps and flee, but the sight and the horrible presence of white demons that had dropped from the sky. These blood-thirsty monsters had surely flown from unhallowed graves to play their vicious games on vulnerable mortals. They were clearly fashioned of fleshless bones packed with cold earth, and were no doubt impossible to kill. No one even tried to challenge the attackers. Who would dare go against fiends from hell? And for their part, the invaders knew that all they had to do was kill anyone who was not covered in white river clay. Any other man youth or indeed woman was the enemy. While they let females and young boys, terrified out of their minds, run off into the night, the attacking forces cut down as many of the Bernician warriors as their wearying muscles would allow. They needed to provide a lesson for the sake of their king, Paega, who would demand it for the death of Acca and all those who had fallen with him in and around the trenches.

When it was over, just six of the Mercians lay dead and another dozen injured. Among those who had fallen was the stupid Aedelhun, who had refused to strip off his clothes and plaster himself with white clay. It was not known if he had fallen under the sword of an enemy or a friend. Certainly, once the battle-lust was in the heads of the attackers, their brains buzzing with the slaughter of the foe, they would not have stopped to ask a man whose side he was on. They took it for granted that if a man was not pure white, he was the enemy.

When the thegns reconvened, they thanked Osric profusely for his clever plan and promised that Paega would know who had saved their lives. Osric tried to tell them that it was the Thief who came up with the scheme, but they would not listen. Even when they learned that the Thief was the first one to make the shout, 'They're coming from the sky…' pretending that he was a Bernician and filling their hearts of the with the dread of being overrun by demons, the thegns merely nodded and no praise was forthcoming for a man from over the North Sea. Instead they feasted and drank their mead, praising the gods and the 'wanderer' from the East Angles.

THIRTEEN

There came a day when Osric was back on a fresh tour of duty on Uffa's Dyke, but was not on watch on the wall. Bored with the company of warriors in the long hut which served as their barracks he was drawn to the natural world beyond the camp. He took himself on a long walk, following a rill which cut through the snow like a dark snake. The morning was cold and clear, with puffs of cloud decorating an otherwise pale blue sky. Indeed, Woden and the other gods were probably all still abed, for there was no visible or audible activity in the heavens. On this ramble he encountered a few beasts: a weasel with an unidentifiable prey, a wild dog which was so emaciated its ribs could easily be counted, a robin or two out looking for worms along the stream's bank, and a bunch of rooks in the leafless branches of a hornbeam. Osric had his bow and quiver of arrows, but felt no desire on that pleasant winter's morning to kill any of the creatures of field or forest.

He was warm enough, having breeches of fox fur strapped with leather thongs to his legs and a heavy cloak, fur hat and mittens. He was about to turn back, feeling he had gone far enough into the outeryards of the countryside, when he caught sight of a ribbon of smoke wavering up from behind a low hill. Curious, for there seemed to be no other villages or farms in this area, he trudged through the deep snow and over the rise to find a stone building which was clearly occupied.

Now normally the Angles and Saxons avoided these lone remainders of the Roman occupation of the land, considering them unlucky. Some ignored the idea of bad omens it was true, and Osric wondered who was brave enough to do so here.

He entered the inneryard of the occupant and yelled.

'Hey! Who's in there?' He took off his quiver and laid his bow against the wall of a well. 'Can I enter? I am unarmed and of a friendly nature.'

There was no reply. Osric repeated his request. Still no reply. He was about to pick up his hunting weapon and leave the occupant to his privacy when the door to the dwelling flew open and a voice cried, 'Come in, but I am at stool.'

Osric wrinkled his nose. 'Well, I'll wait until you've finished what you're about and then come in.'

There was a short wait, then an elderly figure appeared in the doorway adjusting his breeches.

'Ah, a boy,' said the elder, 'come, come. You'll want refreshment. Are you a Mercian or a Celt?'

'Neither,' replied Osric. 'An East Angle.'

'Then you'll be hungrier than I thought, for you must have walked all the way from the East coast to the West today.'

'What are you saying?' said Osric, impolitely, 'that's several day's ride.'

The elder smiled. 'I'm sorry. I didn't mean to offend your sense of propriety young fellow. It's just my sense of fun. Please come in and partake of a drink of elderberry juice and some seed-cake. I made the cake myself, so it's very good. What takes you out into the wilds? Are you lost?'

'No, elder, I'm one of the guards on the wall. I just thought the world looked inviting today and decided to accept its invitation to walk.'

The old man nodded. 'Very commendable. I heartily approve. Life is not to be wasted. If you see an opportunity for a stroll and time to contemplate the beauties of nature, immerse yourself in profound thoughts on the world and its ways, philosophise on the condition of men, then you must take it. Too many young fellows simply idle away such time, moaning about their lot in life, dreaming about power and wealth they will never have...'

'I believe you think me capable of deeper thought than is possible,' interrupted Osric. 'I simply decided I preferred the quietude of the outeryards to the stinking confines of our billets.'

'Ah, modest too. A very admirable trait. Yet, you have a refined way of speaking young man. You're not a churl, I can see that much in your bearing.'

'I was once a prince, my father the king of the East Angles. He was murdered. I escaped the same fate by running away as a youth. Now I am an outlander in a region which puts up with me, but does not recognise my former status. I make a living, when not on the wall, shoeing horses with two good friends, also outlanders.'

'Thank you for that history. Now, cake and drink?'

Osric, sitting by the blazing fire, was grateful for the hospitality and sat there eating, contemplating his surroundings. The stone walls did not, as he had been told they would, hold the winter inside. Instead the room was warm and cosy, and he began to envy the elder's ability to keep himself detached from the rest of humanity.

'How do you feed yourself?' asked Osric, studying one wall of the room which was covered in a wooden structure full of holes. In the holes were rolls of parchment: dozens of them, tied with pieces of string presumably to keep them from unravelling.

'Why, I hunt, of course, like anyone else. Age has not robbed me of my former skills as a young stripling. And in the fine weather I grow my vegetables and fruit, gather nuts from the trees and wild seeds from the plants – and indeed, herbs from the river banks. I survive quite well, better than most.'

'How are you called?'

'They name me Godric-of-the-Borderland.'

Osric nodded towards the rolls of parchment.

'Are you a priest?'

'Of sorts. You would be more accurate to call me a man of learning. I spend my time trying to solve the mysteries of nature and mankind. You'd be surprised how interesting such things are.'

'And what are all these?' Osric's arm swept round to indicate the scrolls.

'Ah, they were left by the Romans. They're called *books*. I've collected them from various old houses such as this one. Some of them have been eaten by mice and rats, but others were kept in stone or wooden boxes and so luckily remain intact. Do you speak Latin?'

'What's that?'

'The language of the Romans. A prince should be a learned man. If ever you find it possible to return to your old status, you should learn to read and write both Latin and your own language.'

'I can read and write a bit – not Latin though.'

'Would you like me to teach you?'

Osric thought about this for a while, then asked, 'What would be the point?'

'The point, young man?' The elder laughed. 'Why, swords do not make good kings – knowledge does. Do you want to be a good king?'

'If ever I get the chance.'

'Then learn, fellow, learn.'

'Is there anything in those *books* which will help me regain my father's kingdom?'

'There is everything. There was once a famous king of the Romans they called Julius the Caesar – he wrote several books, copies of which you see there in those pigeon-hole shelves, describing the battles he fought. He used ploys he called "strategies" and "tactics" to win those fights. He was one of the most successful leaders of armies that ever lived. Some of his tricks on the battlefield he learned from a man who went before him, one they called Alexander the Great. These are tried and trusted ways of winning battles, young man – what is your name?'

'Osric of the east Angles.'

'Well, Osric. Do you want to learn how to conquer or not?'

Osric drew in his breath, thinking that surely one of the gods, Woden or Ing, or even Loki, must have led him to this dwelling, to this old man called Godric. He was conscious too of the fact that the Thief knew some of this 'knowledge' and had used it to get them out of that scrape with the Bernicians. Osric had a feeling that he was about to become a little more elevated than most young men of his age.

'Yes, yes indeed I do.'

Thereafter, whenever Osric had the time, he visited Godric of the Borderland in his home and was a diligent student of both Latin and Roman conquests.

Lord Ing:

Such promise! The young man values education. Now there's a great advantage, when seeking character. This is what the intellect is for: learning. Give me a brave, strong warrior with a good brain and a grasp of knowledge over a brave, strong warrior with a wooden head and no interest in furthering his knowledge any time. Pit them against each other and you'll see the difference. Nine times out of ten wooden-head will be chewing worms and dirt while the student walks away.

While the Thief and Osric were thus engaged once more on the wall, Kenric was hard at work shoeing horses and wondering why he had ever left his home with the South Saxons since this is just what he would be doing there.

'I came away looking for adventure,' he grumbled to a horse which seemed to be listening politely to his complaints as he drove nails into its hooves, 'and all I've found is the same work that my father did before me.'

'What are you saying to my mount?' called the owner of the beast, suspiciously. 'Are you bewitching the animal?'

'Would I be doing that to one of my best customers?'

'Am I one of your best?'

Under his breath, Kenric replied, 'Yes of course you are – you don't know how to ride and you go through horseshoes like I go through charcoal for the furnace.' Out loud however, he said, 'You are indeed, sir, since you look after your mount like a noble, making sure she's well shod...'

When the last customer for the day had left, Kenric went down to the open ground where men drank mead around blazing log fires, even in the winter months. He was not often one of their number but he felt lonely now that his two companions were on wall duty. Kenric purchased a jug which contained far too much mead for a young man to drink at one sitting. He bought it with a promise only, of giving the mead seller a cheaper shoeing next time the man brought an animal to him. Then he sat down, pulled his woollen cloak tightly around him for it was indeed a cold night despite the fires, and listened to the story-poems while he combed his hair.

There was a ceremonial whetstone, a beautiful object with an iron boar at its head, which was passed from man to man as the tale proceeded. The whetstone was made of greywacke, one of the hardest stones known to an Angle or Saxon. It never went into Kenric's hand, of course. He was considered far too young to know the great old tales of crossing the swan-road to this land – stories like *The Wanderer* and *The Seafarer* – beautiful tales beautifully told in verse in the language that these tribes fresh to the island had, after several generations, developed into a new tongue. They called it 'Englisc'. It was not as lyrical as the Walha they heard from those over the border, which was almost like singing, but it was *their* language and as such they spoke it with proud relish and it fell on men's ears with a flavour of its own.

Kenric, listening to the tales, found himself being wafted away on ships with blossoming sails that sped across the swan-road.

> '... warriors, with joyous tears
> use the splendour of spears,
> the swords piercing hearts...

Then on to the journey to find:

117

'... storms crash on cliffs
deep waves with rifts,
before the falling frost
fetters the land-lost...

To reach the point where:

'... winter darks keep
the night shadows deep.
A malice of men
returns yet again
from the north...'

Old battles are reborn in the flames of the fires and the men listening have shining faces and shining eyes. None were there, but they know the tales handed down from grandfather to grandson. There was a seamless thread that ran back from these descendants of those who came in their wooden ships looking for a new land. Some simply settled and mingled with the Celts, while others found it necessary to fight and die for their right to remain. The old princes and those who followed them were driven west, into the corners of the island. In the distant north there were other Celts, but they were too far away to be of any bother to the kingdoms now occupied by Saxons, Angles, Fresians and Jutes. Kenric had heard that it was mountainous country in the far north, similar to the terrain from which his ancestors had come.

Later in the evening, when he was a little drunk from too much mead, Kenric found himself talking to a pedlar who had recently been in his home realm. Once the man had turned away from him, Kenric was shocked to realise that a wedding which had taken place amongst the South Saxons was that of his older sister. And – and that it appeared she had married a man she hated! How could that be? He clutched at the pedlar's shoulder and asked him to repeat what he had said. The man was a little startled and then annoyed by the insistence, but eventually confirmed his tale. Kenric stumbled away from the fires, going back to the forge, where he fell asleep on the warm floor and slept until morning. Initially, when he awoke, he forgot what he had been told the previous evening and went to a nearby stream to dunk his head and restore some sense to his thinking processes.

Once his faculties were back in sober order Kenric's mind dwelt on the fact of his sister marrying a man she despised.

'Surely this is not a union she agreed to,' he said to himself 'And with Ma and Da dead there's no one to question it.'

Kenric had no brothers, but there were cousins who might have intervened, if they felt this was a forced marriage. It was a mystery and one Kenric felt he needed to investigate. He was fond of his sister, who had raised him after his parents had been killed. Something was not right here and Kenric was determined to find out if his sister was being wronged. He wasn't sure what he could do about it, since the man responsible was a powerful noble, but he couldn't just let it lie.

Arming himself with the sword his father had made for him, and with provisions in his carrying sack, Kenric went out into the pasture where Magic was grazing. He knew that Osric would be angry if he borrowed the prince's horse, but there was nothing else for it. Kenric wasn't going to walk all the way to the villages of the South Saxons. That would take too long and his business here would suffer dreadfully. Perhaps the old farrier might even take back his customers?

'Now, horse,' he said to the wary Magic, who was looking at him approaching out of the corner of its eye, 'you know me for a friend. You've seen me with your master and we are the best of companions, an't we, eh? So if you'll just let me get a rein on you and let me up on your back, all will be fine.'

Magic snorted and backed away, his nostril's flaring. Kenric knew by the horse's reaction that he was not going to accept the youth on his back just like that. It was going to be a longer process than first hoped. He was going to have to woo the mount and spoil it first with a few bribes. One thing was in Kenric's favour. He knew horses and he was used to making friends with them. If you were going to nail a blistering-hot iron hoop to a horse's foot, you had to gain its trust first or get kicked. Kenric had a voice spread with butter when it came to quadrupeds and they eventually allowed him to stroke them and finally to hammer on shoes.

'Oh, oh, that's no way to treat a good friend, now is it, horse? Look, look what I've brought you.' Kenric opened his palm and the weak sunlight fell on some golden crystalline cubes. 'Honey. *Honey.* Even the word sounds good, now don't it, my lovely steed. Come on, have a sniff. Have a chomp. You know you like it.'

The horse now had a whiff of the honey cubes and his eyes did not stray from their glittering shapes. After a moment or two, he stepped forward and stood looking at the sweets, his breath hot and musty on Kenric's cheek. Kenric flattened his palm as the nose came down and the teeth gathered in the delicious food. Once they had been taken, Kenric reached into his purse and took several more cubes out, feeding them one by one to the greedy horse. Kenric then left Magic to his pasture and went back to the forge. The following day he returned to the meadow and was gratified to see Magic come trotting forward to receive another batch of honey cubes. After five days of wooing him, Magic was ready to accept Kenric on his back. The only problem was that Kenric was no rider. He had been on horses, leading them to his father's forge, and indeed his own workplace, but riding out over the countryside had thus far been a pleasure denied him.

Finally Kenric set off, heading south-east towards the land of the South Saxons, his own people. In the time the Thief, Osric and himself had been companions, Kenric had grown and filled out more. He was no longer the scruffy urchin who had wandered under the gallows where Osric had sat contemplating his own future. He was now a thickset young man with a strong eye. A boy no longer. Magic trusted the weight and the strength of this farrier on his back and knew he was in good if inexperienced hands. The youth was no natural horseman, no expert when it came to the canter or gallop, but Kenric was learning fast. The fact that Magic had been raised to know light-framed elves on his back made him a little friskier than a normal mount, but he was well able to cope with the extra muscle and bone.

After two days of riding and seeing no habitations except isolated small holdings, Kenric came across an amazing sight. It was a village – yet much more than a village for there were broken dwellings which stretched over a vast and rolling landscape – with buildings made of stone and solid wood. No wattle-and-mud walls here, at least not many, but taller dwellings with marble pillars holding up the sky and even the floors of these halls and homes were fashioned of stone, some of them forming pictures made of coloured chips of quartz and other minerals. These were the faces of men and women, perhaps gods and goddesses, and of animals, flowers and fishes, and warriors with weapons in their hands and helmets on their heads.

But the natural world had attacked this huge village of brick and stone. The streets were not level but wildly undulating, with tufts of grass splitting paved areas and places where shrubs had crashed through plates of solid rock. Here and there a tree had burst from below and was now mature and flourishing. Some had trunks as thick as a horse's girth. Many of the buildings were lopsided, or had collapsed completely to be clutched by fists of vines and creepers. Clearly these dwellings had been abandoned long ago allowing the plant world to retake old ground. Once this landscape had been forest and field, with brooks running through and moss growing on the banks: now the green owners had returned with a vengeance.

Kenric rode Magic slowly through the streets of stone. Magic had never needed shoeing, being an elfen horse. Nevertheless his hooves clattered noisily on the stone streets, echoing through the buildings. Here and there were ivy-covered statues of men swathed in marble robes, some life-size, others even much larger, staring down on the pair as they moved through the place. There were regal eagles with broken wings on the tops of ridged roofs made of red tiles. Many of the edifices of the buildings were embossed with scenes of chariots, battles between armies, horses and other creatures Kenric had no names for.

It was an awe-inspiring place and one that had been glanced at in the poems of the Angles and Saxons. There was a hint of giants living in a time before Kenric's people came from over the swan-road – that stretch of cold green sea that separated an old home from a new one. Kenric had heard stories of men clad in metal who ruled here once – perhaps they were the giants? – but who had returned to some far-off land that lay even beyond the old country where Kenric's ancestors had held sway.

Suddenly there were three armed men in Magic's path in a narrow cobbled street on which Magic's hooves kept skidding and slipping.

'Where'd'ya think you're goin'?' asked one of the greasy-looking long-haired men of Kenric. 'Don'tcha know this is our inneryard?'

Kenric nodded. 'Good day to you, friends. I am just passin' through and mean no trespass.'

'Well, whether you mean it or no, you've gone an' done it, an't you, eh?' said another of the men, the one with the warhammer. 'I'm thinkin' you need to pay a tribute, since you're an intruder in our private inneryard. Don't you know,' he swept the warhammer in a circle, 'this here all belongs to us?'

'You built it, did you?' snapped Kenric. 'Stonemasons, are you?'

The faces of the three men turned thunderous. They looked at one another with narrowed eyes and the first one who had spoken said, 'I think you'd better get off that there horse, sonny, and be on your way lessen you want a caved skull. You can leave her with us, an' the rest of your gear. We'll find a use for her and any other goods you've got on you. You can leave quiet like and think yourself lucky to be alive.'

Kenric drew his sword and set himself on Magic's back.

'You think you can take me, do you? There's brave for you. If you stay where you are my horse will ride over your bodies and on the way I'll take a head or two from the shoulders that own 'em. Would you like to try me?'

The men looked a little uncertain now and the one with the warhammer stepped back to give himself more room to swing his weapon.

'You can try me as soon as you like,' he growled, his voice thick, stupid and slow, as if heavy with the effects of too much mead.

On his own volition Magic suddenly sidestepped and slammed one of the other two men against a wall with his left buttock. Kenric heard the crack of ribs and the exhalation of air from lungs. The man screamed and fell to the ground as Magic sidestepped once again. However, the rogue on the right side had grabbed Kenric's leg and heaved upwards to unseat him from his mount's back. Kenric almost toppled but managed to snatch at a handful of mane with his free hand. Now Magic lashed out with his offside left leg, catching this bold robber in the gut with a hoof and flinging him backwards.

Kenric righted himself on the horse's back and urged his beast forward. The fellow with the warhammer was in the act of swinging his weapon when Kenric's sword cleft his skull lengthwise down to his breast. There was a horrible moment when the two halves of the head fell away from each other, the startled eyes parting company, the mouth revealing two tongues. Then the robber's body folded like a sack and sprawled on the cobbles, brains and blood mingling in the gaps between the flints. The two halves of the severed skull cracked like nutshells on the flint cobbles. The metal warhammer bounced and clanged on the stone. One of the other men looked up at Kenric and groaned, 'There's more of us!' but then he vomited down his front.

Kenric realised he was in a dangerous place, full of rogues and bandits, and knew he had to leave this massive ghost-village as quickly as possible. No doubt the scum who lived here had been banished from their tribes and had gathered to prey on passersby and travellers. Pedlars would probably give it a wide berth and hunting parties simply skirt it, there being nothing in amongst the stone dwellings to interest them. He noticed now how the place stank, too, of faeces and rotting rodents and other creatures killed and left to decay by the inhabitants. There was no thought of cleanliness in this strange inneryard. Disease was probably rife amongst the scoundrels and scallywags that prowled its streets. It was not a wholesome place to stop and rest one's head in any case and he and Magic were pleased once more to be out in the open fields and woodlands where the air was clean and sweet.

That night Kenric came across the small farmhouse made of turf and stones, with unshaven timbers supporting it against a rock overhang. Remaining on his horse he called to the occupants that he was a lone traveller who meant no harm and requested a bed for the night. Eventually a woman of uncertain age came out and looked him up and down before saying, 'Have you the price?' Kenric told her he had a bag full of iron nails. He was then invited in to the dwelling, which smelled of earth and dry grass, and was much more pleasant than would have been the shit-covered streets of the place he had just left behind him. There were five occupants in all, in this inneryard, three of them children and the other two women. There was no man at that time, but the master of the home arrived later, a questioning frown on his forehead.

'Just a lone youth-traveller,' said one of the women, explaining Kenric's presence. 'No harm in him.'

'We hope,' grunted the farmer, who had two hares strung together and slung over his forearm.

Once the fire had been built up and there was meat and corn boiling in the pot, Kenric got speaking with the farmer. Kenric explained that he had been in the place of the stone dwellings and mentioned the giants who might have owned them. The farmer laughed and shook his head, a few dead leaves falling from his hair where he had ridden too close to the low-hanging branches of dormant trees.

'No giants, young man. No giants. They were built by men of a mighty army who once occupied this land. An army controlled by a city called Rome, which lies a thousand miles away or more. They had tradesmen they called 'engineers' whose slaves cut the stone under their instruction. There were stone carvers too, and wood carvers, and men who knew how to lay wide straight paths across the landscape along which their armies could march quickly. I should know all this, because my grandfather was one of them. He was not from the original city, but from just across the water, recruited by the men who had come from a hotter land than this one. He was a Gaul and when the great army left these shores, he stayed on the piece of land he had been given to farm, *this* land which I now work myself. Once a man had served twenty-five years in the Roman army he was given such land as a gift for his services. Now I have to defend it against brigands and men who are worse than the dirt under my sandals – foul creatures who only want to take what is not theirs. Thieves, robbers, rapists, men of no worth whatsoever. But I hold my own. I hold my own.'

Kenric tried to sort all this information out in his mind. He could not quite understand how men of a place that was so far from the shores of his island could conquer and hold a foreign land. His expression told the speaker what he was thinking and the older man explained that the Romans were men of great invention, who had homes heated by underfloor fires and had running water in their kitchens. Their methods of fighting made them masters of the world, with such formations as phalanxes and turtles, whereby their spears were like the spines of a hedgehog and impenetrable, and their metal shields covered them completely like an iron cloak. They were invincible, said the farmer. You would think, he added, that those tribes they conquered being more numerous could have overwhelmed them, but the Romans made all those they fought and captured into Romans themselves, until the whole world was in the tight control of one huge, mighty army.

Kenric was amazed by this story and said he had seen floors made not of wooden planks like the floors of the Angles and Saxons, but of chips of stone which formed pictures. 'A bit like the Mercians then,' he said, 'and that turtle thing you told me about, like our shield-wall, though our shields are not made of metal which I think must be too heavy and cumbersome for a warrior to be lithe and quick in battle, but of strong, seasoned alderwood and thick, tanned leather.'

'Ah, much greater than the Mercians. There were more of them than there are stars in the night sky. That's one reason why they couldn't be beaten in battle. And the skills they had! Our minds have lost the ways and wherefores of such wonderful skills now, many clever things which the Romans taught us but which have since vanished on the back of the wind. There may be some, who knows, who've been taught by their grandfathers, but I don't know of anyone who still has the knowledge. We've got our music and our poetry, and our stories survive through the memories of strong-minded men, but much was lost when the Romans went home.'

'And what happened to them? Do we know?'

'Only that they left because they were under attack from yet another powerful foe – they called them *barbarians* – warriors without learning, whose only purpose in life was to destroy what others had created. There are some on this Earth whose only skill is to rape, burn and kill those they overrun. They farm no land, they build no bridges or permanent homes, they tend no livestock. They simply take from those who have these accomplishments and kill them without the thought that tomorrow there will be no one left to steal from, no one left to make or grow what is needed to sustain life, and thus their brains rot in their skulls as they look around for more tribes to destroy, finding none because they have laid waste to every living thing.'

The farmer was growing fiercer and more furious with every word he spoke, until he hardly made sense any more, he was lost in a great welter of angry words and raging sounds. One of the women came to him and stroked his head and neck until he had calmed down and was able to sit with his back arched and his great head hanging low over the fire as he stared into the flames. Kenric was wise enough to say nothing, but simply sat and ate the gruel served him by the younger of the two females. He still only partially understood what the older man was talking about, but he decided it was better to keep any further questions locked in the back of his throat.

Kenric slept by the fire and in the morning thanked his hosts for their hospitality. He had already given them a handful of iron nails in payment for the shelter and the meal. Magic was in a lean-to outside the croft and looked a bit put out at having been tethered for the night. *Don't you trust me?* his expression conveyed to Kenric, *do you think I would run away? Shame on you!* Kenric led the horse out and let him graze for a while, before mounting and saying, 'You can eat later, when we stop for a rest.'

Kenric and Magic rode on. At noon the rain came down in torrents. It became a miserable journey for both man and beast. Not long after midday Kenric halted and took shelter in a wood. There was no lightning, which might have been dangerous, though the sound of thunder could be heard behind some distant hills. Once the rain dropped in intensity to a mere drizzle, Kenric led Magic out into open ground once more and walked beside the beast, holding the elfen steed loosely by its rein. After walking for a short while, Kenric was startled to find someone strolling beside him, humming a tune in a low deep tone. When the person next to him, a tall lean handsome fellow, saw that he had been noticed, he spoke.

'I suppose you didn't see that god post, back there?'

'What?' cried Kenric. 'Where did you come from?'

'I asked my question before you asked yours,' replied the tall man, pursing his lips. 'I think you should answer me first, out of good manners.'

Kenric stared back along the trail he had taken. Indeed, he saw a carved tree trunk standing by the path a short way back.

'No, I – I was…'

'Preoccupied?' offered the stranger.

'Yes, I suppose so.'

'The gods can get pretty shirty if you don't recognise them and give them due deference, you know. You should be careful. Your preoccupation might be mistaken for contempt.'

'Oh, I would never be like that to the gods.'

'Like what.'

'What you said. Ignorin' them.'

The man nodded. 'That's good. You should always show respect to those who are more powerful than you. Now, I understand you're off to do harm to someone? You wish to challenge a warrior to mortal combat. Well, be very wary of doing so, my friend, because the warrior in question is very skilful at killing people. He's twice as big as you, twice as battle-wise, and he'll eat you for breakfast.'

Kenric was astonished. 'How – how do you know all this?'

The man laughed. 'I can see it in the way you walk. Your gestures, the determination on your face. The rage in your heart is like a beacon to those of my kind. And of course, I heard about your sister, so it doesn't take a genius to put all the bits together – though I am a genius, of course, so I can reach an answer that much quicker than those who are not quite so clever as I am.'

'Who are you?'

'Ah, well that's for me to know and you to find out.'

Kenric laid a hand on the hilt of his sword. 'I don't think I like you much,' he said to the fellow who was beaming down on him with a very smug expression. 'Where did you spring from, anyway? One minute I was walking on my own – well, with my horse – and the next, you're there.'

'Not *your* horse, now is it? That's a big whopping lie for a start.'

Kenric was beginning to get very frustrated and angry.

'Hey. What business is it of yours? My friend's horse, or my horse, it really don't matter, do it? Not to the likes of you.'

'The likes of *me*?' the man chuckled. 'Ooo, we are getting het up. And let me remind you that I can walk where I please, say what I want so long as it's not insulting or obscene, though I do like a little obscenity sometimes, within reason of course, nothing too shameful, and do what I want if no one objects. You seem to think these fields, these hills and valleys belong to you. No sir, they do not. They belong to us all: men, beasts, elves, giants, gods, what have you. Even that flea crawling over the curl you have hanging from your forehead. This is a world we all inhabit equally and unless you're prepared to challenge me to combat, I shall remain here by your side, chattering away, annoying the very devil out of you if I wish to.'

Kenric automatically brushed his curl with a sweep of his hand and then became furious when the stranger laughed and nodded.

'Sir,' he said after a while, 'I would like you to go away.'

'You don't want my help? In the business of fighting Oscetyl?' The stranger's face took on an expression of musing. 'Oscetyl. Now there's a fellow misnamed. *Divine Kettle*. That's not a name for an oaf, now is it? His mother should have known better. He should have been called *Disemboweller* or *Headseverer*. Something that reflects his skill at his trade. Anyway, you're confident of your own skill in being able to overcome this great murdering giant of a warrior, who has slain more adversaries than you've had hot meals, so I'll leave you to get on with it.'

A moment later there was a sort of wavering in the air, as if a heat wave had passed through the area. Then instead of a man standing next to him, Kenric found a pure white horse with red eyes. The beast whinnied and nuzzled Magic for a moment, before galloping off over the fields and into some distant woods. Kenric stood and stared for a long time, realising what he'd done, or rather not done.

'A shapeshifter,' he murmured to himself. 'One of the gods?'

'Loki,' replied a voice behind him. 'You've just rejected the assistance of the great trickster god, Loki. What are you thinking?'

Again, Kenric jumped, startled. He turned to see Sethrith, the beautiful witch standing there in a sort of chiffon dress with a ragged hem. Under the dress she could see her naked form and his eyes bugged. Sethrith frowned.

'I asked you was that a wise thing to do, Kenric?'

Kenric almost exploded with frustration. 'What is this place?' he cried, looking around him wildly. 'Why are creatures like Loki and you poppin' up from nowhere? Is this sacred ground?'

'Yes, of course it is. The long low mound you're standing on – not very visible, I have to admit – is the grave of a great king. That's why the god post is back there, to warn you of where you're treading. Anyway, you'd better be on your way. You want to make the land of the South Saxons sooner rather than later, don't you? Even though it means you're going to be cut to pieces by a berserker with muscles like boulders. Pity you told Loki you didn't need him. You might have lived otherwise.'

'You,' cried Kenric. 'You could help me fight Oscetyl.'

'Sorry, I don't do that sort of thing,' replied Sethrith. 'I'm a pacifist.'

'Wha – what does that mean?'

'It means I don't kill people, or even help to kill people.'

'Oh.' Kenric was bitterly disappointed, both with himself and with the two otherworld creatures who, it had to be said, could have been more clear about what and who they were. 'Well, there's nothin' more to be said, is there? I got to go and fight this bloody bully, 'ause I can't turn back now. My sister's in trouble and I'm goin' to help her, whether it means the end of Kenric or no. An' that's that.'

'You're very brave,' said Sethrith. 'Foolish, but brave.'

Then she too vanished into the rain-laden skies.

Kenric, feeling depressed and upset, mounted Magic and then continued towards the land of the South Saxons. It was true; he was probably going to die at the hands Oscetyl, who was indeed a giant of a man. But what could he do? He was not particularly close to his sister, Eostre (named after the goddess of springtime), but she was blood of his blood. Their father was dead, so Kenric regarded himself as head of the household and protector of his family. That family consisted of him, Kenric, and his sister Eostre. They would probably both die once Oscetyl found out why Kenric had come home to the tribe he had turned his back on.

FOURTEEN

'He took my *horse*?' cried Osric in anguish. 'He took Magic?'

The old man who lived in a ditch close to the forge was enjoying himself. He knew just how to get under the skin of his neighbours who made too much noise with their banging and clanging, and was not interested in an old man's complaints.

'Rode off, that ways,' said the elder, waving vaguely at the horizon. 'Said his sister was in trouble, so he's off to kill the man who's troubling her.'

The Thief laid a hand on Osric shoulder. 'Look,' he said, 'Kenric's sister obviously sent him a message. What was he to do? He couldn't run all that way and get there in time, obviously, so he borrowed a horse.'

'Not just any horse,' moaned Osric. 'An elfen horse. I can't imagine what I'd do if something happened to him.'

'To Kenric?'

'No, to Magic.'

The Thief frowned. 'You don't care what happens to your friend?'

'Of course I care,' replied the distraught Osric, 'but I care more about my wonderful horse. I'd like them both to be safe, of course, but I'd like Kenric to die saving my elfen beast. He is so beautiful...'

'Kenric?' questioned the old man.

'No, my horse!' Osric was beginning to get exasperated with these stupid questions. He knew what he had to do. He had to hire some horses and he and the Thief would go after Kenric and Osric could reclaim his mount. Why didn't Kenric hire a horse, instead of stealing *his* horse?

Osric did not start off in pursuit of Kenric and Magic straight away as he was obliged to attend a feast in the Great Hall. This feast was the usual block reward to warriors who had returned from duty on the wall. The Mercian king was generous towards his thegns and ordinary warriors, as every Angle and Saxon king should be. To his thegns he gave armrings – gold and bronze – but to the rest of his warriors he simply gave a slap-up feast and an evening's entertainment, all provided by the royal house. The men, young and old, looked forward to eating at the king's tables, where mead and food was served in great quantities.

129

There was fish – perch, trout, herring and eels – along with shellfish such as oysters, mussels and cockles. Meat in plenty, with pork, beef and mutton, accompanied by side dishes of purple carrots, parsnips, peas, beans, cabbages, onions, leaks and wild roots such as burdock. There were buttered bread and cheese too, naturally. It was a wild evening, with a great many songs, poems and some dancing, and much bragging about feats and prowess.

Osric, who had not seen the king since the battle with the Bernicians was stopped and spoken to by the lord of the Mercians.

'I hear you did well in that little scrap the other month.'

'Scrap, my lord? Oh, yes. Shame about Acca.'

'Ah,' sniffed the king, 'he was never much. Now, I expect you're wondering why you weren't rewarded for your part in that fight? No armring for Osric.'

'My part?' Osric immediately forgot his father's advice about modesty. 'My friend and I saved the rest of the army from being slaughtered.'

'That's not the way I heard it, though indeed it may be very true. Anyway,' Paega waved and arm, 'it wouldn't have been expedient to reward an East Angle. Now had you been a Mercian born, then you might have got something. You'll always be an outsider here, boy, so don't think you can wheedle your way into becoming one of my hearth-companions, even if you do come up with clever battle schemes.'

'The thought never entered my head, my lord.'

'Good, keep your head locked against such things. Ah, the stories are about to begin – some of them are about me, you know...'

One of the stories was about a warrior named Halfdan-the-black, a fierce and powerful brute who set out to kill a young man who had had the temerity to ask for his daughter's hand in marriage. The would-be bridegroom was escaping with the cattle he had brought to pay for his bride. This slowed his progress down as he crossed hill and dale and traversed woodland and swamp. It being the back end of winter, a wide river he came to was still frozen solid. Bravely he drove his bulls over the ice, hoping to reach a dense forest on the far side before Halfdan could catch up with him. But the enraged Halfdan reached the river before the boy and his beasts could enter the forest pale. Halfdan yelled his threats, told the youth he was going to gut him and use his innards to decorate the bushes. He set off across the ice in the path of the boy. Midway over, however, the harassed cattle had defecated and left large dollops of their steaming dung. By the time Halfdan reached that spot the hot cow shit had melted the ice. The huge and heavily-weaponed Halfdan crashed through into the freezing river and died before he could be helped. The young man returned to Halfdan's village and was reunited with his love, whom he married the day following the memorial service held for the dead father of the bride.

This story brought to Osric's mind his brilliant escape from the treacherous thegns who had murdered his father, but he said nothing of this to others. His father had told him not to hold himself up as superior in anything, to always be modest and cheerful, and to leave it to others to boast and brag. Boasting and bragging were part of being a warrior, but Eorl had been a fine-spun king with genteel views.

Another tale told of a too-clever warrior, who finally choked to death on his own shrewdness, and another whose dreams had weight and were so heavy that one night he was crushed to death by a leaden nightmare. Many of these stories were familiar and had been heard time and again, but on the odd occasion an old man wrenched a new one from deep in his memory and delighted his audience with a fresh adventure which usually ended in the death of one of the protagonists.

Sometimes those feasting had disagreements and there were bloody fights at the table, but these were swiftly set outside to be finished off, since the queen liked the evening to end on a gracious and civilised note, with music from the lyres and wind instruments filling the hall. Many of the drunken men went home with tears in their eyes, as the melodies and poems were often sad. They returned to their wives and children with small gifts from the king, vowing they would follow their lord into hell and back, should this be deemed necessary. The next day they rose from their beds with headaches and stomach problems, knowing they would be driving an ox-wagon or cart, or plying some other hum-drum trade that day. When they were on guard on the wall, all they wanted to be was at home in their warm hovels with their warm wives in their warm beds and yet no sooner did they get home to their families and ordinary work, they wanted to be back on the wall. Men are contrary creatures, not really enjoying the excitement of being on the fighting line when they were there, yet missing it when they were bored with their everyday lives.

Lord Ing:
Who said that? Whoever it was, this is so true. Men are never completely happy with their lot. Make a man rich and he wants power. Make a man rich and powerful and he wants acclaim and to be honoured. Make him all those things and he wants to be loved.

The last is the most difficult to obtain, especially when you possess the others. You might have to rid yourself of wealth, power and the trappings of success if you want to be loved and cherished.

Although he knew the business would suffer, Osric asked the Thief to join him in riding to the land of the South Saxons. It was a dangerous thing for an Angle to do – different for Kenric who was himself a Saxon – but Osric was desperate to be reunited with his horse. No man he knew had ever owned an elfen steed and Magic was his most treasured possession. He even became maudlin and started dreaming of returning to his elfen wife Linnet, though he knew this strange marriage would not work in the long run. These thoughts led to other girls he had fallen in love with – daughters of kings and kitchen maids – and to a certain wondrous-eyed witch. Osric indeed was a flawed young man whose heart was ready to fly out of his chest at any young woman whose beauty was exceptional. His mother would have told him to look deeper, into the souls of the girls he lost his head to, but that would have done little good. He only listened to his parents when they told him something he wanted to hear, like a lot of youths struggling to become men.

The Thief, although this was not the land of his birth, had a universal cunning about him and his sly skills enabled the pair to avoid many dangerous encounters, both with the landscape and with rogue bands of warriors. It was now Weodmonath, the weed month, and travelling was a hot business. They did not need to circumnavigate marshlands, the dryness having hardened the paths through them well enough to use. However, any marish or bog they encountered needed to be traversed in daylight. No man would spend a night in such a place, where ghouls and ghosts were as numerous as peat hags on a moor. Even during the bright daylight the two men kept their eyes peeled for any weirdness that might threaten them. Once, a small, strange old man about as tall as a human's shin-bone popped out of the ground and jabbered at them, but they were almost across the bog by that time and managed to ride off at speed before the horses had time to be spooked.

Once, Osric thought he saw a band of elves out hunting, but he could not be sure because all that he actually witnessed was a changing of the light patterns beneath some willows and yews. These two were the favourite trees of the elfen and if a hunting party stopped to rest, they would do so under the light green and dark green, which often grew together. Indeed, a boar being hunted by elves would head for a thicket with willows, having learned over the centuries that elves would be loath to ride full tilt into a growth of these trees, for fear of damaging the hanging fronds. Unlike mortals, elfen archers did not make their bows of yew wood, but of horse-tail hair stiffened with golden resin from a live oak. The hair was woven into cords then the cords plaited and reeved. Their arrows however followed the human fashion and were of ash, whose grain is straight and true, of course.

On another occasion they saw a fully-grown dragon flying above the trees of a distant copse, but luckily heading away from them. The great leathery wings flapped slowly. The long neck, like the long slim tail, stretched out in a straight line. It was a beautiful sight and one to be stored in the memory. The Thief remarked that Osric seemed to have something about him which attracted creatures from the other world and guessed it was because the youth had been touched by the gods. Osric said he did not know, but certainly while the skies were blue, with puffs of white cloud, he felt able to talk about such things without feeling concerned. However, on one night there was a great dry storm, with Thunor throwing his crooked javelins of fire about the sky, and Osric wondered whether some punishment was about to be meted out to him for indulging in all this talk about the otherworld beings. Woden on a Wild Hunt passed over the very place where Osric and the Thief were camping, but it was indeed just a passing, no fire and light rained down on the pair. Still, the lightning bolts continued to crash on the horizon and Osric decided it was time to hold his tongue about whether one was blessed or cursed by being close to the Wyrd.

When it came to the natural world, birds such as kestrels and magpies seemed to bring a touch of normality to the wilderness that spread its marshy and forested places between habitations. Indeed, after dragons and storms, lynxes and wolves would have been welcome sights. One evening neither man was paying much attention to the world around him, each being weary after a long day's ride under a hot sun. Suddenly a host of those elves of the bird world, long-tailed tits, were flushed from a bush and fled twittering into the scarlet-tinged twilight sky.

Osric stared at the bush, wondering what had disturbed the creatures when he saw a flash of white buttocks. Someone was squatting, relieving themselves under a natural dark hedge of butcher's broom. Osric turned away to give the man or woman some privacy. This was a fatal move, for standing a little further away in the shade of some high brambles was a group of men. While his back was still towards them they set off running past their comrade who thought they were coming towards him in order to tip him over in jest. They ran past the man halfway through his toilet and were on Osric before the prince had time to unsling his bow or draw his sword. He was thrown to the ground and held there by several feet until finally they let him up. Osric rose, dusted himself down indignantly, then faced his attackers.

'Well, well,' cried one of the men, 'what have we here? Not just a traveller, but a fully-grown prince who is worth a bag of gold any day.'

Osric's spirit plummeted as he recognised the voice, manner and features of the speaker. It was Sark. one of the thegns from the East Angles. This was the man who had been shitting behind the butcher's broom and he came forward at first grunting in displeasure at being interrupted. Now he had seen who it was who had been apprehended by his men he was rapturous.

'We were on our way to the Mercians to purchase you, but now we can keep the price of a traitor and regicide for ourselves. I'm certain King Eadgard would wish us to.'

'I am no traitor,' fumed Osric. 'Eadgard murdered my father...'

'Yes, he said you'd say that. Yet we all know you're the murderer.'

Osric snarled. 'And how do you know that?'

Sark looked a little taken aback at the fierceness of Osric's question, but then he gathered himself and growled, 'There are those who saw you do it.'

'Those being Wulfgar and his henchmen. Did they tell you I killed Finnan and Holt too? Well, that much is true, at least I was responsible for their deaths. When they were chasing me, they fell through the ice, being heavy oafs without the strength of mind to recognise that I was lighter and quicker across the sheet. Listen to me, Sark, I did not kill my father. I had no reason to kill him. Getting rid of Eorl would not have given me the right to be king. I would still have to be declared ruler by the thegns. And who would agree to having a green youth for a ruler, especially if he was suspected of killing his father? None. None. *None.* I loved my father,' Osric's eyes were wet and hot with anger, 'I still love him, for he's lodged in my heart. His spirit is with me always. I will avenge him some day. Eadgard and Wulfgar will die, hopefully by my hand. Yet, I can see by your face you do not believe me. You think all this is a bundle of lies. Well, then, you'd better kill me, hadn't you – and take my head back to your great ruler, Eadgard, who I'm sure will reward you with gold rings. However, I ask you one boon, and that is not to kill...' Osric looked round for the Thief and realised that he was nowhere to be seen. '...not to kill my horse, who has had no part in this affair and is completely innocent.'

Sark's complexion darkened. 'Are you trying to make a fool of me, boy?'

'Well now, that wouldn't be difficult, would it, since you've been made a complete fool of by others...' Osric did not finish the sentence because Sark struck him a blow on the head with a club and knocked him out cold.

When he came too, Osric found himself bound to a tree. The warriors who'd captured him were sitting around a fire, arguing. One of them, Saewine, was questioning Sark's non-belief of Osric's side of the story. Saewine was commenting on the fact that Eadgard had become very aloof and arrogant recently and that their new king had made one or two bad judgements in his rulership. One man he had hung recently had turned out to be completely innocent of the crime he was supposed to have committed and it looked like Eadgard's son was the real culprit.

'We should not simply wave away the prince's account,' said Saewine. 'We should look into it further.'

Sark was firm. 'And how do you propose to do that? Sneak around the villages asking for witnesses? We have witnesses. They all say they saw Osric murder his father. These things can go on and on, without going anywhere. I'm happy to turn the boy over to King Eadgard and there's an end to it. If you want to accuse the king of murder, then you must do it on your own. None of us will back you up.'

There was a murmuring of assent amongst the warriors. None wanted to re-open the likely cause of death of the old king. Things were as they were and stirring up doubts amongst the ordinary people could be a very dangerous thing to do. Sides would be taken, men would be accused and counter-accused, and civil war would follow. There would be executions and more murders, and the settling of old scores nothing to do with the real cause of the war. People used a time of shadows and dark nights to get rid of neighbours they had grudges against and relatives they had always hated. No one wanted civil war. It was the ugliest of events turning brother against brother, cousin against cousin, even father against son. Best to leave things as they were and hope that justice had been done correctly.

Osric remained tied to the tree overnight. He prayed at first for the gods to bring devastation down on his captors and enemies. When that failed, he called to the wind to carry a message to the elves. They did not come either. Nor did any local creature of the otherworld. Osric felt abandoned. Also, while he was thus held by his bonds, crows and rooks came and jeered at him, stalking round and round his tree. Then two magpies came and perched one on each shoulder until Osric managed to bite one on the tail and they flew away in a flash of white, black and blue, shrieking insults which only *corvus* could understand. Why he was made a jest of by this particular family of birds he was unsure, but he guessed it was because when he was a young boy he had thrown stones at them to protect the tribe's crops and he supposed that crows, rooks, magpies and jays never forgot an insult to their kind.

And where was the Thief? Run away, obviously. Osric couldn't blame him. But he also couldn't help feeling a little bitter. The Thief was so good at self-preservation. He had obviously assessed the situation immediately and had slipped into the shadows before even being seen by the warriors. That was a skill which took half-a-lifetime to learn. But now he had left Osric to a band of half-wits. Like a lot of the warriors who formed the heavy set of the fighters, Sark was not known for his intellect. He was a good fighter, perhaps even a great one, but it was all muscle and no brain. Now Osric could hear them arguing about whether or not to kill him before they returned to the east Angles. Sark was arguing that Eadgard simply wanted justice and justice was not a thing that needed to be delayed.

However, they didn't kill him immediately and so Osric went through another day tied to his new friend, the tree. Night came again and he knew that they were moving the next morning, returning to the villages they came from. Whether they had decided to take Osric back alive he did not know. Part of him would be going anyway: his head most probably. Osric's limbs were seriously aching now. Despite it being summer he was cold at night and the chill was getting deep into his bones. He slept fitfully, waking in starts and staring around him, hoping that somehow the elves would come, or that the god Ing would save him a second time.

Just before dawn the miracle happened. He felt his bonds loosen. Someone had cut them from behind the tree. He did not even have to look round to see who it was: he could smell him. It was the Thief. Once the cords fell away, Osric rubbed some feeling into his wrists and ankles. He tried standing up but found he had to steady himself by holding on to that damned tree. Then, when the giddy feeling had passed, he stood up straight and turned to see the Thief holding his elfen bow, quiver and his sword. He strapped on his blade, slung his quiver over on shoulder and his bow over the other. The Thief pointed silently to a pond nearby and made a gesture by which Osric knew that the Thief had stolen *all* the weapons in the camp and thrown them into the water. None of the warriors could arm themselves.

Osric then trod softly to where Sark was sleeping. He drew his sword very slowly and carefully, while the Thief looked on with wide eyes, obviously wondering what the young man's intentions were. But Osric did not have murder in his heart. He was not that kind of creature. He knelt down and with one hand firmly over Sark's mouth, he placed the sharp blade on the man's throat. Sark's eyelids flew open, but before he could struggle Osric whispered, 'Don't move, Sark, don't move, or I'll slit your throat. Now listen to me. Listen carefully. I have you at my mercy. I could kill you very easily with one swift slice, leaving your blood to drain on the turf. But I'm not going to. Do you know why? I'll tell you why. Because I am not a murderer. I told the truth. I never killed my father. That was Eadgard and Wulfgar. Remember when you return to your so-called king, that I let you live and that I am innocent.'

The Thief had brought two fast horses close to Osric, one of which he mounted. Osric leapt from his kneeling position onto the back of the other and the pair of them charged out of the camp. The Thief had removed the hobbles from all the other horses and they scattered at Osric's charge through them. The other warriors were on their feet the moment they heard the yell of their leader, Sark, and they began to run after the horsemen. Indeed, Sark was particularly swift on his feet and almost reached up to unhorse Osric, but the prince kicked him in the teeth and Sark went hurling to the ground, cursing and yelling obscenities. Soon the two companions were well ahead, leaving a band of miserable warriors behind them.

After a while of riding, Osric turned to the Thief and said, 'Thank you, my friend. I thought you'd left me to die.'

'I left releasing you until they had grown confident, unwary and lackadaisical, otherwise we might both have ended up on a gibbet.'

Osric nodded. 'You did exactly right and your ability to steal things was useful too – getting rid of their weapons was a brilliant act.'

Osric was getting to like the Thief more and more as time passed. The Thief was supposed to be a coward, liar and – naturally for a thief – he stole things. Well, yes, he would admit to all those traits, but sometimes they were useful in order to help his friends survive. And Osric could not afford to be choosy in his companions. If he lived a normal life he might disapprove of someone who was adept at removing and keeping the property of others, but life was far from normal. His world had been turned upside down and those people he found and accepted in that topsy-turvy place were not ordinary law-abiding individuals. They were criminals and vagabonds.

The pair rode under a grey mare's-tail sky, streaked with the threat of rain. The Thief said that soon there would be wild horses in the heavens, their hooves thundering on the clouds, but he was wrong. A downpour came but there was no black storm with thunder and lightning – just interminable rain. The two men continued on, Osric determined to reach the South Saxons as soon as possible. Days stretched into more days, until they came to a strange mound that was like the belly of a pregnant woman, a swelling on the earth. The horses refused to ride over it and Osric soon learned why. A young woman appeared, a beautiful young woman, whose features he did not recognise. But when she spoke he knew instantly who she was and his heart began beating faster.

'Sethrith, you do not look like yourself!'

'Oh, I have no self to look like. I am many forms. They are all amazingly lovely though, aren't they?'

'Well, the two I've seen so far – definitely.'

'Your friend passed over this spot just over a week ago.'

Osric felt his stomach harden. 'Yes, riding my horse – riding Magic.'

'He is on his way to kill a man twice his size and ten times more experienced in the ways of fighting. I believe that unless he gets help, Kenric will die. Are you on your way to do that? To help your friend?'

Osric didn't want to answer this question because instinctively he knew that Sethrith would not understand a man's anger over a stolen horse.

'I just want to find him,' he said, 'and speak with him.'

All the while he was talking with the witch, the Thief had hung back, unwilling to eavesdrop. Now the Thief called, 'I'll gather wood for the fire, while you two are exchanging pleasantries. With that he dismounted, hobbled both horses, and strode off towards a nearby copse.

Sethrith said, her eyes intently focused on those of Osric, 'So now we are alone at last.'

'Yes,' replied the young man, his legs suddenly losing most of their strength, 'at last.'

'Do you want to make love to me, Osric? I know you want me.'

He stared at her long-flowing auburn hair, burnished copper in the twilight. His eyes travelled down to her gold-green eyes, then further down to the small but unavoidable breasts that were visible beneath the flimsy chiffon garment. The lust in him rose like a tide of hot lava. His hands shook as he dismounted and followed the floating witch dumbly over the meadow to a place where the turf had been lifted by the roots of five oaks planted closely together. There was an opening in the ground, where the roots arched and lifted the sward, much like the entrance to a fox earth. Sethrith disappeared down this dark hole and then her slim white arm hooked out again and a pale finger and beckoned him.

Osric continued to stand where he was, staring into the blackness of the interior of this underground chamber, wondering if he was going to his death.

'Shall I come down?' he asked, weakly, trying to make up his mind. 'Do you want me to follow you?'

There was no answer, which he already knew anyway. Eventually he gathered his courage and entered the hole feet first, dropping down inside a tomb-like chamber the size of a small room. There was a strange ethereal glow inside this earthen place to which his eyes soon adjusted. The floor under his feet was soft and yielding, an ideal bed on which to take this willing female.

Yet, yet, he was patently aware that he was about to copulate with a witch, an extremely dangerous indulgence for a mortal youth. And he knew also that this was not 'love', it was pure lust. Witches were not mortals. They had their own unfathomable rules, weird culture and more importantly their own otherworldly idea of morals, which a mortal might not even recognise as a true set of ethics. This was not like making love to an elf. This was entering into a union with something close to a demon. There was the possibility, the very real risk, that he would be consumed by fire the moment he entered her. He was being wrenched apart inside by two great forces: desire and fear. He desperately wanted to have sex with this otherworld being, yet equally he rather hoped to walk away afterwards whole and healthy.

139

'What are we standing on?' he asked, looking down at the floor of the chamber, shilly-shallying while he tried to make up his mind. 'It's very soft.'

'Butterflies wings.'

He peered intently at the floor and indeed the chamber was covered with a thick layer of the wings of butterflies and moths, colourful even in the eerie light which seemed to come from the witch herself. Yes, there were those butterflies with eyes on their wings. What were they called? And those, with the white flashes. And gatekeepers and meadow browns. How strange! There was something aesthetically wonderful about such a beautiful carpet. He asked her if this was magic.

'Magic has nothing to do with it,' Sethrith said, simply. 'They were dropped by the bats.'

'Bats?'

'Yes, didn't you know that bats eat the bodies of butterflies and moths? The wings fall to the floor.'

Indeed, there were three or four, floating down now.

Osric looked up. He saw with a shudder of distaste that the ceiling of the earthen chamber was thick and black with the bodies of bats. They were jammed in crevices too, that lined the walls. Not just one kind of bat, but several different species, their hundreds of eyes glittering as they stared at him. He let out a yell of disgust and backed towards the exit to the chamber. It was not that he was afraid of these creatures of the night, but he could feel them shitting on him, the droppings landing in his hair and on his shoulders. There was no way he could make any kind of love or even lust to Sethrith underneath this wretched mass of watchers.

'Where are you going…?'

But Osric had already scrambled through the hole and out into the twilight. It was just growing dark and no sooner was he on his feet than a swarm of the chamber's inhabitants followed him, their tiny wings and bodies brushing the bare skin of his face, leaving the stink of their hairy forms in his nostrils. Osric, trapped in this swirling cloud of flying mice, flapped his arms and yelled, trying to get out of their way. But still wave on wave of aerial mammals continued to swish around and past him, until finally he was finally able to run for the trees. Once there he put his back against a trunk and sank down to his buttocks. He was breathing heavily, but not now from lecherousness but from exertion. After a while he was aware of a form standing over him, peering down at him. It was not the witch, but the Thief.

'So, did you satisfy your carnal desires?' asked the Thief, his language revealing the stiffness of a foreigner who knows he's asking a very personal question.

'No, I did not,' replied Osric, emphatically.

'Did you lose the inclination?'

'Indeed I did. The place was full of bats.'

'Which caused you to reconsider.'

'Which put me off completely.'

The Thief seemed to accept this explanation and nodded his head, but whether in approval or simply affirming his own thoughts, Osric didn't know.

What the young man did know was that his flight was only partly to do with his dislike of bats. It had suddenly entered his head that he was in a subterranean chapel where carnivores ate the bodies of their prey. It struck him forcefully that he might, in agreeing to a union with the witch, also be consenting to a fate similar to that of the butterflies and moths. His mind's eye held a brilliant image of his youthful body being greedily devoured while his stringy arms and legs fell to the floor of the chamber to lie amongst the inedible discarded bits of flying insects.

They saw no more of Sethrith that night and Osric spent much of the time when he should have been sleeping simply staring at a hole in the ground.

FIFTEEN

Quite late in the evening Kenric arrived in the village where his sister lived. He knew if he did not immediately get down to the business of challenging his sister's unwanted new husband to single combat he might falter. So he placed Magic in the care of a stable owner and then made his way to a fire around which sat a group of Saxons. Some were warriors, some farmers, some herders. The scene was quite jolly, with mead drinkers telling stories or offering to play the lute and sing. One man was already deep into the story of the founder of the Saxon race, Mannus, son of Tursco. The speaker was elderly and had to keep clearing his throat of phlegm to continue his account, which had many round the circle fidgeting impatiently, until finally a younger man stood up and said, 'Well done, well done. Now we have heard what our brother had to say and it was well said, but it's time for some music.' With that a flute player immediately pierced the evening with a bird-like trilling before launching into a melody that was cheered by all.

Kenric sat down between two warriors and greeted them. 'Be whole.'

Both men turned to stare at him and one said, 'Who invited you to separate two good friends, churl?'

'No one,' replied Kenric, ignoring the snarled put-down. 'You wouldn't know a warrior by the name Oscetyl, I suppose?'

There were raised eyebrows.

'And what would you be wanting with Oscetyl?'

'I'd like to offer to fight him.'

The man on his left let out a huge guffaw of laughter, which his good friend soon joined in with. They laughed until the tears ran down their cheeks and decorated their chins with jewels that glittered in the firelight. Others glared at them because they had rudely interrupted a rather beautiful song, but when one of the two explained what had occurred, there was more laughter, until the whole arena was rocking with merriment. People passing by, on their way to their dwellings or going about an evening's chores, stopped to ask why the jollity and could they join in. When they were told what was afoot and the rather slight form of Kenric was pointed out to them, they too shrieked with laughter and swayed on their heels.

'All right, all right,' growled Kenric. 'You've had your fun, now what about it, eh? I know what Oscetyl looks like. I've seen 'im. Big bastard, yes, I'm aware of that. Now where can I find the bugger?'

'He'll be skinning the wolf he killed today with his bare hands,' cried one of Kenric's tormentors. 'That's where he'll be.'

'Which is it?' asked Kenric. 'Is he skinnin' with his bare hands or did he kill the wolf with 'em?'

'The last one,' cried one of the warriors, hardly able to speak through his laughter. 'But he'll do both to you – kill you with his fingers and skin you with his nails.'

This brought hoots of mirth and finally with a sigh Kenric got up and walked back to where he had left his horse – or to be more accurate – Osric's horse. There he paid the owner of the stable a dozen mixed bronze and iron nails to stay the night, sleeping on the straw alongside Magic. The man grumbled, looking at the nails in his hand and said, 'Ain't you got no coin?'

'Coin?'

'Yes, money. Where've you bin? We use copper, gold and silver discs now, to pay for things, not bloody bits of iron.'

Kenric had seen coins before, of course, and the Thief had told him that the Norsemen used them as common currency to purchase things with, but the practice had not yet crossed the ocean to the land of the Angles and Saxons. At least, it hadn't until now. It seemed a funny way to buy things. How could you trust it? What if you sold something to a stranger then found no one would accept the coin you had received in payment? Gold was gold, but you wouldn't part with it just to sleep on straw in a stinking stable, would you? Gold bought expensive things, like slaves and cows, and maybe a wife. And silver wasn't far behind gold. Copper? That sounded very untrustworthy. The coins that Kenric had come into contact with so far were used mostly as jewellery or melted down to decorate the hilts of swords and daggers, or helmets.

'What's it called, this using coins?'

'Called money.'

'Well I 'aven't got any.'

The stableman sighed. 'So the nails'll 'ave to do then, won't they?'

Kenric bedded down in the straw next to Magic. The familiar smell of the horse and his dung brought some comfort to the young man. Magic seemed to like him being there too, in these strange surroundings. Kenric was able to drift away to sleep thinking about what he would say to his sister, should he survive the contest. This Oscetyl was a fiend of a man, who had already beaten two wives to death. The assembly called the Thing, always held on Thunor's day, had judged both deaths as 'accidents'. Oscetyl had powerful friends in the main village – not the village in which he lived, but the one where the king had his Great Hall. In this particular village he was unopposed in most things, being big, callous and brutal. There was no other to challenge him, even though he was not actually a thegn. The lord in charge of the village was the old man Kenric had seen and heard at the symbel fire. The elder who had been giving the long tedious account of their Saxon ancestors.

When morning came he was woken by one of the two warriors he had sat between the previous evening.

'He's waitin' for you, down by the river,' said the smug messenger. 'I told 'im you were going to cut off his bollocks and stuff 'em in his mouth.'

'Whatcha do that for?' said Kenric.

'Well, he was yellin' about what he was going to do to you, so I thought you needed to trade a few threats with him, to balance things up, like.'

'Thanks for nuthin.'

Kenric rose and went to the water trough to splash his face. Then he strapped on his seax, stuck a dagger in his belt, and began the walk to the river. He knew where he was going. This had been his own village before he decided to travel the country. The warrior looked surprised and said, 'You're not going to run then?'

'No, I've come a long way to do this.'

The other fellow fell into step with him and they walked side by side, with the warrior saying, 'You're a brave lad, but a dead one.' Then, after a minute he added, 'Don't I know you?'

'I'm Edmund-the-farrier's son. Used to be.'

'Ah, knew I seen you before. Yes, stripling of a boy. You're not much more than that now. Anyway, what d'you mean, used to be? An't you his son no longer?'

'He's dead.'

'Course he is, but you're still his son.'

'I suppose.'

By this time they were walking down the slope of the bank to the water's edge where the giant Oscetyl was swinging his warhammer back and forth, practising on invisible enemies. He was indeed a huge man, the biggest warrior Kenric had ever encountered. Standing there, with the backdrop of the blue sky behind him, he looked even larger than Kenric remembered. Long, blond, matted locks fell from his head down past his short thick neck leaving dirty smears on his deerskin vest where the ends flicked back and forth. His shoulders were massive. There appeared to be an oaken beam under the same vest, though Kenric knew this was not wood but solid muscle. He had the waist of a woman and the legs of a bear; the small neat blue eyes of a child and the hands of an ogre; the voice of a girl and the mind of a boar. Oscetyl was a grotesque mixture of the weak and the strong, the lovely and the foul. His singing bordered on the sublime, but his personal habits were disgusting.

A crowd had gathered on the top of the slope, ready to watch the slaughter. Kenric was amazed to see Osric and the Thief in the front row. He gave them a feeble wave and after a moment's hesitation, Osric returned it. Then Kenric marched up to Oscetyl and said, 'You ready?'

Oscetyl peered at him with those tiny eyes and said, 'Ready – but why? What've I ever done to you?'

'I just don't like you,' said Kenric. 'Your breath smells.'

Oscetyl wiped a hand over his mouth and his eyebrows rose. 'You want to kill me for *that*?'

'Can you think of a better reason?'

A furrowed brow, a pursing of the lips. 'No.'

'Then let's get to it.'

Lord Ing:

Sorry to interrupt the flow of an exciting passage, but you need to know that Osric's friend has made a grave mistake. He is about to fight to the death with an innocent man. I use the word 'innocent' in a specific, not in the general sense. That is, he is guiltless of beating the farrier's sister and forcing her into marriage. Indeed, Coelwin hardly knows the fellow. Yet Oscetyl has performed some terrible acts that would leave men gasping with horror and disgust. Indeed, spitting babies on a spearhead might be regarded a tame atrocity next to some of the barbarous acts of this great wooden-headed malefactor.

Kenric's heart was racing now, too fast, ahead of his brain. All he wanted was to get this thing over. He had a plan, of course. Osric had taught him that. One always had to have a plan when going into combat, single or otherwise. His plan was to strike the first blow, because if he didn't manage to do that, he was surely meat for the crows. Oscetyl now stood with his legs apart, the warhammer in its backswing. Before the huge warrior could bring the weapon back for the killing blow, Kenric drooped and appeared to faint, falling in the dirt at the feet of the giant. Oscetyl looked puzzled but, 'Feigning won't save you, you little turd.' The big man then began the downward arc of the warhammer, aiming at the body near his feet.

In the process of delivering a fatal blow the giant man stepped back with his right leg to gain more leverage. In the split second it took to adjust his stance Oscetyl's young opponent suddenly came out of his swoon and lunged forward, hard downwards, pinning the giant's trailing left foot to the ground with a dagger. Oscetyl screamed like a maiden in labour, his warhammer descending to find nothing but clay.

All this in but a moment.

The warhammer lifted again, with an angry blubbery sob from the lips of the giant, but Kenric had scuttled through his legs. Kenric swiftly swung his seax at the pinned foot, and with three or four hacks chopped it off at the ankle. Another, much louder scream from Oscetyl as he crashed to the ground. Kenric, quick as a rat, sprung to his feet and swept the sword again, the blade edge finding the short thick neck it was looking for. It went halfway through. The scream changed to a gargle and blood bubbled forth. The second blow of the sword almost got through, but it took a third swipe to separate the head completely from the body. The head rolled down the slope to the river's edge, teetered for a moment, then with a *plop* dropped into the flowing water. The body still jerked and twitched for a few minutes after the decapitation, but once Kenric had vomited, the heat and the occasion being too much for his youthful constitution, this too had ceased.

When he looked up again, he saw the crowd. There were open mouths and dazed expressions. For a few minutes no one up on that slope seemed to believe what had just occurred. Then Osric yelled – a cry of triumph – and punched the air. The Thief allowed himself a smile and a nod. All others remained silent. There was no cheering, no cries of 'Winner'. They seemed rooted to the spot, unable to comprehend that the biggest bully in the village had been slain by a youth. Then, in ones, twos and small bunches, they began to drift away. Two men came down to look at the headless corpse and one kicked it, but this was the only indication that anyone approved of the killing. Kenric climbed the slope to where his two companions stood.

'I took your horse,' he said to Osric. 'Forgive me.'

SIXTEEN

Osric waved a hand. 'Oh, that's not important. Think nothing of it, Kenric. We followed you because we were worried about you.'

Kenric didn't miss the sideways glance that the Thief gave Osric and knew this was not the case. However, he could not concern himself with Osric's possessiveness now. He had to find his sister and inform her she was now a widow. This he passed on to the other two. They agreed they should accompany him and then perhaps, once she had been given the good news, they had better get out and ride for Mercia. There had been no permission from the king of the South Saxons for this single combat to take place and all three knew that strangers entering a village, killing one of the inhabitants (however loathed that man might be by the populace) was not acceptable. The Frithguildsmen would demand an enquiry and there was no guarantee Kenric would walk away with all his limbs or even his life. Oscetyl might be a favourite of the king or one of his hearth-companions and demand blood for blood. Certainly he was highly thought of by at some of the nobles in the royal hall.

They found Kenric's sister, Coelwin, scrubbing clothes at the village washhouse. She looked up and saw her brother coming. First there a frown appeared on her brow, then it cleared and the woman, looking careworn and drab, smiled.

'Brother! You've come home!'

'Not for long,' replied Kenric, as the other two held back. 'Just come to set you free. Just killed your husband in single combat…'

Coelwin let out a shriek. 'What? Don't make jokes like that.'

'It's not a joke,' called Osric. 'We saw him do it. Chopped his head off.'

Coelwin's mouth fell open and her grey face switched back and forth, studying the expressions of these newcomers and her brother. She was gauging whether this was an elaborate jest – a distasteful one, but a jape none the less – but the expressions on the faces of the three men, especially the older one dressed all in black, told her that this was the truth. Her husband had been slain by her younger brother. She screamed and threw a twisted bolt of wet clothing at Kenric, crying, 'You bastard! You killed my man? Why? In the name of the gods, why? He did nothin' to harm you. He spoke well of you and said he was lookin' forward to meeting you.' She sank to her knees and sobbed for a moment, while Kenric gaped in disbelief. Then she said, 'What will become of me now he's gone? What about the baby in my belly?'

Kenric stared at his sister. 'You're with child?'

'If he's a son,' she said, fiercely, staring up at Kenric, 'I'll tell 'im what you did and send 'im out to get you. I will, Kenric. I will.'

At that moment a man came between the hovels and marched over to them.

'All right, what in hellmouth is goin' on here?'

'Oscetirl!' cried Coelwin. 'You're alive.'

The man, short and thick limbed, with a barrel torso, looked down at himself and replied, 'Well I was when I left home this mornin'.'

'But they said you were dead. Kenric said he'd killed you.'

'Kenric?' repeated the man. 'Your brother's here?' He looked over the three men and said, 'Which one is he?'

'I'm Kenric,' said Kenric, after clearing his throat. 'I think there's been some sort of mistake. Your name's Oscetyl?'

'Oscet*irl*.'

'Ah, that's where I went wrong,' said Kenric. 'I thought my sister married that great lunk Oscetyl and I knew she hated 'im. Now I've gone an' killed a man without any good reason.'

'Oh, that was you, was it? I 'eard about that,' said Oscetirl.

Coelwin humphed. 'Village is better off without 'im.'

'And we had better be going,' interrupted Osric, 'before the Frithguildsmen come and take you away, Kenric. We don't want you dangling from a rope before the day's out. You can ride the horse I came on, because I'm reclaiming my mount.'

'Who're these two?' asked Oscetirl. 'Friends of yours?'

'Prince Osric of the East Angles,' replied Kenric, with more pride in his voice than he intended, 'and the… that is, he's a Geat from over the swan-road. We've sort've got a business together, a forge.' Kenric was a little embarrassed as he added, very quietly, 'shoein' horses.'

'You're a farrier?' cried Coelwin. 'You told our father you never wanted to do such a menial trade – an' what's a prince doin', shoein' horses? An't he rich then?'

'His father was murdered and he would've been murdered too, if he hadn't left quick. Now we've teamed up, us and the… the Geat here.

We've got a nice little business goin'. The king of the Mercians has his warhorse shoed by us. We're sort of famous really, in the north west.'

'So, he's not really a prince at all, but a runaway? If he's left his realm, someone else's been made king,' said Coelwin.

Osric said, 'I don't care what I am, right at this moment. My father told me to call myself the Wanderer. We need to mount and ride, before there's a mob after us. You know how things turn very quickly. You were a hero a few minutes ago, but by tonight you'll be a killer of the most beloved man in the village.'

Coelwin looked at her brother with moist eyes. 'Will we see you again?' she stepped forward and hugged him. 'My little brother.' Then to Osric, fiercely. 'You look after 'im.'

'I will,' came the reply. 'Just as he looks after me. We – we are like brothers now, aren't we Kenric.'

Kenric seemed a little surprised by this claim, then his face broke into an enormous grin. 'Yep, brothers – that's what we are.'

Oscetirl then stepped forward and clapped a hand on Kenric's shoulder.

'I'm not *like* a brother-in-law – I am one. Now that I've met my new wife's family, for you're all that's left of it, I like what I see. A fine youth. Don't be a stranger. Come and see us again when all the fuss has blown away. We'll look forward to that. We'll keep a stew boiling. Now, on your way.' Oscetirl then stared at the Thief. 'And you, I don't know who or what you are. Very mysterious. Yet you seem to be trusted by these two. You're welcome also, should you pass by.'

'Just remember to lock up your valuables,' murmured Osric. Then seemingly on reflexion, added, 'No, I shouldn't have said that.'

The Thief just shook his head.

The three companions left the hovel and went to the stable to fetch their horses. The stable owner muttered something about the killing, but they took little notice of him, anxious as they were to be well away from the village before noon.

The journey home through the outeryard wilderness was no less eventful than the one going, the trio having a near encounter with a group of Ettins, the less aggressive of the tribes of giants. These loose-limbed ogres ambled by ululating to one another, the sound on which their language was based, frightening every bird and mammal for miles around. The three humans managed to avoid being seen by hiding with their horses behind a massive harrow, a rustic altar fashioned of granite

with flint and sandstone insets, until the giants had passed by. The
mortal auras of Osric, Kenric and the Thief were surely disguised by the
huge harrow and, more than likely, by the density of the rock from
which it was fashioned. The altar had been raised in praise of Freo, the
goddess of magic and sister of Ing, since a fierce battle had been fought
in this place. Freo is always entitled to half the souls of those slain on the
battlefield (the other half going to Woden) and therefore both winners
and losers would want to appease her. The three companions, having
used her altar to escape the notice of the Ettins offered prayers of thanks
to Freo that night.

Two days after that, it was Walpurgis Night, and again the three had
to hunker down while the air was as full of witches as it was of bats.
They crossed back and forth across the moon with hideous shrieks and
insane laughter. Despite the fact that the men had hidden themselves
under a lean-to on the edge of a forest, one of the witches detached
herself from those in flight and landed next to their hide.

'I know you're in there, Osric,' she called. 'I can't stay, but I want you
to know I'm keeping you safe.'

It was Sethrith, of course.

'How did you know we were here?' called Osric, fearful of being too
loud in case he attracted attention from one or all of the others swishing
above the woodland.

'We *all* know you're in there, but I have asked that you be left alone.'

'Are you – I mean, do you look like you normally do, or are you in
that body you were in when you met me the other day?'

'I didn't meet you the other day. Oh, *oh*, now I recall. That was my
sister you met. She was playing a nasty game with you. You ran away
from her when she offered herself to you, which made me glad. You
might have ended up as a pile of grey ashes, Osric. There's always a price
for making love to a witch. You surely know that? And listen, I *always*
look the same, Osric. You shouldn't be so gullible. That particular sister
you met, you should try to avoid her next time. She loves to bed mortals.
She would sacrifice a dozen men for a single orgasm.'

'You have other sisters?'

'Seven hundred and twenty-one of them.'

'Real sisters? Not just other witches.'

'No, they're my real sisters. We were all born on the same day, by the
same mother, but not of the same father.'

'Weird,' muttered Kenric, 'but then, you know: witches…?'

'Anyway,' said Sethrith, 'I am your guardian tonight, so you'd better be nice to me next time we meet.'

With that she was gone and the companions spent the rest of the night with hellish sounds filling the atmosphere and black shadows criss-crossing the moon in swarms. The next day dawned pleasantly, with a warm sun drying the dew on the grasses. The witches had all gone, to that place where witches dwell, their crofts somewhere deep in the forests or in the caverns of the Earth. Now the month of Drimilce had arrived, the month of the three milkings, when cows are ready to give up their treasured liquid thrice times a day. It is a good time, when winter has definitely been put away for a good while. The hares had stopped punching each other and the winds were softer and warmer, and indeed the showers which usually came in Eostremonath only came on the odd occasion.

'No wonder we've been beleaguered by otherworlders,' grumbled the Thief, as he readied his horse for the day's ride, 'I've just chased away a cofgoda. He was hidden tucked inside my horse blanket. Did you hear him giggling as he left?'

'A house Wight? You must have picked him up somewhere in the village. And he's been with us all this time?' said Osric, as if he were talking about a flea. 'Well, he won't last long out here, so I don't know why he's so happy. There're no dwellings within ten miles of this place and he'll be nothing but a wisp of dust before he reaches one. At least you've got rid of him. Now perhaps we can have a peaceful rest of our journey without being bothered by witches, giants or elves.'

At the sound of the last word, Magic gave out a poignant whinny, having no doubt been reminded of who he was missing, now that he had mortal on his back the whole time.

PART TWO
WARRIORS

ONE

Once the three were back in their forge in Mercia, Osric realised he had a dilemma. If he wanted to get revenge on Eadgard, the only way was to raise an army to fight the murderer and usurper. This he did not want to do, because it would mean his enemies would be his own people. Osric could hardly lead mercenaries against his friends and relations and expect them to thank him for it. Of course they would never, after what was bound to be a bloody encounter, elect him as their king no matter that his father had ruled them well and wisely. He might be of royal blood, descended from the gods, but the East Angles would probably find a way of getting him executed for bringing death and destruction to their villages.

Thus two years passed with the three companions, two of them now grown to men, working as farriers and earning themselves a place in Mercian society. Indeed, most of their neighbours regarded them now as Mercians and had forgotten they were incomers from another realm. With Paega it was different. The king still refused to recognise Osric's claim to the kingship of the East Angles, but Osric had now come to accept this fact. Just as he had come to accept being treated like a churl. The three incomers had learned that Paega was a harsh ruler and was not above punishing severely those who fell out of his favour, on occasion using the death penalty. Osric had also learned from others that his father Eorl had been humiliated and treated with disdain by Paega whenever the two had come together. Osric had known that the East Angles, like most of the Angle and Saxon nations, were subject to Paega's overrule, but he had not realised – naturally his proud father had kept this from him – that Paega treated all the subject kings with utter contempt. The Mercians had for a long time been the dominant nation on the island that the Romans had called Britannia. Osric could not see that changing in the near future, not with warrior-kings like Paega rampaging through the land with his superior army and his lack of any regard for other peoples, other tribes. He was indeed a cruel and unforgiving master.

That said, the Thief and Kenric were naturally happy enough to drift on through without a thought for the future, but the grievances in Osric would not let him rest. One day, one day he had to put matters right, firstly and mainly with Eadgard and Wulfgar, and until that time the anger and hate would gnaw at Osric's guts, telling him he should be doing something to make that happen.

Solmonathtide arrived, with many of the children and adults burying cakes in the ground in honour of the gods. Osric was shoeing the horse of a thegn called Dudda, meaning 'round man' and he was indeed a short fat little man, though handy with a warhammer. Dudda would strike at the knees of his opponents and then crush their heads when they were lying in the dirt. Dudda was getting impatient with Osric, who was a little slow having no help: Kenric was away at market and the Thief was serving on the wall.

'Not finished yet?' grumbled the chubby thegn. 'I'm supposed to be out there hunting by now.'

Osric was about to apologise, but at the same time suggest that if Dudda had come in earlier, he would indeed already be out with the hunt. However, while he was mulling his answer over in his head, a figure half-entered and then stood in the doorway, the light of the day behind him. All Osric could make out was the shape or silhouette of the person, who seemed to have rather pointed ears and stiff upright hair. The eyes, though, glowed brightly in the gloom at the back of the forge, the flares from the red-hot charcoal in the forge picking out gold flecks. They did not sparkle, exactly, but they took on a strange luminosity which was eerie to look at. Dudda seemed startled by the sudden presence of this stranger and took a quick two steps back, treading on Osric's toe which caused Osric to let go of the hoof he was holding and the horse to snort in disapproval.

For a few moments all three men and the horse formed a tableau which stayed frozen.

Then Osric called, 'Can I help you? Have you a horse to shoe?'

'No horse,' came the chimed reply. 'I walked.'

Dudda cleared his throat and asked, 'Walked from where?'

'Oh,' the dark figure waved an arm towards the light behind him, 'from over there.'

'Has the place a name?' asked Dudda.

'Yes, but it would mean nothing to you. I wish no conversation with you, anyway. I came to see my father.'

Dudda frowned and Osric could see that the fat thegn was wondering whether he ought to give this offhand stranger a lesson in manners. In order to try to prevent any unpleasantness, Osric swiftly asked, 'What's the name of your father. Perhaps we can point you in the right direction and I can get on with my work.'

'Yes,' growled Dudda, growing bolder now that the shock of this newcomer was behind him, 'what in hellmouth's foul breath is his name?'

'Osric,' said the stranger in that musical tone he employed. 'His name is Osric.'

Osric dropped the hammer he was holding and it clanged noisily on the anvil, making Dudda jump again. In the meantime, the stranger stepped fully into the forge and with the light of the coals on him, he nodded.

'Yes, you are my father,' he stated melodically. 'You are Osric, the prince from the East Angles. I have been told to ask the question, "How are you?" And this question also, "Are you well?" These are not questions elves would ask, but since I am from your inneryard, my father I wish to be – how is it said? – civil and polite. Oh yes, I have to say also, "Be Whole", which is the other greeting I have been taught. It would not be good if you were elfshot and had fallen sick, which I can see is not the case, so I have no need to apologise for my clan. My mother sends you greetings and says even though she does not love you any more and believes you were a very clumsy being when compared to her new life-mate, she still thinks of you sometimes because you are a mortal and therefore you were an unusual lover.'

Osric stared at the slim, delicate-looking youth standing before him. He had an almond-shaped face, slightly-pointed ears and nose, those tell-tale eyes and long thin fingers – longer than most – with wrists you could encircled with your thumb and finger. The youth appeared at the same time brittle yet with the promise of suppleness and agility in the hinterbody. He was quite short for a human, coming up to Osric's shoulder, but there was no diffidence to be seen in his stance, no insecurity. In fact when Dudda grunted, he stared right into the fat thegn's face with a certain effrontery, quite unwilling to hide the fact that this grunt offended him.

'What are you looking at?' snarled Dudda. 'Show respect for your betters.'

'Betters? I do not believe you are a better man than I.'

'I'm a thegn, one of the king's hearth-companions – look, what do you think these are? Earned in battle. Eh? You piece of straw. You pond weed.'

Dudda flashed his armrings, some of bronze but at least one of gold.

'It does not impress,' said the boy.

Dudda suddenly drew a dagger from his belt, but before he could do anything with it, the youth's hand flashed out and grabbed his wrist. They stood there for a few seconds, Dudda straining to release his arm, the stranger simply holding his ground. After a minute, Dudda began to whine, which turned quickly to a scream, until finally he dropped the weapon on the floor. Osric kicked the dagger out of the way and then laid a hand on the young man's forearm. 'Let him go,' he said, gently.

Indeed, Dudda's own arm fell to his side, where he nursed it for a moment.

'I could have you killed for that!' he said, his breath coming out rank and hissing. 'I'll have you whipped first…'

'I don't think so,' Osric said. 'Do you want to go to your fellow thegns and admit that this dainty boy forced you almost to your knees? I wouldn't. Even if they didn't laugh in your face, which I suspect they would, they would snigger behind your back. Do you want to look a fool? See here, I'll knock in another couple of nails and you can take your warhorse and go without payment. A free shoeing, how's that?'

'Forget the nails,' spat Dudda, 'I'll have him finished elsewhere. You,' he nodded at the boy, 'you watch your back. I'll see you again.'

With that, Dudda gripped the mane of his mount and led the beast out of the forge and was soon gone.

Osric then turned to the boy, who stood looking at him with a fondness that was disconcerting.

'Now,' said Osric, 'tell me who you really are.'

The youth's narrow eyes opened a little and his wide, wide, thin-lipped mouth curved upwards into a new moon crescent which might have been a smile.

'I am Quercus, your son and the offspring of my mother, Linnet.'

A rock the size of a man's fist formed in Osric's throat. He shook his head, vigorously. 'No, no, impossible. Why, Linnet and I only – that is it's only been three years – not longer…'

'Ah yes,' the smile on the lean face grew wider. 'My mother said it would be a great shock to you, to find you had son almost fully-grown, but, you see, I have elf-blood in my veins. I am half-elf, am I not? Elves grow to maturity very quickly, much more quickly than mortals. We are like wolves or the wild boar. No sooner do they enter the world than elves are left to fend for themselves, having to grow quickly. Indeed I did not mature as swiftly as those who had a purity of elf in them, having a mortal's blood in my veins. I was quite slow and shamed my mother.'

'My son?' whispered Osric, wonderingly, staring at this beautiful young man. 'My own son? I can't believe it.' He felt his heart fill with fondness for the boy. 'I have not long reached manhood myself, yet here you are on the brink. So, what do we do? Do we embrace like mortal father and half-mortal son? Or would that be distasteful to you?'

The boy stepped forward and hugged him.

Then he stepped back, saying, 'Father, you are so tall and strong and brave looking. See how your muscles gleam in the firelight. You have a broad face that is ugly to an elf, but I suppose is passable for a mortal. Your strength must come from your trade, which is a respectable one. Elves do not shoe their horses, but working with metal as you do, you are like the elf Wayland Smithy, who made exquisite swords and jewellery for mortals, until he broke free of his chains. I am not ashamed of you, Father. I thought I would be, but I am not.'

'Well, I'm pleased about that.'

'Yes, you will make a good father for me and I will make a good son.'

Osric began to busy himself with his tools and the fire in the forge, all the while thinking, thinking. Finally he turned and said, 'I'm still not convinced. How do I *know* you're my son? Even if I accept that elves grow to maturity much swifter than mortals, how can I be sure you're my son? I only have your word for it.'

'I don't understand,' came the chimed reply, the pixie face frowning. 'I've told you I am your son.'

'Yes, but you could be telling a lie.'

The look of shock that appeared on the face of the creature before him dispelled any doubts that Osric had. Clearly he had made a statement that was so incredibly wrong it had penetrated deep inside the half-elf and stained his soul, if indeed elves had such things. Perhaps half a human soul and half what went for such in an elf? Were they two separate halves or were they mixed, merged at birth? Osric felt all at sea. His mind swam with the various complexities of two creatures from separate worlds producing at child. Had they started a new race of beings, a completely different...?

'Elves do not *lie*.' Quercus's voice filled the forge with incredulous anger. 'How *dare* you accuse an elf of not telling the truth? It never happens. Only mortals tell lies. Elves only ever speak that which is, never that which is not.'

'I'm sorry,' replied Osric, 'but you are not an elf.'

The heat went out of the person standing in front of him.

'I – I am – I…'

'You are half-and-half. Perhaps the liar in you is the mortal half?'

The melody in the voice was now stifled by deep sorrow the boy felt on hearing this statement.

'I – I wish I were *all* elf. I do. I wish it with all my heart. Then I would know who I was. Instead I am neither elf nor mortal.'

'Perhaps, my son,' said Osric, gently, 'you are both fully man and fully elf, the two in one body. Perhaps you are greater than you think you are. Instead of diminishing you, your special place on the Earth raises you above the ordinary. Your mother Linnet and I have been blessed with a son who is greater than each of us. The sum of Osric and Linnet is a creature who strides two worlds, not one who has fallen between them. You have the wisdom of the elves and the wider knowledge of the mortals. Men travel far with having to trade, experiencing the rawness of the weather's terrible storms and sudden changes. Each individual society of men needs to meet with foreign cultures, needs to invent tools and make discoveries when they are faced with disasters or to make life easier for themselves. Elves live very narrow lives in their woodlands, simply hunting, making love and cohabiting with nature, with the odd foray into the world of mortals. Elves have all the time in the world for deep contemplation and seeking the inner meaning to profound questions. Thus they have wisdom which can only be found by the odd hermit in the world of men, but elves are not physically and mentally hardened to deal with life beyond their sylvan glades.' Osric paused, then added, 'And this is longest speech I have ever made of any consequence. I don't know where it came from, but it's drained me. The gods, I think, are speaking through my mouth. I hope you appreciate the effort.'

'You believe I am your son?'

'I could not do otherwise, seeing your expression when I suggested you may not be who you claim. However, I'm not sure we should tell anyone. I think it should be a secret between the two of us. Don't get me wrong,' Osric placed a hand on the shoulder of Quercus, 'it's not that I'm ashamed of you. I'm immensely proud and if I could say you were my younger brother, I would do so. But look at me – I don't look much older than you. We would be a laughing stock and, you know, mortals are suspicious of elves, who play tricks on them all the time. We need not tell them that you're part elf. By the way, what did you do to Dudda? Was it overpowering strength?'

'No, I did it with my eyes, not my hand. I looked into his brain and made him believe my strength was that of ten men. He could have wrenched his arm away at any time, but he was convinced that this was impossible.'

'See!' cried Osric. 'The wisdom of elves. The power of persuasion.'

'Be whole! And who do we 'ave here? A strange-looking lad.'

Kenric had entered the forge and stared at Quercus.

'Ah, Kenric. This – this is my cousin, Quercus,' replied Osric, 'and I'll thank you not to call him strange. It's true his mother had a hard birth...'

'Pulled him out by his ears, by the look of them.'

Quercus flashed Kenric a look which made the man step back and say, 'Whoa! No need to get upset. Just jokin''.

Kenric was now a strapping man, at least two fingers taller than Osric and a good hand wider at the shoulders. Whereas Osric's muscles were smooth and rounded as stones on a seashore, Kenric's bulged like lumps of rock. He was obviously physically very strong, with thick muscled thighs and a waist that hardly tapered at all on its journey from his hips to his chest. The face had no malice in it whatsoever, just an underlying layer of humour. No one, looking at that visage, could imagine anything lying behind it except benign intentions and a cheerful disposition.

'Ah, Quercus is a bit sensitive about his ears, Kenric. So I wouldn't go along that track if I were you. I ought to tell you, he just sent Dudda running with tears streaming down his face, so tread very carefully.'

Kenric beamed. 'This little drop of milk? Braced Dudda?'

'And sent him running...'

'... with tears down his cheeks. Well, well. Hard to believe, but if you say it's true, Osric. So, young man, how old are you? Fifteen summers?'

'And as many winters, sire.'

'I thought so. No need to call me sire though. Call him sire – he says he's a prince – but I'm from more hardy, worthy, humble stock. Princes? They're not much good to the world, are they? But farriers, now there's a set of men who you can trust with your hearts and heads, as well as your horses. Whatsay, lad?'

Still within the hearing of Quercus, Kenric added, 'He's a bit thin, an't he? Looks like you could snap him like a reed. Your cousin, you say? I do see a likeness, though – he's got your dainty looks, that's certain. That long hair falling down his back? It's got a strange hue to it. As if he's borrowed it from a barn owl. Your cousin. Hmm. Is he stayin' with us, or movin' on? I don't mind. Just asking.'

'Staying.'

'Fair enough.' Kenric offered Quercus his weapon hand to shake, but it was clear the boy did not know what to do with it, so Osric told him, 'Take hold of the fingers tightly and shake the arm, Quercus.'

The youth took Kenric's thick-fingered, calloused hand in his own slim appendage and stared into the farrier's eyes. Kenric's grin vanished instantly and he yelled and swiftly pulled his hand away, nursing his fingers.

'Gods and devils,' cried Kenric, 'he's got a grip on him.'

'I told you so.'

'By the by,' said Kenric, 'the Thief is back. He'll be along, presently.'

And indeed, within a short while the Thief trudged wearily into the forge. Being quite a lot older than the other two men, his time defending the wall against the Walha had taken it out of him. Once he had bathed and changed his dusty clothes he was introduced to Osric's 'cousin', but Osric and Quercus realised by his expression that he knew instantly what Quercus was. Whether the Thief thought he was half-elf or whole, they did not find out because the Thief was not one to delve into matters that were clearly kept from him for a reason. He simply nodded, without offering his sword hand to be shaken, and retired into the background.

'Bad time on the wall?' asked Kenric.

'No worse than usual,' replied the Thief. 'The Walha almost overran us one day, but luckily they ran out of daylight. They're wild men, all right. I hear Paega is going to offer to take some into his army, next time he goes to war. He said as much at the Thing yesterday. Better to have them on your side than on the other.'

'Expensive, though,' muttered Kenric.

'Yes, but Paega is one of the richest of the kings of the Seven Realms.'

'Eight, if you give Umberland its two separate kingdoms,' interrupted Osric.

It was true that Umberland had split into Bernicia in the north and Deira in the south and was now under two separate kings.

Osric went on, 'What have you heard about Paega going to war, then?'

161

'Ah,' said the Thief, 'you want to know if he's going against Eadgard? No, I think not. It's the Deirans again. He seems to have trouble getting them to pay tribute. Edwin Hafface refused to send the annual payment. Paega had his messenger thrown in the wolf pit, poor bastard. I'm glad I'm not young and fleet of foot. If you refuse to go, you're executed by your own king for treachery and if you do go, you're tortured and killed by the king to whom you deliver the damn message. The only thing to do is set out to take the message and then abscond halfway. You may be hunted down, you may starve through lack of resources and friends, but at least you stand a chance of getting away with your life.'

'I'm fleet of foot,' said Quercus, but without any puffed pride in his voice.

'I would wager a ton of gold on that,' said the Thief, eyeing the boy's build and suppleness. 'I expect you could outrun a deer.'

'Almost.'

Osric said quickly, 'Well don't go telling anyone about that particular talent outside of this inneryard, Quercus, or you may attract the wrong attention.'

The light of the day had now given way to the shadow of the night. Lamps were being lit. Torches were blazing at the entrance to the Great Hall. The three men and the boy settled down for the evening by the forge, which still glowed with the embers of the charcoal. The Thief, weary though he was, made them a meal. He was the best cook amongst them, though of course no one had tasted anything made by the hand of Quercus yet. The boy simply told them he was useless when it came to preparing food and Osric was aware that elves did not cook, ever. They did not eat meat or fish, only raw vegetables, so anything Quercus produced would be looked on with disgust by Kenric, who was a true carnivore. Indeed, the meat was badger and Quercus was horrified when he was told that.

'You eat *badgers?*' he cried.

'We eat anything with it's back to the sky,' replied Kenric, without apology, 'otherwise we might starve.'

Quercus said ruefully, 'I shall sleep on my side tonight.'

This made the others laugh and the poor elf-mortal did not know what to do with himself.

Lord Ing:
And there you have it, the surprise that young Osric left behind with his elfin wife, Linnet. Certainly the father of the boy has taken it well.

Two

During the night Osric made use of a bergamot vial in order to visit his dead parents. He wanted to ask them to help him solve his problem on how to avenge his father and regain his place in the kingdom of the east Angles. 'Father, Mother, I do not necessarily wish to be king, though I wouldn't shy away from the duty, but I do want one day to return to my own people.'

However, the dead have dull minds, which grow duller the longer they spend in the world of the spirits. His parents, both intelligent people when they walked live on the Earth, were at a loss as to how to help him. So on his way back to Middangeard, the land of living mortals, Osric was audacious enough to stop by the Rainbow Bridge that led to Esageard, home of the gods. He was of course stopped from crossing by Hama, the Ese god who guards the entrance to the bridge.

'Where do you think you're going, mudlark?'

'I need to speak to Tiw, the god of war.'

Hama laughed. 'Oh, do you? Just like that? And perhaps you'd like to chat to Lord Woden, or Seaxneat, or even one of the goddesses? Frige, Freo or Eorthe?'

'Well, that would be nice, but my question concerns war, which I believe is the province of Lord Tiw, is it not?'

'Listen, wanderer of the skies, you've got as much chance of getting into Esageard as I have of getting into Eostre's bed...'

At that moment a figure, wearing a blue cloak and carrying a spear the haft of which was made from an ash tree, appeared out of the cloud-mist, striding down to the end of the bridge. The form was huge and burly, and the sun seemed to shine from *within* his body, for by his massive genitals that swung in the air, he was most assuredly male. Long, lustrous locks hung from his great head halfway down his back and Osric now noticed that the walker only had one eye, the other having a closed to a thin black line. Here indeed was the greatest of the gods, Woden, Lord of the Wild Hunt, Lord of the Gallows and the Dead, God of Magic and Wisdom, High King and Master of the Runes, God of Poetry and Mantic Ecstasy, consort of the goddess Frige. On each of his shoulders sat a raven, the names of which Osric knew were Huginn and Muninn, and at his heels slunk two wolves, Geri and Freki.

A shaft of fear pierced through Osric's soul. He took several paces back as the god advanced to the end of the rainbow bridge. He was right to be terrified. Even Hama, one of the gods himself, was clearly afraid at the approach of great Woden, whose temper was known to cause terrible storms, earthquakes and volcanic eruptions, though all knew he could be gentle when it pleased him. There was a sternness to the chief god's one eye, however, as its look penetrated the brain of the mortal before him, giving Osric a sharp headache that intensified until he felt as if his head was going to burst like a seedpod under a hot summer sun.

'A little correction, visitor to my sky,' boomed Woden, 'Lord Tiw may be allowed to indulge in the sport of war sometimes, but I am the overriding god of that terrible exercise to which mortals seem forever addicted.'

'My lord,' replied Osric, his body shaking and creaking like a crack willow in a high wind, 'I beg forgiveness for my stupidity.'

'And you,' said Woden, halting suddenly and causing the two wolves, to rotate on the spot, 'Lord Hama will *never* get into the bed of the goddess Eostre, that sweet lady of springtime and the dawn.'

'As I said, my Lord, I have as much chance...'

Woden swung back to face Osric before Hama had the opportunity to finish his sentence.

'Well, now that I'm here, what is you wish? Who are you, anyway?'

Feeling small and insignificant, wilting below the glare of this god-giant, Osric stuttered out his problem, that of wishing to recover his place amongst his people, yet seemingly only having one option: to take the realm by force of arms, which would of course make him a murdering tyrant and a traitor in the eyes of those people.

'My name is Osric, Lord,' he said at the end of his explanation, 'once prince of the East Angles.'

'Osric, Osric,' muttered Woden, stroking his long beard, 'I seem to have heard that name before. Wait a moment, aren't you the farrier who assisted my groom? You warned him about Sleipnir eating acorns I seem to recall. What are you doing, forever wandering about Neorxnawang anyway? Mortals don't usually come this way unless passing by on their walk to the land of the dead.'

'Visiting my parents in that very place, my lord. I seem to have the ability to do so in my dreams.'

'Ah, I like a man who knows his duty to his mother and father. Both dead, eh? Well, I am most grateful for your advice about the acorns. I knew that, of course, since I know everything, but my groom had not been told. So, since I like you, Osric of the East Angles, I shall give you some advice regarding your dilemma. I will not fight your wars for you. I do not do that. I won't even assist you in your own war. I don't do that either. But I will tell you what I would do, if I were you…'

And the great god Woden then explained to Osric his best course of action, given the circumstances of his troubles.

After listening to the great Woden's advice, Osric went on to visit with those wisps of vapour that were his dead parents. He discussed his plans with his father at great length, then talked with his mother. However, as he took his leave from them, he turned and called out, 'Oh, by the way, you're grandparents now.' He watched as their misty forms swirled in agitation, and he was left wondering whether this unrest on their part was because they liked the news or because they were disquieted. Indeed, his personal life and its quirks were the last things he was concerned with at that moment, after having spoken with the greatest of the gods and walked away unharmed. Osric had heard stories of men who had died of fright at the mere sight of the Lord of the Wild Hunt. There were those whose attention had been on the sky and had seen the god riding through thunderous high regions and whose eyes had burned to blindness in their sockets. One woman, on accidently catching sight of Lord Woden striding through a Middangeard woodland, shrivelled to the size of an oak gall. Her husband, who went looking for her later, found her wizened likeness in a fist-sized, lumpy knot of wood lying on the forest floor and took this quaint aberration of nature home to decorate the table on which the children ate their meals.

ᴛHᴙᴇᴇ

When Osric woke he went straight to the Great Hall and entered. King Paega was sitting at the long table with some of his thegns discussing something. There were raised eyebrows as Osric approached and the king's two closest gesiths or hearth-companions rose immediately and braced him. These were Horsa and Headho, fierce warriors who took their duties of guarding their king very seriously. Horsa's eyes were roving Osric's form, obviously looking for a weapon. Headho simply stared into Osric's face with an indignant enquiry blazing forth.

'You dare to enter here unannounced, farrier?'

'I wish to speak with the king,' replied Osric, simply.

Horsa said, 'You and a hundred others. If you have a petition...'

'I wish to speak to him now on a matter of great importance.'

Headho stated, 'Tell us then and we'll tell the king.'

'No – I must speak to him directly.'

'You *must?*' cried Headho.

'*What in the name of the gods is going on over there?*' shouted King Paega. 'I'm trying to plan a war here.'

'That's precisely the reason I'm here, my Lord,' called back Osric, though in a softer tone. 'I wish to offer my services.'

'Who is it?' the king peered through the gloom inside the windowless hall. 'Step forward, man.'

'It's the farrier my Lord,' called Horsa and Headho, in chorus

'Well nudge the fellow forward. Ah, yes, I know you, farrier. What's so important that you interrupt a war council? I hope you haven't come to ask for my daughter's hand in marriage. You haven't a hope in that direction. I'm saving her for a prince...'

'I am a prince, my Lord.'

'Yes, but one without a princedom. What good is that? Marriage to a pauper prince isn't going to increase the size of my empire, now is it?'

Osric had once considered asking the king for his daughter's hand, but had refrained knowing he would come away with a kick up his backside for his impudence. He was glad about that he hadn't done so now, because he'd seen another girl in the village who was prettier than the king's daughter, though he would never dare say so. Osric of course fell in love at the drop of a yew-bucket and changed his mind daily about who was the lady with whom he wanted to spend the rest of his life. He admitted to himself that he was rather shallow when it came to love and that the problem with eternity was that it lasted forever.

'This has nothing to do with your daughter, Lord. I wish to lead an army in a war…'

The king threw himself back in his great wooden chair and tossed the dagger he was using as a pointer clattering onto the table.

'Oh well now, if I'm not needed to lead my own army into battle any more, I can retire and play singlesticks with my grandchildren, can't I?'

'No, no,' Osric approached a little closer, which had the nobles at the table shuffling a little, 'I did not mean that, my Lord. You are, I'm told, about to make war with the Umbrians? My plea is that you allow me at the same time to lead an army against the East Angles. I would need just a few Mercian men, but hope to recruit some of the Walha warriors, who I'm told are good fighters.'

Paega stared at this upstart farrier come prince-of-nowhere for a good few minutes.

'You want to retrieve your father's kingdom?' he said at last. 'You've been angling after that ever since you came here.'

'Yes, Lord. I wish to avenge my father's death and regain my place among the people of the East Angles, it's true.'

'I'm told that it was you who killed your own father.'

'Lies, my Lord, put out by Eadgard, the usurper.'

'And just say I believe you, what's in it for me? You get a chance of ruling your father's realm, but what does that give me? I'll have to pay for warriors and provisions, and the Walha don't come cheap, even if you do manage to get them to follow you. The main aim of the Walha is to flatten Mercia and have us all in slave manacles, so I don't give a great deal for your chances there. Come then, what does King Paega get out of you conquering the east Angles.'

'A loyal ally for the rest of your life and the life of your successor.'

'I have an ally in the East Angles. They are one of my subject kingdoms.'

'But I'm talking about a *loyal* ally, my lord.'

The king sighed. 'Hmmm. You use clever words, boy, and some of them ring true. I'm not going to argue that it would be comforting to have a reliable buffer between my kingdom and the East and South

Saxons. Someone to cover my flank to come in if we are ever ourselves attacked while fighting the West Saxons.'

'My Lord,' said one of the thegns, sounding shocked, 'you're not taking this idiot seriously, are you?'

King Paega stared at the thegn. 'I take any good idea seriously.'

Osric's heart lifted. 'Lord,' he continued, 'I will also make good the cost of such a war once it is won and I have a kingdom's coffers at my disposal.'

'And if you lose?'

'That's not possible, but if it were to, I would shoe your horse for nothing for the rest of your days on the Earth.'

This remark brought a roar of mirthful approval from the thegns, who hammered the table top with their dagger pommels.

'I'll give him this,' cried Horsa, the tears soaking his tunic, 'he's got more gall than can be found in a dozen pigs' bladders.'

The king stared at Osric for a while, then said, 'Come back when I'm less busy and we'll talk.' He turned away, but then turned back again, saying, 'You might even get to marry my daughter yet, if you've got a kingdom to offer her.'

More raucous laughter from the warriors in the room, then Osric was ignored and made his way out of the Great Hall into the sunshine. Osric walked on, feeling slightly humiliated and a little aggrieved.

Osric was later called to the Great Hall where he found the king alone. The talk was brief. Paega would indeed sponsor an attack on the East Angles, if Osric managed to boost the army that was to take the field with Walha warriors. Osric would have to negotiate for warriors from the Walha people using his own cognizance. This was his chance, said the king, to exact revenge on Eadgard and Wulfgar, so he warned Osric not to waste the opportunity. Osric was then dismissed from the king's presence. He thanked the king and left the hall to find his two friends and his elfmortal son. When he told them his plan they showed surprise but didn't argue with the idea.

'So, how do we get these Walha-men then?' asked Kenric. 'Stand on Uffa's dyke and yell come and join us?'

'No,' replied Osric. 'When I was on the wall the first time, I met one of them, a man named Tomos from Powys, who spoke our language. I intend going into the land of the Walha to find him and ask for his help.'

The Thief sucked in his cheeks. 'You won't get ten steps before they cut you down.'

'I'll take that chance. In the meantime, while you're waiting for me, you can find out what the king is giving us in the way of warriors, though I suspect they won't be up to much. I'm happy as long as they have two legs, at least one arm and can see and hear reasonably well. I'm fairly certain he'll want to take the best to Umbria, so we mustn't get too excited by our share of the locals. As long as they look the part, they'll do for my purposes.'

Again there were raised eyebrows from the other two, but they didn't argue with him. They got together some provisions for him, a purse full of nails and some tools to buy his way out of trouble if he needed to and sent him on his way.

Throughout this conversation, Quercus had said nothing. However when Osric prepared to leave he stated that he wished to go with him.

'No, I think not, Quercus. You need to stay with Kenric and the Thief.'

'No, I need to go with you. I need to be with my... cousin if something terrible happens to him. I can be of assistance if there are travails.'

Osric tried to argue but Quercus was determined. In the end, after a long debate, Osric gave up and agreed. The boy was determined to go. He told his father that if he was forbidden to join him, he would follow anyway. Osric could hardly imprison his son to prevent this, so wearily he nodded in assent and they prepared for the journey together.

The evening before the pair left for the land of the Walha the king held a gathering for an Ierfealu, the traditional round of ritual toasts dedicated to the deceased. After the Ierfealu one of the thegns reminded those present that all Angle and Saxon kings were descended from the gods and therefore were touched by divinity. They were not gods, said the speaker, for even the founder of the race, Mannus son of Tursco, could not call himself a god, but kings were indeed set above ordinary men. There followed a list of the gods belonging to the Ese and the Wen, long and complex, but all Mercians knew their names and their strengths.

The speaker started with Woden, chief of the gods, god of war, poetry and mantic ecstasy and consort of Frige, and went on to list all the major gods – Osric could not help a quick glance at his son when Ing's name was intoned – followed by the lesser gods.The speaker rushed through the latter in order to get to the horn of mead before it was totally quaffed, after which he spoke of the codgofas and spat on the floor to emphasise his distain for these house wights who tormented ordinary humble folk in their homes.

The only god which was not mentioned by name was Loki, the trickster, that devious being who on hearing his name was quite likely to have come down disguised as a mortal to mingle with the guests, causing mayhem before the evening was out. You couldn't trust Loki to stay away if he saw the chance of creating mischief – and Loki devilment could end in terrible slaughter.

After the pantheon came the reckoning between inneryards who were at loggerheads with each other. There were those inneryards who were feuding with their neighbours and the king told them to settle their differences on this night or feel his wrath, because, he added, their selfish squabbles disrupted the lives of other, peaceful inneryards. A grith, or pact of peace, had to be agreed between the parties at war with one another. If this was not done, the king intended sending the Frithguildsmen to arrest the troublemakers. The king then emphasised the thews, the virtues and honour of the Angles and Saxons in order to hammer home his point.

There followed another round of the symbel, the drinking horn passed from one to another, toasts, oaths, boasting, followed by songs and stories. Osric noticed that though his son put his lips to the drinking horn, he did not appear to swallow any mead. Elves, Osric knew from living with them, did not approve of drinking liquid which robbed them of their faculties. He wasn't sure whether this was a good thing or not, but he didn't admonish his son or force him to drink. Obviously the boy, being half-elf, was concerned enough to observe the customs of his mother's society.

Lord Tiw:

You were probably expecting Lord Ing, who's been following this mortal's progress and favouring him with nudges in the right direction, probably because he's fathered an elf, or rather half-elf. However, we've now moved into my inneryard, that of WAR. This is no light choice. War is a terrible human action which always brings the brother of War, namely Chaos, into the room. Men go trooping off to War singing songs of glory and bravery and trudge back home again with hollow hearts, vacant eyes and smelling of Death – an odour which they can never wash away.

The next morning, a day with a clear sky and mild temperature, the pair set out, riding double on Magic's back to the wall. Osric was a sturdy man now, but Quercus weighed less than a sack full of leaves. The world seemed at peace with itself, with rills gurgling as they trotted by, the leaves of trees glistening in the brightness and the scent of herbs and weeds in the air. Birds flew up from the bushes as they approached, all but one yellowhammer who steadfastly refused to break off his trilling and who stared at Magic belligerently when they passed his twiglet perch. Other creatures, too, scattered before the hooves of the horse: weasels and stoats, rodents, the odd grass snake, a flashing hare that zigzagged away. Even a slinking fox crossed their path, well ahead, glancing warily at their approach. It seemed that all was right with the kingdom of Paega, before he went off to start a war.

On arrival at Uffa's Dyke they left the elfen steed in a stable. Osric didn't want some foreigner taking a fancy to his horse and keeping him for himself. The pair then clambered down the far side of the wall, into the ditch, then up again to level ground on the far side. There were no Walha-men guarding the far side of the wall. Uffa's barrier was built to keep the barbarians out, or at least keep them contained. The Walha were not worried about being attacked by the Mercians. They would have welcomed it. They knew their own hills, mountains and valleys, and would have enjoyed picking off an enemy who were lost, unsure and insecure in a strange land.

The kingdom of Powys was just on the other side of the wall and the pair were able to stroll to the first village without hindrance. The moment they walked into a group of dwellings however, there were wide eyed people transfixed by their presence, staring at them in disbelief. One man immediately reached into a doorway and came away with an axe in his hands. He yelled something at them in his lyrical language, which though melodic was obviously a black threat. Osric held up his hands to show he was carrying no weapons. Quercus did the same. Their attacker however stood in front of them, clearly enraged, yelling and yelling, until an elderly man stepped in front of him and said something quietly to him. The axe-wielder wilted a little and shuffled back, to let the old man speak to the intruders. The elder faced Osric and spoke with a stern voice, as if to a child.

'Are you lost, *dieithryn*? You are in the wrong place. This is Brythoniaid.'

They had obviously been recognised for what they were, because the old man spoke to them in their own language. Osric knew that the people Mercians called the Walha called themselves the Brythoniaid. He shook his head.

'I know where I am. I have come looking for a man called Tomos.'

The white-bearded Walha's face broke into a wide grin.

'Powys is full of Tomoses. I am one myself. Is it *me* you seek?'

Osric felt daunted. 'No, not you, old one, but a man I met on the other side of the great wall. There were three of them. There were twenty raiders, in all, and only three of them survived the fight. He said his name was Tomos, but I didn't realise that it was a common name among you – you Brythoniaid. This raid took place almost two years ago. Tomos and his companions were exchanged for Mercian prisoners held by your people.'

Osric knew he was pronouncing the word 'Brythoniaid' badly, stumbling over the vowels, and this again made the old man smile redly, his mouth being almost toothless. There was quite a crowd around them now, mostly curious, though some still wore antagonistic expressions. The old man turned to the gathering and spoke to them in his own language. There were many nods and some pursing of the lips. Eventually the old man turned back to Osric and Quercus again.

'We know the man of whom you speak. What do you want with him?'

'Forgive me, old one, but I must speak with Tomos and with no one else. I mean no harm. I wish to ask him for a favour. One he owes me, though the favour I require is bigger than the one I gave to him. I must let him decide.'

Again, a sage nod from the elderly Walha, then a quick look at Quercus before he said almost in an aside, 'This is one of the faerie. Does he belong to you?'

'The boy is my son, Quercus,' replied Osric, deciding that the truth would be more to their advantage than a lie, 'his mother is a proud and beautiful elf.' Then the sentence that followed was as much for Quercus's benefit as the elderly Walha's. 'I love her very much.'

'Ah!' The elder's eyes shone. 'An elf, is it? An elf named after the oak tree that we all depend upon, whose wood makes the best houses, the best boats, the best tables for our food and drink. Here's an exotic day to have an elf walk into my village!' He reached out and pinched one of

Quercus's pointed ears and to give the boy his due, Quercus did not pull away or even flinch. 'An elf, or even half of one, is welcome anywhere in this kingdom, eh? So you, you made love to an elf, Mercian. I won't ask you if was any different, unless you want to tell me.'

'I think I would rather not, the boy being within earshot.'

'Of course. Forgive me. Though naturally, curiosity overwhelms a man, even one whose escapades in the bed are long behind him. To come across the lover of an elf-girl is something quite unusual. Follow me, I will send word for the Tomos you wish to speak to. In the meantime, you'll both be welcome at my humble dwelling. An elf in my house. My wife will be tickled, so she will. Tickled to little pieces. Is it good luck to have an elf in the home? I'm sure it is. Now there's excitement for you. Lovely ears, he has too. Lovely. Come. Come. You are safe with me. They want to cut off your head,' he waved at the crowd, 'but I won't let them. Not until you've seen Tomos and spoken your piece. Then we'll decide what to do with you.'

Osric and Quercus were at worst unsettled, as they remained the guests in the house of Tomos the village elder. They were well fed, probably on mutton, and had soft beds of straw, but there were those in the village who came to the doorway and without entering glared at them fiercely. Many had lost relatives in battles with Mercians and were obviously unhappy at having two of the enemy in their yard eating and drinking their fare. Osric yelled at one of them that he was 'not a Mercian' but the man shouted back, probably not understanding what was being said to him and thinking he was being flung an insult.

Tomos-the-elder's wife was a toothless hag who looked much older than her husband and whose mouth was continually open revealing the cavern within. She clearly was tickled to have an elf in her home and touched Quercus whenever she thought she could get away with it. Each time she did so, she glanced down at her fingers, probably expecting twinkling star dust to have come away on them. She seemed puzzled and a little upset when nothing showed. Perhaps somewhere in her ancient brain was the idea that before Quercus left her home she would be transformed back into the pretty young girl she had been many decades ago. Osric could not blame her for her, for although she looked generally healthy, she was crooked of limb and bent over almost double, shaped like a bracket. That dancing, long-legged, fair-skinned creature that once she was lived only in her dreams and wanted to come out.

Clearly Tomos-the-elder had a lot of authority, for though many in the village would love to have had two heads on pointed stakes to gloat over, none seemed to have the courage to enter and take them. It was two days before the younger Tomos arrived and entered the hovel. The strong, dark man stood there in the sunlight glancing through the doorway and studied Osric for a moment. Then he stepped forward and placed a hand on the Angle's shoulder, saying, 'My best enemy.'

Osric nodded. 'And mine.'

'You risk your life coming here,' said Tomos, his eyes on Osric's. 'You're lucky to have reached this far, so you are. Why have you come to find me? Is it gold you bring me? Or perhaps a herd of cattle?'

'I appreciate the jest,' Osric replied, 'but I'm on serious business. I need men for a war against my own people. Let me explain...'

And he did, outlining his plans at great length. Tomos, now sitting at a table, took it all in without a murmur, though sometimes he glanced at Quercus while Tomos-the-elder nodded and indicated by his expression that yes, this was the elf he had told everyone about,. When Osric was finished the Walha rubbed his calloused hands together, hands that had built the drystone walls around his village, hands that had killed Angles and Saxons, hands that had farmed the valleys, and he sighed.

'This is a lot to ask for the small favour you gave me.'

Osric nodded. 'I know it. But then I will be deeply in your debt and you may call on me when you wish for repayment.'

'Listen, there's a lot of don't knows here. I don't know whether I can gather any men for this enterprise, especially since there's nothin' in it for them. Not straight away, anyway, though you may be a king afterwards. I don't know that I really want to leave my wife and family when the harvest is coming closer. I don't know that I'll ever need another favour from you, Osric. I just don't know...'

'I simply ask you to try, Tomos.'

FOUR

Tomos arranged a meeting with several chieftains of the Walha. They gathered under a rock hang which overshadowed the main village of these fierce people who had been driven out of the eastlands by the tide of Angles, Jutes and Saxons that had flowed over the channel from the continent. They had been displaced, but not conquered, their princes and kings now holding the west of the island with great determination and stubbornness. No one was going to take their mountain country from them without the loss of many many lives.

Quercus and Osric watched as Tomos spoke to the ring of chiefs, studying their faces. They looked darkly aggressive. Once or twice one or two of them glanced towards Osric, but their eyes were like flints. Attempting to read their expressions, Osric's heart sank in his chest. There was no way these burly Walha were going to accede to Osric's request. He could see it in their stance, their grim visages and, once Tomos had ceased talking the language that Osric could not understand, in their loud voices. The chiefs all began shouting at Tomos, their voices harsh with apparent anger. Mouths yelled what sounded like ugly oaths and actually Osric began to fear not only for his own life and that of his elfen son, but for Tomos too, for they shook their fists in that man's face and snarled and growled and howled like wolves.

Tomos eventually came over to Osric and smiled.

'They'll do it,' he said. 'We leave tomorrow.'

Osric rocked back on his heels. 'What? But what was all the rage about? I was convinced they were dead set against it. The arguments...'

'Oh, that's just their way of deciding things,' said Tomos. 'If they hadn't wanted to do it, they'd have just walked off without a look, muttering to themselves. The meeting wouldn't have lasted the length of time that it did. However,' he looked over his shoulder at the chieftains, who were still yelling at each other, 'I didn't tell them the whole plan, Angle, otherwise they definitely would not be coming. I made it sound as if there was going to be a great battle with plunder to be had.'

'But,' said Osric, with consternation in his spirit, 'what will happen when they find out what my plan actually involves?'

175

Tomos shrugged. 'We'll deal with that when we come to it. Now, give them a rousing speech in your own language – you can hardly do it in ours – and that will seal the agreement. Some of them understand a little Englisc. Go on. Inspire us. Give us a great stirring speech that will put fire into the blood of these warriors. Send us on our way with our bloodlust high and visions of great deeds in our eyes. Just as in battle the whirling bullroarers raise the temperature of our blood and souls to a wild pitch of enthusiasm for the hearts and heads of the enemy, so let your words fill us with the same spirit of joy for the deliverance of death to our enemies.'

Osric cleared his throat. 'Men!' he cried. 'Chieftains of the Walha – that is, the Brythoniaid – we are set for a glorious task, the plan which was given me by our great god, Woden, Lord of the...' there were glares and Osric suddenly realised that of course, Lord Woden was not the god of the Walha and he glanced across with a flutter of panic at Tomos, who interrupted with the roar, 'Aeron, god of slaughter! Cicolluis, god of the Celtic army!' There was a great cheer from the Walha chieftains who waved their fearsome weapons in the air. Osric, cleared his throat again, and thinking he was on firmer footing cried, 'I am in your great debt, Brythons, for assisting me in my task of regaining my father's kingdom. I am here because you are the greatest fighters in the world. I who have fought against you can attest to that. Man for man, you stand alone and hold your ground. There, my praise for your courage and fierce manhood forces me into poetry, poor though I may be at such art.

'So, I thank you for your patience with me, a one-time enemy, and perhaps even a future enemy, for we cannot say what the Wyrd will bring. I have been told by Tomos-the-elder that you have the King of Britannia among your people. A giant by the name of Bendigeidfran. I would rather have such a one fighting for me, rather than against me, though I have also been told that he would never fight alongside an Angle, no matter how just the cause, so we must do without him. Tomorrow we set off and will be joined by an army of Mercians. They will be small in number, because...' Osric paused and reconsidered his next few words, realising that if the Walha knew King Paega was away with the greater part of his army fighting Umbrians, these canny chiefs might decide to divert their army from the agreed aim and instead conquer Mercia while the king and his army of Angles were far away and unable to stop them. '... small in number because the Mercians regard it as a great honour to fight alongside the Brythons, so therefore only the best fighters were chosen.' There was a great deal of ironic laughter following these words as they were translated for those who did not speak Englisc and Osric knew he had gone a little too far with his flattery. He finished his speech, with a rather lame ending and afterwards Tomos said to him, 'If you're going to be king of a people, you'd better brush up on your rhetoric my friend. That speech might have inspired an army of voles, but I'm afraid we have five-year-olds who could do better with inspiring warriors.'

'My father is a fighter, not a priest,' said Quercus, defending Osric fiercely.

Tomos looked Quercus up and down, as if seeing him for the first time, saying, 'He's a big boy for his age, eh? Your son?'

'You must have heard,' said Osric, 'that he's half elf.'

Tomos nodded. 'And you must tell me about that, sometime, Angle – an interesting story, I'm sure.'

The Walha chieftains gathered together their army, seven hundred strong.

There were the greatest of the warriors with their named swords – *Cigyddwr* (Slaughterer) – and others in the same vein. These elate, mostly horsemen, were followed by the spearmen, slingers, archers, huge muscled fellows with warhammers and axes. Then came a hotchpotch of banner-carriers, whirlers of bullroarers, boys with choppers and daggers, musicians with their drums and wind-pipes, youths carrying standards from which hung hairy skulls and bunches of blackened testicles sliced from enemies in previous battles. Behind these came the cooks and cattle drivers, the supply wagons, the women who liked to watch, fire-makers, the water-carriers, the ox-cart handlers, the priests and the scribes to record the battle. In fact, everything and anyone needed for a successful campaign in foreign territory.

Osric and Quercus went ahead, hailing the sentries on Uffa's dyke, warning them not to fire any missiles or cause a great alarm when they saw the army of the Walha coming over the slopes towards them. There was naturally a flutter of panic among the guardians of the Mercian kingdom, but fortunately the officer in charge of the wall that day was a sensible thegn who knew of Osric's mission and had been told to let the army of the Walha through the kingdom of Mercia. In order not to upset the Mercian public and to keep the Walha from knowing there were mostly only old men, women and children left in the villages, Osric diverted the army around the Mercian inneryards into the wild outeryard beyond. Then he went back and collected those warriors who had volunteered to fight with the Walha against the east Angles, where Kenric had been waiting impatiently having gathered them.

Indeed, the Mercians who had decided to fight an eastern war instead of a northern one were not all sad men, some of them were prime warriors. Their reasons for joining one war over another were various, but at least Osric did not feel disgraced by the quality of the Angles who were to fight alongside the Walha. He praised them and told them they would receive their reward in Neorxnawang heaven, which had them sniffing and privately thinking they were looking forward to a few trinkets while still here on Middangeard – on terra firma.

The two armies came together, that is alongside each other, eyed each other warily, and settled down for the first night. The Mercians swore the smell of the Walha was as overpowering as stagnant ditch water and the Walha told each other the odour of the Mercians was worse than the stench of a dead cow's guts. (Quercus thought the Walha insult was the most colourful of the two). The fact that both armies stank of sweat, faeces, ancient re-used cooking fat, piss, animals, uncured hides, last year's cheese and this year's dried fish, and all the other stuff that armies stink of when on the march had actually nothing to do with what they thought of each other's way of life. Myths are powerful things in the minds of men and though occasionally there is a sensible regarding of the truth, men enjoy believing that their culture is superior to that of all others, that they themselves are all that is good and noble, and that their neighbours represent everything that is foul and unjust.

Still, they knew they were going to have to get on with one another for the next several days, perhaps longer, and so they settled down and put up with the fact. The same full moon shone its yellow night beams on both armies, the same stars spread their canopy over both camps and the same night air filled the lungs of the sentries on duty. On the pale of the two groups, one or two friends were made between the separate nations: men who swore they were not like their colleagues and whose minds were open to new ideas. Indeed, Osric realised it was a fact that men could like each other as individuals and yet dislike each other as nations. Probably, before the campaign was over and done with, there would be firmer friendships between individual Walha and Mercian warriors than would ever be the case between Mercian and Mercian, or Walha and Walha. In the centre of each camp, however, where there was little or no contact with the 'foreigners' alongside them, there were warriors who were certain that the shrivelled heads and balls that hung from the other camp's trophy poles were from cousins of theirs.

Tomos had been made general of his army for this campaign only, since he had initiated it. Osric was naturally the leader of the Mercians. The two men were intelligent enough to settle disputes between rivals justly, so that all could see there was no bias. They set off over the outeryard, the wild landscape that lay between Mercia and the east Angles, wondering what strange things might befall them in the wilderness. Indeed, marshlands, swamps and dark forests were where the creatures of the otherworld were likely to be found. Elves might live on the periphery of villages of mortals, but giants and dragons and their kind stayed firmly in wild places where chaos and unearthly happenings sprang from the bogs and fens. There were also bandits out there, some roaming in large numbers, but nothing which this army of Walha and Mercians could not easily stamp on with half their number.

Indeed, even on the first day they lost two Mercians to a nixie, a water spirit, who lured the men out of their depth in a dismal lake where the reeds grew taller than a mortal. The nixie in the guise of a beautiful young woman stood tall amongst the reeds and called to a group of warriors filling their yew-buckets with water. Two of the fools rushed in to claim her and disappeared after thrashing on the surface for a few minutes, during which the nixie shrieked with laughter. Then she too went under the water, presumably to eat her prey, and was not seen again.

On the second day, the outriders saw a group of giants ambling over a hill in the distance. They were Thurses, the giants that Osric had helped the elves to battle when he was with his son's mother: savage creatures bent on destruction. On seeing the outriders, the giants broke into a clumsy run towards them, no doubt hoping for an easy kill. But the army was close behind and once the Thurses saw almost two thousand mortals streaming over the downs they took flight, their great horny feet thumping on the hard earth, leaving the world juddering and trees trembling in their wake. When they thought they were far enough away, the giants turned, hooting and hollering in their strange, deep, echoey language, probably shouting threats and oaths, and daring warriors to follow them into the forest. Some excited men did indeed dart forward, ready for the chase, but were called back by their superiors and told to control their emotions. What man amongst us, though, would not like to brag of a battle with a giant that had left the monster dead amongst the bloody weeds on a meadow?

The army surged forward, the animals and birds scattering before the many feet wondering if they would see the dawn of the next day. On the fifth morning, as they were getting close to their enemy, the army saw the wondrous sight of a fully-grown green dragon flying northwards towards the land of the painted men. The beast came low but happily ignored the mass of humans spread out on the fields beneath it. There was some intent in its flight, as if it too were on a mission. Men marvelled at the length of this creature, amazed by the yellow ridged belly that looked impenetrable to ordinary weapons, enjoyed the sight of the slim, vicious jaws and the long elegant tail that flailed the clouds behind it. Then it was gone, off to where the Picts lived and fought their border battles with the Umbrians, leaving only the faint smell of burning in its wake, as if fire had streaked across the sky. The Walha afterwards claimed they were unimpressed by this low flyer with its bat-like wingspan through which the sunlight shined green. They maintained the red dragons of their region were far larger, far more ferocious, far more capable of dealing out death.

FIVE

The army of Walha and Mercians halted on the bank of the river that separated the outeryard wilderness from the villages of the East Angles. The same river that Osric had crossed on ice to escape the murderers of his father. Men were running hither and thither and families were being evacuated, in anticipation of an attack. King Eadgard and his henchman Wulfgar were readying warriors for war, but as yet they did not know against whom. Osric sent them a message to inform them that he had come with an army ready to destroy them if they did not surrender immediately. That destruction could be avoided, said the message, if the East Angles handed over certain people in order that justice might be carried out. Since both their new king and his chief thegn were top of the list, Osric knew what the answer would be.

The messenger returned with the expected reply: the easteners would fight to the death. He had barely escaped with his life as the king wanted him thrown into a wolf pit. However, many of the nobles argued against this action, saying that to kill a herald was dishonourable and the gods would be angry at such a blatant disregard of the thew. There were so many voices raised against the king and his hearth-companions on this matter that the messenger was able to sneak away and get back to his boat, where Walha were waiting to row him across.

Many of the Walha and Mercians were pleased at the reply, believing there was great glory to be had in battle. They wanted a fight. There were armrings to be won, praises to be gathered. They wanted their thirsty swords to taste blood and to leave the slaughtered ones on the field, never to rise again. They wanted their spear-points to bite into the enemy's hide. These were warriors whose sole occupation was war and when it came they were eager to throw themselves into it. Many of them had not seen combat before – young men with appetites – and though fear might be touching every heart, they were raring to prove themselves in a bloody engagement.

The next morning the two armies faced each other on opposite sides of the swiftly flowing waters. There was a small island in the middle of the river. Osric had remembered this place from his childhood, when young boys dared each other to swim out into the fast currents to reach

181

it. Now it was time to put his plan into action. He had told Lord Woden that he did not want to meet his own people on the battlefield: that he would never kill his own relatives and former friends, even though many would accept that he had little choice. Lord Woden, being the wise god that he was, offered Osric a second choice, which he was now going to execute, despite the fact that his eager army would hate him for it.

Osric stepped forward with Kenric at his right shoulder and Tomos at his left.

'Eadgard!' he yelled, over the swirling rapids, 'meet me on the island for single combat. If you win, my army will depart in peace. If I win and you remain still alive, then you will leave the East Angles and be banished for life. If you win, then I will be dead and no further threat to you. What say you, usurper? Murderer of my father, liar, man without honour, wastrel, foul leavings of a common pig?'

As expected, this challenge caused great consternation in both armies. The only Walha who had prior knowledge of it was Tomos. The only Mercian who knew what was coming was Kenric. These two turned about and faced the army who had marched across the country in order to take part in a war. Now this army was being robbed of its purpose. Angry sounds and threats filled the air. Kenric and Tomos did their best to stem the uproar with their own voices.

On the other side of the river there was a debate taking place. Men were arguing there too, but there was much more at stake for the East Angles. They had their villages to protect, their womenfolk and children to think of, their land and crops to worry about. If they fought a battle and Osric's army won, all would be laid to waste on their side of the river, since Osric would not be able to control a rabble army with hot blood flowing in their veins after winning a war. They would be entitled to plunder and pillage, to taking the women and children as slaves, to burn the fields and the houses, to destroy every piece of enemy ground that came within the reach of their sword arm. If they could avoid a conflict, the East Angles would do so, and this offer of single combat was like offering them a ripe plum in the middle of winter.

In the end, as Osric knew it would, the offer was accepted.

Osric stripped to the waist, left his elfen bow and sheath of arrows on the bank and with Kenric and Tomos boarded a boat for the island.

On the far side, Eadgard did the same, with two thegns accompanying him.

Both armies began to find places to sit on the ground, one of them groaning in disappointment, the other happy that their king was a mature fighter with many kills to his name. Eadgard was no coward, nor was he a weakling. When Osric's father was king, Eadgard had protected Eorl with great cunning and skill as a fighter. He was still in his prime, a large man with a scar running from the centre of his forehead down alongside his nose on the left cheek to the corner of his mouth. The man who had given him that scar had his eyes torn out by Eadgard's fingers and rammed down his throat, where they choked him to death.

Osric arrived at the island first and stood there, swinging Kenric's seax sword, limbering up. Then came the other boat and Eadgard leapt ashore, snarling like a dog. Wulfgar was grinning like the oaf he was, while his companion, a thegn Osric recognised as his once best friend when growing up, remained impassive.

The king said, 'You stupid puppy. I've been praying for this moment.'

'Never mind the talk,' Osric said. 'You can do that later, when you're lying on your deathbed. Now is the time for swords to bite flesh. Are you ready?'

The two sets of seconds stepped back from the combatants.

Osric went in first, stabbing wildly, despite his promise to Tomos beforehand to remain calm and deliberate. Eadgard parried the blows easily, turning the point of Osric's seax away from its target. Next Osric tried slashing, attempting to break through Eadgard's guard, but always metal met with metal, edge with broad blade. Eadgard looked as if he was enjoying himself. This furious assault of Osric's went on for a few minutes, then Eadgard seemed to decide it was time to take the offensive and he too went in with strong sweeping strokes, attempting to sever a limb or even a head, or failing that to penetrate Osric's heart.

Now that the combat was under way, there was cheering and yelling, jeering and gesturing from both watching armies. They had all settled down to enjoy the fight, each supporting their champion and sneering at the efforts of the opponent. The remarks were colourful and competition was fierce for extracting a laugh or a cheer from fellow supporters. 'Stick it in his belly!' or 'Chop his head off his shoulders!' were commonplace, but something like, 'Joint the bastard and roast 'im – I don't mind making do with the scrag end! I've only got bread and cheese in my pack!' brought a peel of laughter and further jibes to ripple along both banks.

However, while Osric's attack might not have been the best, his defence was easily the equal of Eadgard's. To the consternation of the king, who all could see was expecting to end the combat with a few well-placed strokes, Osric proved nimble on his feet and quick with his sword hand, leaving just empty air for Eadgard's blade to whistle through. Soon both men were visibly tiring, unable to break through their opponent's defence and deliver a killing blow. After quite a time, with the two fighters weaving back and forth, managing to avoid any contact with metal, Eadgard suddenly yelled out, '*Hold!*' and quickly lowered his weapon.

Osric stepped back, thinking the king had had enough, and was preparing an elated speech in his head. However, Eadgard simply said, 'I need a drink of water.' The king went to Wulfgar, where a goatskin was offered and taken. Then some whispering went on between the king's men and the king himself, obviously they were trying to find a strategy for dealing with this upstart ex-prince.

Osric too was grateful for a drink. He quizzed Tomos and Kenric in the same manner, asking if they could see a weakness in the king's guard. They offered one or two pieces of advice, but there was no real plan forthcoming. When the fight began again in earnest, nothing had really changed. Both fighters were expert at defending and both lacked any real scheme for breaking through the other's guard. Gradually the pair tired again and then things came to a head when both attacked at once, defences abandoned, and suddenly it was all over. Osric received a stab wound in the right side of the chest and Eadgard was slashed open from the base of the neck down his left side to his hip. The injuries were severe enough to cause both fighters to fall to the ground, but neither could take advantage of the other for the final *coup d'grace*. The two of them were dragged back to the boats by their seconds and carried off to separate shores. There Osric was bundled into a cart and the Walha and Mercian army rumbled off westwards, honouring the promise to depart should their champion prove not to be the winner of the combat. The fact that was no winner or loser slightly mollified the complainers, but not a great deal.

SIX

Osric drifted off into a dreamland which was full of pain, yet felt a place of safety, of security. Every so often he came near to the surface of consciousness and was aware of someone playing a harp. Indeed, he was even aware that the instrument was not of mortal making, but had to be a faery harp, since the music it produced was sublime and otherworldly: the music of the spheres. No human could produce such a sound from a harp made by the clumsy hands of a mortal, even one an expert in such craftsmanship or in the art of playing. This had to be a faery instrument and its strings of which plucked and stroked by faery hands. Thus he knew without question that some ethereal creature was in the tent and was producing this beautiful sound which soothed his raging mind and was gradually giving him the peace and tranquillity he needed to get better.

Once he woke up fully, to see a lovely young woman busying herself by a brazier glowing with hot coals. He recognised her as the witch-girl, Sethrith and he asked her in a croaking voice what she was doing.

'Looking after you,' she replied, turning to reveal her features to him.

'Oh – do I need looking after?'

'You've been severely wounded. I've been tending to your hurt. That Tomos didn't want me to go near you and wanted one of the Walha women camp-followers to nurse you, but Kenric would have none of it. He told Tomos that I was one of your women. Huh!' Sethrith reflected a moment on this, then said, 'One of your women! As if I were a slave girl and not a free witch.' Her voice then took on a more practical tone. 'Witches, you know, are very good at healing. We have knowledge of natural cures and can use unnatural ones if they don't work, though the latter have a price which might mean giving something of your soul to those in the world of the dark. Fortunately, nature seems to work on you. You'll find a poultice of goldenrod and yarrow on your chest. Leave it where it is. You're not whole yet.'

He thought about this for a while, but in any case was too weak even to lift his blanket to peer at the injury.

He said, dreamily, 'You could help me by coming under the blanket with me – just to keep me warm.'

'I think such an act, attractive as it seems, would kill you. You will be dead within a few minutes. I am a witch. You are a mortal. We would make love and I would have to eat you afterwards, as a female spider eats its mate. Anyway, I don't think you realise how sick you are. By the way, your wife has been here and I don't think she would appreciate finding me in her husband's bed.'

Osric was surprised. 'My wife? Linnet?' He recalled the sound of the faery harp and knew now the identity of the instrumentalist.

'Yes, a very skinny female elf. Your son brought her. They thought you were going to die. When she found out I could keep you alive, she left me to my devices. Personally, I don't think she was all that concerned for your welfare.'

Osric sighed. 'When an elf ceases to love, it's like a door slamming.'

'Oh, I'm not sure she has stopped loving you. I could see the love for you flickering in her eyes like candlelight. Not burning brightly, but there just the same. Osric, she is angry with you. Very angry. She could not stop talking about her new "life-mate", who apparently is the epitome of all that an elf should be. To hear her talk, you would think she had married the king of the elves. But that was just to conceal her real feelings. Ha! To think even an elf could hide feelings from a witch. We are their match, I can tell you.'

'Sethrith,' he said, 'will you marry me?'

She smiled at him. 'Don't think I'm not flattered, Prince Osric of the East Angles, but the fact is, if a witch marries a mortal she loses all her magical powers. I couldn't give those up on a whim. They're too precious to me. You must find a woman who has less to lose than Sethrith.'

Osric sighed again. At that moment a figure entered the tent and walked over to him. It was Quercus and the boy peered down at him. Quercus's elfen eyes were full of concern. His mother might be angry, but Quercus himself clearly loved his mortal father without reserve. There was nothing but hope in their depths.

'Father, are you feeling better?'

'A little.' It was still very strange being addressed as 'father' by a youth who looked only a bit younger than himself. 'Still very weak.'

'You must rest. I hope the noise of the battle did not disturb you.'

Osric was fading back into sleep now, but the words that Quercus had just spoken alarmed him a great deal.

'Did we attack the East Angles?' he moaned. 'I gave my word...'

'Father, you must not worry about these things. They're not in your hands. All will be well, I promise you. Rest. Sleep. Recover . . '

The wounded man heard the last few sounds coming from his son's mouth, but they were unintelligible to him. His understanding had slipped away somewhere and he was left with nothing but a dun world, a twilight place, where shadows walked and sometimes even danced, but all sensibility was beyond his ken.

Lord Tiw:

Well, good. For a moment there, I thought there would be no War, just single combat on a shabby piece of turf. Where in the annals of great deeds will you find single combat? There needs to be ditches full of blood, severed limbs scattered over the battlefield, lopped heads, pierced hearts, bellies disgorging their guts – all these and more, in their hundreds and thousands. Two men fighting? What is that? A nothing.

Yet, I was not disappointed in the end. There was indeed a healthy battle. The wind of another morning blew over the corpses, its lifting of a piece of clothing here and there the only movement on the field – until of course the crows arrived to crop out eyes and the stoats to tear out tongues.

When he woke the second time, still in the same tent, Sethrith was nowhere to be seen. This time Osric was almost fully *compos mentos.* Finding himself alone, he sat up and yelled for assistance. When no one came he climbed slowly from the litter on which he had been sleeping and staggered towards the doorway of the tent. However, before he could reach it, two men entered: Tomos and Kenric. They both smiled at him and helped him back to the litter, where he sat on its edge and stared at them.

'How long have I been out of my head?'

'Long enough,' said Tomos. 'We need to be getting home.'

'Listen,' Osric said, flexing his arm and getting some pain from his wound for doing so, 'something's been worrying me. Quercus spoke of a battle. I gave my word, Tomos, that we would not attack the Angles. My honour...'

Kenric grinned and Tomos shook his head.

'We attacked no Angles, rest yourself on that one. No, no, Osric. But, you know, my warriors were very disappointed, so they were, to march all the way across the country and find no fight, no spoils at the end of it. I had a hard time keeping them down. If they could have got at you, they might have done you a mischief for robbing them of their battle with your kinfolk. The Mercians were no better, see. Kenric and myself, we had a difficult few days holding the army together and stopping them from going back and carrying out a slaughter.'

Osric blinked. 'But – so, this battle Quercus spoke of?'

'Well, there you have it, Osric. There you have it. The gods thought to supply us with a ready-made enemy, just when we needed it. While we were on the march, slow like, to keep you from slipping off early to Neorxnawang, we came across an army of East Saxons, on their way to fight the Jutes below the great river. So we obliged them with the war they wanted and gave them a good thrashing. Then there was a bonus. The Jutes had come up looking for the East Saxons, knowing there was to be a tussle and so we laid into them too.' Tomos lowered his head for a moment in a sign of respect. 'We lost several good men. Quite a few more wounded and once more we have to proceed slowly across the landscape.

'But on the sunny side, my Angle friend,' and here he smiled, 'we took a lot of gold, a good bit of silver, some fine fabrics – silk even – and a whole lot of slaves. Weapons too. Enough spoils to go round and fill the pockets of my warriors and the Mercians also. Funny day, it was, us fighting alongside bloody Mercians, but there you have it. I'm sure I'll witness stranger sights before I die.'

'A great battle – and I missed it?'

Tomos said, 'There'll be more to be had, during your lifetime, man, so don't fret about one battle.'

'What about Eadgard,' asked Osric, hopefully, 'is he dead?'

It was Kenric who shook his head. 'No, still alive, so we've heard.'

Osric felt despair. 'Then I'm back where I started.'

However, despite the fact that Eadgard was still alive, there was a feeling of great achievement and satisfaction in the camps of the Mercians and the Walha. They had fought two battles and had proved their worth. It was probably a good thing Osric had been lying on his litter, unable to command the army when they met first the Saxons then the Jutes, because he would no doubt have tried to avoid a confrontation, there being only the base spoils of war to reward the winner. Osric was a man unusual for his time in that he did not approve of fighting for fighting's sake. He needed more than the love of glory for sending men to their death. Be that as it may, the thing had been done and his warriors were cock-a-hoop with the result.

That evening the two separate camps celebrated their double victories, the Mercians with a tremendous wassail, the Walha with singing. Indeed, Osric and the Mercians were amazed at the beauty of this male choir of almost seven hundred strong, whose lusty voices filled the night air with song. They had never heard such a sound before in their lives, since their own singing tended to be of the loud and boisterous kind, with little regard to tunefulness. The soft tones, some baritone, some bass, some tenor, none of which would have meant anything to an Angle, all melding together to make a music which filled the hearts of those listening.

The Mercian warrior, Yffi, sitting with his companion Hengist by the campfire, listening to the mellow sound which had silenced their storyteller, said, 'Hengist, are those *tears* I see running down your cheeks?' Hengist, wiping his face quickly with the back of his hand replied, 'Don't be stupid, Yffi. Why would I be crying? It's the smoke from this damn fire, getting into my eyes.' This exchange was typical of many happening within the camp of the Mercians and around the fires of the Walha it was even worse, for Walha men openly gave way to their feelings.

The army was again on the march the next day, tramping over the outeryards of the largely uninhabited midlands towards the country of the Mercians. One night, while they were camped on the edge of an upland moor, a band of peaceful dweorgs emerged warily from their holes and caverns underground and offered – for a price of course – to turn some of the drinking cups and ornamental gold and silver into attractive armrings with sacred patterns on them. Dweorgs being the best metal workers in either the Otherworld or Middangeard, the offer was swiftly accepted and the lumpy pale creatures who lived deep in the earth brought up their tools. They also brought their own fire, for subterranean fire has special properties. It comes from the molten core of the world and has powers to transfer a magical luminescence to the raw material that is melted down by its heat. What the wind-world faerie did with starlight and moonlight, the still-world faerie did with molten lava.

This subsurface race produced the most exquisite jewelled armrings from the gold and silver. These ornaments were sorted into two lots, one pile for the Walha, the other for the Mercians. Osric ordered the Mercian pile to be kept complete, for only a king can be a gold-giver and reward his warriors for their loyalty and bravery in battle. The fact that King Paega was not there, on the battlefield, made absolutely no difference. What the Walha did with their share of the gold was their own affair, but the Mercians had to wait. .

The dweorgs were suitably rewarded, too, being such crafts-creatures as to rival Wayland Smithy in their metalwork. They took their tools, and their fire, back down below the earth to their deep, dark chambers, the ceilings of which were covered in limestone fangs and the floors with upward-pointing tusks. Here their hollow, echoing shouts of joy were contained by upturned bowls of limestone, drowned by the gushing of underground rivers, heard only by bats and sightless snakes. Here they marvelled at the grain in the polished wooden staves which was their price for their work, for they lived in a world of roots and flints, and *their* treasure was the hearts of oak, beech, birch, hornbeam, willow and elm, unobtainable except through trade with those who lived on the surface. They could indeed venture out of their earthen homes to steal such bounty, but at the risk of their lives, for dweorgs are such light-blind creatures that a crow might peck out their living eyes with impunity, or a lynx or bear bite off a toe without fear. Dweorgs have a terror of the unstoppered vault of the open air, which seems to them so vast and unending they need the reassurance of the creatures who live up in this high-ceilinged, sweeping world where one cannot see the beginning or end of it, a place of freezing mists and wild currents of wind could force themselves into their fragile lungs and slow their heartbeats.

That evening Osric spoke with Kenric and Quercus.

'Well,' he said, 'it looks like my venture has been a failure. I am destined to spend my life amongst the Mercians as a farrier. Not a bad life, in the main, but not one my father would have chosen for me. I would have preferred to live amongst my own people, but again, you, Kenric, have also left your ancestral tribe. And you, Quercus, have left your birthplace. The Thief, too, has even crossed the ocean to find a new home. We are all destined to be outcasts for our time on Earth.'

Kenric said, 'I don't think the expedition has been a total failure, Osric. Look, you gave Eadgard a solid whackin' there. He's not goin' to recover from that for a good while. At least he's got something back at last, for all the wrong he's done you and your dad, eh?'

They were in the open air, camped by a wood. A skein of geese flew overhead and Osric followed the arrowhead of birds towards the horizon.

He said, 'Yes, at least I gave him something to hate me for, other than the fact that I'm the son of the man he murdered.'

The geese suddenly did a panicky u-turn still in their v-shaped formation. Out of the sky to the east came a swiftly-flying, young, black dragon. The dragon caught up with the end of one arm of the v and scooped up the whole line of geese into his cavernous mouth. Then he turned and took the other line of the hapless birds head on and they too disappeared down its throat one by one in rapid succession. This amazing event took only a short time, then the well-fed creature with the leathery bat-wings, fiery mouth and long, long, tail shot upwards into the clouds.

'Did you see that?' asked Quercus, his mouth hanging open.

The other two nodded and Kenric said, 'It's a dangerous world out here in the outeryards.'

'It's a dangerous world in the inneryards, too,' replied Osric. 'However, we must get back to our forge.'

'Osric,' said Quercus, obeying that man's orders not to call him 'father' in company, 'you must not give up hope of regaining your ancestral realm. The world of mortals is an unpredictable place. Sometimes things happen that are not laid down by the Wyrd. Of course, it is very unusual for a mortal to deviate from the primal law of the ur-law laid down by the Wyrd, but you, Osric, are an unusual man.'

Osric was not sure that he was much different, essentially, to any other man that walked Middangeard, the Middle Earth, but he was touched by his son's idea that he was special.

'Thank you, cousin, for your kind words.'

The next day the Walha detached themselves from the army of the Mercians, with Tomos saying, 'If we march into King Paega's inneryards with you, he will be nervous. We are, after all, his traditional enemy. He wouldn't trust us and I don't trust him. That's how it should be. Now, Osric, the plunder has been divided equally between the two of us, so we can quite happily be on our way back across the border.' He took Osric's hand on the good side of his body and shook it vigorously. 'You will always be my friend and I will always be yours, whatever happens in the future. You never know, we might come up against each other when you serve on the wall again, so I make no promises that we won't find ourselves in battle against each other. If I kill you, it will be as a friend, not as an enemy.'

'I shall *never* take up a sword against you, Tomos. Never.'

Tomos, big black beard quivering, laughed. 'Ah, you say that, Osric, but you don't know. You never know. This world is an uncertain place. You might have to, my friend. But, hey, until that hopefully never-coming day, be whole, Osric.'

'And you too, Tomos. My thanks go with you. And say a heartfelt hello and thank you to the old Tomos, who gave me such good hospitality.'

Tomos and his army left for the border, swinging in a northward arc to avoid the main villages of the Mercians. The smaller ones, on the fringe of the Angle realm, would get a fright when the Walha warriors skirted them, but there would be no chance of a confrontation, the Mercians being so few in number in those regions. They might even hide when they saw the Walha coming. The Walha warriors would enjoy seeing the Mercians run for cover. Mercia was a large and powerful kingdom. King Paega had never lost a battle and extracted annual tribute from many of the realms that filled the land below the great wall that separated the Painted People, the Picts, from the kingdoms in the milder-weathered southern landscapes. Even the West Saxons, another powerful people, had not escaped the edge of Paega's sword.

Lord Tiw;

Now the fight in the North, that's what I call a War. You can trust a king like Paega to slay enough of the enemy to make the battle worthwhile. That's what you do. You humiliate the foe, leave his numbers so depleted it will take him two generations to get back to normality. Oh yes, there's the king for me. Crush the foe, stamp on his face, leave him utterly spent, leave widows wailing and tearing out hair by the roots.

The Mercian army, with a pale Osric at their head, rode and marched into King Paega's village in triumph. The king himself was back from his war with Deira. Horsa and Headho scowled at Osric when he rode past them in the market place. These two thegns raced to the Great Hall to tell the king the upstart had returned. Osric must have failed, they argued, or he would not be here in Mercia, but ruling his own kingdom of the East Angles.

'Not necessarily,' argued Paega. 'The boy is stupid, but honourable. He may have just led my army back to me to thank me for the loan of it.'

At that moment Osric entered the hall followed by men carrying treasure chests looted from both the East Saxons and the Jutes.

'My lord,' said Osric, 'I failed.'

'Ha!' cried Horsa and Headho in unison, nudging each other.

'Quiet,' muttered King Paega. 'So, you failed in your mission to regain your father's realm?'

Osric nodded. 'I fought single combat with Eadgard. We were both seriously wounded and he was taken away by his thegns and I by my men. As you can see, I recovered. As far as I can ascertain, he too overcame his wound.'

'You're wrong,' growled Paega. 'My spies report that he's dead.'

Osric felt the earth sway for a moment and he almost lost his balance. 'Dead? I killed him? But...'

The king snorted. 'You may have had something to do with it, but he didn't die of his wounds. He died in his bed of the fever that fills the lungs with water. Perhaps your friends the elves had something to do with it? Anyway, you couldn't have claimed your victory because it wasn't your seax that took his life from him, but a sickness of the chest. Kings should not be subject to such ailments.'

'I agree and I think they are not,' replied Osric, 'since Eadgard was never a king.'

Paega smiled at this, his closely-shaven face glistening.

'Well said, lad. However, you're back where you started because Wulfgar has taken his place and proclaimed himself Lord of the East Angles.'

Bitter feeling surged through Osric on hearing this. 'I suppose I could not have expected anything else. Damn his eyes and liver.'

'That's as it is and things as they are. Now, I understand you gave your word to the East Angles that you would not wage war on them if you were unsuccessful in your single combat.'

'That's true, my lord.'

Paega's eyebrows were raised. 'And you kept your word?'

'Indeed, I was surely bound to. Frith, my lord. The virtue of honour? My soul would have been stained forever if I had broken my word.'

Horsa and Headho laughed out loud at this, but the king waved a hand gently to quieten them, though there was an amused smile on his face.

'Very commendable. You gave your word to a murderer, the man who killed your father, and were bound in all honour to keep it.'

Osric drew in breath. 'Well, when you put it like that…'

'How else is one to put it? You were dealing with a cockchafer whose honour had not only been stained, but lost in a pit of sins against the gods. You could have recovered from your wounds and returned to your old country to slaughter its people. This should have occurred, boy, and I would have been enraged had it not been for the fact that your army found two other armies to fight instead. I have heard you had a brace of battles, one against the Saxon, the other against the Jute. Are these the spoils of those battles you bring me here?'

Osric swallowed his anger at the way things had turned out and nodded at the chests which had been laid at the feet of Paega and opened to reveal the jewels, fabrics and other riches within them. 'These are yours, my lord. I have also taken the liberty of having armrings forged for you to hand out to the warriors – we met some dweorgs who fashioned the rings for us. I have a list of the names of the bravest and most intrepid of your warriors – those who performed with particular skill and courage.'

Osric handed the parchment to Paega, who took it and nodded sagely as he read the names, as if they were those he expected to be there. On occasion his eyes widened a little, probably finding one that he had not realised had such worth in him, his grim mouth stretching a little to register his approval. Finally the king finished reading and rolled up the parchment, saying, 'Your name is not on the list.'

'No, my lord. To my regret I did not take part in the battle…'

There was a quiet chortle from Horsa and Headho.

'… unfortunately I was lying without conscious thought on a litter recovering from the single combat with Eadgard. I only came to myself after the battle was over and therefore took no part in it, not even to offer strategy or tactics to Tomos, the Walha leader of his army. You will however see the names of my good friend Kenric on the list and also that of my cousin Quercus, both of whom I am told performed with outstanding bravery and success. Quercus did not take part in the killing, but he did tend the wounded in the midst of savage fighting without regard for…'

Paega interrupted, seeming out of patience.

'Young man,' said the king, 'you are much too honest to go far in this world. You'll never make a king, I'm afraid, despite your antecedents. I will reward each and every one of the men on this roll of honour. Additional to that, I will also reward you, yourself, for the success of your single combat. Whatever the outcome of the fight, he died and you stand there, breathing air. You performed with great bravery. Single combat is never easy. Going into battle with ten thousand men around you is preferable to preparing for and going off to fight to the death with one opponent, especially a larger and more experienced one. I would liken it to waiting for the dawn to arrive when you expect to be hung or drawn for a crime. The agony is in the waiting and the turmoil of thoughts swirling around in your mind.

'Your reward is both gold and flesh – you shall marry my daughter, Rowena.' With that the king snapped his fingers and the beautiful raven-haired Rowena, youngest of the king's three daughters, came from a corner of the Great Hall wearing, as her name suggests, a pure white gown that accentuated the darkness of her eyes and hair. She looked ravishingly beautiful. Osric was astonished by the loveliness of the woman who stood before him, her head bowed but her eyes turned up to stare at him. There was a little smile on her face. However, he had no wish to marry this maiden, despite the fact that it was obviously a great honour to be given the opportunity.

'My lord, my lord,' cried Osric, hastily, 'the honour is too great. I'm sure the girl, that is Rowena, has no love for me, a grubby though hard-working farrier.'

The king snorted. 'What's love got to do with anything? Anyway, she's already called you a 'beautiful young man' in front of the queen and myself, a statement that almost made me vomit down my jerkin. You will marry her and that's final, whether she wants you or not. It'll be a bad day when women have the choice of their husbands. What trash they'll come up with then, I don't doubt.'

'Well,' said Osric, 'I am greatly honoured, to be sure, but I'm already married my lord.'

The king's head jerked backwards. 'To whom? And if so, why have you been making eyes at Rowena here, if you already have a wife in your bed?'

'It's,' Osric found himself giggling nervously, 'it's a bit strange, my lord. I have no wife in my bed. My wife is an elf by the name of Linnet, who resides in the forest above the river which separates my home villages from the outeryards. She cannot leave her kind, or she'll simply waste away. Elves, you know…'

'I don't want to know about *elves*,' yelled King Paega, 'I've never heard of such nonsense. You can't marry an elf. They're not human. It just doesn't count.' He calmed down for a moment. 'You'll have to, at some time, tell me what it was like – you know, beneath the sheets with a female elf – I'm intrigued, I must admit, but as an impediment against you marrying my daughter Rowena, why it's ludicrous. You owe no allegiance to such a marriage. It's outside the laws of mankind. No good can come of such liaisons. What next? We'll have half-elves running around the kingdom causing all sorts of havoc, souring milk churns and stealing butter! Utter chaos. I take it there were no offspring that emerged from this union of fools?'

Osric was torn between the truth and the bent truth, knowing that if Paega discovered a 'half-elf' was running wild around his kingdom, he would have Quercus banished at the very least, executed at the very worst. In the end he went for the latter option, since he did not regard himself as a fool, nor his dear Linnet. So indeed, no offspring emerged from 'a union of fools'.

'Nothing like that has happened, my lord.'

'Right, Rowena will take your hand in marriage and you'll be my son-in-law before the end of the month. Those two idiots there,' Horsa and Headho, 'will find themselves outranked by the one they've been making jokes about all week. They don't think much of you, you know, so once you're family you might want to send them to the wall for a few weeks as ordinary warriors, to teach them a bit of respect. It's what I would do and what I would expect from any son-in-law of mine.'

The looks on the two faces of the nobles was enough to set the king roaring with laughter and even Rowena let out a few sniggers.

'You don't want me, do you?' Osric asked the beautiful Rowena. 'I mean, I've done nothing to gain any stature. I failed to lead my army against the East Angles.'

'You are a hero,' she said, simply. 'You fought single combat against a man with twice your experience in warfare and you triumphed.'

'Well, not exactly…'

'Enough of this debate, farrier. You can't win against my daughter anyway. She's far too intelligent for the likes of you. You two are getting married and that's an end to it. Now go and prepare yourself, while I make the arrangements here.'

Osric was in a daze when he left the king's presence. Yes, the king's daughter was lovely. Too lovely, really. When a woman was that beautiful it often happened that she believed the world should be laid at her feet. Dazzlingly beautiful women, despite the fact that it was merely an accident of birth that they were so, expected to command. A husband of such a woman might be running around most of the time, satisfying his wife's whims, especially if she were the daughter of a king and he, the spouse, a mere jumped-up farrier pretending to be a prince. It did not bode well for Osric's future and on the way back to the forge he even thought of marrying the first single female churl that he came across, to thwart the king's plans. Some of those farm girls and kitchen maids were quite pretty and would possibly be grateful to become the wife of a farrier. Then again, he reflected miserably, sometimes they weren't all that grateful and they too wished to rule the house. No, it was only love that sorted it all out. Love put both groom and bride on a level footing, and led to that wonderful state called compromise, with no swayer in the home.

In any case, if he did marry the first lovely wench he came across, the king would have him executed for treason.

When he arrived back at the forge, his three companions crowded round him.

'What happened?' enquired the Thief.

'Are we to get gold armrings?' asked Kenric.

'What terrible news did you hear?' questioned Quercus.

His half-elf son had obviously seen by his expression that all was not well.

'I am commanded to marry Rowena, the king's youngest daughter,' said Osric, with a sigh.

Silence followed this piece of information for at least two minutes, then Kenric said, 'Well, you always fancied the maid.'

'Lady,' corrected the Thief, 'she is a princess, remember.'

'You cannot marry anyone,' cried a distressed Quercus, 'for you are already married.'

Osric knew this news was particularly upsetting to his son, since it was his mother who was being dismissed out of hand.

'I told the king that and he poo-hooed it. Said marriage to an elf didn't count.'

'Didn't count?' cried Quercus. 'Of course it counts. Linnet is your wife.'

The Thief and Kenric stared at the half-elf, probably wondering how he knew the name of Osric's elfen love.

'Well, though, Quercus, you know,' bumbled Osric, 'I think she married again after I left, didn't she?'

The boy's face fell and the misery showed through the elfen features. 'I had always hoped – that is – I wished you and my mother might one day…'

'Get back together? I think not, son. She could never leave the elfen glades and I could not confine myself to living a life in a hundred acres of ground.'

Kenric's mouth had fallen open. 'Son? You called him *son*?'

'Yes, Quercus is my – my offspring,' growled Osric. 'Elves grow to adulthood much swifter than mortals. I think you,' he nodded at the Thief, 'have already guessed there was something a bit strange about our relationship. Well, there you have it. Father and son. And both proud of the fact. However, this does not solve my problem. How to get out of this marriage. Yes, she is a lovely woman –' Osric's tone drifted off into a dreamy note '– and yes, of course I would like to bed her. Who would not? Creamy skin, lovely shape, nice eyes… but there, no, *no*, I think it would be all wrong. I do not love her. I once thought I did, but now it has come to marriage I see the folly of my feelings. They were shallow ones, interested only in the coupling and not in the living-with. I'm sure it would be a disastrous marriage of two quite different souls.'

'Indeed,' said the astute Thief, 'she would rule the roost.'

'There is that to take into consideration,' agreed Osric, as if he had not already thought about this aspect of the affair and acknowledged the importance of it. 'Also the fact that I would have to spend a great deal of time with her father.'

'The gods save you from that!' Kenric said, emphatically. 'The man eats like a pig and flies off into a temper at the least imagined slight.'

'It's all part and parcel of being a king,' agreed the Thief. 'No one dares to curb the temper of a king or tell him not to speak with his mouth full.'

'So,' said Osric, looking hopefully at his companions, 'how do I get out of this unwelcome marriage?'

All eyes were on the floor or ceiling. Indeed, no one had an answer.

SEVEN

Before the marriage was to take place, there was the ring-giving ceremony. King Paega obviously enjoyed this exercise. He loved being seen as the generous, benevolent lord who rewarded his people for their services. And, to be fair, those who were rewarded loved it too. They were heroes, exalted amongst their fellow warriors, men who had shown great courage in battle. Kenric was one of these and the now well-built and strong-jawed man was pleased to receive his silver armring (gold being reserved for thegns and the king's hearth-companions) even though he had little regard for the ring-giver. He stepped forward, *jogged* forward, when his name was called, while Osric, Quercus and the Thief cheered him from the side-lines. The king looked a little bored at this juncture, having dealt with the gold armring receivers, but still this did not spoil the day for the men from the farriers' forge.

It was a double ceremony, taking in five battles: three fought in the north against the Umbrians and the two in the south, one against the East Saxons, the other against the Jutes. The greatest warrior of the day was of course King Paega, who always fought in the vanguard surrounded by his nobles, and was indeed one of the fiercest and most ferocious of fighters. A savage man with the warhammer and a skilful man with the sword. He was, it could be said in all truth, the most feared and expert killer in all the lands of the Angles, Saxons and Jutes, admired by men and women throughout the island. It was no wonder he received tribute from many different realms and held sway over a vast landscape.

Osric was given a special ceremony all to himself, no doubt at the instigation of his bride-to-be. Rowena would not want her future husband to be seen as someone ordinary, but a man of great renown and special powers. A man of great character, fortitude and bravery. Thus this particular ring-giving, the presentation of the best of all the gold armrings decorated by the dweorg metalsmiths, took place last in the Great Hall of King Paega of the Mercians.

There were two flying dragons etched into the shiny surface of a ring that was a finger-length wide – the largest of all the rings that had been given that day – three beautiful wolves that prowled the edges of the ring, and two ravens that perched together, faces turned towards each other. Embedded in the metal were garnets from a far distant land that no one knew the name of. These dark-red gems, polished to a tone that resembled fresh drops of blood, had come across the world through trading between neighbouring nations, until they finally came to a full stop in Mercia. The only other place they could go would be over the short stretch of sea to the next island where a king called Diarmait mac Cerbaill was busy turning the religion of his clansmen around by ordering his people to pray to one god alone, a solitary deity imported from a hot land thousands of miles away. The armring was indeed a thing of great beauty and worth, and even as Paega was presenting Osric with this honour his eyes glittered a little and those who knew him realised he was wondering whether he was making a mistake and should keep the object for himself.

Osric argued that he had taken part in none of the battles, but the king told him to hold his tongue. He had, he was reminded, defeated King Eadgard in single combat: or at least, been responsible for his death. This event had changed the face of power across the wider landscape of the Angles' land. Osric didn't think there was a great deal of difference between an East Angles ruled by Eadgard and one ruled by Wulfgar, except the latter was probably a tad more vicious and cruel than the former. However, he knew he was not going to influence the ceremony at all with his protestations, so he accepted his lot and received the armring with great dignity and solemnity, thus impressing all who were there for the treat. They wanted their heroes to be great heroes. Modesty was not a trait that Mercians or indeed any other nation on the island thought becoming. You swaggered, you boasted, you showed you were the great man with the wild spirit, and everyone loved you for it.

'Well, I'm glad that's over,' said Osric, once the four were all back in their inneryard again. 'Not that the warriors didn't deserve their rings. They did. So did you, Kenric. I was told you fought like a leader of men. That you used your head as well as your fury. To fight two battles, one after the other, and be victorious in both – well that takes some doing. And you did it, you and Tomos and the others.

'But as to the ceremony. That's more for King Paega's sake than ours. He likes handing out largesse. Bountiful Paega. And as for that queen of his, Beornwynne, she sits there looking smug and fat as if to say, "Look at me, aren't I clever to marry the biggest bruiser in the kingdom? And now I'm as powerful as he is."'

'The queen is not fat,' interjected Quercus. 'She has an ample figure, but it is more voluptuous than over-heavy.'

'I like them a little slimmer,' retorted his father.

'And you're going to get one as thin as a reed,' said Kenric, pouring another measure of mead for the Thief, who was by this time in the evening, usually quite mellow in his cups.

'She's not *that* skinny,' replied Osric.

'Thinner than I like 'em.'

'Well, let's not get into an argument about taste. Something that princes naturally have imbedded in their bones and sons of farriers spend a lifetime trying to acquire, usually without success.'

'Whoa!' cried Kenric. 'Insults already. An' it's only just dark.'

Osric grumbled to himself after that, trying to concoct a plan for getting out of the coming wedding. It was true he fell in love with almost every pretty girl he met, but once marriage was mentioned the object of his passion became a lot less attractive all of a sudden. Suddenly that sweet voice had an undertone of a squeaking gate and jarred on the ear, the beautiful complexion was a bit too floury, the big wide blue eyes protruded somewhat and the pert pointed breasts looked dangerous rather than inviting. He did not know how it happened, but all of a moment the delightful pretty red-headed faun became a sly-looking, mean little vixen.

He was still brooding on this when he went out into the wood yard to collect logs for the fire. When an invisible someone spoke to him out of the thin air, he thought it might be Linnet, but then he recognised the voice as being that of Sethrith. He was going to get no peace from friends, he realised, from either the mortal world or the otherworld. One usually looked for solace in one's hearth companions, but Osric seemed to be the exception to this rule. His acquaintances enjoyed baiting him and arousing irksome feelings.

'So,' said the ethereal witch, 'what have you got yourself into now?'

'Oh, Sethrith,' said Osric, in a heartfelt manner. He dropped the bundle of wood from his arms and reached out to hug her. She stepped back and said, 'You are spoken for, Osric, are you not?'

'But I don't want to be,' he replied, miserably. Then he brightened. 'You – Sethrith, you're a witch. Magic me out of this quandary.'

'Now, you know if I could do something like that, I would have made you king of your beloved East Angles before now. I can't interfere with your ur-law, laid down by the Wyrd at your birth. Your life is in their hands, Osric, and they would take away my magic if I started changing the live-patterns they have set out.'

'Quercus tells me that it's possible to deviate from one's ur-law.'

'In little things. Very small ways. This is a big thing. Marriage. One of the biggest in a man's life. Birth, marriage, death.'

Osric snorted and was foolish enough to let his frustration with his lot run away with him. 'Then what can you do? You're supposed to be a witch. I haven't seen you do anything special yet.'

A frown appeared on Sethrith's normally smooth pale brow.

'Well, I did save your life after you were mortally wounded by King Eadgard – but that's just a little thing, really.'

Osric stared at the young woman standing before him, not knowing what to say.

'And if you like,' continued Sethrith, 'I could change you into a toad for the day, just to teach you some manners.'

'I'm sorry. Sorry,' blurted Osric. 'It's just that I don't know what to do. But I shouldn't take it out on others, I know. I've hurt my son, Quercus badly. He was hoping I would get back with his mother, you see, and he's very upset with the situation. With me.' He made a face then said, 'Have you come for any good reason? Or just to gloat? I know what a pathetic creature I am, Sethrith. You don't need to tell me.'

'I came to offer you my congratulations, but I see what is required is an offer of sympathy.'

'I'm being pathetic, aren't I? When really I should be grateful. This marriage puts me in a position of great power. The son-in-law of the king. I should be celebrating my good fortune. Yet… yet, I can't help feeling this is one of the biggest mistakes I'm going to make in my life. I genuinely don't want to marry this woman.' He stared at Sethrith. 'You. It's you I should be marrying, if anyone. But you're a witch and can't marry a mortal without losing your powers.'

'And you have to ask yourself, does this witch want to marry *you*?'

'Oh, probably not.'

'Well, I'm fond of you enough to come and warn you. One thing I can do is look into the plots of others. This wedding is the prelude to your murder, Osric, so be warned. Once you are married you will be given the duty of ambassador to Bernicia, accompanied by your new wife – who, by the way, is not all she appears to be, but… well, you'll find out – and that wife has been instructed to kill you in your sleep and blame

Ewin, the king of Bernicia. This will give Paega the excuse to go north again, capture and execute Ewin, and take over Bernician completely. Bernicia is not strong enough to oppose him. He will then be king of both realms.'

'Lord-of-the-Gallows, that's a monstrous plan,' cried Osric. 'He would really have his son-in-law murdered in order to justify his actions in the eyes of others?'

'Even Paega needs the approval of the masses, Osric. If he were simply to march on Bernicia and kill its king, the Bernicians would forever be steeped in hatred and in revolt. He needs to be seen as the just and righteous punisher of evil, if he is to take a whole fiefdom for his own.'

'Well, I shan't be that easy to kill, you can be sure of that,' snarled Osric, as he contemplated this scenario. 'Thank you for the warning, Sethrith. I am in your debt.'

'I must leave you now.'

She looked so beautiful, standing there in her gossamer dress, her lovely body visible through the material, her bright wide eyes shining, her long lustrous hair burnished by the sun, it brought a lump to Osric's throat. She vanished before he could add anything to what he had already said. Once more in his life he felt hopeless and helpless, subject to the vagaries of the winds of change.

Lady Freo:
So, Ing's favourite mortal is to marry a second time? Is he not already wed to one of my elves, a female of exceptional beauty and disposition? My brother needs to choose his favourites a little more carefully. I am inclined to take this prince out onto the moors and leave him to die.

Lord Ing:
Hmmm, my sister is unhappy with this match, as am I, but the young fellow is not marrying out of love or even lust, he's being forced into the match. If she takes him out into onto a moor in his sleep, then I'll simply bring him back again. I must speak with her before she does something stupid. This prince is, after all, a father to a half-elf.

The wedding took place in the middle of the Winterfylleth-monath, the first full moon of the cold season, the moon that belongs to hunters. In this month, once the lunar orb was in full bloom, there was indeed a hunt almost every night. The king and his thegns revelled in charging around in the moonlight, scattering moonshadows and spearing boar and deer. There was sacrifice and feasting and general wassailing, the drinking horn being used with great abandon and much mead going down the throats of churls, thegns and craftsmen of all types, from farriers to butchers to swordsmiths, to bakers to washerfolk and of course sluggards and wastrels.

Woden, too, with his spectres, and occasionally gods like Ing and Loki, swept through the night skies on the Wild Hunt with mouths of thunder and eyes that discharged lightning. The one-eyed god on his eight-legged steed chased down the celestial boar with his band of ghosts-riders, sometime high above the earth amongst the clouds, sometimes lower and skimming bushes on in the outeryard wastelands. Careering over moor and woodland, over village and farm, the huntsmen wheeled and turned with the terrified quarry, scattering birds from their nests and frightening any creature on the ground. Those mortals who were unfortunate enough to witness the terrible sight expected to die before the morning sun rose in the east.

The wedding was, naturally since a prince was marrying a princess, a magnificent affair. The Great Hall was filled with dignitaries both royal and common, from several different Angle and Saxon nations. The king of the Walha was there, too, a truce being declared amongst all Mercia's enemies for the period of the wedding. It was rumoured that the Fairy King was among the guests, along with the King of the Elves, but since these were invisible invitees, no one could be sure this was fact. The one king who did not attend was Wulfgar, Lord of the East Angles, which was just as well since there would have been a blood-bath not a marriage, had he turned up with his thegns. King Paega might have been able to step back from his enemies for a few days, but Osric was not made in the same prosaic mould as the King of Mercia, being more inclined to give in instantly to heightened emotions.

All those who did attend brought wonderful gifts of gold, silver, gems, perfumes, textiles, weapons, tools and slaves, all of which Rowena quietly salted away in one of her houses guarded by several loyal thegns. It was doubtful that Osric even saw any of these wedding presents and was so distracted he probably wouldn't have been interested in them anyway. He wandered about in the fine wolfskin cloak, given to him by the king, its cowl having a silvery sheen, wondering how he had come to this beginning, or perhaps it was an end?

Indeed, he was caught up in the fever of the excitement for who could not be, with servants rushing around everywhere, colourful tents and awnings appearing like toadstools covered in morning dew, feasting tables being laid, banners and flags flying, and marshals roaring from every corner, making sure that preparations were perfect and on time, or someone would be sorry. Queen Beornwynne, mother of the bride, was in the centre of this melee, yelling orders with the loud voice of a tin-pan pedlar, marshalling the marshals, yelling at Osric to keep out of the way because he wasn't important yet and was a bloody nuisance, fussing over the caterers, greeting the guests in quite a different voice to her supervising one, and kicking young kitchen boys up the backside when they got in her way.

Osric began to feel that being married to Rowena might not be such a bad thing, if this was an exhibition of what you could do with your royal power. Also, he was a lustful young man and was looking forward with great anticipation to the bedding of his bride, who would undoubtedly be a virgin.

Then, too, he would at last be wealthy, surely? Yes, he had to be on his guard in case the prophecy that Sethrith had spoken turned out to be fact. However, it was possibly that the witch was jealous and the tale was either untrue or exaggerated. He, Osric, could still enjoy the fruits of being a noble while keeping a weather eye out for any skulduggery. So why not let things take their course and take advantage of the fact that kings usually let their son-in-laws dip into the treasury pot.

The actual ceremony went well, though Osric was in a daze most of the time. On the periphery of the crowd he could see his three companions: his son, looking glum; his best friend, Kenric, grinning; the Thief, looking calm but serious. When the formalities were over the dancing, the music and the feasting began. On occasion it started to get riotous, but the queen's guards moved in and threw the troublemakers out into the dirt. So, the evening moved on, sometimes swiftly, sometimes slowly for Osric, until the time came when he escorted his bride to the bridal chamber, which he did with all the jeers and cheers of the drunken crowd in his ears. He was excited. Indeed, she was a beautiful woman. She smelled wonderful, she looked wonderful, she was soft-skinned, clear-eyed and very sweet.

Once in the chamber, he stared at her, his sexual desire rising, when suddenly the king entered the room.

'So, that's that over,' said the king, in a weary voice, 'and time for you to be on your way, young man.'

Osric started, stepping backward quickly. 'On my way, Father?'

'Home. To your forge, or wherever you sleep.' The king frowned a little. 'And don't ever call me 'Father' again, or I'll have you flogged.' He looked at his daughter for a moment, then said, 'On the other hand I don't want you going with bawds tonight. No doubt the lust is raging through your veins in anticipation of bedding my Rowena and if you can't have her, you'll go and find a churl wench. Spearing a tart tonight would be very disrespectful of my daughter. You'll sleep here until morning, but not in her bed. On the floor, or on that bench in the corner.'

'But, I'm *married* to Rowena.'

'Yes, you are, thank the gods. Now that little Bernician shit Ewin can stop asking me for her hand. Ah, you look puzzled. Well, the reason I wanted you to marry Rowena was so I didn't have to make an alliance in marriage with my enemies, who continually press me to let them have Rowena for a wife, the youngest and last of my unmarried daughters. I want no close ties with any of them which might cause me to hesitate about going to war against one of them. If she's married already, they can't have her, can they? However,' he sounded off-hand, 'neither can you. Rowena doesn't want you. You will come and chat with her on occasion, if she requires you to, but forget anything to do with under the blankets. That's never going to happen.' He laughed. 'Now, I don't want to see you here when I come back in the morning. By then you will have said your goodbyes to your wife and have left. Oh, by the way, my third steed needs shoeing this week.'

With that the king left the room, leaving Osric stunned and devastated. The young man turned to Rowena.

'What do you have to say about this?'

She shrugged. 'I just do what I'm told. I'm a girl.'

'But, we could – you know – do it now, and then he'll have to...'

'Osric,' she sighed, 'you don't understand. I like girls.'

'So? Girls are lovely creatures. I like girls.

'You really don't understand. I like girls in the way that you like girls, to do things with.'

He stared at her for a few moments, assimilating this strange piece of information, then recalled that there were boys who liked boys, though it was never spoken of openly. It made sense that girls might like girls in that way too. It was all a bit too much to take in for one day, especially on his wedding night. The worst possible end to it all: he had been forced to marry a woman he did not love and even denied the compensation of taking her to bed at the end of the day.

'I've been destroyed,' he said, sitting down on one of the chairs in the room. 'I've lost my father's kingdom, I've lost my princedom and now I've lost the woman I've only just married...'

'You haven't lost me, Osric, because you never had me.'

'That's true, but I've lost my self-respect and I'm going to lose the respect of every man in Mercia – and beyond.' He was suddenly horrified to think that this fiasco was going to reach the ears of Wulfgar. 'I'll be a laughing stock and I'll be dead within a week, because I won't be able to stop myself from challenging any bastard that uses me as a target for their jeers. I'll either be killed by one of them or I'll be executed for murdering them. It's monstrous. Your father will rot for this.'

'This?' she laughed at him. 'This is nothing. My father has done things that would make you blanch. Things that would make you sick to your stomach. He won't rot for this, because when the judges get round to this small event in his life, he'll already have been pilloried for things that would curl the toes of Woden.' She paused, then, stroking his hair gently, added, 'No one will hear about this outside this village. My father would decapitate the first man who insulted me. You will go back to your forge and I will stay here with my father, but everyone will be told we're happily wed – it's just that you love your work with horses. You'll visit my home often, especially in the evenings. Walk in the twilight and smile at the people you pass. Bid them a fine evening and tell them there's a meal on the table prepared for you by the Princess Rowena. This much will be true. On occasion you'll stay the night on a single bed and leave in the morning, in the grey light of a new dawn. Again you'll smile and wish them a sunkissed morning, wink at the men as if to say you've had a night they would envy in the bed of a beautiful woman. Nod at the women and say how fine they look and how you wish them good grace, and may they be canny at the market. Everything will be as it should. A man must work and a man must do the kind of work that he enjoys and suits him best. There, I'm finished.'

He spent a long hard night on an oak bench, then late in the morning, feeling as low as he had ever felt, went to the forge. On the way there he spoke to villagers he passed, smiling like he was mad with joy.

'Be Whole, Tresca, may your children be strong.'

'How is your back today, Ornoth? Perhaps the elves will stay in the trees this morning and not bother you?'

'Esel, how beautiful you look in the dawn's light. I can say that to you now, because I'm a married man, and there can be no mistaking my intentions.'

When he reached the forge, two men were working, the thief at the anvil hammering out a shoe, Kenric at the forge, using bellows to get the fire to a white heat. The half-elf was out somewhere communing with nature as was his wont. Kenric and the Thief watched in puzzlement as the newly-wedded man put on a leather apron. Their mouths dropped open when he picked up a hammer. Their eyes went wide with disbelief as he snatched a pair tongs from a hook on the door in his free hand. Then Osric removed a red-hot lump of iron from the open mouth of the forge and began to hammer it into some sort of shape. Sparks flew in a shower as he struck the metal, falling like bright rain on the dirt floor.

Finally, Kenric spoke. 'You've come to work.'

'Looks like it,' grunted Osric.

'Well, I thought you'd be out hunting this morning – I saw the king go by with his thegns just after dawn.'

'Did you now?' Osric continued to work, not looking up.

'Well, shouldn't you have gone with your father-in-law?'

Now he looked up, grinning impishly, 'After a night alongside his daughter? The king is a man like us. He knows that I wanted a little bit longer between the blankets… hellmouth,' his face lost its false smile, 'you might as well know, I've been kicked back here. It was all a ruse to fool Ewin of Umberland and other chieftains who wanted to marry the king's last daughter to their sons or brothers. Everyone wants to be family to Paega so he'll leave them alone. The king, on the other hand, wants no such ties which would inhibit his ability to go to war. No, I didn't bed the princess, nor will I ever. They used me like the fool that I am. One day,' Osric stared at the misty horizon where the trees began, 'I will have that bastard Paega at the point of my sword, begging me not to pierce his heart. One day.'

The Thief nodded, making a sympathetic face.

'In the meantime,' said the foreigner to their land, 'we have horses to shoe and the day is short, so let's get to the work.'

They did so, none of them with more energy than Osric, who was trying to work the boiling fury out of his system.

EIGHT

Three days after the wedding, King Paega sent a messenger to the forge demanding the presence of his son-in-law. Osric took off his leather apron, wet his hair and smoothed it down, put on his best jerkin, and off he went full of hope. Surely Paega had had a change of heart and was going to put Osric in with his family? Perhaps he had even ordered Rowena to satisfy her husband's sexual needs? Not that Osric wanted a woman who clearly did not want *him* but it would bring her closer and make life more comfortable. They could muddle along quite happily in a nice large house: a place that could accommodate his three companions as well as himself.

'You're going on a state visit with your wife.'

Paega was breaking his fast, gnawing with smacking sounds on a cold haunch of venison that had been last night's supper. There was congealed, white fat around his mouth, making his lips look bulbous and shiny as he slobbered over the meat. His queen was looking at her husband with an expression of distaste, and tugged irritably at the cuffs of the long sleeves of her dress, a sure sign that she was getting angry. The queen did not like noisy, sloppy eaters at the best of times, especially when she was working at her loom and needed to concentrate.

'A state visit?' repeated Osric, tonelessly. 'What's that?'

'In order to keep the tributes coming in, without having to decide whether to go to war every five minutes, I've decided to send people like you, family, on state visits to my subject-kings. While you're there you can gauge the general mood and send a messenger back if there's revolt in the air. Some family members are less important than others. You, for example, mean very little to me. I'm telling you this, since there's the obvious possibility that you'll be taken and used as hostages. So, put on your best clothes, grab your new bride, and set off up north to the Bernicians. There you'll stay with Ewin for a few weeks, letting him show you off to that dim-witted, snot-faced populace of his. Watch yourself, though, because he's as sly as a weasel, that man. He smiles too much and the smiles are cold and unfriendly.'

'Your daughter. Isn't she important to you?'

'Yes, of course she is, you oaf. But Ewin would never harm Rowena. He's besotted with her. He's more likely to arrange an accident to get rid of you – get you out of the way so that he can marry her himself. That's another reason why you should watch you back. I shan't be very happy if you go and get yourself killed and I lose my lovely daughter to that prick in the north.'

'Can I take my companions?'

'Take who you like, but I want you on your way by noon.'

So, thought Osric, Sethrith's prophecy begins to take shape.

Osric went back to the forge and told the others what was happening.

'Someone's got to stay with the forge,' said the Thief. 'I'll do that. The rest of you can go with Osric.'

Quercus was excited. 'I'd like to see Bernicia, though they say the winds up there are cold and cruel, and the rain can be endlessly merciless.'

'Nice,' muttered a sarcastic Kenric. 'Cruel and merciless weather. I'm looking forward to it.' He went off to find his seax.

When they were all ready, they set out on horseback for the Great Hall. There they found Rowena waiting impatiently, sitting on a litter. A number of warriors, some mounted, others on foot, were milling around her. Two maids were standing by the litter, one of them a beautiful girl of around eighteen summers. This young lass was holding Rowena's hand and she smirked at Osric when he glared at her. Osric rode up on Magic knowing he was looking very heroic and handsome on his elfen horse, but realising this image would mean nothing to either of the hand-holders.

'Time we were off,' he barked. 'Everyone ready?'

'We've been ready since the cock crowed,' replied Rowena, snuggling down amongst the animal hide blankets which covered her.

It was indeed quite cold. The men were all in wolfskin cloaks or thick woollen garments. Many had bound their feet and had leather that, unlike their summer sandals, covered each of their whole feet. Fur hats were pulled own over their ears. It was going to be an uncomfortable journey and why the king hadn't waited until the following spring was beyond both the farrier-prince and his princess.

The march north-eastwards was slow. The wilderness on the way to Umbria was even more rugged and craggy than the Mercian scenery, toothed with great black rocks that jutted from vast windswept heather-covered plains. Osric realised what a gentle childhood had been his. The countryside of the East Angles was docile, with soft, sloping downs and quiet rivers. This landscape was shaggy and harsh, with deep sweeping dips and wild dales through which fierce brown rivers crashed. There were high waterfalls and waterforces at every turn. In the upland places the freezing winds cut people in half and in the low valleys the shadows were as solid as ice. Osric cursed his father-in-law for sending him out in the winter, to a kingdom he knew nothing about, in order to spy on its ruler. One of the party had already died on the march, an elderly female companion of Rowena's and it was certain others would succumb to the terrible weather over this exposed landscape. Paega was a foul man and if Osric disliked him before, he despised him now. The Mercian king had no finer feelings for any of his people. Even his daughter was a thing to be used for his own purposes. Paega was self-serving tyrant, interested solely in personal power.

The weather did not abate. Sleet, snow and rain dogged them almost all the way. There were two wagons of supplies, the wheels of which kept getting bogged down or caught in frozen ruts. These had to be heaved and levered out every two or three miles. Though they were able to stop at poor outlying villages, who were forced to offer them a roof over their heads, the hovels these half-starved villagers lived in were pitiful defence against the onslaught of the cruel, scything weather. They lay on the straw-covered floors of shelters whose roofs were like sieves, the thatch having been eaten by rats or robbed by nesting birds. It was difficult to make fires in the pouring rain, even under lean-tos of staves and hides. It was indeed a terrible, miserable march which had the warriors cursing their grandmothers for giving birth to their mothers and thus bringing they themselves into the world. Rowena never stopped complaining about being cold, wet and hungry. By the time they reached Bernicia, having passed through the smaller realm of Deira where the fearful inhabitants shut themselves inside their dwellings, they were all as miserable as could possibly be imagined.

Ewin of Bernicia was there to meet them when they arrived. After a string of profuse greetings he led the main party to the Great Hall where a roaring fire in a weather-proof building the size of a large barn awaited them. The Mercian warriors were sent to huts on the edge of the large village where they were pointedly ignored by the Bernician warriors they had been fighting against not so long ago. Palpable hatred was in the air and not surprisingly so, since the slaughter had been rather one-sided.

Ewin was a thin man with thin straight hair, though which you could see his skull, and a hook nose. Some said he was a follower of the passive god imported from a land far over the seas: the one god that Paega hated so much for being both foreign and womanish. Perhaps it was *because* Paega loathed this deity that Ewin was secretly in favour of it. He offered Osric his sword hand to shake and the long thin fingers and palm felt like a slice of yesterday's bacon: cold, greasy and unpalatable. Rowena simply ignored any effort to gain her attention and Kenric went straight to the kitchens to fill his belly with hot soup.

Rowena asked for her quarters and was taken away along with her maids with the promise that there would be a feast that evening in the Great Hall in her honour, in answer to which she blew out her cheeks. Osric introduced Quercus as his cousin and the boy said he was delighted to be meeting the king of the Bernicians in his own home, admired the Great Hall with a sweep of his hand, and seemed to mean every word it. Osric was then offered a bench on which to place his weary behind and was told that his horse along with others would be fed and watered.

'We have stables here,' said Ewin proudly, as if the Bernicians had invented them and owned the only stalls in the Britannic isles, 'so your mount will be cared for and will be kept warm and dry.'

'Thank you, my lord,' replied Osric. 'And thank you for your hospitality. I'm sure it must run against the grain to be hosting the family of your most hated enemy, but I assure you this is no wish of mine. I was ordered here by Rowena's father to spy on you and, like you, I'm subject to his whims.'

This candid speech widened the eyes of his host.

'Oh,' said Ewin, 'we really don't hate King Paega...'

'Well you should,' interrupted Osric, 'because he despises you.'

Ewin said nothing to this, his eyes not meeting either Osric's or Quercus's.

Osric continued, 'But I wouldn't feel put out by that, because he despises all other kings, all other peoples, in fact anyone who isn't King Paega. I thought I might as well be straight with you from the outset. By the way, if at any time you think it might be a good idea to take me hostage in order to have some sort of control over King Paega's intentions, forget it. He despises me too and regards me as a he might a kitchen boy. Rowena of course is his daughter, but I'm told you have a

212

weakness for her, so would not dream of using her as a counter in this game of wars.'

Ewin flushed. 'I would not harm a hair on her head.'

'Just so.'

Osric did not tell the Bernician king that if he was dreaming of one day having Rowena for his own, that she was already captive by her handmaid.

'Right then,' said Ewin, after a few more moments of reflexion, 'well we have a feast arranged for this evening. Probably not as grand as the ones you're used to in Mercia, but I think we can give a good account of ourselves. Your servant,' he nodded towards Kenric, 'can sleep with your guards in the stables. Off you go, fellow. My own servants will take care of your master while he's here.'

Kenric gave Osric a long look.

Osric said to Ewin, 'He's not my servant, he's my friend – the best friend a man could wish for.'

Ewin looked taken aback. 'But he looks like a blacksmith.' Kenric's shirt was open at the front. 'Those burn marks. They were surely caused by flying pieces of hot metal? My own blacksmith has similar marks.'

Osric opened his own shirt to reveal similar dark flecks on his chest. 'As do I. We were farriers by trade, my lord, before we pulled ourselves up by our own sandal straps and decided to become princes.'

'Decided to become princes?' Ewin's jaw had fallen open. Then his face hardened. 'You are jesting with me. I do not like to be made a fool of.'

'I'm sorry for that, but I want you to be under no illusions about who and what we are, my lord. I myself was once a prince, of the East Angles, but my father was murdered by the man who now calls himself king in my father's place. As a young man I had to flee from my own people, accused of patricide, for naturally the usurper blamed me for my father's death. I then met with this man here, an itinerant farrier, and we went into business together. He taught me all I know about shoeing horses and fashioning harnesses. I am more proud of my skills in that occupation than I am of my princely upbringing. Finally, the king of Mercia called me to his Great Hall and ordered me to marry his daughter Rowena, in order to take her off the market, since he did not want her wedded to kings like you. Oh, and by the way, we will require two bedchambers. Rowena is still a virgin of sorts and wants nothing to do with me in that respect. Give us a room anywhere, my lord, and my friend Kenric, and of course my cousin, Quercus, will share it quite happily.'

'Still a virgin?' murmured Ewin, dreamily.

'Indeed, my lord. No man has managed to break into that fortress yet.'

There was a long silence, then King Ewin studied Quercus, before whispering in Osric's ear, 'The boy had a bad birth? His head looks squeezed.'

Osric whispered back, in full view of his companions.

'Just so, my lord. They had to pull him out of his mother's womb by his ears, which as you can see are elongated.'

'But,' the whispering continued, 'he is sound of mind?'

'He sometimes speaks in a strange tongue, a language which we believe belongs to the elves,' murmured Osric. 'We are not sure of the parentage of the boy, but it is possible his father is not his father, if you get my meaning. His mother, not wanton but a woman whose eyes were not always on her husband, denies any involvement with a third person – but *women*? How many of that sex tell the truth when it comes to such things? They need comfort and affection to survive, and if the husband does not supply these, then they will seek them elsewhere.' Loudly now, 'But I love the boy for all that. He is my own flesh and blood, so to speak, of my greater family, and is my constant companion.'

During this exchange, which could be heard by Quercus, the boy's face was contorting as if he had some foreign object stuck in his nostrils and he was trying to get rid of it without using his fingers. By the time they were led away to their room, Quercus was obviously bursting to chide his father. Osric shook his head the moment Quercus opened his mouth and said, 'Now don't attack me, boy. I meant nothing of what I said. I know it was all lies, but that's how mortals work.'

'It seems a strange way to make friends with a king.'

'He believes I've been candid with him and therefore will trust me – the rest was just a punishment for calling Kenric a servant. Now, we must get ourselves ready for the feast tonight. Kenric, how's your thirst? Do you think you can manage a horn of mead?'

'I'm famished more'n thirsty, though I could quaff a jug of water.'

'I'm sure Ewin will have more than water on the menu.'

There were roasted wild boars, calves' hearts and livers, cooked game birds including ducks and swans with their plumage replaced and their posture in the same attitude as if they were swimming on a lake, blackbirds and various other songsters fried in butter, mushrooms a-plenty, dried fruit, berries, cheese, bread, elderberry drinks, apple juice both alcoholic and without fermentation, biscuits made of wild seeds, and much much more, including of course the horn of mead which was passed round the table. Rowena demanded to be included in the ritual symbol, which surprised King Ewin but he shrugged his thin shoulders and acquiesced. Osric had already witnessed Rowena's drinking prowess at the twelfth night wassail, the toasting of the cherry and apple trees, and knew her to be somewhat formidable at dissipation. Whereupon the princess proceeded to get very drunk and began to sing bawdy songs which the warriors and nobles pretended not to listen to. Her maids got inebriated along with her and later in the evening were all carried off to bed, two of them unconscious, leaving their mistress still up and laughing raucously at some of the stories that the men were exchanging about their amorous conquests.

'When I was a youth,' Osric was bragging to Ewin, 'I visited the Wih and spoke with Lord Woden while on my way to my dead parents.'

'Surely, Prince Osric, that is the wine talking,' cried one of the thegns. 'You visited the inneryard of the gods and spoke with their lord? I think not.'

'Would you care to fight me, to prove I am a liar? roared Osric, already deep in his cups. He leapt to his feet with a sword in his hand. 'I tell you I was there and I gave Lord Woden advice on curing a sickness which his horse was suffering.'

'You cured Sleipnir of a sickness?' cried the thegn, jumping over the feasting table. 'That is surely the biggest lie of all. Why would the horse of the greatest god we have in our skies need a mortal to cure it? Why, Sleipnir is surely a god-horse itself, with the power to cure its own sickness if need be. I think you make stories out of your dreams the way your mother makes butter out of milk, by stirring them with a big stick until they become solid enough to spread among gullible warriors.'

'Intereshting,' Rowena said to King Ewin, nudging him drunkenly. 'Will they kill easch other? Who d'ya think will win, eh?'

'Certainly I cured Sleipnir of a colic caused by eating too many acorns,' replied Osric to the thegn, 'and you are an ignorant man if you think that Sleipnir is a god-horse. Woden's steed was once merely a workhorse who pulled a wagon for a giant who was commissioned by Woden to rebuild the walls around Esageard, the home of the gods, when they were threatened by attack from hostile giants.'

King Ewin stood up and intervened.

'This is true. Woden did indeed ask a giant to rebuild the walls of Esageard. I was taught this story by the priest who educated me as a boy. However, the giant wanted, as payment for his work, to sleep with Frige, the wife of the Lord of the Wild Hunt. A time limit was set on the building of the walls, which if not finished by a certain date, would cause the builder to forfeit his payment.' Ewin was now in full flow and both the thegn and Osric had cooled down and took their seats on the benches again, glaring at each other on occasion, but also listening intently to Ewin's recounting of the tale of Woden's horse. 'Once the walls were almost complete, but the last stone had not been laid, Woden asked the trickster god Loki to intervene. Loki then changed himself into a mare to distract Sleipnir, thus preventing the giant from finishing the job on time. The giant was naturally very angry when thwarted of his payment and threatened to tear down the walls again, but Thunor crushed his head with his great hammer, so solving the problem. Woden kept the giant's eight-legged horse for his own steed – but Ragnar,' Ewin severely addressed the thegn who had taken issue with Osric, 'Sleipnir is indeed a giant's dray horse, not a god.'

Rowena cried, 'Fight! Fight! Fight!' but no one took much notice of her and soon one of her maidservants staggered back into the hall to collect her mistress and take her off to bed. Kenric had already collapsed and was under the table with the hounds, who were alternately chewing bones and licking his face. Quercus was sitting stony-faced by his father and quietly told that man that he'd had enough to drink and it was time to retire for the night. Osric shrugged and allowed himself to be eased off the bench. Between them they dragged the curled, sleeping Kenric out from his comfortable home under the long table, then bade the king goodnight, telling the delighted Ewin that it was the best feast they had ever been to and was far superior to any they had experienced in Mercia, both for entertainment and food. The wine, added Osric, was especially of the highest quality, which was probably why all his Mercian guests (including Rowena and her maids) had gratified themselves so deeply. Osric said he hoped they had not disgraced themselves, but for his part he felt the hospitality had been of the highest level: so convivial and thoughtful- including the kind offer of a fight to the death – that they had unwittingly overindulged.

NINE

The following day there was a hunt. King Ewin did not go: he asked to be excused, saying that hunting was not a pastime he enjoyed. He preferred his books.

'I read Latin,' he told Osric, 'and am interested in this god that the Romans brought with them to this isle. I have several rolls of Roman parchment I wish to study today and I would only be a hindrance to you hunters, who have the gift of sure sight and skill with weaponry. No, indeed, my body is not made to be perched on a horse and galloped at full speed towards a wild boar.'

Osric wondered how such a man fared in battle and Ewin admitted that he guided his army from a safe position on the field.

'I know what to do. I know what is to be done. But I cannot do it myself, naturally, so at a certain point my senior thegns take over. Then all I can do is watch and wait, and hope for a successful outcome.' He sighed. 'I have not known many victories. My own brother, who was king before me, was killed by Paega who then quartered him and hung the four quarters in an old oak for the birds to feast on. Poor Edgar. Now, *he* was a huntsman. He knew how to stick a pig. Me, I just get in the way of those who know what they're doing with a spear in their hands.'

For much of his spare time in Mercia, Osric had continued with the education he had received under his father's tutorship. There was a priest in Mercia called, appropriately, Godric-of-the-Borderland, who had agreed to assist with Osric's studies and Osric. Kenric had joined him for a while, but the farrier's son soon got bored with 'learnin' letters and runes' and Osric had carried on alone. Now Osric felt the equal of any man of learning, be he priest, king or demi-god. It was, he appreciated, important to know about the world and its ways, if you were to rule a realm. It was true, there were kings who remained ignorant of the information contained on parchments and in books, kings who relied on their priests and scribes to assist them, but Osric did not like having to rely on a second person for his information. What if that person were not a true friend, or provided false information for fear of being discovered ignorant, or was a clever man with ambition and manipulating the king into a position which was untenable? So he admired a king who felt it necessary to educate himself, although he also felt that such a king was missing a great deal in life by not wishing to hunt. The hunt was a glorious thing and made the blood sear through one's veins like a hot, red river.

So, the hunt went out without the king, who instead of going to his library went straight to the bower where he knew he find Rowena.

There was a thick rime on the landscape, which shone like silver in the glancing light of a low, weak winter sun. Grasses were stiff and crisp under the hooves of the mounts, whose ankle-fringes sparkled with the hoarfrost thrown up by their iron-bound feet. Frozen streams crackled under the same bay-shaped hammered iron shoes and the branches of trees hung low with the weight of icy moisture. Around the riders and hounds, wildlife scattered in all directions. This was a time of empty bellies, when caution was thrown to the winds and animals would rather have a full belly than be safe from all harm. It was difficult to stop the dogs chasing sprung hares or racing after foxes that had been started by the sudden arrival of their deadliest enemy. However, sharp commands ruled the day and the hounds, though somewhat bewildered, heeded the call to *stay*. Theirs was a world contained by the height of the weeds and though they could hear the thrashings and smell the redcoated quarry, they did indeed remain as a complete though restless pack.

They found the boar and they found the deer. The hounds howled with pleasure as they chased the quarry through the undergrowth. Horsemen followed, whooping and yelling in excitement, crashing through the bushes and ducking under the low branches of trees. One man who tried to jump a ditch was unhorsed and broke a leg. He had to be littered back to the village.

Another was struck by a sapling that had been bent forward by the breast of the horse in front, then let go like a whip which lashed the face of the hunter. This man, whose cheek had been bared to the bone, leapt on the back of the horseman who had caused his injury and beat him with his fists, yelling his fury for all to hear. Most laughed. Osric was annoyed at the foolery and told everyone to get on with the hunt proper and not get distracted. A noble asked who he was, to give orders to Bernician nobles and Osric threatened to fight the man if he did not do as he was told, thus adding to that which he had been arguing against just a few moments earlier. Quercus, who had also joined the hunt as an observer, asked his father to calm down so that they could they indeed get on with the purpose of the day.

Finally, they killed the boar and then, some time later, a fawn. Quercus slid from his mount and cradled the deer in his arms as it died, speaking to it in the tongue of the elves. When the light went out of the creature's eyes, Quercus laid the fawn on the grass and stepped away from it. The boy was caught between two races: on the one side he was elf, who only hunted prey that sprang back to life the next day; on the other he was mortal and felt the fire race through his veins when the hunt was in full swing and the beast was finally cornered and cut down. Only once its life-blood was staining the earth did he feel regret and then great remorse for the act. Now he was the object of derision and wonder, for his gentleness and concern.

'What did you say to the beast?' asked a curious hunter. 'Did you ask it where its mother was so that we could kill her too?'

'I merely wished it good speed to where it was going,' replied Quercus, 'and begged its forgiveness for our cruelty.'

'Ha! Speak for yourself, boy. I wager you'll eat its flesh tonight, after it's been on the roasting spit, eh?'

'No. I do not eat meat.'

The warrior raised his eyebrows.

'No meat? What about fish?'

'Nor fish.'

'Are you mad?'

'Yes,' came back the simple reply, 'as mad as the aelfen.'

The man looked into this strange boy's gold-flecked eyes and felt a ripple of fear of the unknown go through his body.

'Well,' muttered the man, 'each to his own, I'm sure,' and rode away to join the leaders of the hunt.

Quercus had hoped to meet some of his mother's beings while out in the meadows and woods on the hunt, which was one of the reasons he had joined it. However, the elves, giants, dweorgs, nixies and their kind were only to be found in the wild outeryards well away from the contamination of mortals. It was true that elves did shoot their poisonous darts into mortals who strayed a little too close to the pale that separated the two worlds, but the faery stayed wrapped in the shadows of trees and bushes, remaining unseen by humankind. Giants, too, came to wreck villages and farmsteads in the night, but were always gone in the morning, far out amongst the peat hags on the moors or deep in the thick forestlands. The hunt that day did not stray far enough beyond the borders of the cultivated fields and the pastures where domestic stock was put out to grass. In truth the Bernicians were a fairly home-tied bunch of people, who were overcome with dread at being a lost and wandering soul in any wilderness that contained those creatures which were spoken of by old women and had haunted their dreams as children.

Osric, riding beside his best friend, took the opportunity to speak with him, knowing they could not be overheard.

'Kenric, these people lack leadership,' said Osric, firmly.

Kenric stared at his friend. 'What? You meanin' to take over the kingdom? You'll need to swat Ewin first and one thing I know is, you ain't a murderer, Osric.'

'No, no. I wasn't thinking of taking Ewin's place. I was thinking of getting rid of Paega. I could not go to war against my own people of the East Angles, but I wouldn't mind going at Mercia.'

Lord Tiw:
War yet again! Oh, joy. This is better than the coming of Springtime.

Kenric was clearly shocked. 'How did that get in yer head? King Paega is the most powerful ruler on this island. He's killed more kings than you've killed flies. Besides, he gave us a home, didn't he?'

'He allowed us to remain in Mercia, you mean, Kenric. I've since learned from Sethrith that Paega plans to have me assassinated to give him an excuse to make war on Bernicia and execute Ewin. I'm not going to wait until that prophecy reaches its climax. As for Paega being powerful, he's a man like you or me. He's got to die sometime and he's getting too sure of himself. He's getting older. Why, he must be forty-five years at least. I think his battle skills are becoming blunted with age. We could take him, if we planned it carefully and had a strong army at our backs. I'm sure Ewin would love the chance to see Paega grovelling at his feet in humiliation. That or chopped into pieces and scattered in the swine pens for the pigs to eat.'

'Ewin has just suffered a big defeat by the same man you're offerin' to go against. Ewin's thegns must've been thinned to the bone. How many of them do you see around the Great Hall? Not many. Only a few of 'em are left alive. Would you expect those who walked off the battlefield in that recent war to follow you, a stranger, over every wild bit o' country, to go after the one man who's thrashed 'em each time there was a to-do between Mercia and Bernicia?'

'The tribute,' said Osric, 'is a killer, too. Bernicia is drained of the meat, grain and vegetable resources needed to get the people through the winter. Paega is a rogue king who sucks the best of the goodness out of his tribute realms and leaves them the dregs to survive the months of harsh weather. Many die of starvation and lack of warm clothing. We've been lucky, you and I, and the Thief. These people haven't. Nor my old clansmen. I can remember Mercian raiders stealing our cattle, pigs and sheep and when we retaliated they sent an army against us to teach us 'our place' in the heirarchy of the kingdoms.'

Osric paused and narrowed his eyes against the cold wind. Already the hoar frost was taking its toll on the Bernicians. Those inneryards out on the edges of the realm were suffering from lack of food now that crops had been taken in and nothing could be grown. Most of the summer's and autumn's harvests had been confiscated during a recent visit from the Mercian collectors of the six-monthly tribute. The villagers were surviving on wild roots and nuts, along with what they had managed to hide from the plunderers. It was mostly the churls, the underclass, who were suffering, but put a weapon in their hands and the promise of rich sustenance if they came through the fighting – why they would surely follow a strong leader onto the battlefield, even though the enemy were Mercians.

'Might I politely remind you, Osric, that you ain't fought a battle yet?'

'You can do that, Kenric, but I won't take any notice. I think I learned enough from my father to know that every battle is different and that you have to think on your feet. The Mercians simply go in with weight of numbers and superior weapons. They can afford to give good strong swords and spears to every warrior. Their warriors too are fit and healthy, having had a life in which food was not scarce. In keeping the other realms subdued and scrabbling around for bits to survive on, they ensure that their men remain the fittest and strongest on the isle. It's self-fulfilling. You are the best at fighting because you keep the others struggling to stay alive on your leavings and if these weakened creatures rise up against you, you knock them down again and take, take, take.'

'You ain't said how you're goin' to break this cycle.'

'By using my brains on the battlefield. Paega has no real strategy and hardly employs any original tactics…'

'Wow, you've learned a lot of fancy words from that Godric!'

'Yes, I have, and a lot of practical stuff too. Godric has shown me Latin books in which the strategies and tactics of Roman generals are written down. This land was ruled by the Romans before we came. Some of them stayed when the armies went back to their home country. Oh, I know a lot of them were from Germania and Gallia, auxiliaries they called them, and not really from Rome itself, but still those families who went back to Rome left their books and parchments. Godric has managed to obtain many of these. They liked to write about how they won their wars, the Romans did, and Godric had me study the battles. They were excellent warriors those men from Rome. I've learned a great deal from their descriptions of great conflicts they had with our own ancestors, back in the old country. A great deal.'

Osric stared at his friend coldly.

'I intend to kill Paega and subdue the Mercians, bending them to my ways. What happens after that will depend on whether they accept me as their new ruler. If I have to slaughter all the thegns and rebellious warriors to get my way, I will do it without hesitation or compassion. They deserve what's coming for supporting a king whose greed and ambition has filled the graves of many burial grounds. Many mounds, those earthen pillows which cover Angle and Saxon fields, are the work of Paega. It's time he had a tumulus of his own to lie in for eternity.'

Kenric stared at his friend as they rode side-by-side back to the Great Hall. He was left to wonder what changes had recently taken place in his friend's heart. Perhaps it was the manipulations of King Paega that had finally broken Osric's link with acceptance of his lot? To be ordered into a loveless marriage and then commanded to go and spy on another king was to treat a man, a former prince, like a kitchen boy. There was now an iron in Osric's blood, perhaps even in his soul, which had crept in over a long period. They were now both in their mid-twenties, healthy men whose strength had been developed by years of working at the forge. That metal they had hammered on the anvil was now in Osric's veins, swirling around that muscled frame, hardening his resolve, his determination. Kenric knew of course that he would follow his friend into any conflict, but he hoped also that he might be able to somehow temper this new ruthlessness.

When Osric arrived back at the Great Hall the guards tried to stop him entering, but he brushed them aside. When he entered the gloom inside and peered through its murk, he saw why. Lying in a corner under wolfskin blankets was Rowena. Next to her, naked from the waist up at the very least, was King Ewin. The king sat bolt upright and let out a groan when he saw Osric. He then reached over and shook the sleeping form beside him. Rowena rose from her pillow sleepily, her breasts spilling out over the wolf's fur. Then she saw Osric and gave a little laugh. Yet a third person then emerged from underneath the blankets, that of her maid, who blinked rapidly on seeing Osric, then dived down underneath the hides again, clearly terrified that some horrible blood-bath was about to ensue

'Look,' said Ewin, spreading his hands, 'she asked me.'

Osric began to draw his sword from its scabbard, then on reflection slammed it back down again.

He ignored Ewin and said to Rowena, 'I thought you only preferred girls?'

She shrugged. 'I'm not averse to a bit of variety.'

'Well, that's up to you, but thankfully this means we're not married any more – Ewin, you can have her with pleasure.'

Rowena's face took on a grim expression. 'Of course we're married,' she said.

Osric yelled, 'Kenric, Quercus. Come in here, quickly.'

His companions were by his side in seconds, Kenric with a drawn seax.

'What's wrong?' cried the farrier. Then, after glancing at the make-shift bed on the floor said, 'Oh, I see.'

Quercus turned his back on the scene, clearly upset.

'You're both witness to this adultery,' Osric exclaimed. 'She has defiled the marriage bed with her wanton behaviour.'

'There was no *marriage* bed,' muttered Rowena.

'Which makes it all the more easy to accept your betrayal, otherwise I might have to decapitate a king, a princess and a maid, probably all with one slice since you're all knotted together there.'

'My father will kill me,' snarled Rowena, 'and you, if you reject me.'

'And that thought didn't enter your mind when you crawled into bed with that skinny worm.'

'I am a king!' shouted Ewin. 'You speak to me with deference!'

'You are a slimy bastard who steals the wives of other men and I haven't yet given up my right to take off your head.'

'Cuckold!' chimed in Rowena. 'Cuckold! Cuckold!'

'Or yours,' added Osric, reaching for the hilt of his sword again.

His hand was gripped by that of Kenric's.

'Yet, things have turned out for the better, haven't they? These three can get on with their greasy games, while we plan a war, Osric.'

'Don't worry, my friend,' said Osric, turning his attention towards Kenric, 'I'm not serious. I couldn't care less who she goes to bed with and I'm grateful for a reason to reject her as my wife.'

'You can't do that,' cried Rowena. 'You can't.'

Osric turned back to her with a sympathetic face. 'I'm sorry, Rowena, but I have. No man would expect me to stay with a woman who not only kept me out of her boudoir, but took another man instead. By the by, I'm aware you've been told by your father to kill me. How was it to be? A dagger in the heart while I slept? Poison? Well, I'm happy to tell you that you can give up the idea completely, because after today I don't want to see your face again. If you so much as step inside a room which I am already in, I will kill you myself. You'll have to work all this out with your father. He may not be around much longer anyway, so if you wait awhile you'll find your fear of punishment from him unnecessary.'

A puzzled frown appeared on her normally smooth brow.

'What do you mean, not around much longer?'

Osric didn't answer. He simply turned on his heel and left the hall.

That evening, in the middle of the feasting, he stood on his bench and to the astonishment of King Ewin addressed whole hall.

'I am gathering an army,' he cried, addressing the thegns. 'It is my intention to attack Mercia and rid it of King Paega. I will need warriors, strong men, at my side. You Bernicians have been whittled down in numbers, but there are still fighters among you. I can see it in your bodies, in your faces. My companions and I will march against Mercia in the spring, when the snows are gone. Who will join me?'

There was utter silence in the hall. Ewin's mouth had dropped open.

The king said, 'I gave no permission for this!'

'I need none,' replied Osric, firmly. 'This is my enterprise, not yours. You may join me if you wish, but you will be subservient to my commands if you do.'

Cyneric, one of Ewin's thegns and a hearth-companion of the king leapt to his feet and braced Osric.

'Who are you to come here and start giving orders?'

Osric remained calm and although there was now a sword in Cyneric's right hand, he made no move draw his own weapon.

'I am no one at present, but I intend to be the king of Mercia before the next year is out. You Bernicians, and your cousins the Deirans, have been humiliated time and time again by Paega and his Mercian armies. Ewin here might be your rightful ruler, his ancestry in the gods of this land, but he will never lead to you victory. He is not a man of war, as we can all plainly see.' Osric paused, before continuing. 'I myself do not like war. Yes, it is glorious when it's in progress, with nobles and warriors winning armrings and great honours, but it also leaves orphans, widows and cripples in its wake. Paega will never stop raising arms against Bernicia, so why not take the initiative and attack him first? War is going to come again, so let it be on our terms, at a time of our choosing, rather than that of the warrior-king of Mercia.'

'Surely, you are a Mercian?' cried someone else. 'Why would you...'

'I'm no Mercian. I am a former prince of the East Angles.'

There was a buzz of conversation following this, which swept the room. Men began arguing in small groups, nodding towards Osric, some of them with affirmation written on their features, others angry and hostile. Kenric sat stiffly on the bench, his hand on his seax. Osric's proclamation could go either way. The three men might be attacked at any moment by those loyal to their king who felt he had been insulted, then again there might be a swell of opinion supporting Osric and his plans. Contrarily, it was Cyneric who seemed to be in favour of the plan. Eventually he stood up and hammered the table top with the pommel of his sword.

'Quiet! Silence! You're like a bunch of geese.' When the hall had gone relatively silent, he continued with, 'Now I, as you all know, am loyal to our king Ewin. A man who betrays his lord is a man without honour. But what the outsider says is true. We can sit on our arses and hope that battle will not come, but we'll sit in vain. It *always* comes, and it comes from the same source as ever – Mercia. I propose that we leave the decision to our king himself. He need not put his weight behind the project, but merely give us the right to form an army outside his dominion. Lord,' he turned to the brittle, upright man on his left side, 'what say you?'

Ewin stood up and cleared his throat. Osric wondered whether the insults he had recently thrown at Ewin would affect his judgement. After all, he was a man with a man's pride, even though an ineffectual king. But after glancing down at Osric, Ewin said in clear even tones, 'Let us destroy the bastards who would ruin my kingdom!'

For a moment there was utter silence as the warriors and thegns (there were no women present at this feast) tried to divine whether their king meant Osric and his companions or King Paega and the Mercians.

'Let us march south-west,' cried Ewin, who could be a very good orator when he'd partaken of enough mead, 'and trample Paega's face into the mud!'

In no doubt now, the warriors in the Great Hall let out a tremendous cheer and hammered the tables with their sword butts.

'Let us tear out his guts and hang them from the same oak from which he hung my brother's limbs,' yelled Ewin, now well into his stride. 'Let us twist his testacies from his groin and dangle them from my spear head! Let us rip out his tongue and nail it to the doors of the Great Hall. Paega, I spit when I say the name,' and indeed several men close by wiped faces that were in the line of the spray, 'and men will ever thereafter hold it in contempt. I will piss on his grave. I will shit on his tomb. I will scatter his bones over the dunghills of wolves and wild dogs. I will...' and there was much much more, but now very few were listening. They were all talking excitedly about their personal plans for the coming war, forming pairs of companions who would watch each other's backs, wondering what they would tell their wives, the majority of whom would approve of the proposal having lost children to slavery and starvation. The whole of the Great Hall was abuzz with excitement.

King Ewin leaned towards Osric, who was on his left, and murmured in his ear, 'I'm not fond of you, Osric of the East Angles. No one likes to be insulted in front of the woman he loves, especially a king. However, I've been called worse by my late brother and my former wife. Indeed, my wife even had the audacity to criticise my poetry: an insult that made my hackles rise as on an angry wolf. I almost slew her on the spot. However, that bastard Paega I hate with every fibre of my being. If you can deliver his head to me, I might change my mind about my feelings towards you. We could even be friends one day – but not yet. Oh dear me, no – not yet. The wounds to my pride are still fresh and the blood from them not yet dry.'

Osric nodded at the king and then grinned at Kenric.

'Well, that bit's over,' he said. 'Now we need to get our plans in place.'

Osric was thinking that it was time to sniff the bergamot again, to take a new journey to Neorxnawang and his father and mother, and to perhaps by chance meet with one of the gods while passing Esageard. If he could get Woden or Ing on his side, then of course there was no doubt as to the outcome. However, he knew that the gods rarely intervened in mortal affairs, not to the advantage of one man over another, and when they did there were always quarrels amongst them as to which mortal should be favoured. Probably, Osric decided, it would be best to leave them out of the equation, since if they did get involved gods like Loki could turn a certain victory into a messy defeat, simply through being what he was, a trickster.

PART THREE
LITTLE WOLF

ONE

It was Modranecht, Mothers' Night, and the Bernicians were celebrating all over the land. Other realms would be doing the same. Blodmonath had come and gone, that month when the cattle were slaughtered and blood flowed into basins for the table. On Mothers' Night there was a splendid feast in the Great Hall to honour the Idisi, that group of female ancestral spirits who controlled the battlefields of mortal men, making decisions on who should live and who should die. Osric was especially keen on placating the Idisi, since soon he would be leading an army into a war that he had to win.

During the feast, all men and women rose to leave the Great Hall and followed the local priest, an influential old man called Coifi, to enter the wooden-framed temple dedicated to Tiw. Here they pleaded with Tiw to give them victory in their coming battles with the Mercians. Osric heard that Rowena was among those who prayed to Tiw and Kenric and Osric wondered what she was praying for. Was she asking for the death of her own father? Or was she requesting the death of Osric? Osric had already ordered a tight guard to be put on Rowena, so that she did not warn her father of the plot against him. All men and women who left Bernicia were checked for written messages and interrogated for unwritten ones. Osric felt confident that he could keep his ex-wife from informing her father and mother of the coming storm of war before the army was ready to march.

After the feast Osric went to his room, lay on his bed, and lifted a vial to his nose. The scent of bergamot instantly propelled him heavenwards, to that path he had followed before to where the spirits of his dead parents now dwelt. He passed the god Hama, who was as ever guarding the Rainbow Bridge that led even higher into the cloud kingdoms of Esageard, where the rest of the gods played their godly games, made love and hunted. Osric had half a mind to attempt a visit to Freo, Ing's sister and a war goddess, but he knew it was impossible to get past Hama. It would have been good also to speak with Tiw, the god of war and combat, but to get close to such a deity would probably mean death.

Some gods had several functions. Tiw was also the god of justice and the sky, while Freo was goddess of fertility and of course one of the rulers of the elves. On the other hand Thunor, the son of Woden, was in charge of thunder and lightning: he would ride across the heavens in a chariot pulled by goats and he loved to strike oak trees with his thunder bolts. Frige was the goddess of love and the consort of Woden while Eostre herded in the Spring and took care of the dawn and rebirth of the day. Bealdor provided light for men to see by. Wuldor's arts were hazy and beyond the ken of mortals, as were Geat's, Helith's and Hretha's. Not all the gods and goddesses revealed their powers and responsibilities to ordinary men. Woden's priests, like Godric, probably knew what they were about, but mere sons of kings might only wonder and guess what went on in that place they called Esageard.

'Father,' said Osric, once he had found the wisps of vapour that were his parents, 'do you approve of my plans?'

'I have been told of what you are about to do, my son,' replied Eorl in the hollow tones of the dead, 'but I do not understand what it will achieve.'

'Why, Father, I shall be ruler of the Mercia. This is a powerful realm and from there I can march on our old home and destroy Wulfgar.'

Now his mother said, 'But you know you cannot kill your own people and level their homes and burn their crops.'

'No, Mother, I can't. But with another army, more powerful than before, I can force Wulfgar and his companions to meet me in combat. It will be between just them and me and my companions. I have two good friends who will help me in the fight, perhaps more, with Tomos the Walha. You see I have made friends with men not of our nation: warriors who lived in this land before we came across the sea. I am a man full grown now and I must avenge the death of my father the king. Please bless me in this act or I will find it hard to go into battle.'

'My son,' said his father, 'your plans seem to be sound and I fully concur with your scheme. How you carry out the deed is a matter for you alone and your conscience. It is a foul undertaking, revenge, and would that it was not necessary, but a murderer and usurper cannot be permitted to profit from his terrible crimes or there will be chaos in the land. Go, and my thoughts and prayers go with you.'

His mother blessed him and said she wished she could take him in her arms, but alas she was insubstantial and such an act of affection was impossible.

'This is one of the hardest things to bear,' she told Osric, 'to know that we are nothing but mist at the mercy of the winds.'

Osric left his father and mother, once again passing the Rainbow Bridge and wistfully thinking it would be good if he could recruit the gods to his mission. However, a single glare from Hama sent a gust of fear through Osric's body and he hurried on, back down to Earth. He woke on his bed and was satisfied with the visit to his parents. A man needs his father's blessing behind him if he is going to put all before him and wager on one great effort to achieve his ends. Then, if he should fail, he will not sink into a pit of despondency thinking he has been arrogant and foolish, since others of great importance have endorsed his plan.

The next morning he held a council of war with Ewin and Kenric. They had sent a messenger to the Thief who would hopefully soon he on his way to Bernicia to join with them.

'Now,' said Osric, 'as I've told you, I've studied Roman battles using the books my friend Godric has collected into a library.'

Kenric blinked. Already this homespun young man was lost with words like 'library' but Ewin leaned forward with a keen expression.

'I have one or two of these battles in my head, especially those of a great Roman leader called Julius Caesar. Caesar was a brilliant fighter, with many many victories, but in fact the one battle I wish to copy is not one of his. It's a Roman *defeat* that I want to use. The leader of the army that won that day was called Hannibal and he fought two Roman generals, as they were called, at a place called Cannae, where there was a river... Anyway, no need to go into it in detail now, I just want you to know that the two Roman generals, Paullus and Varo, were as arrogant as King Paega and believed their army to be invincible. You have to know that the Roman army at the time was indeed the best trained, the best commanded, the best disciplined. The Romans hardly ever lost a battle on land. Sea was different. They weren't good sailors, but their land battles were brilliant. However, on that fatal day, fatal to Rome that is, General Paullus died on the battlefield and Varo was in great disgrace when he returned to Rome having lost 75,000 men...'

'What about the other side. Who were they? How many men did they lose?' asked Kenric, now intensely interested in this account.

'Hannibal's army lost only around 5,000 men. Hannibal came from a city called – now what was it called? – Carthage, yes, that was it. It doesn't matter really. These places, they're too far away and too different from our villages to even imagine what they're like. If you look at what the Romans left here, the stone buildings, stone statues of men and pictures made of bits of coloured stone which decorated their inneryards, why, they couldn't have been anything like us at all. We're very different from them – except when it comes to war. We can't copy their houses but we can copy the way they fought their battles. We can use their brains to defeat the Mercians, who've had it all their own way for so long they're over-confident and will expect our warriors to start running away after the first clash. We won't run. We can't run. We must stand our ground and trust in the gods that our warriors are just as good as Paega's. One or two cowards will of course desert the battlefield. And traitors will change sides. That always happens. But in the end, if you have faith in me, we'll prevail and be victorious against Mercia.'

Ewin murmured. 'Wonderful. It will be wonderful, if it happens.'

'It will.'

Kenric then said, 'But – but what about numbers. We've only got, I dunno, a third of the warriors that Paega can muster, if that. You know, if he feels really threatened he can call on the South and West Saxons, and the Jutes, to swell his numbers. They'll have to fight for him as subject kingdoms. Perhaps even the East Saxons…'

'I've sent Quercus to the Walha, to ask Tomos for his support. We may not get it, but you know, they do love a fight, almost as much as they like to sing, those people from the mountains and the valleys beyond Uffa's Dyke.'

'Still, they won't be enough, not if we're to stand a chance.'

'Quercus has reminded me,' said Osric, 'that there's another world alongside ours. I aim to recruit witches, giants, dwarfs, elves and any nicor monsters that'll come with us. Oh,' he held up his hand, 'I know they won't all come. We'll be lucky to get even a few. But think of it – witches and giants fighting alongside mortals – it'll scare the Mercians silly. You know how they fear the elves, who are forever firing their darts into Mercian hides and causing sickness to enfold them.'

Ewin clapped. 'Let's have a tumbler of mead, to celebrate our plans?'

'Why not,' replied Osric. 'I'm as dry as a badger's sett in summer.'

However, when Ewin called for the mead, it was Rowena who brought it.

Osric, fearful of poison, refused to drink it. Rowena regarded him with contempt and lifted the jug to her own lips and swallowed, then smacking her lips said, 'There, am I about to drop dead?'

Osric shrugged and allowed his beaker to be filled.

Rowena then stared at him through slitted eyes.

'Are you going to kill my father?' she asked. 'Is that what this meeting is all about?'

'We're going to try,' replied Osric. 'I'm sorry.'

'He's done you no real harm – you, Osric.'

'Are you telling me he didn't order you to assassinate me?'

Rowena sighed. 'He did tell me to kill you and blame Ewin for the deed, it's true.'

Ewin let out a gasp, but Osric laid a hand on his shoulder.

He said to Ewin, 'I knew of the plot, so there was no real danger to either of us.' Then to Rowena, he said, 'Your father hasn't managed to carry out his plans with regard to me, but to others he's done terrible harm. He's killed thousands of men who would rather be out in their fields, tending their cattle, growing their crops, for no other reason than greed. Yes, others do the same, I know, but I don't believe in that way of life. Prosperity comes with peace as well as with war. There needs to be a stronger cause for war than just increasing the power and wealth of one man.'

Osric paused and breathed deeply, before going on.

'On a personal level, while he lives and keeps his powerful grip on the Angle and Saxon peoples, I shall never be safe. He sees me only as a useful tool to expand his empire. If I become king of the East Angles he won't think twice about going to war against me. So, why should I not take the war to *him*? And if I should be successful and destroy him, why should his death be any more special than the death of any other warrior? He has lived by force and plunder, increasing his power year on year, and now he's the one who needs to protect his property and wealth.

'You know, we might lose. Your father has never lost a war yet. You should be concerned for us, not for him.'

While this council was in progress, a mute pedlar arrived in Mercia and. using sign language, requested audience with King Paega. He was refused, Paega's thegns dismissing him with typical contempt. The pedlar did not however take much notice of these self-important lords and waited until Paega emerged on horseback from his inneryard to go hunting. The pedlar then rushed forward and grabbed the king by the ankle, gesturing with the staff he carried. One of the thegns raised his sword to cut down the elderly man, but Paega stayed his hand.

'What do you want, elder?' asked the king.

The pedlar pointed to his mouth, which he opened, showing the king that there was no tongue inside. Then the pedlar quickly took off a leather strap he was using as a belt which had been wrapped around his waist three times. The leather was adorned with what appeared to be centripetals and swirls. These markings were not intelligible in any way, but appeared to be for decorative purposes only. Then the old man wound the long strap around the staff in a spiral, starting at the top and twisting it down to the bottom of the oaken stick. As the leather strap overlapped itself, the fragments, the strange markings, became whole letters. When the spiral was complete there was a message there, intended for the knowledge of the king of Mercia. Paega read the words on the staff and his eyes revealed emotion: first anger, then contempt.

'Give this man a piece of gold,' said Paega, studying the words on the leather. Then under his breath he muttered, 'Well, Osric of the East Angles, you treacherous whelp of a mongrel bitch, you're about to join your mother and father in Neorxnawang. March against me? I'll have your head on a stick in the fouling pits of my warriors, so that they can shit on you the morning after the battle. March against *me*? You little snot. I've trodden on slugs with more brains.' He stared into the distance, as if he were addressing a huge audience. 'My warriors have swept the land clear of ambitious kings,' he said. 'Prince you may have been, when you filled your nappy-rags in your infancy, but now you're nought but an idiot farrier with ideas dribbling out of your ears like wax. I'll have your bladder for a fool's balloon and feed your testicles to my hawk – that's your destiny, my dear son-in-law.'

A few days after the feast in Ewin's Great Hall the Thief arrived in Bernicia, dishevelled and dirty. He had escaped Mercia in his usual fashion, slipping away like a fox in the murk of the early dawn, scrambling behind hedgerows and crawling along ditches. There had been warriors out looking for him, but the Thief had long been adept at smelling danger on the air, and he had slipped out of the forge by the back way and was off into the wilderness before the first thegn stepped through the doorway of the forge. He had had no sleep for two days and had drunk water from puddles, but apart from that the Thief was well. A nicor had tried to entice him into a pond at one point, but the Thief was such an old hand the crafty water-monster was wasting his breath. The

Thief had outwitted heroes and dragons, and was not likely to be fooled by the meanest and most insignificant of supernatural beings.

'He knows,' the Thief told Osric and Ewin. 'Paega. He knows your plans. A traitor came with a message wrapped around a staff.'

'How did that happen?' cried the king. 'We have been checking everyone who leaves Bernicia.'

'It was an ancient and clever device,' replied the Thief. 'I heard it was used in a land called Persia over a thousand years ago.'

'Anyway,' said Osric, not too upset that King Paega was on to him. 'I'm glad you're here. Paega would have found out sometime. You can't make war plans in this land and keep them secret. Someone is bound to talk.'

Once he had seen that the Thief was fed and watered and given a bed to sleep, Osric left the village, riding Magic into the outeryard wilderness. A hound who had recently taken to Osric accompanied him. The bitch was called Hreda, after one of those several goddesses whose occupations remained a secret of Esageard. She seemed to adore the prince and at one point Osric began to wish that Rowena and this hound would change souls. He felt it would be better for everyone, not just himself, if Rowena actually liked him.

Once in the outeryards he called a name.

'Sethrith! Sethrith! Where are you?'

He stared over moorland hemmed in by dark forests, and wondered if his witch-girl could hear him. A marsh harrier settled for the night. The wind blew over the long reeds sending waves through them and they emulated the sea. No witch appeared, though, out of the moor's reedy hair. He called again and again, but still here was no sign of Sethrith. Darkness fell and the moon's yellow light brought shadows with it that played touch-and-run over the peat hags. Hreda whined, clearly uneasy out here where there was no bang and bustle of humans going about their business. She had been raised in the confines of the village and knew nothing about the wilderness.

'Sethrith, damn you, come to me!'

A tawny owl replied, asking who he wanted. Then there was a terrible screaming: probably a hare with an ermine at its throat. Hreda jumped and stared around her, before slinking forward to lie between Osric's legs. Then something slithered through the grass at his feet and Osric too jumped. A shadow passed over the moon and Osric looked up at those bright-ice stars that filled the sky.

Where was she? She had always told him she would come when he called.

'Seth...' and there she was, gliding over the reeds like a white ghost. A shiver went through Osric when he saw this sight. He was reminded starkly that he was dealing with a creature not of his kind. 'Where were you? I've been calling for ages.'

'I was a long way away,' and she glanced up at the moon.

'Up there?'

'Somewhere up there. Then I got tangled in some high branches, wondering which direction you were calling from. What do you want?'

'Oh,' he was thrown for a minute, as he tried to recover his composure. He wished he were some place where there was lamplight. 'Well, it's this. I've decided to go to war again. This time not against my old enemy, but against King Paega.'

'Why?'

'It's a means to an end. First I need Mercia.'

'How can I help?'

'I was hoping you would fight for us. It would be good to have a witch on our side – we need all the help we can get.

'How about a hundred witches?'

He stepped back, almost treading on Hreda's tail. The dog scurried away, now under the legs of Magic, who stood placidly waiting for her master some distance away amongst the thorn bushes. Sethrith crooned something and both Hreda and Magic made animal sounds, which seemed to please the witch. Osric gathered his thoughts. A hundred witches! What havoc could such a number wreak! Why that would be marvellous. He had no idea how witches fought in a battle, but just the thought of them would frighten any mortal out of their wits. Even if they did nothing, they could look terrible to mortals, and might send many a man back to his wife with hair-raising tales of horrific visions.

'A thousand witches would be too much to ask.'

'They are yours, Osric.'

He sighed in satisfaction. 'Now, what about giants?'

'I could get you a score of Ettins, but not Thurses. Thurses would simply be hell-bent on destruction and would kill everyone, no matter which side they were on. Ettins could be controlled a little more easily. Would you like Ettins?'

'Yes, I would. And dweorgs?'

237

'Some of those too, armed with their hammers.'

'Excellent. What about a dragon?'

She shook her lovely head, her hair throwing off sparkles of light.

'Not a dragon. Most of them have now gone north and, like a Thurse giant, they would simply burn without favour. In any case, they would not fight for *you*.'

Osric was shocked. 'Why not?'

'You killed one of their children.'

He suddenly remembered the small dragon he had shot to death with his elfin bow and arrow, when he was still a youth.

'Oh, I see. How old was the dragon I killed? I had no idea it was a child.'

'Only three-hundred years of age.'

Osric laughed. 'How is that a child-dragon?'

'Every hundred of their years is equivalent to ten of ours.'

'That still makes it thirty years of age. I was only around seventeen summers myself. In that case it was a fair fight.'

'Tell that to a fully-grown dragon.'

He grumbled, 'Oh, all right. No dragons then. They're a bit unwieldy in any case. Difficult to control, I imagine.' His mind went elsewhere for a moment as he went over his plans in his head. 'I wonder if Quercus can get some elves…'

Sethrith said, 'They won't kill for you. Not outright. If you did get them, they would only use their darts to poison the enemy, who would not die immediately.'

'Well, they could go amongst them the night before the battle.'

'Yes, they could. Would you feel that was ethical?'

'In what way?' asked Osric, rattled a little.

'Well, it's a little sneaky, isn't it? Not a manly thing to do, poison the enemy. It's the sort of thing queens do to family they don't like.'

Petulant now. 'Oh, all right. Yes, unmanly.'

'Witches, giants and dwarfs – it will be a formidable contingent of creatures from the otherworld.'

'Yes it will. Thank you, Sethrith. We shall need help. I believe Paega can muster over five-thousand warriors, while I a mere two-thousand. We shall be fighting two or three kingdoms of Saxons and Jutes, as well as Mercian Angles. Paega's influence is spread very wide. I shall have to be extremely clever to win this war and I don't have the kind of brain that Godric owns. I'll need advice from others. The gods give me the humility to accept their suggestions. I know what I can be like if I think I'm being told what to do. You must be there to stop me from being foolish.'

TWO

Over the winter the Bernician and Deiran warriors trained for the coming war. They seemed in good spirits, considering they were probably all going to die. Paega would not let any of them live if Osric lost the battle. He could be somewhat merciful if he was the one starting the war, but there would be no leniency for those who had gone to war against *him*. Probably he would enslave the whole nation: kill the young boys, the old men and women, and herd the young women back to Mercia to be used as workers in the fields and kitchens – and the bed chambers, of course. The king would take over Bernicia and Deira completely, put his own people on the land, put in one of his thegns as the new ruler and therefore wipe out the Bernicians completely.

Lord Ing:
This prince has now burnt his bridges. It's difficult to see how he can win against a seasoned warrior like Paega, who's never lost a single war. Lord Woden would not permit any of the gods or goddesses to intervene on behalf of either of the warlords: that way would lead to battles within Esageard, god against god, which would create terrible chaos. However, I have an idea that I can persuade Lord Woden to go on a wild hunt the night before the battle. He doesn't need much urging to carry out his favourite activity.

Quercus returned from over the other side of Uffa's Dyke to say that Tomos could provide five-hundred men.

'Just five-hundred?' .

'Yes, Father, but he did say at first that you would be lucky to get any at all – they have no love for Angles beyond the border.'

'Well, in this case, they will be killing Angles.'

'Which is what I told him and thus he was able to muster half-a-thousand volunteers. I also told him that once you are king of Mercia the Walha can expect a bond of friendship. You must meet with them, my father, and make a pact of peace with those wild, hairy people. Tomos admits they will no doubt still raid and steal any cattle they can find just over the wall, but he and I think that's a small price to pay for a peace between two nations.'

'Hmmm. I'm not sure we can persuade the owners of the cattle and sheep to agree on that, but we'll manage that when we come to it. We haven't won the battle yet and, even if we do I might be killed and so might Tomos. I think I'll leave such problems until it's absolutely necessary to deal with them.'

When the spring finally arrived, Osric gathered his army together to march to the south end of Uffa's Dyke. To do so they had to navigate between Mercia and the East Angles and had enemies on both flanks. Fortunately the forced march had been kept secret enough to prevent Osric from being intercepted by either of his foes. He needed to get his army in a position of advantage. There was a bend in a river to the south-west, which mirrored the place where Hannibal had beaten the Romans. Once he had turned in that direction, he knew he was going to make it to the ground he desperately wanted for the battle.

Tomos met him in the cradle of a curve on the great river that separated the country of the Walha and the land of the West Saxons. The army had the river at its back, which was normally not a good position since it meant retreat was impossible. However, Osric was determined to follow Hannibal's tactics to the letter. Hannibal had the curve of a river at his back and therefore Osric chose a duplicate position for his army. Osric knew that he should wait for the afternoon sun to be as far and low in the west as possible, so that it shined in the eyes of the attackers. However, it was unlikely he would be able to use this tactic, because Paega would no doubt attack in the morning. No commander worth his salt was going to hang around until the afternoon.

Ewin had not accompanied the army. He was not a warrior-king and said if death was coming he preferred it to do so while he was writing poetry. And so Osric had complete control of his army. Once they were camped and the supply wagons were all in, he called a meeting of his senior commanders in his tent.

'Tomos, Cyneric, Kenric, we've made it here. Now we need to prepare the field of battle to our advantage. The first thing is to graze the cattle and sheep, and get the area over which the enemy will charge bare of grass. If our domestic stock doesn't eat it, then we'll pull out the grass by its roots. We have men a-plenty for such a task.'

'And women,' reminded Kenric, thinking of the camp-followers.

'And women.'

Tomos and Cyneric looked bewildered.

Tomos asked, 'What do we do that for? Get rid of the grass? It doesn't make any sense.'

Osric told him the reason behind this strange preparation of the battle ground and after he understood he was satisfied.

'Good,' Tomos said, 'and next?'

'Next we dig trenches and fill them with clay pots. Make sure all warriors are armed at all times, with spear, sword if they're sufficiently rich to have one, wooden shield and iron helmet. Paega is cunning enough to send a small force to attack us while we're making our preparations and I don't want the men to be surprised. He'll need time to get his army together, but he's always got his hearth-companions ready.'

Kenric's turn to be puzzled. 'What for? The cookin' pots, I mean.'

'Paega's cavalry. The pots, broken or whole, will make it more difficult for the men and horses who fall into the trenches to get out again.'

Tomos nodded. 'Good.'

'Now,' continued Osric, 'the formation of the warriors.'

Cyneric said, 'All right, it's my turn to ask. What's a formation?' Do you mean the *shield-wall?*'

Cyneric, like most Angle and Saxons commanders, knew only how to charge the enemy, or defend with lines of warriors using their alderwood shields as a wall.

Osric explained. 'We need to arrange the battleline of men according to their strengths. I want the strongest warriors on the flanks and the weakest in the centre. I know this is contrary to conventional thinking, but I want to copy the Battle of Cannae to the letter. I've never commanded an army, I've never even fought a battle. I have to use the brain of a long dead warrior chieftain and trust to it. Do you agree?'

Tomos and Kenric nodded, and Cyneric said, 'We have to, I suppose,' but he didn't seem wholly convinced by the argument.

Osric then dismissed his commanders, but, before they left, Kenric brought out something wrapped in a soft cloth.

'This is for you,' said the farrier. 'I made it.'

'What is it?' asked Osric, taking the weighty object. 'It feels like a weapon.'

'Sword,' replied Kenric.

'But you made me one before.'

241

'Not like this. This one's special. I've hardened the iron.'

Osric unwrapped the sword and found a beautiful weapon. Like most swords used by the Angles and Saxons, it was double-edged and straight bladed. The tang was covered in a beautiful hilt with an upper and lower guard, a pommel wrought in the shape of a falcon's head and the leather-wrapped grip. Inlaid on the pommel were precious stones and slivers of gold and silver. The guards were similarly decorated with the addition of mythical animals. The blade itself had an ashleaf pattern which ran the whole length, a natural consequence of the twisted rods of iron which had gone into the hammering. The weapon had been sharpened to the point where he felt confident it could sever a single blade of grass lengthways. Finally, the sword had a fuller – a long groove down the centre of the blade – which reduced the weight and allowed blood to flow freely when the weapon was in use. In the hands of a skilled warrior, this was a deadly sword and deserved to be named by its owner.

'Oh, Kenric, you are a talented ironsmith indeed. I shall call this sword *Rowena* after my ex-wife, for this sword is as sharp as her tongue.'

The others laughed, but Kenric said, 'You'd better not let her hear you say the last bit – let her think it a compliment.'

'You're right, my friend. No sense in getting petty.'

Osric swished the weapon, this way and that, testing the balance, which appeared to be perfect.

'Does it have a sheath to go with it?'

Kenric grinned. 'Of course.'

The farrier produced a carved wooden scabbard which was lined with fleece, greased to keep the blade from rusting. Around the neck of the scabbard was a golden frog – a metal band to prevent wear – and it had a golden chape at the bottom. A single meerschaum bead was attached to the neck of the sheath by a small strap: a charm to ward off evil and protect the weapon's owner. The scabbard was attached to a baldric to sling over Osric's shoulder to carry the sword. Indeed, the whole gift was a handsome one, and fitting to go with his elfen quiver and bow.

'A thousand thanks, my friend,' said Osric, laying a hand on his shoulder. 'One day soon you will either be a celebrated thegn, a man of high position in the king's hearth-companions – or you will be dead.'

'That's pretty comfortin', that last bit, 'cause if I'm dead, I won't be worryin' about where the next meal's comin' from, will I?'

Now that the gift-giving was over, Osric visited the wagons that had brought weapons and food. Water could be had from the river and Osric had provisions in place to prevent Paega's men from drinking. They would have supply wagons too, of course, but those provisions would be limited. A man can go without food for two weeks and still be able to fight, but three or four days without water is thelimit.

All the freemen had been armed for the march, of course, but there were more spears and javelins in the wagons. The spear was the 'dart' of the elves, for that was what the throwing spear was called. Ewin had provided for the whole army and was not a mean king. The length of the spears ranged from the height of a man, to a third more in length. The longer spears would be used by the second and third rows of warriors when they formed the shield-wall, over the shoulders of the front rank. The spear was the main weapon of the rank and file warrior. Osric remembered a line from the poem *Beowulf*, which the Thief had taught him:

'Henceforth spear shall be, on many cold morning, grasped in the fist.'

Next, Osric checked the swords, which were of lesser quality than those blades carried by nobles, princes and kings. They consisted mostly of seaxes and scaramaxes: iron-bladed weapons. The ordinary seax was not much more than a knife, but the long-seax, which Kenric preferred was of sword length. The scaramax too was longer than the ordinary seax being the length of the lower part of a man's arm, from elbow to fingertips. Handles were mostly wood, but some of iron. Some were pattern-welded. Some of the blades were decorated with incised lines, and often bore the name of the maker, such as, *'Kenric made this weapon'.*

Among the axes, there were long-handled battle-axes and throwing axes, but normally only very strong or big men carried one of the former.

The bow was not the favourite weapon of the Angle, though there were those who called themselves archers. Stacks of arrows filled one of the wagons: shafts with fire-hardened points, or with leaf-shaped or triangular bone or antler heads. Some indeed had iron arrowheads, several with barbs. The string of the bow was woven animal hair or gut.

Many warriors also carried a sling-shot, being hunters with these weapons.

Finally, there were the items for protection: the shields and the helmets. The shields were circular and constructed of alder planks glued together with a metal boss in the centre. The round shield was often covered in leather to give it further strength, along with bronze studs and decorative shapes in the manner of animals. Mostly they were painted a bright yellow. Helmets were made of iron, some elaborate and others basic. The fine, decorated helmets worn by the thegns would mark them out as great warriors and to be feared in combat. No ordinary fighter, even if wealthy, would wear a helmet that proclaimed him to be a warrior of superior prowess. Their money would be spent on a chain mail vest, for being a man of substance they would not like to leave the world on the battlefield, while a thegn might regard that end as something to be proud of and, while not seeking it, not shying from it.

THREE

On the third day, Paega's army arrived to confront Osric's men. The numbers of the Mercians were awe-inspiring. They filled the hollows and the low ridges of the gentle hills so that the landscape beyond was completely obscured. Tents and war-banners flapped in the wind which, along with the bull-roarers and horns, created a fearsome, aggressive noise. Their fires almost turned night into day, they were so numerous. The Thief guessed there were least seven-thousand warriors, if not more, now camped a wide length away. Quercus took a ride in no-man's-land, being a half-elf easily able to dodge the arrows and spears from ambitious Mercians. He returned to reveal that there were indeed Saxon contingents among the Angles. From their banners and standards, Osric learned there were West and South Saxons, and a small number of Jutes. Paega was leaving nothing to chance. He was going to swat this upstart son-in-law, this treacherous prince-come-farrier, as a man will slap down a wasp. Already his temper was evident from the number of heads on spiked poles: those who had displeased him in some way during the march across country.

Moreover, Paega had somehow heard that Osric was recruiting supernatural creatures to assist him in the battle and had brought some of his own. There were huge, strange, black dogs called *barghests,* which roamed the perimeter of Paega's camp. These animals were savage and terrible, with fiery-eyed stare that froze a man in terror. They stood as high as a tall horse though still on all fours and would rip warriors to pieces so that not a bit of flesh would be recognisable as a body part. The bones they would crunch to splinters then spit them out in a deadly spray of darts that would kill a man in his tracks. Also in Paega's camp were dark elves. These were cousins of Quercus who lived not in the light, the forests and fields, but underground in deep caves. Paega must have promised them something extraordinary to get them to come out of their black holes, for they hated the daytime and had to severely squint in bright sunlight. The dark elves, however, would not fight with light elves standing against them and Quercus promised Osric to get his own elfen clan to simply appear on the battle field to negate Paega's creatures.

245

Osric's army was in a complete panic.

'We didn't expect this many,' said Cyneric, gesturing at the massed warriors that filled the outeryards beyond the river. 'Not this many. There's only twenty-five-hundred of us to stand against them.'

Osric replied, calmly, 'You did know how it would be, but now you're letting your eyes tell your head and heart what to do.'

'But we don't stand a chance!'

Kenric said, 'You have to trust in Osric.'

The Thief said, 'And in the gods.'

Quercus added, 'Also the elves.'

Cyneric was agitated. 'But how can I control my warriors. They're all convinced they're going to die, to the very last man. I walk past their fires at night and I can hear their voices are full of dread. They won't fight well, in that mood.'

'Cyneric,' said Oscar, 'we both know that men are affected by the jitters just before a battle. It's natural. Once the fighting starts, however, they'll throw themselves into it as they always do.'

'But they are so many...'

'I know, and we are few, but Hannibal will win the battle for us.'

'He's not here. He's been dead for centuries.'

'Still, he will win it for us.'

At that moment a warrior entered the tent and cried, 'There's a messenger here, from King Paega. He says if we leave now, he'll spare all our lives.'

Osric replied, 'Was the message for you, or for me?'

'For you, lord.'

'Then let the messenger tell me what Paega is offering – I don't need it second-hand. See him in.'

A few moments later Osulf, one of Paega's most trusted thegns, stood before Osric.

'Go home, boy,' said Osulf in an insulting tone, 'you're out of your depth.'

Osric allowed himself a laugh. 'And that's the message?' He turned to Kenric, 'Have this idiot thrown into the wolf pit.'

Osric was rewarded with seeing the blood drain from Osulf's face.

'I come under a banner of truce.'

Osric's voice grew louder, 'Then give me the proper message, or I'll treat you as a spy. Paega would not call me "boy" when I have an army at my back, or tell me I'm out of my depth. You are a messenger between two commanders, nothing more. I am the lord of this camp and you are nobody, understood? One more insult and you will indeed feed the wolves tonight. I'll not be a butt for your arrogance.'

Osulf looked at the ground, clearly angry, but he spoke the real message.

'Lord Paega has graciously granted you leave to go from here with your army unharmed. You are to be gone by the time the sun rises and you have King Paega's word he will not pursue you. He gives no promise that he will not post you as an outlaw in Mercia and that he will not send men to end your life. He holds no personal grudge against Bernicia, knowing you have persuasive powers and have charmed King Ewin in some way to assist your rebellion against Bernicia's rightful overlord. The only person he holds responsible is Osric of the East Angles. These are truths and these terms he swears on the heart of the god Woden and awaits your answer.'

'Hmm,' said Osric, pacing the floor of the tent, 'he hasn't asked for my surrender because he knows he won't get it and I have no doubt there are infiltrators who are now in my camp giving my men the hope they are going home.' He stared first at his companions, then at Osulf. 'He's trying to turn my army against me.'

Osric went out of the tent and stood on a hillock.

With his army all around him, he yelled this message.

'*I am Osric, leader of this army. I shall fight the Mercians whatever message their king sends or whatever terms he offers. If any man is afraid, he should leave now. If need be my companions and I will fight alone. No man will call you coward if you go this instance, but know that those who remain will have to fight to victory or death!*'

There was a stirring amongst the warriors as they discussed this offer and Osric could hear one or two saying they should go, for who were they fighting for but a man with a personal grievance? Others, however, were arguing that they were fighting for Bernicia against Mercia, who had subjugated them for too long, and that if those who were afraid wanted to go back to their wives and tell them they had run away, then they should indeed leave. But remember they would go to their graves without honour.

Eventually, the buzz died and men settled around their campfires once again, their voices lower and less excitable. Very few warriors left the camp. There might have been others who wanted to leave, but dared not because their comrades would jeer or despise them. There may have been those who would have liked to walk away, but knew that without warriors willing to go with them, the journey back to Bernicia was a long and dangerous one. There were no doubt those who wished to go, who were indeed afraid they would die in the coming battle, but who conquered their fear by remaining and trusting their own fighting ability and the gods.

Osric returned to those in the tent.

'Osulf,' he said, 'tell your king we are going nowhere.'

The Mercian noble looked astonished.

'You'll all die. Every last one of you.'

'I'll remember you said that, when my sword is pricking your throat.'

'We shall seek you out, on the battlefield – Horsa and Headho, Assel, Sigeberht, even Dudda. If we take you alive we'll give you to Godescealc and you know what he does to prisoners. There's also a butcher's helper, a fellow called Thark, who says he wants to carve pieces from your body and that, he says, is his skill. I feel pity for you, Osric of the East Angles, for your enterprise will come to nought.'

With that, Osulf left the tent and was escorted back to the Mercian lines.

Once the Mercian thegn had gone, Kenric said, 'An' we 'aven't even *got* a wolf pit.'

They all laughed.

FOUR

Paega was not too unhappy with the message from Osric, when Osulf returned and gave it to him. He had expected nothing less. A man does not gather an army and march into enemy territory without intending to use it.

He told his thegns, 'Osric will soon learn what weaklings these men of North Umbria are. I shall unleash my warriors, my slaughter-wolves, who will scythe through this rabble of an army and send the survivors home with tales of terror and death.'

Sigeberht, the most senior and trusted of Paega's hearth-companions and ruler of a subkingdom of 3,000 hides, nodded in approval.

'My Lord, our ash-spearmen are ready. Those who wield the blood-swords are ready. Even the kitchen boys with their seaxes are ready...' there was a stamping of feet and thumping of fists on tables. 'We should attack as soon as possible and drive these fools into the river. Have they no better sense than to have a river at their backs? The cowards among them will run from the fight and drown. There is no avenue for retreat. A few thousand weak men? We'll cut through them within the time it takes to breathe five breaths. You, my lord, will be victorious as ever and you shall have this Osric's head on a spike.'

The king, always a brutish man but now in his later years, thick of limb and girth, with a large head and pock-pitted face, said, 'I want this upstart boy captured alive so that he will undergo this "blood-eagle" that I've heard about. It's a fitting end for an East Angle, whose King Eadgard introduced the torture to this land. I want his ribs broken and his lungs pulled out of his back to become the wings of a bird. I want to see him to die in great pain, but more than that, in great indignity and distress. I shall hang his guts from a tree for the rooks and crows, and yes, the head on a spike. Brook me? *Brook me?* Ungrateful bastard. Did I not give him my beautiful daughter's hands in marriage? Did I not bring him into my own household? Treacherous snake. Foul dog that bites the hand that feeds it. I cannot wait to cut out his foul heart."

There were those in the room who might have reminded their king that he had humiliated a young prince by treating him like a stable boy, forced him to marry his scold of a daughter and sent him against his will

249

to be an ambassador in a kingdom where he was likely to be assassinated by resentful thegns. In fact, Paega, in his arrogance had not been true to the thew in offering the proper hospitality to a youth of rank and consequence. However, none dared to put such thoughts into words.

A messenger interrupted the king's ranting by rushing into the tent.

'My Lord,' cried the man, 'there are boatloads of warriors crossing the river from the other side and joining with prince's army.'

Paega stared at the warrior, his face black with rage, then he said in a low deep voice, 'The Walha. He's being joined by the Walha. That's why the mongrel has the river at his back. So that the Walha could come to him. They too shall pay.'

Tomos shook sword hands with Osric and nodded at the men pouring out of the river-craft behind him. Seven-hundred-and-fifty men,' he said. 'More than what you asked for.'

'All are welcome,' said Osric. 'Thank you, Tomos. Now, you must be given refreshment, you and your warriors. Then I shall explain the battle plan to you.'

Tomos raised his eyebrows. 'You have a *plan*?'

'I have a plan. A good one, used once before. And it worked the first time, so there's no reason not to think it won't work again, for us.'

Tomos looked around him. 'I was told you would have witches and giants, and dwarfs on your side?'

'They're coming just before the battle. You know what such creatures are like – they're quite shy – not the witches of course, but the others.'

'You trust them to come?'

'My good friend Sethrith the witch has promised.'

Tomos said, 'Then indeed, I hope she is a good friend, but for my part, man, I would sooner trust a serpent than a hag.

'She is no hag, I assure you. An enchantress might be a better word. Or even a sorceress. But not a hag.'

Tomos looked at Osric sideways and drew his own conclusions about the relationship between this mortal and the witch-girl.

Osric continued. 'I believe Paega will attack tomorrow. I hope he will attack tomorrow.'

Tomos said, 'I was told you had all the grass uprooted between their army and ours. Very strange, Osric.'

'No, you'll see tomorrow. Hopefully the wind will be in its usual direction for this area – west to east – otherwise we'll be in trouble. Hopefully it won't rain tonight and the ground will be dry.'

'I think you're half-mad, Angle.'

'Only half?'

They both laughed.

Lord Ing

I do not wish to boast – well yes, in fact I do – my persuasive powers have worked again – just a simple suggestion to Lord Woden, which he has grasped eagerly – too easily really, so perhaps the brag is unwarranted? But it doesn't take much to get the Lord of the Wild Hunt on his horse and charging about the night sky.

That night there was indeed a wild hunt in the skies. The one-eyed Lord Woden on his eight-legged steed, along with grisly companions, the spectres and ghouls who accompanied him on this frenzied chase, charged and swept around the heavens pursuing the wild boar. The phantasmal hunters, some of them dead fairies, others damned mortal souls, followed the savage hounds on horseback, screaming and wailing with delight, their laughter loud and demonic, and likely to drive any mortal within hearing, insane. Time had torn black holes in their grotesque faces through which the wind whistled and wailed. Eyes were bright and feverish with excitement. Insubstantial forms changed shape with every twist and turn through the blackness of the night. They swallowed moonbeams with their cavernous gaping mouths as they rode. The hooves of their ghostly mounts threw up divots of cloud behind them and their lashing manes and tails tied knots with loose bits of darkness. Roaring and rampaging through the atmosphere, this lunatic group of hunters were sometimes hurtling along the ground, sometimes just above it. Any mortal in their path was swept up with the mad riders and lost forever in the demented onrush.

Osric went around his camp, reassuring the warriors that this heavenly cacophony did not spell disaster.

'This is for our benefit,' he told his warriors, 'and to terrify the enemy.'

Indeed, in Paega's camps the men were horrified by the wild hunt, which they had always been told by their elders meant catastrophe was coming. They got no sleep through both the noise and the worry. Some men slipped away and set off across country heading for home, convinced that their lord's army was going to be butchered. Others sat hunched and shivering, pondering on their personal fate the following morning. The king himself took little notice of the raging in the heavens. Paega was not unsettled by any act of the gods, for he was descended from them, they were his ancestors. While his army cringed and trembled, King Paega slept off the mead, waking only to have a stinging piss in his bed-bowl and to curse Osric for his audacity and betrayal. The king was not a man to be frightened by sights and sounds. In fact, he was not a man to be frightened by anything. Years of battle had deadened his nerves to fear. He had seen it all before, had ever been victorious, was confident of winning the coming battle. Paega was made of the same iron as his sword.

The following morning the two armies readied themselves for the great conflict, drawing up battle lines. A good portion of Paega's conscripted Saxons and Jutes had left under darkness, unwilling to fight for a king who oppressed their people. Still the numbers in the Mercian king's army were superior to those in Osric's. The ratio was down to two-to-one in favour of the Mercians. Osric felt quite buoyed by this improvement of his chances of victory, even though he knew that many Bernicians in his ranks were inexperienced fighters. He had the Walha, and the Bernician thegns at least had seen battle before, against Paega.

Osric was thankful that there had been no rain during the night. In fact thankful that dry conditions had lasted for over a week before the battle. He watched keenly as Paega's army arranged themselves in their usual formation: the king in the centre with his most trusted nobles around him, all on horseback. In front of them the toughest, most battle-hardened of the warriors. Then on the flanks, the weaker and less trusted: the Mercian freemen churls with their spears and the slave troops on the left flank, the remainder of the conscripted Saxons and Jutes on the right. Still further out on the flanks was the cavalry, ready to sweep round and mop up the devastation which Paega expected to cause when the charge came. Osric had predicted the formation and was ready to arrange his own troops.

'Now remember, I want the weakest men in the centre,' he told Kenric and the Thief, 'and the strongest on the flanks. Tomos and his men on the right flank, the Bernician thegns and their best warriors on the left.'

The Thief looked astonished. 'Do you know what you're doing? I keep telling you, the strongest should be in centre, to meet Paega's thegns. They'll come at us like a battering ram and smash through. I've seen battles, Osric, I've been on their fringes and have run from them when necessary. I know how they're fought.'

'Trust me,' said Osric, calmly and determinedly. 'I do know what I'm doing. Now, as for the cavalry, I want them to charge their opposite numbers, Paega's cavalry, but when they get close I want them to dismount and use their bows. Using a bow while on horseback is extremely unreliable. Paega's cavalry will not have bows, they'll try to get in close to use their spears and swords. I want them shot out of their saddles before that happens.'

'Right,' said Kenric. 'Got it. An' where'll we be.'

'In the centre. I've already given Tomos and Cyneric their orders. Now let's get to it.'

King Paega watched the movements of the foe with equally keen eyes. He saw Osric commanding a motley band of churls in the centre of the line and the strongest troops, the Walha and battle-hardened Bernicians on the flanks.

'Doesn't the boy know anything about warfare?' he murmured with contempt. 'This is too easy, Sigeberht. We shall hang this upstart heath-walker from the gallows and Woden's guileful birds shall pick out his eyes. Woden's ravenous beasts shall devour his liver. Watch for the full moon tonight and you shall see a brace of ravens cross its face, whose names are Huginn and Muninn. Listen beyond the middle hour and you will hear two wolves howling deep in the darkness: Geri and Freki. Woden's beasts will feast on the sword-waving but cowardly traitor, Osric of the East Angles, as they leap on his corpse.

'When we are finished today, the serpent Nithogg shall feast on the blood and flesh of the Umbrians, as indeed it eats adulterers, murderers and oath-breakers. I shall send Osric's spirit to the Hall of Cowards, whose doors face the cold north, its walls made of serpents woven together like wickerwork, while our heroes will be winging their way to the *Waelheall*, which has a ceiling of golden shields and whose halls have more than six-hundred-and-forty doors, there to feast on the great boar, *Saehrimnir*, who comes back to life every morning so that he can be hunted again.'

With this speech, which was meant to fill his hearth-companions with pride and honour for their lord, he fell silent and watchful, planning the action.

Paega had placed his Hwicca slave-troops and the Celtic boys stolen from Walha villages on the flanks, knowing they would be slaughtered. He had no use for them, except as a distraction for the enemy. Today he was going to finally wipe out the Umbrian thegns, so that Bernicia and the tiny Deira could become Mercian. He would send nobles of his own hearth into these kingdoms and those realms would become Mercian. King Ewin, he would execute immediately.

'Are we ready, Sigeberht?'

'The sooner over, the better,' replied his closest thegn.

'Start sending missiles from the field-weapons,' ordered Paega, who had recently had this artillery fashioned from pictures left by the Romans in their mosaics, the only Angle or Saxon leader to recognise the worth of such inventions, 'we'll thin their ranks with rocks and iron spears before the main attack.'

So, the air was soon full of great stones and javelins of iron that fell amongst Osric's men. The damage was minimal, however, since these missiles were slow to travel through the air and the army could part quickly to let them through or allow them to drop on an empty space. Osric had no large ordnance of his own, so he merely called on his men to be alert. He was waiting for his supernatural reinforcements to arrive, hoping they would be in time to help thwart the attack from Paega which he knew would follow the rain of rocks from the sky.

At that moment Sethrith and seven covens of witches arrived on the battlefield, swooping down from the sky, most of them beldames, one or two of them, Sethrith for example, young novitiates. Their armour was not chain mail, but the linked and knitted bones of dead men which rattled when they moved. Underneath the bone-armour, to protect their wrinkled skins, they were clothed in rough-haired badger-hide. Over their breasts they wore human pelvises and their faces were covered by skulls, their intense fiery eyes peering through the sockets, their hairy noses poking through the nostril holes. The weapons they bore were skillets and fire-pokers, assisted of course by any magic in their power. They shrieked and howled, as witches will, with ear-splitting notes so that the men in both armies had to put their fingers in their ears to prevent deafness or madness. The Mercians were filled with a terrible dread knowing they were going against these creatures. Even the warriors of Osric's army were chilled by the sight and sound of these foul beings and they, being on the same side in this war, really had nothing to fear.

Then the giants came along the river bank, Ettins, a score of them, their feet drumming the hard earth with a slow, solid beat. They were big square-shaped creatures, almost as wide as they were tall. They had thin, straggly locks hanging from their flattened pates and their tiny eyes peered out through a veil of hair. Everything about them was dull and heavy-looking, from their stubby, stump-like fingers to their brick-shaped teeth. In their hands they carried huge stone clubs or the trunks of trees with a root-clump still clinging to mud. They moaned as they walked, as giants will moan, as if just to move from one place to another was a waste of precious energy and time. Great lumbering beasts they were, that trod on bush and shrub with no regard for any natural living thing, whether useful or pretty. If a domestic dog or a wild fox did not get out of the way, it was stamped flat as a cow pat and the perpetrator did not even bother to look back. Even as they took their place in the battle line, a heavy spear shot from a Mercian field-bow struck one of these beings in the forehead and he fell like an ancient oak, the ground juddering on impact. His fellow giants wailed in deathly-hollow tones but none inspected his fatal wound. They simply took their place in the line with backs towards the river.

Once the giants were in position, their females indistinguishable from males, some swarthy dweorgs – those lumpy dwarfs with clever metalsmith skills – came up from underground, bursting out of the earth like moles and blinking in the bright daylight. Several were armed with iron hammers and others had axes made of flint lashed to hornbeam roots. Some too had spears of limestone stalactites, while the shorter fellows, only waist-high to a mortal, each had a rope-handled rock to whirl around their heads. The language they used was deep and dark, full of harsh consonants and drawn-out vowels. They were continually on the move, like fish in a shoal being chased by a predator, or ants under attack, and milled around amongst the mortals getting in the way of each other, bumping into friend or relation.

Finally, over the Mercian army, a huge dragon with monstrous wings and a long, long tail gracefully glided. The shadow thrown down by this mighty beast threw the whole of Paega's army into a panic. Even the king himself shuddered when he looked up and saw the colossal shape of the creature. Though the dragon was high up, men crouched and cringed, as if the beast were going to descend upon their heads.

Though there was no attack from the dragon, it had unnerved Paega's army and the king had to ride along the lines reassuring his warriors.

'Stop cowering, you fools! It's gone, over the hills and far away. Look, it's not coming back. It's gone for good.'

By the time he was back in place and ready to give the order to attack, it was almost noon and the whole morning had passed. Indeed, the stored water in his camp had been used up two days previously and there were no wells or streams nearby. The only water to be had was in the river and parties sent out along to distant banks had been attacked and harried by Osric's skirmishers. Survivors had returned with their vessels empty. The Mercians were now extremely thirsty and many were tired, having been kept awake by the wild hunt. There was nothing for it but to attack, however. King Paega looked along the lines of his thousands of warriors, the magnificent banners and standards fluttering in the wind and pride filled his chest. On his own spear were the scalps of three kings he had beaten in battle. Brave, brave men. Stalwart fighters. Strong, as hard as greywacke stone, almost invincible. Yet Paega had trampled them into the ground. Who would not dread such an army, led by the most feared and skilled warrior-king on these islands?

'Now!' he yelled. 'Three gold armrings for the man who brings me Osric of the East Angles – alive!'

A hoarse cheer went up and the name of 'King Paega' came from a seven-thousand throats.

The front line of Paega's horde of warriors charged across the plain towards the river, their feet raising dust on the ground that Osric's men had cleared of vegetation. The prevailing wind had not failed Osric. Soon the yellow dirt was billowing up in clouds from thousands of soles and heels. The charging men had trouble seeing ahead and were choking. Already they were desperately thirsty and dry dust turned their throats and tongues to harsh sandstone. Before long, in their near blindness, the lines began to break up, some men running faster than others. Foot-warriors began to run into one another, while thegns on horses surged too far ahead, their riders screaming battle cries. The bullroarers fell silent as these instruments clogged. Drummers were denied their rhythmic beat. The charge began to turn into a shambles as men lost their companions in the dust storm and their confidence was sapped.

Those who halted, coughing and spluttering, were trampled by the hordes coming up from behind. Still the main body of warriors thundered forward: some four-thousand men, like a giant herd of blind cattle. From the ridge far behind, the reserves waited to be called into the fray, many desperate to be part of this great victory.

The horsemen, their warlord-king among them, hit the wide ditch just a hundred strides before Osric's front line. Horses tumbled through the bracken disguising the ditch and went down, screaming and whinnying. Men yelled in shock as they were thrown through the air. Osulf, to the king's right, hit the ground head-first and Paega heard the snapping of his neck. Assel, a cousin of Osulf, landed on his legs, both of which shattered, the fractured shins piercing through the skin and showing white ragged ends. Mercifully a riderless horse came on and crushed his head with a hind hoof, ending his dismay and pain. For several minutes it was chaos as men fought to regain their feet, or to squeeze from under a thrashing horse. Osric even thought of charging at this point, but reminded himself that he needed to stick to Hannibal's battle plan and charging greater odds was not part of it.

Those Mercian riders who did not break their spines, or a vital bone, quickly got to their feet and urged the foot-warriors coming up behind to join them. However, many of the horses in the dirt channel could not get out, their legs caught in broken pots, and they impeded the onward rush of warriors, scores of whom fell into the same ditch and were lacerated by the shards of the shattered crockery. Some were so badly cut they bled to death, still calling for water to slake their thirst. Soon the many hundreds behind the front ranks were running over their comrade's bodies, which choked the dry channel. Mostly men's eyes were on the river, hoping that they could scythe through Osric's front line and go on to reach the water.

King Paega's nobles, those that were still able and whole after the fatal ditch, gathered about him and called for order amongst his warriors. They now regrouped and the king, savage with rage, called for a second charge against Osric's line. Here the stalwart churls and farmers were presenting an unbroken row of round wooden leather-covered shields, the bosses gleaming and sunlight dancing among the bronze-studded surfaces of the protective line. This was the famous defensive 'shield-wall' of the Angles and Saxons: difficult for any attacking enemy to penetrate since rows of spears protruded like the spines over and through the wooden wall. All that could be seen above the wall were the iron helmets of those warriors behind it.

Paega and his warriors flung themselves at this barrier with great fury and vehemence and the wall was forced backwards by their onslaught. Indeed, Paega was triumphant when he saw the ranks of the foe wavering, bending towards the river, giving way under the onrush of the Mercian centre, not understanding that this was precisely what Osric had been counting on. The king cried out that the enemy's shield-wall was collapsing, that those warriors would soon be eating the dirt at his feet. He called for the slingers to send their stones over the shields and the air was soon full of a hail of flints. Then, under this umbrella of pebbles, Paega urged his men forward in a strong spearhead attack, expecting to force his way through the weak line. The shield wall bent back even further, a flexible line rather than solid as it normally should be.

Yes, the foe's centre was giving way, but out on the flanks it was a different story. The Walha had sent the Saxons and Jutes on the foe's left wing running back to the forest. These Mercian allies were there unwillingly anyway and had only put up a token fight before retreating in numbers. They felt no allegiance to the Mercian king and felt no loss of honour leaving him to a fight of his own making. In fact, for a brace of hares each they would have joined with Osric's men. Soon Paega, though he did not yet know it, was a thousand men short of his original seven.

On the other flank, his Hwicca slave-troops were being cut down like reeds under a sickle-wielding thatcher. They were hopelessly untrained for war, since no Mercian really trusted them with weapons. Some were fleeing like the Saxons and Jutes, others were dropping their arms and falling to their knees, awaiting their fate. Cyneric was having similar success to Tomos, on the other flank, and this side of the battlefield too saw Paega's men fleeing for their lives towards woodland.

The flanks dealt with, Cyneric and Tomos turned their forces inward, to come at Paega's main force from two sides. The Mercian king was caught in a pincer, being squeezed tightly into a central knot by the two enemy flanks. Mercians were soon battling to get out of the crush, some going down under the feet of their comrades. Arms were pinned down by sides and legs were static, having no room to move forward, backwards or sideways. Somehow the vanguard managed a retreat, forcing its way back through the mass of warriors, the hearth-companions protecting their warlord-king and getting him to safety at the rear. Dudda, that simple noble, was standing by his lord and king when an arrow entered his right ear, the point coming out of his left. He turned to look at Paega, an expression of surprise on his face, then slid to the ground under the feet of companions. The Mercian thegns were depleted, but still numerous and vengeful enough for a second attack. The dark elves and the black dogs had not yet been used, but Paega needed a respite to gather his thoughts, realising now that he had to remain cool and calm. This was not a battle he could win by crushing the enemy with sheer numbers or with blind rage.

Out beyond the foot-warriors, beyond their flanks, Paega's cavalry was being massacred by the horsemen of Osric's army. The Bernicians and Walha riders under Osric's instructions had first ridden and then dismounted. They then stood their ground and waited for the charge of the Mercian cavalry. Predictably it came and the archer-horsemen proceeded to shoot the Mercian riders out of their saddles as this foolhardy enemy rode straight at them. Riderless steeds began to tangle with the Mercian cavalry and caused further mayhem. Some of the enemy tried to leave the field, riding out of the dust cloud towards the distant forest, but wild-haired witches intercepted them and dragged them from their mounts, then beat them to death with skillets and pokers. Those horsemen who managed to get through this havoc got only as far as their baggage train before spells cast by the witches caused sprouting branches and leaves to come out of their ears, mouths and eyes, and the orifices below their waists. These unfortunates dropped from their steeds as living, walking clumps of foliage. Here they thrashed and stumbled around in terror, frightening the female camp followers, who ran away from this scene of abominable transmogrification.

Now Paega's black dogs were let loose, creatures almost the height of a man, and these beasts went hurtling into the Bernician lines snatching up warriors in their savage jaws and tossing the broken bodies aside. Sethrith and her witches began to take on these demonic creatures, sealing their jaws with magic so that the dwarfs could club their shins and bring them down to hammer their heads. Soon the giants had waded in with their stone and tree-trunk clubs, smashing the black dogs, breaking their backs, crushing their skulls. It was not long before those creatures who had survived the witches, dwarfs and giants, fled from the field howling with anguish.

Elsewhere on the battlefield, Paega's men were in dire straits. Many were so thirsty they had run on through the Bernician ranks to the river to drink. Others were locked in by the pincer movement and those in the centre were still struggling to wield their weapons while their comrades on the edges were being hacked down. Tomos's Walha were cutting a swathe through the flank of the enemy from the right and Cyneric's Bernicians were wreaking similar havoc with the foe on the left. The Mercians, still in the greater numbers, were being squeezed like a piece of fruit, their blood flowing on the earth like juice.

Those who managed to break away from the melee fled the field in the only direction they could go, which was north-east along the river bank. Here they were slaughtered by the giants who kicked and punched them into the flast-flowing waters, where many drowned. Paega's army started breaking up and scattering in full flight. Osric had forbidden his men to pursue them, knowing that only if he could keep his army as a unit would he be victorious, for Paega still commanded a sizeable number of warriors. The day was not over until King Paega was dead or captured. Indeed, until the Mercians had no warrior-king to inspire them.

The witches, giants and dwarfs, though short in numbers, were terrifying the enemy with their might and magic. The giants were simply picking up bunches of Mercians and throwing them into the river. Those that could swim went for the far bank, not intending to get back into the fight. The witches had produced short staves from within the folds of their flowing garments, which transformed anyone they touched into a base creature: a toad, slug or worm. Mercian warriors were fleeing in large numbers as they saw what was happening to their fellow fighters. The dwarfs remained on the periphery, chopping away at the legs of those who tried to go back into the fight. Osric, seeing all this happening around him, lost some of his battle-heat and actually called to Paega to surrender, so that the killing and the transmogrifications could cease.

King Paega, however, blew a long, wailing note on a golden horn, the sound of which drifted over the meadows behind his lines. This was a signal to a great horde of dark elves, who had been lurking in a forest on a ridge, ready to come out and begin their slaughter. They carried black bows and black arrows, the latter tipped with deadly poison, and seeing their lean dark shapes flood down the slopes towards the river filled Osric's men with fear and dread. These creatures of the otherworld were taller than ordinary mortals and in their gaunt, sallow faces were buried eyes that had never known pity or compassion. Paega had promised to send the dark elves three-hundred young children, probably to be used as slaves or even worse as cattle, in payment for their help. They came with no battle cries or grand gestures, but simply slid silently en masse down the slopes, their wicked, gleaming teeth visible as their mouths salivated at the thought of feeding on the enemy dead. Some of Osric's men, on seeing these menacing creatures descending on them, were terrified and ran from the field and down towards the river.

However, before the dark elves reached the bottom of the gradient a similar signal went out from Quercus and from the far side of the river came a wailing reply. Then out of the woods on the distant bank the light elves came riding, crossing the water on their beautiful horses, whose hooves barely touched the surface of the river. On reaching the shore they rode through, high over and around the mass of fighting men and straight at the dark elves, who had stopped in their tracks. The light elves formed a line at the bottom of the incline, facing their dark brethren. There was an exchange in that strange high-pitched language of the elves, between the respective leaders, and soon the dark elves were striding back up the slopes down which they had come, yelling what sounded like insults and obscenities at their cousins still sitting on their horses in a quiet dignified line, watching them go.

The light elves then left the way they had come without any fuss.

'What happened?' asked Osric of his son Quercus. 'What did they say to each other?'

'What you would expect, Father. Thorn told the dark elves that they would have to pass through the line of the light elves if they wanted to proceed.'

'Thorn? My old friend. And they were afraid to do that?'

'Not so much *afraid*, but unwilling.'

Osric said, 'Well, I don't understand but I'm grateful… So, my elfen mentor Thorn was leading the light elves. I should have guessed.'

At that moment Osric was attacked by a Mercian thegn and had to leave his son's side to deal with the threat.

King Paega, Lord of the Mercians, set about rallying those of his nobles who were still on two feet and also the remnants of his vanguard, along with the reinforcements he had left in the rear. He prepared to make another charge. The order was then given and, having learned nothing from his initial attack, the shape of his force remained that of an arrow-head. The Mercian king was still attempting to pierce the weak centre of the opposing army. This time Osric ordered that centre to open up and let the charging Mercians through. With terrible ferocity and wild cries the Mercians drove their wedge right through the middle of their foe to reach the river bank.

Paega realised his mistake when he found himself and his men with their backs to the wild flowing waters of the tidal river. The enemy closed in around him. He still had many warriors, but they were mostly scattered. Even those who had remained by him, almost two-thousand, were looking for avenues of escape. They were hemmed in by Osric's men, who now encircled the exhausted attackers. Clearly the Mercians were going to be cut down in their dozens if they did not surrender. Some were prepared for this, prepared to die for their lord, but others thought that the waste of life was unnecessary, that such action was a warrior-king's indulgence

Sigeberht was one of these who knew the day to be lost

Thus Paega's most trusted thegn and closest hearth-companion cried out. 'Enough my lord! Can't you see? The Bernicians and their allies have overwhelmed us. Let the killing stop!'

An enraged King Paega swung round with a murderous expression on his face and cried, 'Traitor! Where is your honour?' and struck Sigeberht down with his sword.

This act horrified even the Mercians who saw it. They parted from their lord and left him standing alone with the bloody sword in his hand. Osric then went forward, *Rowena* in his grasp, stained with the hot blood of fallen Mercians. Osric then engaged Paega in single combat. With all men now exhausted, arms by their sides, the warriors of both armies simply stood watched this duel.

The pair clashed blades and tried to find an opening in the opponent's guard. It was clear that the older and more experienced Paega was the better swordsmen. His eyes glittered with excitement. Now it was one against one. The Mercian king was confident of victory. A man against a boy! The contest was his for the asking. At one point the pair paused, both fatigued, and stepped away from each other to recover their breath. Paega used this break to jeer at his foe.

'Brook me, eh boy? You have a long way to go to be a man yet!' crowed the Mercian king. 'I'll have your entrails on my blade and then the fighting will begin again. I'll not leave the field until either your men are all dead, or my Mercians are all in their graves.'

It might have been the last part of this sentence that motivated Horsa's next move, or perhaps the callous murder of the king's closest noble and his best friend by the royal hand. Clearly, whether King Paega won or this single combat or not, Mercia had lost the battle and would be cut down to a man if they continued to fight. So Paega's once faithful noble stepped forward and struck the king down. Horsa's sword descended onto Paega's head and split helmet in twain. Headho then followed, driving his own blade through Paega's heart before the king hit the ground.

Horsa cried, 'Over! It is over. Lord Osric, we ask to be able to leave with our wounded and our dead.'

A great cheer went up from the ranks of Osric's small but able army. They had won. Some of the Bernician nobles could hardly believe it. They had been under the thumb of the Mercians for so long and had lost every battle until now. They walked around with dazed expressions on their faces, while the Walha tended to their wounded and began gathering up their own fallen. By nightfall, there were so many mounds of dead warriors, in truth most of them Mercians, it was decided to make mass graves on the bank of the river and put enemy and friend in with one another. Horsa and Headho insisted on taking the bodies of Paega and Sigeberht home to give them a ceremonial burial fitting of their rank and status.

When Osric asked about repercussions from those still in Mercia, Headho replied, 'There is no one back there except children and women. Even most of the old men are here today, for Paega wanted the largest army he could muster. Now we have lost at least a quarter of our army to Freo and Woden, who share the dead between them. Another quarter are wounded and some of those will die too. There is no one to accuse us of disloyalty to our king. He was clearly mad to want to lose a whole nation of warriors for the satisfaction of his own pride.'

'You realise that I am now going to proclaim myself ruler of Mercia?'

'That's your right. We've been defeated. You will be a hated king and will have to survive many assassination attempts, but that's up to you.'

Osric nodded. 'I don't plan to take up kingship, only temporary rulership. You need your own king, hopefully a less vainglorious one. I simply want control of your army for the time it takes to regain my own realm. Go on your way now. I will come to the main village when we have finished our own orisons and obligations to the dead here and then we can discuss things further.'

Headho nodded. Then he walked away, his head hanging low. Horsa too looked utterly miserable. These Mercian thegns had for so long now, perhaps their whole lives, been part of the ruling realm of the island's kingdoms. They had subjugated all the regions around them and had been lords of all they surveyed. Now that was at an end, until perhaps a new Mercian king arose with the same lofty ambitions as Paega. Until then they had to suffer the humiliation of a defeated people: defeated not only by a numerically lesser army but by those they considered their inferiors. They dragged themselves from the battlefield and Osric knew that unless he showed clemency as their new ruler, they would show enough defiance to thwart his own plans of regaining his father's kingdom.

Lord Tiw:

Well, that was a good one. I enjoyed that. Who would have thought that those Bernicians and their allies - most of whom do not pay any regard to gods such as myself, Lord Ing - could defeat such huge numbers. It was all in that plan, I suppose, that the young East Angle had in his possession? Strategy, he called it. Strange word. A battle is a battle as far as I'm concerned. You shouldn't need plans. Just get in there and hack away until they're all dead on one side, or they throw up their arms.

₣I₩Ɇ

Lord Ing:

So, all's well. Our side won. I had no doubts. And those dark elves. They need a talking to, sometime. I expect my sister put them up to it. Elves should not go meddling in the affairs of mortals, any more than gods do.

You have to leave men and women free to make their own mistakes, though I do think sometimes they go to extremes. Greed and hunger for power are the motivators. My Lord Woden understands the second one, but none of the gods really know what it is to be avaricious.

Once the observances for the dead were over, especially the Ierfealu – the round of ritual toasts dedicated to the deceased – Osric called his friends to his tent. The solemn funerals, eulogies and elegies had taken several days and Osric's men had since had time to reflect on the bestiality of man's basic instincts. War, Osric decided, was a strange activity, full of contradictions. Prior to the battle, the men were usually pensive and fearful of losing their mortality. During the fighting they were often swept up in fiery heroism and blood-letting, the fever of death and destruction boiling in their blood. After the killing and maiming was over, they were mostly appalled by the experience, having to contend with guilt and grief, and their feelings of the horror of the acts. Many spent the post-war days staring into space or with their heads in their hands, probably wondering why men – sensitive scholars and spiritual leaders, artists and writers, philosophers and craftsmen – are brutish creatures underneath, savages really.

The women who had accompanied Osric's army had tended to the wounded and were still nursing them. The camp followers of Paega's army had done likewise with their own warriors. Many would have died without these non-combatants, who risked their own lives to be near their loved ones. There had been conquerors in the past who had taken revenge on their enemy by slaughtering the women and children who had followed their men to the killing grounds.

Osric was now a rich man, having captured the Paega's baggage train, which was full of the king's personal treasure. There were gold armrings in caskets, which Paega would have given to his own nobles once the battle was over. These were now passed out to Osric's thegns, the Bernician warriors, with great ceremony. Osric had risen in a day from rebel to lord. He was now an armring-giver, not yet a king, but close to becoming one. Those who had stood with him on the field of blood would ever regard him as their lord. They had seen the determined ferocity of his sword arm and the skill of his elfen bow and they were greatly impressed. He would now go on to claim the king's place in Mercia, where he knew he would not be welcome.

'Those of you not yet rewarded,' he told his army, 'will soon be given your due – there is more treasure in Paega's Great Hall, which is ours by right of conquest.'

Already from the body of Paega, the victorious thegns had taken a shoulder-clasp of stupendous beauty, wrought-gold inlaid with blood-red garnets, wonderfully worked by the artist who had made it. This had been given to Osric by his men. Paega's fabulous sword and dagger were also Osric's, and in the baggage train were beautiful cloaks of dyed wool, wolfskin, bearskin, and other cured hides, woven blankets, many other items of great value. Paega's magnificent helmet was ruined but there were other helmets, some of them just as splendid as the one the king died wearing. These were all gathered and held by the Thief, who almost surrendered to the instincts of his lifelong trade, but managed to resist by sheer force of will.

Osric thanked his friends profusely for their help and promised Tomos that at least for the foreseeable future there would be peace between the Walha and the Mercians. This is what the Walha had fought for and of course they expected no less. The Walha were given their share of the treasure captured from the baggage train and Tomos was elated by the victory, though, like everyone else, in deep sorrow for those comrades lost on the battlefield.

'Our cause was good, though,' said this dark-haired fighter, 'and men were fashioned for war, which is both glorious and abominable. We took many heads.'

Indeed they had a wagon full of severed heads of slain Mercian thegns (mostly the good-looking ones which are often mistakenly believed to have belonged to the strongest and most skilful warriors) to flourish in front of those who had not joined them in the march to war. 'I shall go back to my own country, back to my people, with the prize that Paega will never again send an army into Brythoniaid to kill our people. Mercia as a nation will take a long time to recover from this defeat.'

'When I leave this region for the East Angles, I can't guarantee the truce will hold,' Osric told Tomos. 'However, as you say, the Mercians won't be in any shape to attack the Walha for a long time to come. They're not so much depleted in numbers, though they have lost a great many warriors, as mentally defeated. It will take them a few decades or more before they get back their old arrogance and to do that they need another Paega. However terrible that king was to others, he had a personality and character that filled his people with awe – he commanded great respect and was feared as much as our great god, Woden – King Paega will not be easily replaced.'

Next, Osric turned his attention to Sethrith, who was also present.

'My thanks to you and your band of witches. We could not have beaten the Mercians without you. Also, I know they have left with the body of their one dead member, but please pass on my thanks to the giants. Why they gave their assistance, I do not know, but it is very much appreciated. Again, the battle would not have been won without them. As for the dweorgs, our dwarf friends, I have already thanked their leader and given them gold for their metalworkers to use. I'm sure we shall see some beautiful jewellery.'

'I shall pass on your words and I have to tell you that the reason the Ettin giants came was because you are reported to have once killed a Thurse giant, one of their sworn and deadly enemies in the otherworld in which we live.'

'Ah, indeed I did kill a Thurse, when I was with the elves.' Osric nodded towards his son, who acknowledged him. 'However, I could not have done it without my elven friends. Speaking of which, Quercus, you must tell Thorn how much I honour him and believe him to be a prince among his kind.'

Quercus said, 'He won't understand that calling him a "prince" is any kind of compliment, my lord, but I will try to convey your appreciation for their help.'

Next it was Cyneric's turn to receive Osric's thanks. Ewin, having heard of the success of his Bernician warriors, had ridden to the battlegrounds and was now in the camp. It was he who presented his best thegn, Cyneric, with three gold armrings and some other pieces of treasure. Cyneric was now a hero among his people and some were whispering that he was destined for kingship, should anything untoward happen to their rather effete current lord and ruler, whose poetry was beginning to become wearisome and repetitive of a long evening in the Great Hall.

Ewin was absolutely ecstatic at the outcome of the war and had taken time to study the ground where his hated enemy King Paega had been struck down, saying, 'And is that stain his blood? I must collect some of that darkened dust in a container to keep in my hall. Do you have his drinking horn, Osric? I would like to have it, if I may, to fill with cow shit and dangle from the doorway. I don't suppose you managed to cut off his testicles? No? Pity, I could have kept them dried in a jar to rattle when I feel a little despondent. I'm sure doing so would cheer my spirit.'

When asked about Rowena's reaction to the death of her father, Ewin pursed his lips and then nodded.

'She shrieked and said that she was going to kill you as soon as she could and that her father had been the kindest and most considerate man that ever walked the face of the Earth – and then she burst out laughing and could not seem to stop for the whole length of a burning candle.' Ewin put his arm around Osric in nonspiritual fashion, whispering in his ear, 'I swear I have no understanding of the princess, Osric. I find her desirable and fascinating, but her mind is a mystery to me. What did you make of her in the time you were married to her, short though it was? Did you have any perception of how her mind worked? I must confess I spend nights beside her wondering if she is fairy or succubus. Tell me, though, do you know her?'

'My Lord,' replied Osric, 'you are asking the wrong man. I do not understand *any* woman, Princess Rowena least of all. They are all an enigma to me and, I think, to any man. They do not say what they mean and they never mean what they say. It's best to treat them as we do the elves, as cryptic, mystical creatures from another world, to looked at, to be admired, to be loved even, but not to be understood.'

'I believe you are right,' replied Ewin, tapping his own chin thoughtfully. 'Yes, I think you are. Very profound, my friend. I shall leave Rowena's mind to Rowena and enjoy the body that encases it, the beautiful casket that holds that enigmatic brain locked away. How wise you are. A warrior and a sage, I think. Yes, I do.'

'You flatter me, my Lord.'

Osric's favours and highest honours, however, were reserved for his closest friend, Kenric. Kenric was made an earl, a noble of great consequence, and given a great deal of the land which Osric appropriated from the Mercians. Twelve hides were taken by Osric and four of these went to Kenric. Two went to the Thief and he himself kept six. The Mercian lords who had previously owned these hides were all dead, killed on the battlefield. Osric made sure the families of the slain Mercians were comfortable, but not rich. He wanted no deaths of children or widows on his conscience.

This was after Osric had entered the main Mercian village, which the Great Hall of King Paega dominated, at the head of his warriors. The villagers and thegns who watched him come in looked surly and mutinous. They were unused to being subjugated and Osric could see that rebellion was already simmering. He did not, however, want kingship of this place and called Headho and Horsa to the Great Hall. With the Thief and Kenric at his side and fifty Bernician thegns within call, he met with this brace of Mercian thegns who had survived the war.

'I want you two to announce your joint rulership of Mercia,' he told them.

They stared at him as if he were mad, mystified by this decision.

'Why?' asked Horsa.

'Because I don't want it and you do.'

The pair looked at each other, then nodded.

Headho said, 'Yes, we would like to rule.'

'Are you able to agree with one another over important issues? Are you able to discuss problems without losing your tempers?'

They said they had grown up together, had been the best of friends since birth and, though they quarrelled over small matters, they rarely argued over big things.

'Then I think you should take my offer, before some other thegn steps forward and gives me a reason to choose them over the pair of you. I wish Sigeberht were still alive – if he was, I would definitely have given the opportunity to him – but he is not and you two are. All I ask is that you comply with my request for an army when I call for it, to march against the East Angles, as we did before.'

Horsa's looks were dark. 'You have plundered our treasures.'

'As is his right,' said the Thief. 'He is the conqueror of your nation. In his compassion he has let you all live. Your own king would have massacred any and all of the enemy left on the battlefield, had he been victorious instead of Osric. You should be grateful you are still walking the world.'

'Who are you?' said Headho. 'You are nothing but a thief.'

'I'm one of those who crushed an army many times larger than my own.'

Horsa cried, 'You did it with witches and giants!'

'And you still couldn't do it with black dogs and dark elves.'

'This man is my trusted aide,' added Osric to Headho, 'and you will be respectful to those who overcame you. As he says, the gold and jewels are mine by right of conquest. You must also respect the thew, the virtues and honour which make a man a man, just as I must observe wealthdeal, the generosity and gift-giving which make a ruler stand above his peers. Horsa and Headho, at the next Thunor's day you must hold a Thing and at that assembly announce your duel kingship.'

The pair still simmered a little, but they knew Osric's generosity was great – he could indeed have had them executed – and they accepted the boon.

'Now I will see Beornwynne, Paega's queen,' said Osric, not looking forward to this meeting whatsoever, 'if she desires conversation with me. However, if she screams and rails at me, or calls me foul names, I will have her thrown into a cage and transported to Bernicia, where they will know what to do with her. Tell her that her son Ramm is safe, that I will not harm him, so long as he does not plot against me. If he does, he will be executed without a moment's hesitation. Is that understood? Tell her to send me the keys to her husband's personal wealth.'

Prince Ramm had not been on the battlefield, but had been charged with defending the kingdom while his father was away at war. He was no warrior, but his status as the son of Paega could easily gather to him thegns willing to sacrifice their lives to restore the kingdom to Paega's dynasty. Just because a man is no fighter does not mean he can't intrigue with the best of them. In fact, the fewer muscles the more likely the deviousness. One needed tools to survive in the harsh world of the Angles and Saxons, and machinations of the mind were as good as physical strength.

The two main duties of an Angle or Saxon queen are: one, to hold the keys to the king's material possessions, and two, to remind him to behave honourably in all things. Beornwynne, however, refused to see Osric – 'that foul supplanter' – saying she wished to be left alone in her bereavement. Osric was both relieved and pleased that he would not have to face the widow. He could deal with male maniacs and murderous men, but women were much, much more difficult. Once he had held the large iron keys in his hand, weighed them thoughtfully with his palm, Osric sent them back to the queen without opening the locks on the chests. This was the last of Osric's duties and he too was now permitted to relax and fall into that pit of darkness that follows a war, there to try to come to terms with his own barbarous nature.

That first night he and his two closest friends went to sleep in the forge which had been cold for quite a while now. There were Bernician nobles on watch to guard them. In the early morning, some Mercian warriors tried to get in to kill them, but they were struck down by the guards. Thereafter, things settled down and Osric began to plan his march to the East Angles and what he would do once there.

One morning he strolled with his thegns through the Mercian marketplace, to purchase some supplies for a journey to Bernicia. As he did so he stopped at the stall of Thark, the butcher, and inspected the meat on sale. Thark stood watching Osric, his eyes flicking this way and that, possibly seeking escape if necessary.

'Be whole,' said Osric. He then asked, 'What will you take for the boar's shanks and torso?'

Thark, thinking the prince had forgotten he knew him, decided to be bold. 'That gold clasp you're wearing?'

'Ah, you've regained your old impetuousness, I see, as in the days when you tried to bully me on the wall. I'm also told you were going to cut pieces off me, after Paega had won the battle, Thark. Are you still of the same mind?'

Thark's face drained of blood. He stepped back and said, 'Please take the boar – it's yours for nothing.'

Osric said, 'No, I couldn't do that. It wouldn't be right. Name your price – a realistic one, if you please.'

'Two woollen blankets?'

'Indeed, the boar is worth three, but I will give you two.'

The blankets were lifted from the bundle which Osric had taken with him for trading, then the prince said, 'Be careful with your boasts, Thark. Don't make threats unless you believe you can carry them out. You're a foolish man, sometimes, butcher, but I'm convinced there may be some good in you. Are you married?'

'Yes, my lord.'

'Do you treat her well?'

'Oh, I do, I do, my lord, for she has given me a son.'

271

This was said with such pride Osric could not help smiling.

'I'm glad to hear it.'

With that the prince walked on and word of this encounter spread throughout the villages, and thereafter the threat of assassination was somewhat less than before. Mercians saw that they had been conquered by a just and compassionate man and though they still hated him for destroying their empire, they also realised that they had been beaten by a prince who was the moral superior of their dead king.

SIX

Osric spent the winter in Mercia and was there to see the joint kingship ceremony of Horsa and Headho take place. Then when the spring came he regathered his army, now swelled by the Mercians he had conscripted – which included the two new kings – and set forth for the kingdom of the East Angles. On the way he was joined by Saxons and Jutes: those who had been conscripted by Paega and spared by Osric, once the battle had been won by the Bernicians and Walha. Osric's army, now swollen by additional bands from several kingdoms, marched on the East Angles. The attacking force was so great, those who knew they were coming also knew that they would be annihilated if they resisted any demands made by its leader.

However, the arrogant Wulfgar rallied his warriors, believing he could crush Osric. Secretly, however, the East Angles were aware that many of those coming to fight them were fresh from a massive victory and full of confidence. They had also heard stories, some greatly exaggerated with the retelling, of Osric's prowess and skill at war. The inhabitants of the East Angles were convinced that the patricide son who had slain his father, King Eorl, was coming to slaughter them. Many of them prepared for death, believing Osric was going to lay waste to the land after he had slain King Wulfgar and had massacred that king's army.

Osric halted his warriors just before the shield wall set up by Wulfgar and his army. Here he stood up in his stirrups and addressed the East Angles.

'You men are fighting under a false king,' he called. 'It was not I who killed King Eorl but the man who leads you to your deaths today. Eadgard, Wulfgar, Finnan and Holt, all conspired to murder my father and place the blame on me. Hand over Wulfgar, and my army will melt away, I give you my word.'

Wulfgar's voice came back. 'The word of a liar and a murderer!'

'You have heard my offer,' called Osric, 'I will not speak with that loathsome creature who answered me. What is it to be? Ask him if he has the courage and vestige of honour to walk out and give himself to me, or whether he will lead you into a slaughter not of your own making, but of his.'

'How do we know you'll go away?' cried an East Angle, from the flank of the shield wall. 'How do we know…?'

'Silence that man,' yelled Wulfgar, brandishing his sword. 'Cut that man down where he stands.'

No one moved, not East Angle thegn, nor churl, nor kitchen boy.

Horsa broke ranks and rode forward. He spoke loudly and clearly.

'I am Horsa, of the Mercians. You all know me from previous battles. I have no love for this man, Prince Osric, but I tell you this in all faith. He is no liar. He is as honourable as any warrior who follows the thew. If he says he did not kill his father, a bestial deed that would make any man sick to his stomach, then he is to be believed. I stake my own life on that statement. I also guarantee that if Wulfgar is given up, I will lead the Mercians in this army back to where they came from. Cyneric of the Bernicians will do the same with the Umbrian thegns and warriors. This king of yours is a foul creature who I have no doubt struck your own King Eorl down, killed him in his bed while he slept, and then put the blame on his son. I speak for Osric, whom I fought in the Battle of Sabrina River, who killed my own younger brother in that fight, who subjugated my people. I leave you time to ponder my words.'

There was silence from the other side for a while, then a struggle broke out behind the shield wall. Eventually, the shields parted and two strong men walked out with Wulfgar between them, holding him securely by his arms. They threw him at the feet of Osric's horse and then walked back to their lines. The shield wall then closed and everyone waited for Osric to strike the huge warrior below him.

'Wulfgar,' cried Osric, 'you will remember how you chased me across the ice of our own river and your companions fell through and drowned? I told you then that I would come back and avenge my father's death…'

Wulfgar sneered and stood tall, waiting for the weapon to cut him down.

'Well, here I am. In those days, at that time, I would have killed you without a second thought. But lately I have been thinking it might not have been you who wielded the actual blade that ended my father's life. I shall never know which of you four murderers actually struck that fatal blow. For that reason I'm not going to execute you,' there was a gasp from both armies, 'but what I *am* going to do you will probably regard as worse than death. Banishment. Henceforth you are an outlaw in several kingdoms – Bernicia, Deira, Mercia and East Anglia. Any man who meets you may kill you without fear of reprisal. No one shall offer you shelter, or food and drink, without fearing for their own safety. Go from here. I never want to see or hear of you again. If you try to return, you will end on the gallows and then on the gibbet, for men to spit on your remains. Leave this place and hide your loathsome self in some fetid hole which you may share with beasts of a higher order. You belong among the slugs and the worms which will eventually feed on your flesh.'

Two Bernicians dismounted and took hold of the burly Wulfgar, stripping him of his fine clothes, then thrust him towards the outeryards, towards the wilderness, naked and humiliated. Wulfgar strode off, his head high, turning only once to raise his fist at Osric, then he was gone into the bogs and marshlands. Someone amongst Osric's army gave out a loud fart – and everyone began laughing. There was to be no battle today, nor any day in the near future. Horsa and Headho could lead their Mercians home, while Cyneric could do the same with his thegns and freemen. Some would stay to protect Osric, for there would still be those with doubts in the villages of East Anglia, and always would be. Some would talk of smoke and fire until they died, because they believed they were more canny than their neighbours.

It took a little time for the truth of past events to sink into the skulls of these eastern people, but eventually they came to realise that they had been fooled by the deviousness of Eadgard and Wulfgar. It's not easy to accept that one has been duped, for one feels stupid and betrayed, but time greases pride. Within a year, which is not a short time in the life of a man who only expects to see fifty summers at the most, King Osric was embedded in his childhood landscape. At the first assembling of the Thing, the people were asked to ratify his position as their king. Indeed it would have been a brave man who said he did not want Osric as his ruler. This was the man who had defeated the Mercians with a lesser army and had destroyed a tyrant. As for Wulfgar, he had ruled by intimidation not with wisdom, and most were glad to be rid of him. Osric accepted that the East Angles were initially afraid of him and were too frightened to get rid of him, but as time passed many came to think of him as a worthy successor to his father and wanted to keep him as king.

He ruled wisely and carefully, remaining on good terms with his neighbours the East Saxons, who lived north of the Dark River, known to some as the River Tamesas,. Kenric sat at his right hand and the Thief on his left: these two were naturally his closest hearth-companions, but other thegns soon pledged their undying allegiance. His son Quercus spent half his time with the East Angles and the other half with the nearby elves. Lord Ing was the household god of both Osric and his son, though Osric was careful to make observances to Woden at all times. No one should ignore the Lord of the Wild Hunt, for he was the ruler of the skies.

He learned one day in the following Lithamonath, known as the First Travelling Month, that it was believed that Rowena had suffocated King Ewin with his bed-pillow and had afterwards proclaimed herself Queen of Bernicia. No one contested her, so Osric assumed Cyneric was happy with this turn of events. It sounded very dark, but then he no longer felt justified in interfering in the affairs of other neighbours and nations. However, musing on Rowena and on his son's mother had Osric thinking of marriage again. There were many pretty girls in the villages of the East Angles – he certainly did not want a marriage to the daughter or sister of another king, having had his fingers burnt the first time, even though it might be politic – so he looked around, studied the women of his own people.

However, lovely as they were and many of them both intelligent and learned women, none really touched his heart. He seemed to have lost that fault of falling in love with every pretty face that crossed his path. He spent his idle time pondering, walking along the river, wondering if he would ever meet another to whom he could give his heart. Of course, the woman he had always adored was unobtainable, a witch-girl who could not give her heart to a mortal. If only... if only... if only. He sighed as a picture of her came to his mind's eye. Lovely. Bright. Full of life and character. There was not another maiden like her who walked Middangeard. Inaccessible, though. The Wyrd could be cruel when laying down a man's ur-law.

One morning, he was sitting on a log on the edge of the woodland, high up over the river, staring down at its silvery form. It was a tidal river and was at that moment coming in from seaward, filling the mud basins and channels first, then spreading over the flats, chasing away the waders who preferred shallows to deep water. A ship came in to the small harbour, a trading vessel, and King Osric could see fabrics and other goods on its open deck. He tried to rouse some enthusiasm for going down and inspecting these wares, but his spirit was somewhat low. Life was comfortable but uninteresting and Osric didn't know how to improve his mood. Then suddenly he became aware of a figure standing next to him.

'Ah, my Lord and King Osric, you're too proud these days to call for Sethrith, the witch?'

He looked up and saw the lovely face of his enchantress friend and smiled. Somehow in thinking of her, she had appeared. There must be magical messages that fly through the air, he thought, and land in the heads of creatures such as Sethrith. He only had to say her name, or even *think* her name, and she came to him. He was pleased to see her and wondered why he had not called her to him before now. Perhaps he had not wanted to see what he could not have: that which was forbidden to mere mortals, even kings with a lineage which led back to the gods.

'Not too proud, just distracted – sorry. Are you whole? I am.'

'Witches don't get sick. Why are you distracted?'

He sighed and plucked a blade of grass to chew. 'Oh, I don't know. I'm thinking I should get married and have a child.'

'You already have one.'

'Quercus? Yes, but he's hardly a child, is he? He shot through childhood like an arrow from a bow. 'No, I mean a family. A king should have a family. It sets a good example.'

'Does it? I wonder.'

'Anyway,' he tossed the mangled blade of grass away, 'there's no one around I want to marry – except you of course – and you're a witch.'

She smiled. 'You would like to marry *me*?'

'Of course. I'm in love with you. You know that. I've told you before. Always have been, probably always will be, but the Wyrd, you know, hates me. It shows me what sort of life I could have, then makes it impossible for me to have it.'

'You fall in love with every female you meet.'

'Used to, but not any more. They bore me now. Even the best of them.'

'But I don't bore you?'

He stared up into her gold-flecked eyes. 'Never in a lifetime, Sethrith. You are the most interesting woman I've ever met. Oh – apart from Rowena, but the interest there is tinged with horror and fear.' He paused, then continued. 'If only you had not been born a witch, I would throw myself at your feet and beg you to marry me. You're the most beautiful and wisest of women. You would make the perfect wife for a king and the perfect life-companion for *this* king. But – but you had to go and be born a sorceress and…'

She put a finger to his lips to stop him from rambling.

'Listen, I never said we could not get married. I only said that if we did, I would lose my powers as an enchantress.'

He sat bolt upright and stared at her.

'You would be prepared to lose your magic? To become a mere mortal?'

'Huh!' she said. 'I could never be a *mere* anything. I am Sethrith.'

He stood up and took her hands. She was wearing a white shift that floated gossamer-like in the breeze. On her head was a wreath of wild flowers – wood anemones, bluebells, buttercups – most of them out of season. Her complexion was flawless and amazingly radiant. Her eyes – well, her eyes were enchanting, as a sorceress's eyes had to be. The small delicate ears and cherry lips completed a picture of a woman who could stop a man's heart in mid-beat.

'So, will you marry me, Sethrith?'

'Yes, yes I will.'

He whispered. 'We have plighted our troth. Neither of us can change our minds now. You realise that?'

'Yes, yes I do, my love, but – but I do wonder what you will think of the *mortal* Sethrith – she is probably sixty years of age and the ugliest of creatures…'

Osric gave out a little shout and stepped away from her.

'No…'

Sethrith laughed. 'Ha! You see. Your affection is shallow and base. You do not love *me*, the real Sethrith. You love only this beautiful form that witches can give themselves. Now you wish to jilt me, do you not?'

Osric swallowed hard, but then said, 'No. I have given my word. I have proposed and you have accepted. We will make the best of what is to be.'

She stepped forward, put her arms around him and kissed his lips. It was the sweetest kiss he had ever tasted. She said, 'I was jesting, my love. I am and will be as you see me now. You have given your word – and I have given mine – thus I have already lost my powers. Now I am as mortal as you. But, I will be sixty-years-of-age one day, and I hope you will love me just as much then as you do today.'

'More,' he said, able to smile again, 'for I shall be ancient too – or in my grave.'

'You are still a young man, my love. Do you know what the people call you, since you conquered Mercia? *Wuffa*. Little Wolf. You are the youngest warrior king on this green and pleasant island. We have a whole lifetime ahead of us. Me, looking after the keys to your treasure and making sure you make honourable decisions and you, wondering whether I'm going to run off with your gold and jewels.'

Excited now, the pair went hand-in-hand to tell the Thief and Kenric of the momentous adventure they were about to begin. The two thegns were in the Great Hall, wearily listening to some a complaint a churl had about a pig he owned, which another churl had decided belonged to him. They had heard the evidence of neighbours, some of whom said the pig was the property of the first churl, while others swore on oath it was property of the second. In the end the Thief ordered the pig to be slaughtered and roasted, and shared between the two men. One of them started to open his mouth to protest, when Kenric said, 'Enough! Judgement's been made. The next man to speak'll feel the flat of my blade.'

The two parties left, with the pig between them, and even before reaching the doorway there seemed to be some conviviality. A feast was a feast, after all, and the porker would make some delicious meals.

King Osric made an announcement to his two friends, while Sethrith stayed outside the Great Hall.

'Congratulate me!' cried Osric. 'I'm to be married!'

Kenric said, 'Not *again*?'

'You've already tried that twice,' added the Thief, 'and both times it's been a bit of a disaster.'

Osric was somewhat hurt by these remarks. 'I wouldn't say my first marriage was a disaster. I had little choice in the matter the second time. Paega would have thrown me into the wolf pit if I had refused to marry Rowena. And for the first, marriage, well, I had to leave simply because I couldn't live with elves.'

'So, who are you planning to marry and leave this time?' asked the Thief.

'Sethrith, and I shan't leave her. She's to be my queen.'

Kenric scoffed, 'You couldn't stay with elves, but you can live with witches?'

'Well, that's where you're wrong, my friend. My future queen is no longer a witch. She gave up magic for me.'

Osric companions seemed stunned by this remark.

Kenric said, 'She's left her coven for *you*?'

'I don't see what's so strange about that. She loves me. I love her.'

The Thief asked, 'Would you give up your kingship, your kingdom, for her?'

Osric was aware that Sethrith could hear all these exchanges, but he was caught on the back foot.

'I – I would certainly consider it, very seriously. I'm not sure what we would live on, if I did – but the fact is, I'm not required to, so it's of no account.'

Sethrith came into the Great Hall. 'So, I'm not worth a kingdom?'

Osric cried, 'Indeed you are, my one love. In fact, if it were necessary for me to, I would do it in an instant...'

'Only if it were *necessary*,' she said. 'But what if it were a whim of mine? – as a witch, I cared nothing for diamonds or gold.'

'But you are no longer a witch.'

Osric felt himself sinking in a mire and had no idea how to retrieve solid ground. However, the others in the room all seemed to be amused by his difficulties and he started to get annoyed.

'See here,' he said, briskly. 'Enough of this nonsense. We have nuptials to plan, so I suggest everyone gets to it. I want this to be a proper wedding, not like the other two. The first had no ceremonial whatsoever, apart from plucking daisies and collecting jays' feathers for the bride's adornments. The second had only the meanest look at the observances of tradition. This one will be done properly.'

Lord Ing:

A wedding! How wonderful. Yet, should I be angry with this new king, for is he not wed to one of my elfen charges? I should be, but am not. To see the joy in these two young mortals is to know that the world is turning at the right speed and the stars are all in their correct places. I look forward to the day. It should prove delightful.

And so it came about.

It took only a week – for Osric was impatient – to prepare for the king's wedding to his bride. The Thief and Kenric were of course groomsmen with serious responsibilities. Theirs was the duty of overseeing all the arrangements. This they did with due diligence and forethought, especially the Thief, who seemed to fall in with the work as if he were born to it. The two groomsmen were naturally only concerned with the formal procedure and looking after their lord. The bride, who had no friends amongst the East Angles, was left to her own devices. She brought in two of her favourite sisters, still witches, of course, to assist her. The women of the East Angles were horrified at having enchantresses in their midst and though they helped prepare the bride, their eyes were continually flicking back and forth between her sisters.

There was an immense amount of work to be done and everyone seemed to be in everybody else's way. People were rushing here, there and everywhere, seemingly dependent on the butchers, bakers, candlestick and dressmakers, yet apparently not getting anything done in the right time. Rush, hurry, haste. The whole kingdom (except of course for the warrior thegns, who simply sat around drinking beer and commenting sagely on the mayhem going on around them) was in a total upheaval. Nothing would be anything like ready of course, for there was so much to do, so little time and so few people to do it.

Miraculously, on the day, everything *was* ready.

Osric looked splendid in a red woollen cloak, his gold and garnet clasp pinning it to his tunic. He wore his ancestral sword, taken from Wulfgar's possessions. The same sword given to his mother by her father to pass on to her sons. Osric had no brothers and so the sword belonged to him alone. It was now his duty to give it to his new wife to be held in safe keeping for *her* sons. The sword Kenric had made for him now hung in the Great Hall as a symbol of the East Angles' independence and freedom from their previous Mercian overlord. Osric stood and nervously waited for his bride to arrive out on the grassy meadow they had chosen for the wedding. With him was the *weofodthegn*, the people's priest, whose duty it was to hallow the site and to call upon the gods – especially Freya and Frige – to bless the ceremony with love and fertility.

The wait seemed interminable to Osric. 'Is she coming?' he said to his groomsmen. His friends appeared to be callously careless of the time she was taking. 'Do you think she may have changed her mind?'

'Patience, lord,' replied the Thief. 'They always do this. I suspect they believe it heightens desire and anticipation, whereas I find it immensely boring.'

'My last two didn't keep me waiting so long.'

'I think,' said the Thief, 'the less we talk about your previous adventures into the state of wedlock, the better, my lord.'

At that moment Sethrith appeared, stunningly beautiful in her pure white wedding dress, decorated with wildflowers, tiny seashells and feathers. She was accompanied by her kin, her two sisters who looked equally lovely, though their wicked eyes belied any quantity of innocence in their souls. Osric's heart was beating fast as Sethrith approached and suddenly he knew he was the luckiest man on Earth. Who would not think so with this lovely maiden stepping towards him about to give herself to him for eternity? He took her trembling, silk-skinned fingers for a second or two and her small hand felt as fragile as a fluttering bird.

They began by exchanging oaths in front of the priest.

'I swear I will love and protect my queen forever,' said Osric, 'and will treat her with the respect and deference a wife deserves.'

'And I,' replied Sethrith, 'will honour my lord and give him equal if not more love than I receive, and will hold the keys to his treasure with responsibility and care.'

Osric unbuckled his ancestral sword and passed it to Sethrith.

Sethrith gave him a new sword, to protect her and her family, with the words, 'To keep us safe.'

The new sword was so astonishingly splendid he had to whisper to her, 'Who made this wonderful weapon?'

'Why,' she whispered back with a twinkle in her eyes, 'Wayland Smithy, of course.'

Osric almost dropped the weapon in amazement.

'Wayland Smithy?'

'Witches and elves, you know. They're as close as thieves.'

The Thief heard this and frowned a little.

'Sorry,' said Sethrith. 'No offence intended.'

Next, the *morgengifu*, the 'Morning Gift' was given to the bride by the groom. This was a gift of money to ensure the independence of the bride and her children, should anything happen to her husband. Sethrith especially was grateful for this tradition since she had no family to assist her should her husband be killed in battle or die of being elf-shot with some disease. And because there were no mortal relatives, the *handgeld*, money which should have gone to her parents or siblings was added to the *morgengifu*. This generous addition was also welcomed by the bride because, having no father, there was no dowry, which was money normally untouchable by the groom.

Next, Osric gave Sethrith the keys to his storerooms and treasure chests and the couple kissed to seal the commitments they had made to each other.

Finally, the wedding rings were exchanged and the priest cried, 'Thus is the marriage complete. You are man and wife. Go forth and be fruitful.'

However, before any fruit could be sown, there was a feast to enjoy, partly held in the Great Hall but also on the village green where even the churls could participate in the marriage of their king to his bride. Osric, having been lowly and poor himself for at least a portion of his young adult life, knew the value of good food and drink. He was generous in the extreme with his stores. No one, not the lowest nor meanest of his villagers, would go to bed hungry on this day of days. Beer was produced in great quantity to jolly the populace while the food cooked. Carcasses of deer and boar were roasting on spits over open fires. Game birds, fish, beef and pork were baked in earth ovens: pits jammed with heated stones wherein meat and indeed vegetables were covered by clay and leaves.

To begin with the churls expected and got a huge cauldron of a pottage of cereals, pulses and vegetables. However, on such a day they were also indulged with as much roasted and baked meat as they could digest. In addition there were vegetables not in the pottage: leaks, onions, cabbage, turnips, parsnips and carrots. The meat and some of the vegetables were flavoured with ginger, garlic or vinegar. On the large tables constructed for the purpose there were bowls of hard-boiled eggs: goose, ducks' and chickens' eggs, along with those of wild birds. Sea and freshwater fish was provided in plenty, including oysters, green pike and eels. Cheese and slabs of butter filled the side dishes. Fresh fruit, such as could be had in the season, lay in shallow bowls to be eaten with cream curdled with mint. Finally there was bread and there were hazelnut cakes in plenty, baked on the same day as the wedding.

'No one will be able to move, tomorrow morning,' warned the Thief. 'If they keep eating the way they are going now, they'll all be rolling around holding their stomachs and wishing the fouling pits were closer to their hovels.'

Osric and Sethrith ate sparingly and slipped away from the feast even before it was polite to do so, but they were eager for each other. They found their bed and began surprisingly gently. After a short while their love-making became more desperate and urgent. Despite the noise of the village going on all around them, they enjoyed each other's bodies to the full: touching, stroking, entering, accepting. It was a long while before they were mutually replete, falling back, breathing heavily.

Then they simply lay in each other's arms, resting from their exciting, frantic love-making, with Osric thinking, *she has retained something of her witchcraft, if she can pleasure her man with such wonderful artistry*, while Sethrith was musing, *it was enjoyable, but not yet completely fulfilling – it will get better I know, for there is more for me to learn and more that I can teach him.*

However, they revealed nothing of these private thoughts to each other. More importantly, their intimacy brought a feeling comfort and security to both of them. The sweet calmness of each other's presence after the hectic wedding feast was wholly welcome in the quietude of their bed-chamber. Sethrith curled up in his arms, aware of his heart beating against her breast, and felt utterly content. If this was marriage, then it was a warm and pleasant place to be. She found herself crying softly and he, feeling the tears fall on his bare skin, was concerned that he had somehow hurt her or had done something to upset her. Through her tears she assured him that all was well and that her weeping was not because anything was wrong but was prompted by happiness. He said he did not understand, because all he wanted to do was laugh and sing, and dance around the room, but if that was how she expressed her feelings of happiness, then so be it, 'Weep on, my love, weep on. I am full of joy too, but the tears won't come, I'm afraid. I shall have to smile instead.'

SEVEN

The pair enjoyed their honey-month, then settled into marriage. Sethrith became pregnant very quickly, for they were both young and vigorous people. Osric was delighted, sure that it was a son. Sethrith was equally happy, certain it was a daughter. Neither was too worried that their prediction might be false. They would love the child whatever sex the Wyrd decided to make it.

One morning in summer, Osric, two of his thegns, Kenric and the Thief went out hunting. They found the deer and followed the herd further than they intended, for Osric had duties as a king and spending the whole day chasing quarry was neglecting his responsibilities somewhat. It was Thunor's day and he had not convened the Thing before leaving, so he needed to get back before the afternoon was over. They lost the herd of deer, which in the end swam across the river, and turned back for home, skirting a dark wood on the boundary of Osric's lands. Suddenly, out of the pale of the trees came a horde of wild men, with a gleeful Wulfgar at their head. He was grey headed, greasy and dirty, his filthy clothes hanging on his lean body. There was a seax in one fist and a scaramax in the other. The outlaws with him carried similar weapons, or clubs and sling shots. One had a warhammer.

'Outlaws,' muttered Kenric. 'Pond scum.'

Wulfgar was triumphant, with some fifteen of his kind at his back.

'So,' he called, 'the boy comes looking for the man.'

The outlaws jeered. Though they had no horses, they had blocked the way back to the village. Osric and his companions realised they had to fight their way through. Almost immediately one of the two thegns charged the outlaws on his mount, wielding his sword. He managed to fell an outlaw in his path, but the others hacked at his legs, brought him down off his steed, and bludgeoned him to death. This attack acted as a signal for the battle to begin in earnest. Wulfgar headed straight for Osric who was of course riding Magic. The startled elfen horse shied as the huge warrior ran up to him swinging the scaramax and Osric slid off the steed's back. Osric's bow was in his hand but the quiver of arrows was attached to the horse. He threw the bow aside and drew his sword, the one given him at the wedding by Sethrith.

'So,' he said to Wulfgar, who had now stopped in his tracks and was taking a fighting stance, 'it had to come to this in the end, eh murderer?'

'Call me all the names you like,' snarled Wulfgar, 'I shall stop your mouth very shortly, forever. Then I shall go back to the Great Hall and kill those who oppose me, after fucking that insipid wife of yours until she bleeds. How does that sound, whelp? Make your blood boil a little? I'll soon let it out to cool on the ground.'

'You always were a stupid man, Wulfgar,' replied Osric. 'You think words are weapons and injure your enemies. They don't. They just make you look feeble-headed and foolish. This,' he brandished his sword. 'This is a weapon…' and he leapt forward and with a skilful stroke took off the end of Wulfgar's long grey beard, at the same time slicing into the outlaw's sternum with the point.

Wulfgar yelled and slashed with the scaramax, missing Osric's shoulder only by the thickness of a fingernail. The pair then set about slicing, hacking and parrying each other's strokes, trying to find an opening. Osric had learned a great deal since his days as a callow youth and his swordsmanship was of a very high quality. Wulfgar was a warrior of old, though, with many tricks in his bag. His talent for cunning strokes was endless and Osric had to watch his opponent's blade very keenly. The young king knew that he did not necessarily have to make a quick killing thrust. If he defended himself for long enough, the ageing Wulfgar would tire. So he watched and parried, fending off the furious attacks by his enemy, waiting for his foe's fatigue to set in and for the strokes of the scaramax and seax to become weaker.

Around the two men, the rest of the battle was in progress. Those on horseback had the advantage of being able to ride off aways, then pick an individual and charge back at that one man. Gradually the outlaws were being whittled down, until there were six bodies on the ground, some of them still, others writhing with wounds. Osric could see all this over Wulfgar's shoulder, careful to watch for any of the outlaws breaking away and coming to assist their leader. None did, though, they seemed preoccupied with the horsemen. The most dangerous of the outlaws were the two with slings, whose stones whistled around the heads of the riders. So far the sling-shooters had been unable to find a target, but once a rider halted his mount and became a static target, the danger of being hit was that much greater.

Indeed, Wulfgar tired, being unable to get past Osric's guard. The big warrior stepped back, breathing heavily. His weapon arm dropped to his side for just a moment and the stronger, younger man stepped forward and drove his sword into the chest of his adversary. Wulfgar looked down at the blade buried just right of his heart, seemingly perplexed. Then his head came up again wearing a savage expression. He slashed with his seax, catching Osric's left arm, opening a wound. Osric pressed harder with his sword, pushing the warrior backwards towards a lone oak. Wulfgar stumbled over lumpy sods of turf, falling backwards against the trunk of the tree. With a mighty two-handed heave, Osric went through the man's body, past his spine, and pinned him to the oak. Then the king stepped away, to stare at the gasping, bleeding Wulfgar, who hung from the trunk trying to wrest the blade from its wooden bed.

'That's it, murderer,' said Osric, 'death is on its way.'

Osric left Wulfgar hanging in order to stem the flow of blood from his own left arm and to look for Magic. The horse was not far away, munching grass, as if careless of the dire danger his master had been in, which of course he was. Osric ran to him, took the quiver of arrows from where it hung around Magic's neck, and proceeded to shoot any outlaw who remained standing. Two of the enemy turned and ran for the woodland, making it into the trees. The others were either felled by arrows or by the swords or spears of the riders. It was over. Wulfgar had given up his final breath and was drooping from the trunk of the oak. Osric went and retrieved his sword, letting the body fall to the roots of its makeshift gibbet, there to be left for the wolves and the crows to feast upon, once the humans had left the scene.

'Well done, my friends,' said Osric, as the Thief bound his wound with a torn piece of shift. 'You fought bravely and well. Now let's go home.'

The Thief remounted and asked, 'Should we bury these men?'

'No, leave them for those two in the wood,' replied Osric, 'though I doubt they'll do anything with the corpses either.'

At that moment, a figure emerged from the edge of the woodland and loosed a sling-shot stone. The Thief was struck in the temple and fell to the ground without a sound. Osric, shocked by the suddenness of this act, fired an arrow in the direction of the slinger. The rogue slipped back into the wood. However, the arrow must have reached its target for they heard a loud groan and the thrashing of a body in the bracken of the undergrowth.

Osric bent over the body of the Thief, to find that his companion of the last few years was dying. He cradled the Thief's head on his knee, as he knelt beside the Geat. The light was fading from the man's eyes. He said, 'In the end, I was not so much a coward, was I?'

'You were among the best and the bravest,' replied Osric, his voice cracking with emotion. 'I shall tell the tales of your courage when you stood beside me in aversity. Your name shall ring out in the Great Hall. It will…'

But the Thief was gone; whether to a better place or not, his soul had flown.

MAJOR PANTHEON

Members of the ESE and the WEN, the two houses of the gods.

WODEN: One-eyed High King and Master of the Runes, God of War, Poetry and Mantic Ecstasy; God of Magic and Wisdom; Lord of the Dead and the Gallows; Lord of the Wild Hunt; consort of Frige and above all, ancestral father-god of all the Old English royal families.

THUNOR: God of Storms and Thunder.

FRIGE: Goddess of Love, consort of Woden.

SEAXNEAT: Founder of the Saxons, Friend of Swords.

EOSTRE: Goddess of Springtime, the Dawn and Rebirth.

ING: God of Prosperity, Passion and Wealth, Ruler of the Elves along with his sister, Freo. Received Aelfgeard, the home of the elves, as gift for his first tooth.

TIW: God of Justice and the Sky, and along with Lord Woden a war god whose name warriors scratch on their weapons.

FREO: Goddess of Fertility, Magic and (with her brother Ing) Ruler of the Elves.

BEALDOR: God of Light.

LOKI: God of Mischief and a shape-shifter.

EORTHE: Goddess of the Earth.

HAMA: Keeper of the Rainbow Bridge that leads to Esageard, home of the gods.

ANDHRIMNIR – the cook of the gods, who prepares SAEHRIMNIR, the wild boar for the gods' supper.

MANNUS: Possibly a demi-god, the founder of the Old English race.

HRETHA: Goddess of Glory.

OTHERS

WAYLAND: Elf once captured and forced to make jewellery for an evil king, who took his revenge by bedding the king's daughter and killing all his sons.

SLEIPNIR: Woden's eight-legged horse.

THURSES: Giants of a particularly destructive nature.

ETTINS: Race of giants, less hostile and aggressive than Thurses.

COFGODAS: House wights.

DWEORGS or DWARFS: Expert smiths. These subterranean creatures made Thunor's hammer and Woden's sword. They also fashioned Freo's necklace, *Brisingamen*.

NIXIE: Water spirit.

NICOR: Water monster.

Also: WITCHES, DRAGONS, BLACK DOGS.

GLOSSARY

ESAGEARD: Home of the gods.

AELFGEARD: Home of the elves.

THING: An assembly, similar to a parliament gathering, always held on Thunor's Day.

HELLMOUTH: Gaping mouth of a huge monster that swallows dead malefactors.

NEORXNAWANG: Similar to Heaven.

MIDDANGARD: The world in which mortals live.

IERFEALU: Round of ritual toasts dedicated to the deceased.

INNERYARD: A homestead enclosure. The inneryard of the gods is called the WIH.

OUTERYARD: Anywhere outside an Inneryard.

WYRD: Fate.

UR-LAW: A primal law laid down by the Wyrd at birth.

FRITH: Peace and tranquillity.
Security and refuge.
Protection and penalty for breaches of the Frith.
Restoration of rights to an outlaw.

FRITHGUILDSMEN: Keepers of the peace and guardians of the Frith.

GRITH: Pact of peace agreed between inneryards.

THEW: Virtues or honour. (Wisdom, bravery, loyalty, truth, friendship, moderation, neighbourliness, steadfastness).

WEALTHDEAL: Generosity and giftgiving.

RITUAL TOOLS: Blot (blood) bowl, silver arm ring for swearing an oath, drinking horn, altar, sprig of a tree.

SYMBEL: Drinking rounds, toasts, oaths, boasts, songs, jokes, stories.

HOODENING: The time when youths carry a horse's skull on a stick from inneryard to inneryard, making the jaws snap loudly.

WASSAILING: Toasting of cherry and apple trees on 12th Night.

WALPURGIS: 1st of May. The night the witches ride in legions across the sky.

GOD POST: An idol made from a trunk of a tree.

HARROW: An altar made of stone.

DAILY GREETING: 'Be whole!' (Be healthy)

GREYWACKE: The hardest stone in the British Isles.

THE ANGLO-SAXON CALENDAR

Monaths (Months)

January. AEFTERRE-GEOLA: 'After Yuletide'.

February. SOL: 'Sun Month'.

March. HRETH: 'Goddess Hretha's Month'.

April. EOSTUR: 'Goddess Eostre's Month'.

May. DRIMILCE: 'Month when cows are milked three times daily.'

June. AERRA-LITHA: 'First Travelling Month'.

July. AEFTERA-LITHA: 'Second Travelling Month'.

August. WEOTH: 'Weeding Month'.

September. HALIG: 'Holy Month'.

October. WINTER-FYLLETH: 'First full moon of winter.'

November. BLOT: 'Blood Month' when animals which would not survive the winter would be slaughtered.

December. AERRA-GEOLA: 'Before Yuletime'.

Christmas. MODRA-NIHT: 'Mother's Night'. Midwinter and birth of a new solar year.

About the Author

Garry Kilworth was born in York in 1941 and has been writing fiction from the age of twelve. His school years were spent in the Middle East and he has travelled widely, having lived and worked in nine countries. After twenty-six years in international telecommunications his first publication was the short story "Let's Go To Golgotha" which in 1974 won the Gollancz/Sunday Times Competition. Since then he has had over 100 books published in several genres: science fiction and fantasy, historical novels, young adult fiction, mainstream novels, graphic novels, poetry. His mainstream novel *Witchwater Country* published by The Bodley Head was longlisted for the Booker Prize. He has the honour of being published in the only Lonely Planet Books' anthological venture into fiction. He was given a Fellowship in the Royal Geographical Society for the historical geography in his 18th Century war novels. Writing fiction has always been a joy. Happily, it is one of those professions which need not cease until the inevitable occurs.

Garry's work has won a number of awards, including a World Fantasy Award and a BSFA Award (*The Ragthorn*, written with Robert Holdstock), the Children's Book of the Year Award (*The Electric Kid*), a Locus Award (*Moby Jack and Other Tall Tales*), and the Charles Whiting Award for Literature (*Rogue Officer*).

The author studied the Anglo-Saxon language and customs as part of his B.A. in English at King's College, London. He has been a volunteer steward at Sutton Hoo Anglo-Saxon ship burial site, where his wife is a guide, for over twelve years. He also lives close to and has visited several times the reconstructed Anglo-Saxon village at West Stow in Suffolk, which is set around the same time as this novel.

Find out more about the author and his work at:
www.garry-kilworth.co.uk

Lightning Source UK Ltd.
Milton Keynes UK
UKHW011310130123
415295UK00005B/609

9 781914 953392